FICTION MANIFESTO.

CANADIAN FICTION MAGAZINE

Editor-in-Chief
GEOFFREY HANCOCK

FICTION MANIFESTES CRITIQUES GRAPHIQUES PHOTOS ENTREVUES

The Best of
CANADIAN FICTION MAGAZINE

**SILVER
ANNIVERSARY ANTHOLOGY**

Edited by Geoff Hancock

Quarry Press

Copyright © 1997 by CANADIAN FICTION for the authors.
ALL RIGHTS RESERVED.
ISSN 0045-477X
ISBN 1-55082-178-4

CANADIAN FICTION is a twice-yearly anthology of contemporary Canadian fiction. The editor invites manuscripts from writers in Canada and Canadians living in other countries. Unless manuscripts are accompanied by a SAE and Canadian stamps or international reply coupons, they will not be returned. Mail with postage due will be refused. CFM is available for exchange lists or any other arrangements that will mutually benefit literary magazines. The magazine is a member of the Canadian Magazine Publishers' Association. It is published with the financial assistance of The Canada Council and the Ontario Arts Council.

Annual Subscription Rates
Individual: **$34.24** ($32.00 + $2.24 GST)
Institutional: **$44.94** ($42.00 + $2.94 GST)

Address all correspondence to
CANADIAN FICTION
P.O. Box 1061, Kingston, Ontario, Canada K7L 4Y5

Back issues of CANADIAN FICTION are available in film and electronic format from Micromedia Limited, 20 Victoria St., Toronto, ON M5C 2N8 and from Xerox University Microfilms, P.O. Box 1346, Ann Arbor, Michigan, U.S.A. 48106 or 35 Mobile Drive, Toronto, Canada M4A 1H6.

Indexed in CANADIAN PERIODICAL INDEX, CANADIAN ESSAY AND LITERATURE INDEX, MLA INTERNATIONAL BIBLIOGRAPHY, INDEX OF PERIODICAL FICTION, and AMERICAN HUMANITIES INDEX.

Printed and bound in Canada by AGMV, Montreal and Cap-Ste-Ignace, Quebec. Distributed to the magazine trade by Canadian Magazine Publishers' Association. Distributed to the book trade by General Distribution Services in Canada and InBook in the U.S.A.

Published by Quarry Press Inc., P.O. Box 1061, Kingston, Ontario K7L 4Y5.

Contents

NUMBER 90-91-92

Geoff Hancock	7	*The Achievement of Canadian Fiction*
Geoff Hancock	13	*Moving Off The Map: From "Story" To "Fiction"*
Leon Rooke	30	*Wintering in Victoria*
Anne Bernard	44	*Siblings*
W. P. Kinsella	60	*Illiana Comes Home*
Mavis Gallant	73	*With a Capital T*
Guy Vanderhaeghe	85	*The Watcher*
Jane Urquhart	120	*Five Wheelchairs*
Keath Fraser	141	*This Is What You Were Born For*
Matt Cohen	167	*Sins of Tomas Benares*
Douglas Glover	191	*Dog Attempts To Drown Man In Saskatoon*
Patrick Roscoe	207	*Scent of Young Girls Dying*
Rohinton Mistry	223	*Condolence Visit*
Frances Itani	240	*After The Rain*
Sharon Butala	253	*The Prize*
Chetan Rajani	283	*The Letter Writer*
T.F. Rigelhof	300	*Hole With A Head In It*
Barbara Gowdy	345	*Ninety-Three-Million Miles Away*
Greg Stephenson	362	*Periodic Table of Escape Velocities*
Thomas Wharton	377	*Dream Novels*
	398	*Tribute to Geoff Hancock*

GEOFF HANCOCK has been the Editor-in-Chief of *Canadian Fiction Magazine* since 1976.

The Achievement of Canadian Fiction

GEOFF HANCOCK

THE TRAJECTORY

Canadian Fiction Magazine is the oldest and finest literary quarterly in the nation devoted to creative prose fiction. And should anyone challenge this claim, my response is the work collected in the silver anniversary issue of the magazine open before you. With 25 years behind us and almost 1500 stories published, *Canadian Fiction Magazine* records the era of the emergence of the Canadian short story from provincial obscurity to the full light of international acclaim.

How to describe this trajectory, which is the narrative of Canadian short fiction? CFM has published social realism, symbol-based and image-based fiction, great slabs of the imagination that slice and whack away at the institutional conventions of fiction. Extra literary problems became the event of the story, once called a fiction, now called a text. The story of our origins. A society in innocence. Our spiritual growth. Our terrible dramas. Our fecund imagination. Our soul's residence in darkness.

Stories published in CFM presented new models of perception. In the grey time of Canada, we answered the question posed by Northrop

Frye: *where is here?* Canada doesn't exist, except as a name we give to an abstract idea, best seen in our art and our fictions. Stories published in CFM have placed special emphasis on a new way to see. Stories in CFM might use a deconstruction model: plot replaced by ongoing incident; characters replaced by consciousness struggling with circumstance; social realism replaced by a sense of situation; form not *about* experience, but *more* experience so that fiction became a record of its own making.

Stories in CFM have used high culture and pop; been avant garde and generic, been comprised of parodies and intertexts; have challenged traditional concepts of character with anti-characters, and marginalized viewpoints. CFM authors have expressed a wide variety of styles, subjects, forms, contents. In the maturing of our nation's fiction, CFM has challenged the conventional definition of the classic short story which consisted of a neat triad of qualities: making a single impression on a reader, concentrating on a crisis, and making the crisis pivotal in a controlled plot.

CFM had to lead the way in the new Canadian fiction, or die. The stories published in CFM articulate a record of the ongoing decomposition of outmoded form. We've transcended the barriers of class, race, region, and gender, while respecting them and allowing them to bloom. We've celebrated the First Nations' writers, the Caribbean Commonwealth, new expectations of women writers, the feverishness of magic realism, of the surrealist vision, the revisions of how fiction is taught and experienced. CFM found the secret passages that led to the future of Canadian fiction. Yes, in a modest way, the magazine has changed the course of history.

MANDATE

CFM has four significant editorial aims. First, to provide an outlet for new and established Canadian short-fiction writers and novelists. Two, to foster a national and international awareness of contemporary Canadian fiction, in French, in English, and in translation from the unofficial languages of Canada. Three, to function as a non-partisan forum for critics and writers, and to encourage discussion of the aesthetics of Canadian fiction. Four, to keep readers informed of current works of fiction in Canada and abroad.

HISTORY

Beginning as a student publication at the University of British Columbia in 1971, CFM grew over two decades to become the premier literary magazine devoted exclusively to short fiction in Canada. CFM has published over 1,000 stories by the best new and established writers and artists resident in Canada and Canadians residing abroad, and has established new standards for traditional and innovative fiction.

CFM has proven to be especially receptive to fictions of the marvelous, the surreal, and magic realism. Through editorials, interviews, and examples, CFM has championed a new generation of Canadian fiction writers. Through the magazine's long history and development, CFM has played a major role in Canadian letters. A detailed history of CFM'S first ten years appears in CFM No. 42, alongside a ten year index. Updated indexes appear every twenty issues. As well as publishing hundreds of important short stories, CFM is proud of many other notable accomplishments:

CFM interviews are the most important introduction to the creative minds behind Canadian short- and long-fiction. Authors interviewed by CFM talk about their narrative strategies, dealing with the possibilities of the blank page, and the demands the contemporary world makes upon their art and craft. For many writers, the CFM interview is the first in-depth discussion of their fiction. Many of CFM's classic interviews were republished in 1987 as *Canadian Writers At Work: Interviews with Geoff Hancock* (Toronto and Sydney: Oxford University Press, 1988). Many others have been reprinted in single author monographs or belles-lettres collections, most recently Margaret Atwood, Josef Skvorecky, and John Metcalf. The CFM interviews are a prime resource intended first for creative writers and second for scholarly study.

CFM has played a leading role in Canadian letters through its Fiction in Translation Series, first from the Quebecois, and secondly from the Unofficial Languages of Canada. CFM has published several book-length anthologies that stand as milestones in contemporary Canadian Translation, most notably issues number 20A, 36/37, which featured a wide range of European, Oriental, and native language fiction by Canadian writers in translation, and issue 43, Canada's first anthology of contemporary Quebecois fiction in translation; issue 60,

Canada's first anthology of contemporary Native fiction, and issues 61/62, Latin American Writers in Canada. The Unofficial Languages issues all received financial support from the Multiculturalism directorate. The purpose of these issues has been to challenge the conventional canon of Canadian literature and to draw attention to the wider variety of Canadian letters and models of perception within a Multicultural Canada.

CFM editorials function as an important forum on the future of fiction. CFM editorials examine the wider possibilities of genre fiction, magic realism, literary magazines (through such symposia as the CPPA Literary Magazine meetings reprinted in numbers 35/36 and 55), modernism, postmodernism, innovation and change in the new shortstory, tactics in the novella and prose poem, and such new developments in narratology as metafiction, tabulation and irrealism. CFM editorials also explore new models of perception such as psychoanalysis and the Assyrians (No. 58), physics and fiction (No. 56), Surrealism (No. 39), specific regions of Canada (Saskatchewan No. 64, new English Quebec fiction No. 63), and problems peculiar to fiction writing (rejection and failure, No. 55). Recent editorials have drawn attention to new writers in Canada (No. 65), regional literary concerns (Ontario Nos. 67/68), gaps in Canadian authorship (the writer and the the nuclear bomb, No. 66), and damage control (No. 70). It is worth pointing out, and proudly, that CFM is one of the few literary magazines to take a written editorial stance on any subject whatsoever.

In the light of the above, the Editor-in-Chief of CFM has published several book-length anthologies which have developed out of editorial ideas first expressed in CFM. The first of these anthologies, *Magic Realism* (Aya Press, 1980), resulted in a well-known three-day conference on Magic Realism and Canadian Literature at the University of Waterloo in 1985 with the proceedings now published. CFM and its editor are widely credited with beginning the discussion on this postcolonial perceptual literary model. Other anthologies — *Illusion: Fables, Fantasies, and Metafictions* (2 vols); *Metavisions, Shoes and Shit: Stories for Pedestrians* (a surrealist exploration of scatological fiction, and a spoof on conventional Canadian literary-anthologies); and *Invisible Fictions: Contemporary Stories from Quebec* (all surreal, fantastic, Gothic, or grotesque) — further explored the wide range of non-mimetic Canadian short fiction. Black Moss Press's anthology *Singularities: prose poems, fragments, and para-fictions: new directions in physics and fiction* grew out of an editorial in CFM No. 56, which examined fictions not normally anthologized. These include stories without plots or characters; fictions without beginning or end, or possibly even without words. The anthology draws attention to the recent theories in fractal geometry, the science of chaos, quantum and subatomic physics, recent cosmology, and contemporary narratology. In 1990, Thistledown Press published *Fire Beneath the Cauldron*, which examined Canadian fiction from the viewpoint of alchemy and Jungian depth-psychology.

CFM related anthologies in fact are a reminder that CFM is the *Canadian Ficciones Magazine*, not the *Canadian Short Story Magazine*, a reference to the inspirational collection *Ficciones* (Fictions) by Jorge Luis Borges which first appeared in English translation in 1964, only six years before the planning of CFM's earliest numbers. Issue 50/51 includes a long essay by Geoff Hancock reprinted in this anniversary anthology on the differences between an unconventional 'fiction' and a traditional 'short story.' That 15th anniversary issue likewise appeared as *Moving Off the Map: from 'story' to 'fiction'* (Black Moss).

In the course of CFM's history, the magazine has made a serious effort to reach an audience beyond that limited to a periodical. CFM No. 63, on new fiction from Montreal, for example, was republished as a book edition on-run with Vehicule Press in Montreal. CFM No. 60, on native fiction, evolved into a major anthology guest edited by Thomas King and published by McClelland & Stewart.

CFM has also been a pioneer in the field of contemporary literary portraiture. The magazine has featured prize-winning portfolios (National Magazine Awards) by Paul Orenstein, John Reeves, Sam Tata, Kero, Helena Wilson, V. Tony Hauser, and Arnaud Maggs. CFM has also published a special issue on the literary portraits of Sam Tata, perhaps Canada's greatest classic photographer. A 50 year retrospective of his career was held in 1989 at the NFB in Ottawa.

From time to time CFM draws attention to specific groups of writers or single authors. In 1985, CFM published 45 *Below: The Ten Best Young Fiction Writers*, in 1988 it published *The Kingston Conference: A New Generation*. CFM has also published single author special issues on Jane Rule, Robert Harlow, Leon Rooke, Martin Vaughn-James, and

Mavis Gallant (which is widely credited for re-establishing her career in Canada).

CFM features an annual Contributor's Prize for the best story of the year to be published in English or French. Previous winners include Leon Rooke, W.P. Kinsella, Mavis Gallant, John Metcalf, Guy Vanderhaeghe, Keath Fraser, David Sharpe, Douglas Glover, Patrick Roscoe, Matt Cohen, Ann Copeland (a.k.a. Anne Bernard), Rohinton Mistry, Frances Itani, Sharon Butala, Chetan Rajani, T.F. Rigelhof, Barbara Gowdy, Greg Stephenson, Susan Crawford, and Thomas Wharton. The stories reprinted in this 25th anniversary anthology have been selected from these prize winning stories.

ENVOI

While this special anniversary issue celebrates the achievement of Canadian fiction over the past 25 years, the publication also marks the end of an era. *Canadian Fiction Magazine* will no longer publish quarterly; rather, the magazine will appear as an anthology twice yearly in the Spring and the Autumn. My appearance as editor-in-chief will be reduced to an occasional role as a guest editor. A new age of Canadian fiction is dawning.

GEOFF HANCOCK has edited several collections of innovative fiction, including *Magic Realism, Illusion: Fables, Fantasies, and Metafictions; Metavisions; Shoes and Shit;* and *Visible Stories and Invisible Fictions from Quebec.* He was the first winner of the Fiona Mee Award for outstanding literary journalism exemplified in such publications as *Canadian Writers At Work: Interviews with Geoff Hancock.* This essay first appeared in CFM No. 50/51 and is reprinted here with minor emendations.

Moving Off The Map: from "Story" to "Fiction"

GEOFF HANCOCK

CANADA IS STILL an undiscovered fiction. So Canadian fiction writers have found a diversity of definitions that imagine what is real about the place. Canadians discover themselves in the linkages, connections, tissues. Michael Bullock says writers are tribal shamans. The poet in a civilized society dreams for his community. "We are Canadians," Robert Kroetsch writes. "We know we are dreamt, but we can't remember what." So we dream our discovery, and in our divergent fictions, we define ourselves.

The short narrative in Canada takes two general directions. The first (story) is the traditional or modernist short story. The second (fiction) calls attention to the artifice of stories. Fiction emphasizes new forms and techniques. Fiction is allied with the post-modern, the medieval, the prehistoric. A fiction is unreliable, its form not yet discovered, the essential mode for Canadians seeking definitions.

The traditional story uses the devices of realistic writing. The writer pays attention to details. Characters are psychologically motivated. The plot has a cause and an effect. A story tells us what we already know, a version of a discovered and possibly not authentic definition.

Thomas Mann notes in the preface to *The Magic* Mountain: "stories must be past, and one might say, the more past they are, the more they are suitable as stories, and for the storyteller, the murmuring conjurer of the present tense." A narrator is secure in the general overview of the story even if the characters are insecure and threatened. But Canadian narrators are not secure, and the 19th-century posture of a German or American or any other narrator cannot be relied upon to write an authentic Canadian fiction.

The Canadian fiction writer is beginning again. The writer must consider the limitations of stories (style, technique, subject) that were set in the past. Does the Canadian writer want the writing of an adventure or an adventure in writing? If the short story is an index to national consciousness, as Gordon Weaver suggests, then the Canadian writer has to find different image clusters, word sequences, and layers of interpretation to tell their own story. The 19th-century conventions had to be abandoned. Unnamed, unlearned, uninvented. Canadian fiction writers moved in an undefined (and unreliable, undiscovered) space that required a narrative poetics far beyond the old style of writing. They did not want the restrictions of comfortable ready-made characters in pre-arranged situations solved by logic, reason, and rationality. Canada: moon country, Eldorado on Ice, mon pays, an unnamed country, the true north strong and free. Such a place required new fictions.

So a new generation of writers began with a different set of premises. They wanted to transform the short fiction of Canada with prose so hot it short circuited traditional structures and created mutants. Fiction had changed, not only in structure, but also in style, and more important, in attitude. "Story," with its formulas, predictable plot contours, and middle class characters, was challenged by "fiction."

Fiction: defining a new territory for Canada. A new aesthetic program for Canadian writers. Instead of "stories," Canadian writers wanted "fabrications, myths, contradictions, and mortal games." The phrase is Pablo Neruda describing Julio Cortazar's fictions. Fiction. The term might as well begin with Jorge Luis Borges' 1949 collection, *Ficciones,* first translated into English in 1964. Fiction: not a living creature. Fiction: the destruction of character, situation, style, and the clichés of language. Fiction: as John Simon said, "the unreality of what we think most real: art." In opening multiple perspectives, a new generation of writers defined their lives, their writing, and, occasionally, their nationalism. But only occasionally. The new generation of Canadian writers were less concerned with nationalism as a reason for literary experience, just as the innovations of Borges altered the short story concept of Poe's "singleness of effect." The fictions were the definition the old critics searched to articulate.

Short stories suggest one view of reality. But fictions urge writers to explore different versions. Many of the new narratives seemed fantastic, ingenious, showing how fiction moved inward, dramatizing the internal processes of the mind at work. A fiction can move from realism to the boundary of reality, or re-imagine the reality in which we live. A fiction can be the summary of several versions of a single work by an imaginary author where real and imaginary authors and characters intermingle.

Fiction alters the way we read stories. External conflict was a thing of the past. The precision of plot was replaced by non-linear, synchronistic imagery. Many fictions seem distorted, grotesque, illogical, and absurd. In fiction, characters might be motivated by fantastic logic, not natural causality. Fiction: the unbridgeable distance between sign and signified. Fiction: a reminder that the ultimate story might never be told.

The concept of the labyrinth occurs frequently in any discussion of fiction. For the writer, fiction is an art that reveals the oldest, most primitive, most constant despair of mankind. As Borges has suggested, in the deepest despair, despair is a comfort. Fiction: the most sophisticated art of all, prose used to search for the centre of the labyrinth and the merging with the infinite. The single moment of the fiction is the centre of the labyrinth, the moment which justifies and explains human existence, the moment the characters seek and then die. Fiction: a response to a crisis of the soul.

The Canadian writer invents any number of containers for fiction. The later fiction of this century has a casual beginning, somewhat akin to the traditional story. Perhaps a startling ending, or more likely a limit of tolerance in a violent situation. Despite a minimum of apparent sophistication, there's a mood of menace and bafflement in these short pieces that make use both of the world and the devices of fiction. Minimal art with maximum effect. These fictions are situated between reality and reflexivity, and so draw attention to the values and complexities of fictional reality.

Other writers locate their fictions in marginal and fringe areas, in the post modern, cybernetic, or hi-tech. Yet others find inspiration in the "paradise of the tale," a library world, a descent into memory. Fiction: self-consciously textual, linked with all other fictions in literary history. Fiction: a disclaim to any originality in literature: all writing as a translation of an existing archetype. Fiction: a link with myth, dream, metaphor, metonymy, magic, paradox, and metamorphosis in both past and present.

In some creative writing classes, the narrative strategies of historical and ancient literatures are examined for their contemporary relevance. The 18th century, Elizabethan England, Etruscan and Roman visual narratives on sarcophagi and victory columns. The middle eastern classics of *Giglamesh, Genesis,* and *Enuma elish;* the medieval romances of *Gawain and the Green Knight,* and *Celestlina,* as well as classic folk and fairy tales are linked to contemporary fictions giving them a strange originality. Fiction: the reimagining of already written stories. (John Ellis in *One Fairy Story Too Many* has already proven the Grimm brothers completely altered the plots, characters, style, and moral tone of the original fairy tales. We thought they were stories when in fact they were fictions.) So we get Leon Rooke's *Shakespeare's Dog.* Derk Wynand's *One Cook, Once Dreaming.* Rikki's *The Butcher's Tales.* J. Michael Yates' *Fazes in Elsewhen.* Andreas Schroeder's *The Late Man.* Jane Urquhart's fabular fictions. Michel Tremblay's contes.

Canadian short fiction includes narratives that fit into the context of literary history as well as those that challenge all efforts at being pigeonholed. Some stories are thematic. But the fictions often reveal little through thematic analysis. Fiction includes many devices: metaphysics, mathematical equations, the manuscripts of old heretics, fake confessions, reviews of imaginary books, parodies of detective stories, phony biographies tinged with jealousy, pastiches of literary criticism, metaphysical detective stories, and ecclesiastical pornography, sealed in cellophane.

Variety gives short fiction strength and its ability to resist easy categorization. Writers on the edge of that new discovery need strong individualities, exceptional responses, and artistic eccentricities to connect tale, teller, and told. Fiction is related to contemporary culture by its cross purposes, failure in communication, and misunderstanding. A fiction might be an updated Socratic method of dialogue that keeps its meaning to itself. Only the personality of the writer shines through.

Fiction is given its momentum, so Sean O'Faolain has said, by "the writer's distillation of personality." What we enjoy most in a fiction is "a unique sensibility." Writers like Mavis Gallant, George McWhirter, Alice Munro, Clark Blaise, John Metcalf, Susan Kerslake, and Leon Rooke write with their whole imagination and personality, not just their intellect. Wholeheartedly, their fiction includes unexpected images, a free access between internal and external worlds. As Mario Vargas Llosa said, writers were either "primitives" or "creators." The difference appealed to was in formal technique combined with a sense of the self. The authorial voice and personality provides the tension between literary play and earnest reality. If telling is a game, then myth must be comic. A fiction succeeds by the rhythms of a voice.

If fiction is a narrative performance, it requires a new set of literary criticisms. A fiction reminds the reader that its existence belongs to the author. Artifice is not only the technique, but even the theme. That's why so much fiction is about non-existent books, places, and characters as described by non-existent authors. Bustos Domecq. Charles Kinbote. Stanislav Lem. Italo Calvino. *The Dictionary of Imaginary Places* by Alberto Manguel and Gianni Guadalopi. As John Barth has said in a famous quote, "Fictions are not only footnotes to imaginary texts, but postscripts to the real corpus of literature." Art: artifice.

Short fiction in Canada was aided in its development over the past 25 years by our need to know our own possibilities. Creative writing workshops and seminars made tremendous contributions. Degree programs such as those offered by the Universities of British Columbia and Victoria, David Thompson University Centre (until it was scandalously closed), York University, Concordia, and informal programs affiliated with colleges, CEGEPS, and a few English Departments, and other programs such as the Banff Centre of the Arts and Fort San in Saskatchewan sharpened literary minds.

Through an intense discussion of the aims, special characteristics, methods, and materials, Canadian short fiction developed a new sensibility. Fiction: match the material to the vision. Fiction: was it linear, or a design in space based on patterns of imagery? Fiction: each prose experience to find a natural metaphor or style that made it different from all other fictions. Fiction: rather than anticipate the literary critic, the fiction writer lives for, and in trepidation of, the workshop experience. Fiction: mixed media presentation: strobes, tape loops, music, an event between literature and theatrical spectacle, edited like a film, or cross-edited like ten channels on TV at once. Fiction: if it works, celebrate; if it doesn't, ask why not?

The past 25 years brought literary translation to Canada from abroad, and showed us new literatures (French-Canadian, Quebecois, the unofficial languages of Canada) within. The giants of world literature descended from the realm of the CompLit specialist to the paperback racks as inspiration for narrative innovation. Fiction: emphasizes transculturalization and the interaction between literatures. The Library of Babel is eternal, found in the City of the Immortals by strolling through the Garden of Forking Paths. Fiction: a reminder that literature draws upon a wide variety of cultures. Canadian short fiction has been transformed and modified by Latin American, Asian, African, Eastern European, and Third World writings. Refusing to follow just the British or American models, transculturalization refuses the colonial process. Short fiction became more integrated, combining author, characters, consciousness, and thought in a personal vision. Canadian writers no longer had to leave the country, but to confront it from new positions. Literary artists from abroad offered stimulating alternatives to realistic writing. Fiction, as William Gass said, was a "figure of life."

As "story" was replaced by "fiction," the future was invented just as the past was recalled. Perhaps this is the key to post-modernism. The past 25 years have been characterized by fictions of uncertainty. The only thing guaranteed is the instability of contemporary consciousness. Literature was created out of literature, and that included philosophy and theology. The new fiction suggested artistic, aesthetic, or religious problems could replace the plot of a story. As Anna Maria Barranchea noted in *Borges, the Labyrinth Maker*, "literary invention vitalizes the abstract, drama and adventure are infused into thoughts which in themselves lack narrative substance."

Fiction was no longer based on ecclesiastical biases. A modern world view was no longer compatible with a linear Christian view of history extending from Genesis to the Last Day, with linear plot and autonomous characters controlled by Providence. Puritan faith suggested human life was a narrative invented by God. A fiction suggested history was cyclical, neo-Platonic, pagan. The emphasis was on a new kind of meaning.

Some writers said this was a time of vanishing forms, of clearing out the brush of dead stories. Fiction: new context, new organization. Fiction: breakdown of something old, breakthrough to something new. So Canadian short fiction changed: in a world that withholds answers, the aesthetics may be more interesting than the truth.

Fictions carry the impossible burden of being themselves and not being themselves at the same time. A "story" reminds us it is a "fiction." The new Canadian fiction takes on many strange perspectives. Anti-fiction, meta-fiction, sur-fiction, trans-fiction, magic-fiction, superfiction. Dream is a background to reality, where dream and reality veil each other. Fiction: exposes the alien element in the authors. Fiction: magical, poetic, illogical. Fiction: a quest preoccupied with its own search.

Even non-literary, non-verbal texts, such as Arnaud Maggs literary portraits, note the fact that the new fictions don't necessarily involve language. The image exists in a world of texts. Even the modest captions say a great deal about transient personalities fixed in a moment, one of forty-eight in a sequence. The processes of artistic and photographic composition probe cultural boundaries. Narrative is not just confined to prose, but includes art, photography, autobiography, formal essays, and criticism. Fiction: an absurd suburb of reality (Robbe-Grillet). Fiction: the art of motionlessness, of postponement, of waiting, of static energy.

"Let's go." (They do not move, from *Waiting for Godot,* by Samuel Beckett.)

The next stage for Canadian short fiction might include the essay as a narrative. The essay can include paradoxes and oppositions, dialogue and discussion, and an unresolved multiplicity of viewpoints. Here the critic as creative writer can confront the alter ego, or offer the essay its own revision and complement. No wonder Borges called essays "the inquisitions." The essayistic short story can explain, discuss, and discover all the personalities in an author, including the non-existent works. As Michael Butor notes, fiction is a means to find unification between the philosophical essay, poetic exploration, and even a way to solve the problems of writing.

The new fictions are formal alternatives to the traditional short story. As contemporary as film, theatre, painting, video, rock and roll music, in tune, so to speak, with the vibrations of our culture. Fictions have their own methods. Their epiphanies might be hollow. The heroes dismissed (or not heroic). The myths might be contemporary, machine age. As Borges notes in *Labyrinths*, "fictions challenge historical time so the imagination can operate with greater freedom." Wittegenstein might have said the limits of language are the limits of the world. But the fiction writer uses language as a rocket to light up what we do not know. Fiction expresses our time, our psychology, our context. Since the spirit of our time is weird, fiction leans towards counter-reality: fantasy, dream, wordplay, new mythologies. Ihab Hassan points out, in *Orpheus Dismembered*, we are in a time of new shapes, new structures, the dismemberment of traditional orders of language. Fiction: poised between extremes of incoherence.

The imagination moves into the void. Narrators are involved in the action. Open to external dangers, internal insecurities. Theirs is a fiction of rapidly changing perspectives: inner monologues, indirect speech, reminiscences: the inner world of little characters, uprooted by the forces of society or authority or genetics. Characters involved in actions that can't always be explained. Michael Bullock's fictions operative verb is "to be." Things "become" other things. Fiction: the end of old orders, old characterizations, old reliable reality.

Realistic stories interpret the world. But fictions are stylized, and not always interpretive. Fiction: intense stylization stylizes the creative act. Fiction: a creation of an author. (Author: a creation of a fiction.) Fiction: as Christine Brooke-Rose writes in *The Rhetoric of the Unreal*, is the meeting of minds in harmony with themselves.

A fiction, unlike a story, suggests that all knowledge is ambigious. The narrating "I" of a fiction is not always a reliable authority. A realistic story teller uses "I" as a narrator of the past. A fiction writer uses "I" in other ways. As a narrator of a continuing unpredictable present, as an abandonment of confidence in history, as an isolated protagonist representative of an alienated generation. Rimbaud: *"Moi, c'est l'autre."*

Flaubert: "*Madame Bovary, c'est moi.*" Michael Bullock observes his narrating self observing the narrator in his surreal fictions. If writers cannot discover Canada, how can the place be known? So there are lessons to be learned from the uncertainty behind "I" narration in Beckett's tales. Borges confronts the multiplicity of selves in "Borges and I" as the living "I" slowly yields to the fiction. If a Canadian has an identity crisis, might the narrating "I" be the dream of another character, or the "narration" of another, and so doubly alienated, doubly fictionalized. Julio Cortazar notes the doubling of "I" and "I, the other" as his characters, like Canadians, unsure of themselves, move back and forth through aquarium glass, jet windows, from the streets of Paris to gladiatorial combat in ancient Rome. The "I" of fiction is diffusive, apart from the material of the fiction, with parts of the personality perhaps succumbing to a different destiny. This is more than an alter ego, or a confrontation with the self. This is a radical change in narrative. Fiction: no longer a clear picture contained within the narrator's purview, but an erratic image where the narrator, the subject, and the medium are brought together into the same imaginative field of interaction, an image that is shattered, confused, self-contradictory, but with an independent and individual life of its own.

The two tendencies of "story" and "fiction" are echoed in most discussions of the short story: continuity and change, tradition and experiment, manners and form, story to anti-story, small press publishing versus large book companies. Two narrative strategies. Story or fiction? Canadians finding new narratives.

Mirrors and illusions characterize the differences between stories and fictions. An often quoted remark of Irish storyteller Frank O'Connor suggests that fiction is like a mirror in the roadway. He says stories reflect the world, and that language has a referent beyond itself. Like Mallarme's *Le Livre*, the great book is a mirror of life, a parable of the Great Creation itself. In Borges' fiction, on the other hand, mirrors are more sinister. Mirrors might simply reflect other books as models for experience. A deadly proliferation of mirrors can pull sinister worlds to us through the pages of books (especially encyclopedias — what kind of Canada might Mel Hurtig's Great Book reveal to us?) Mirrors might well represent the interstices that keep the flow of time from losing itself in infinity. Mirrors, more horrifying, reflect multiple or simultaneous universes that force us to make uncertain choices. Worst of all (from the O'Connor viewpoint) the Borgesian fiction does not mirror the world at all; it is simply one more thing added to the unknown. Fiction in Canada is as real as any other perceptual experience.

A fiction is not a mirror, but an illusion. A fiction does not always point back to a mimetic world. The metaphor of a fiction may suggest what cannot be said by alluding "to that profoundly human second reality that always remains concealed from us." Fables, fantasies, and metafictions suggest fiction is an illusion, a game of words. The writer is a player. The words of a fiction need not capture and mirror all (Mallarme's Great Work), but simply be true to themselves.

Why write stories or fictions? As the French critic Todorov writes, "we quest for what is not known, those mysteries that cannot be explained." Stories and fictions are the means by which we speak our truths. The world is created, perhaps defined, by art. Perhaps, as in Donald Barthelme's fictions, our ultimate reality is in the structures we build. Fiction: our reality, though the words be meaningless exchanges. Dreck, as Barthelme says. As the post-new novelist Jean Ricardou suggests, the world is empty.

Writing replaces the emptiness and establishes itself in the world's place. Writers, then do not re-create, but replace.

Yet each fiction raises and answers the question: what is a fiction? As John Barth noted, the contemporary fiction writer is like Scheherazade, pondering the artifice each night, trying to fulfil the unrealized potential of the eternal, neverending story. Double and triple (or more) endings challenge the concept of closure, or even if a story does end. Fiction has asides, interruptions, and intruding voices. Authorial interruption mingles art, life, and illusion. Fiction: challenging standard conventions.

Characters in fiction go beyond the physical and temporal levels of traditional stories. Characters might have ambivalent sexuality and personalities. Or a fiction might eliminate human characters altogether. Canada's various bestiaries, cosmogonies, legends, cabalistic works, heraldries, and folklores hint that monsters and imaginary animals (Canadian monsters, Canadian imaginary animals!) are mysteriously linked to our destiny. Fiction: cronopios, famas, esperanzas, and nebechs as the essence of the human condition (from Julio Cortázar's

Cronopios and Famas). A fiction can reconsider our vision of Canada, move into other areas of Canadian consciousness, play with memory as well as intellectual constructions. Perhaps even create a new Canadian myth. Fictions are irrealistic. That is part of the nature of short fiction, in its continuing exploration of the psyche and redefinition of self and identity.

That undiscovered fiction of Canada is anywhere we want it to be. As Ernest Volkening said of Gabriel Garcia Marquez, the setting of fiction is not nationalism or regionalism, but "the point of rest amidst the perennial flight of phenomena, the axis upon which the planets and constellations of his narrative inspiration turn." To write fiction, writers needed new perspectives to awaken their political, social, and intellectual consciousness. The centre has shifted — fiction is no longer in North America or Britain or Europe or Latin America. The centre could even be in Canada, pretending to be someplace else.

As George Garret has so ably shown in a study of American short fiction, the relationship between contemporary life and innovative fiction is related. Canada has unemployed, urban violence, a baffling future, closed frontiers, fragmented societies. All this finds expression in fiction. If not in detail, then in a mood of hopelessness or meaninglessness. Things have gone wrong in the present. They may never be righted again. So we get revisionist literary history, new techniques, new forms of criticism. Writers have changed, and with it comes the aggressive young critics looking for original innovative works to explicate. While Canadians don't yet see criticism as an art form (with perhaps the exception of Robert Kroetsch and a generation of graduate students who try to out-Kroetsch him in their explications of his work), the revolution in fiction takes the critic into consideration. Self-conscious fictions, metafictions that contain self-criticisms, and parodies all assume the critic as the ideal audience.

As fiction changed, so did the audience, and with it, the reading of fiction.

Yet the contemporary fiction writer has less faith in knowledge than the traditional storyteller. Perceptions from the outside world can no longer be trusted. Even language cannot be trusted as a means of perception. Fiction: incomplete, fragments, outlines, abandoned works. An irreconcilable antagonism between existence and the imagination. Language matches the intensity and disintegration of a disintegrating world. So a fiction does not always conclude. As Canada cannot completely be known, described, discovered.

Perhaps fictions of the future will incorporate more aspects of our newer realities. Pop culture, super shopping malls, the experience of the working class as critical vantage points for fiction. Perhaps psychic energy will open up new concepts of character. Metapsychiatry — the study of ESP, mysticism, occult phenomena, telepathy, Psi phenomena, intuitive archeology, bioenergetic interaction, energy fields, psychedelic experience, and transcendental states — is an established discipline. Tai Chi, meditation, and various esoteric lifestyles may open up new concepts for short fiction as individual experience in renewed by an inquiry into itself.

After all, if a fiction means anything to a writer, it's a change in the nature of an individual's relationship to society. As in all artistic movements (romanticism, modernism, avant garde, post modernism, post-post modernism), alienation is an aesthetic position. Robert Bly would put individual experience at the origin of all creative endeavour. Canadian short fiction: on the edge of the new, language moving towards the inexpressible.

Yet others argue fiction should be social protest as well as art. Frederic Jameson announces in *The Political Unconscious: Narrative as a Socially Symbolic Act* that literature not only reflects (and expresses) its own community, but also yearns for an idealized one. Fiction by this definition is Utopian and negative by longing for a past, or positive and Marxist as the authors of fiction point us forward to the future we speculate and desire. As history changes, so does an individual's interpretation of it. Jameson's master code is the political interpretation of texts. So fiction deals with class struggle, racism, economic, and social conflict. Fiction should attack the class struggle buried in mass culture, and reveal how capitalism at the end of the twentieth century totalizes culture, and regulates institutions and patterns of behaviour. Fiction suggests our completeness by revealing our incompleteness.

The narrative forms suggested by a generation of feminist critics and creative writers should revitalize fiction. As content of "story" has turned from the family, nature, religion, and heterosexual love to their own bodies, attachments to other woman, physical passion, sexual liberation as well as sexual exploitation and destruction, women shape their material from the very substance of their bodies and lives. As *13th Moon* suggested in a recent double issue on narrative forms, there is a larger world of discourse out there to be reclaimed and discovered. Writers inspired by the meta-ethics of Mary Daly, the archetypal feminine of Nor Hall, the revisionist art histories of Lucy R. Lippard are returning language to its honourable roots by reinvesting language with its original meaning. Scholars such as Dale Spender are rewriting literary history by uncovering centuries of women's writing. Fiction in the 21st century (so close, so new) will be much different: problems will be exposed, named, and hopefully eradicated or at least understood.

Canadian fiction writers have claimed solidarity with many overlapping cultures. As some jazz musicians would say, this is World Music. Synthesis and Juxtapositions. Everybody is from a different background, but it all fits together. French literature and the nouveau roman; American imaginative acts in the 1960s; Latin American writers blending the world's cultural heritage against a baroque colonial backdrop. Canadian writers sought links with the "universal codes" underlying and connecting all fiction. We put Canadian flags on our backpacks and sought to discover ourselves in the nearest library. The world is like a book, and people who stay home never turn the page.

Fiction: the dark irrationality of Kafka; the parables of Ilse Aichinger that reduced representation to basic situations and incidents; the surface reality of Robbe-Grillet; the anti-world absurdity of Ionesco; the fiction of Guy Davenport, linking all of history and artistic innovation; the language of William Gass, existing independently of a story; the intense prose of Jack Hodgins with its hidden myths; and so many others: Duras, Calvino, Artmann, Benn, Roussel, Sarraute, Oe, Abe, Ocampo, Quiroga, Arlt, Handke, Michaux, and the indispensable Cortazar, Beckett, and Borges. Fiction: an experience so intense it suggests another world behind prose. Different notions, frames, conceptions, conniptions that help us shape our fiction material. New approaches. An archeology of the library digging us into our history. And the example of all those foreign critics, their varied theories: Iser, Foucault, Barthes, Kristeva, Bahktin, Derrida, Lacan, and others giving us authority to emulate and rebel against. All fiction: with its own grammars and laws.

Short fiction has entered a new critical age in Canada at the close of the twentieth century. In traditional studies of short stories, the parts were easily identified: grammar, syntax, sentence balance, names of characters, descriptive texture, relationships between characters. These combine with the inexplicable: authorial personality, narrative tone, passion. Wayne Booth's *The Rhetoric of Fiction* suggested a new way of reading beyond the "new critical" methods of Brooks and Warren's *Understanding Fiction*.

Now that fiction is seen as a form of writing, it can be "read" according to the semiotics of culture, theories of information communication, the many varieties of structuralist and post-structuralist analysis. Fiction is now seen as a verbal experience. A fiction can be read with the formalist methods of Tsvetan Todorov or Wolfgang Shlovsky or the "reader-response" theories of Wolfgang Iser and Stanley Fish. Susan Lohafer has written a "practical poetics" based on the sentence unit in *Coming to Terms with the Short Story*. A different approach, based on events, time focus, character, narration, and the reading of a text, is offered by Shlomith-Kenan in *Narrative Fiction: Contemporary Poetics*. Here the analysis of fiction proceeds from the main storyline to deep structure, including the concepts of absence and presence based on deconstructive readings.

As we get new writers, so we get new readers, entering into a fiction via its emphases, its silences, or even, as John Metcalf has suggested, the score of the punctuation. The current university approach to fiction seems keen on the cold cerebral writings of the French *Tel Quel* school, headed by Philippe Sollers. These textualist writers suggest prose is subject to scientific investigation that leads to political activity. According to them, all writing is a "text" and all expression is a "fiction," a creation of history. Reality is either excluded from writing, or is the writing. The text becomes the future of the world written in advance. The arguments of *Tel Quel* in its two phases are dense, subtle, and occasionally persuasive. Clearly, the fiction of Canada has entered an extravagant time for both writer and critic.

How many discourses can we have? Stories are what we are. As Welch D. Everman has written in the *North American Review,* stories teach us how to live, give us a means for integrating our lives and our selves. The many fictions show the shape of shifting personalities, reveal concepts, forces, events, over which we have no control. As Robert Kroetsch has said, in "Effing the Ineffable," narratives are written not because of what they have to say, but of what cannot be said.

As a result, fictions have a disturbing mood. Fiction: elements of paranoia. Characters: improvised, doubtful of their own personality. Struggling for self-definition (in fiction that has characters) in disrupted prose and threatening environment. Fiction: the aesthetic of failure, of sacrifice, of guilt.

Marcel Proust said art is an awareness of life. A century later, art questions its own validity, demonstrates that the connection between words and things is arbitrary, and that language is not always helpful, comforting, or order distilling. Fiction: language exposes the weakness of language. Fiction, as Heinrich Böll notes, can follow the logical consequence of an absurd premise. In turn, the fiction writer struggles to know one is a writer and to act on that knowing. Fiction: a reminder that truth is revealed (if at all) by the making of an untruths.

The diverse voices of Canada's writers enrich our literary imagination as well. Contributors to this anthology have come from many places, all parts of Canada and North America, China, Ireland, India, and Mexico.

Michael Bullock reminds us that surrealism is a philosophy, not an outdated art movement, but a powerful force in the liberating imagination. Two decades ago, Canadian fiction writers had to send their work to England, America, or elsewhere. Now the garrison has collapsed: Canadian writers can send their material to small presses and literary magazines at home.

Yet there is always a crisis in writing. As we move through the 1980s, the neo-conservative right in the western world, including Canada, has reminded us that the economics of literary publishing remain fragile. The Canada Council suffers cutbacks, circulations stagnate, the Ontario Arts Council cancels a promotion program. The bills from post office, accountants, paper mills, bank service charges, printers, and phone company are a constant reminder of the tension between creativity and commerce.

The frontiers of fiction are always moving. Where does a story happen? On the page? In the reader's head as words are reassembled into some kind of order? How do reader and writer participate in the experience of a fiction? Fiction tells us stories about stories. In a time of parodic forms, fiction might come from TV, from movies. From the oral tradition of artless storytelling to the most complex post-modernist innovations, contemporary Canadian fiction embraces reality, and challenges it with reality-warps.

What's next for contemporary Canadian short fiction? Fiction is a shape shifter, existing in the restlessness of the present moment. The life of fiction comes from compulsion, anxiety, recrimination. Stories of magicians, elves, mud, ponds, dying Mexican girls, whales, caves, intrauterine fantasies, Amway, quartets, old TV programs, forgotten movie stars, and ladies on bus rides in China are just some of fiction's contents as revealed in this anthology. Canadian short fiction can accommodate the moral and philosophical fictions of the European and Latin American tradition where ideas are as important as physical sensation in North American fiction. Associative metaphor and image transferring as literary techniques mix with unconscious archetypes and fundamental symbols. The essence of narrative combines logic and intuition.

Perhaps someday a graduate student will send out a questionnaire asking the following: are setting and place important? Are writers and editors optimistic about the future? Is psychology of character important in fiction? Is the drama in fiction found in the event, the language, the characters, or a confrontation with a philosophical position? Will future fiction deal with the abnormal, the mystical, the excremental? What makes Canadian short fiction modern, post modern, post-post modern, or anachronistic? Is form, purpose, or technique more important than the experience of a fiction? Why write fictions at all? Has any Canadian short story writer done for Canada what Chekhov did for Russia? Why have Canadians excelled in short narratives? Will the creative essay ever return to Canadian writing? Will short fiction explore patterns of mediation, content, and opposition between individuals and mass culture and how that culture is experienced? What is the moral effect of artistic change? What will happen to the emotional qualities of short fiction in coming years?

I would like to respond that mystery is essential and central to fiction. We must speak about ourselves and the unspeakable truth that always evades us, as Welch D. Everman has written. The truth may occur in a world of action, or it may be in a fabular and mythic illusion. The fiction may be rooted in long evenings when the talk turns to the neighbours. Or fiction may challenge the concept of plot, character, theme, setting, and closure. A situation may be resolved by logic. Or resolved aesthetically. Or symmetrically, as in a circular fiction. By questioning the possibilities of fiction, we open up other possibilities for fiction.

Of course, we cannot forget the ultimate fiction: ourselves. Rimbaud said, "the art dreams us." Borges reminds us in *Labyrinths,* if the characters of a fiction can be readers, then we, as readers, can be fictions. Fictions are as real in their unreality as we are unreal in our reality. As fictions, our possibilities are limitless. We can be written, and betray ourselves as truth by explaining ourselves as fiction. Fiction reaches the truth by moving towards silence. Canadian fiction is moving, noisily, through its own discovery. Our silence is still in the future. Undiscovered.

LEON ROOKE was born in rural North Carolina in 1934 and lived in Victoria, British Columbia for many years before moving to Eden Mills, Ontario, site of the Eden Mills Writers' Festival. His publications include *Who Do You Love?*, *A Good Baby*, *A Bolt of White Cloth*, *Fat Woman*, and *Shakespeare's Dog*, which received the Governor General's Award for Fiction in 1984. This story first appeared in CFM No. 15 in 1974 and won the first annual CFM Contributor's Prize.

Wintering In Victoria

LEON ROOKE

YESTERDAY MY WIFE LEFT ME, no word of warning, no scenes, I walked in the bedroom and found her packing.

"That's right, jerk," she said, "I'm getting out of your life, you prick, I can't get out of this house fast enough."

Fine, I said, are you taking the kid?

"The kid, the kid, the kid!" she said, "do you even know her name? You bet I'm taking her, she isn't safe here with you!"

What have we done to our women?

Years have gone by since I met one who believed a child was safe with its father.

Not that it bothered me.

I waved them down the hall and out the door, told them if they changed their minds it would be all right with me.

If you want to come back, fine, if you want to make this permanent, fine — no hard feelings on my part.

My wife came running back inside a few minutes later to tell me she'd like to kick my ass, nothing would give her more pleasure.

"Someone," she said, "ought to knock some sense into you before it's too late. If I was only big enough or strong enough or stupid enough, I'd do it myself. Man, would I give it to you!"

I put down the latest issue of Fiddlehead, got up out of the easy chair and bent over.

Go ahead, I said, this ought to make it easier.

The kid was crying, however.

The kid stood in the open doorway, her coat bunched in her arms, saying "Daddy, Daddy, Daddy, bye, Daddy!"

Something is wrong with me, I was touched but barely enough to tell it.

My wife ran up to her, shook her, picked her up in her arms and said "Don't talk to that S.O.B."

Then they went.

Walking, who knows where or for how long, probably without a dime between them.

Too bad, I thought, it wasn't raining.

Since it wasn't I decided to go out for a while myself. Take a walk, Jake, I told myself, be good for you.

My pal Jack was in his driveway the next block down, polishing his Austin mini. Across the street Mr. and Mrs. Arthur C. Pole were raking up wet leaves, trying to set fire to them.

Look at those idiots, I said to Jack — wasting perfectly good mulch.

Not that I cared

Jack threw down his chamois cloth.

"You're my friend," he said, "right?"

Right, I said.

"I can talk to you," he said, "right?"

Right, I said.

"And you'll not take offense, right, you'll not want to punch my head in if I level with you?"

I told him not to worry, we were pals, we had been good friends for a long time, if he had something to say to me to come right out and lay it on me, no hard feelings on my part.

"O.K." he said, "I been wanting to say this to you for some months now."

Go ahead, I said.

"All right," he said, "I will. You've become a big pain, Jake, you've gone wing-wingy on us, nobody can stand your company anymore. It isn't that you don't have feelings, no, I'm not claiming that, but nobody can reach you anymore, Jake, it's a pain being with you, you've become a first-class down-at-the-heels shit-in-the mouth and I can't stand the sight of you, I wish to hell I could never see you again." He stopped then and hitched up his pants and glared at me.

I told him I understood, that I wasn't upset, to get it all off his chest right now if it would make him feel better.

"All right, Jake," he said. "The fact is you've become a bloody cipher, a big zero, a big hulking zombie-fish that I get queasy just talking to! For your own sake you ought to seek professional help, talk to your minister, do something about your lousy condition."

Good, I said, I'm glad you told me, Jack, is there any more?

"That about sums it up," he said. "I've talked it over with my wife, I've talked it over with all the guys, and we are all in mutual agreement that we don't want to have anything more to do with you, we wash our hands of you."

Fine by me, I said, and turned and strolled away, not bothered in the least.

In fact, I felt relief — if anything.

I walked down to the billiards hall and broke a rack and dropped in seven balls the rotation way and quit then, hung up my stick, leaving the rest on the table, it's always that cruddy eighth ball that breaks my streak.

I went over to another table and broke another rack and ran seven more.

I felt all right, pretty good, but I can't claim much elation.

I picked up a pot roast from the butcher shop and walked home and put it in a pot with a potato and an onion and put it in the oven on a slow bake.

I thought it might feel pretty good to sit at home and enjoy a good dinner alone with maybe a glass of wine, take off my shoes, maybe afterwards have a quiet snooze.

In the meantime I checked through the mail, got out my chequebook, paid off some old bills.

I figured it cost me twelve hundred and eighty-four dollars a month just to be comfortable.

To have heat, lights, phone, seven rooms, a car, and clothes.

The only thing I have even a faint objection to is the bird, a canary, that business of eating like a bird is utter nonsense, I can recall times in the past when I've thought the bird was eating me out of house and home.

But he does the best he can, I don't blame him, he's got to get along, I bear no grudges, I enjoyed writing those cheques, I thought that maybe tomorrow I'd go down and watch some of the people when they opened their mails, Stocker's Moving Company and B.C. Hydro and B.C. Telephone and the oil people, thinking surely they'd crack a smile to see that old Jake B. Carlisle had paid his debts in full, no need now to barrage him with further calls, threaten lawsuits, power cut-offs, all that crap.

So there was some mild elation, not much, nothing to shout about, and afterwards I enjoyed a hot bath.

I'm a little tired, I guess, of bathing with other people, of sharing the tub with wife or daughter, I stretched out, closed my eyes, sort of dreamed for a while.

The phone was ringing, it was some guy named Mr. Zoober, something like that.

These people who announce themselves as Mr. Such and Such, I can remember the times I'd strangle the phone and sometimes tell them to go to hell because people who say Hello, this is Mr. Such and Such from Such and Such give me a pain, they're rotten people obviously, they either want to sell you something or tell you they're cutting off your water, in the past such people have really got to me, but this time I was civil, I said, why yes, good of you to call, how can I help you, Mr. Zoober?

He told me he'd like to sell me some insurance, was I interested, and I thought about it for a second or two and then told him well I might be, tell me what he had in mind.

Which he did, and made an appointment to come over that very evening.

I put a few carrots in the pot roast, buttered a bit of bread, poured a glass of wine, and shortly thereafter sat down and had a very nice dinner.

It was during this that the doorbell sounded and I opened it and

Jack stood there with his wife beside him.

Hello, Jack, I said, how are you, how are you, Alice, what can I do for you?

"We were thinking," said Jack, "that perhaps I was somewhat hard on you."

"Yes," said Alice, "you poor man, you see we didn't know that June had left you."

I tried to explain to them that I valued Jack's comments, I appreciated his honesty, that as far as I could tell June's leaving me had nothing to do with it.

"No," insisted Jack, "under the circumstances it was a mistake for me to come down so hard on you."

"You see," said Alice, "we didn't know you and June were having marital difficulties, that changes everything, now we know why you've been such a drip, Jack wants to apologize."

It isn't necessary, I told them, the truth is we hadn't been having any special difficulty, no more so than other couples, that it would be a mistake for them to assume that such small differences of opinion as we had in no way accounted for my recent failures as a person.

No, I said, you're very fortunate to be rid of me.

They stared at me for five minutes or so and then went back to their car and drove away.

I thought it was nice of them to come by like that, a decent gesture, but it didn't matter to me.

I went back in and finished my meal which was cold by that time though I didn't care, if you ask me hot meals are very over-rated.

I noticed about that time that I had cut my finger and figured it must have happened while I was slicing the carrots.

I watched the C.B.C. news on television and nothing much was happening in the world, which was fine with me. I watched a special next, Highlights in the life of Doris Day, and finished off the bottle of wine without much thinking about it.

At eight Mr. Zooker called, right on time, and told me about the various plans and policies a man of my age and income and family status ought to have. He seemed a little worried that I was alone, he asked a few veiled questions about my wife, had a few suspicions about the empty wine bottle, but was obviously most disturbed by the dirty dishes still on the dining table.

On the whole he wasn't a bad fellow, I can't say I much objected to him, and we finally agreed that a policy for fifty thousand or so would do me fine.

I think he was quite surprised when I got out my chequebook and wrote out a big one for him, he seemed to think I had been stringing him along.

He made some joke or other about never losing a customer, and left right away, apologizing, saying he had a few more customers to see tonight, he was aiming for the Million Dollar Mark this year because his company was giving all the Million Dollar salesmen and their families a free trip to Honolulu.

I thought about inviting him back in to write out a bigger policy, what the hell, it didn't much matter to me.

Not much else happened that night, June's mother called and asked what the trouble was, couldn't things be sorted out, she'd always liked me or anyway had liked me pretty much until recently, what had happened to me, was it another girl?

I said, no, it's been years since I felt much attraction for anyone other than June, that her daughter was a fine woman and I hoped she wouldn't worry too much about this, to try to go to sleep and forget it.

"But little Cherise!" she said, "What will happen to little Cherise, don't you love little Cherise!" and crying on and on like that about the kid until I got bored with it all and hung up and got myself a cup of coffee.

I've never much understood how people can go through their lives drinking that lousy stuff they call coffee in the supermarkets, Eight O'Clock, and Yuban and Chase and Sanborn and Maxwell House and Nabob, it's enough to make a person sick, whereas I drink only the dark French roast because there is no better coffee in the world and standards ought to begin with these most common of practices otherwise there is little likelihood they will exist in more important affairs. People all over the world are drinking those lousy brands and thinking this stuff stinks and likely as not going out to murder and rob and cheat all because of the lousy coffee they drink, though I've long-since given up getting worked up over such trivia, it doesn't matter to me, I had my French roast the filter way and stretched out on the sofa and dozed a while before getting up to draft a few letters to people I had been thinking about that day, my mother whom I have always respected and admired and my boss the business man and the girl I had known back in college named Cissy Reeves though I wouldn't know where to send her letter to. Dear Mom,

I said, and told her of the insurance policy of which she was cobeneficiary and enclosed Zoober's card in the event anything unfortunate happened to me and no one got in touch with her because it has been my belief that those guys will not pay off unless a gun is held at their throats.

I doodled a bit on her letter, not knowing what to say, wondering idly about her life and about mine and about her nine other sons and daughters all of whom had turned out to be fairly average people through no fault of hers.

I sealed it up after a while and drew a few kisses on the envelope, it wasn't much of a letter but what the hell.

Next I wrote my boss, telling him not to expect me to show up for work the following few weeks, I was going to take time off, if he didn't like it he could find another guy.

Then I wrote Cissy and that took some time because I found I didn't much remember anything of value about Cissy, she was a fairly regular girl, fairly routine, not especially attractive I guess if one wanted to be objective about it, hard to tell now why I had found her exciting enough to chase all over campus and storm and rage whenever I saw her with another guy, Cissy with her ordinary body and ordinary clothes and a mind certainly that no one would notice in a crowd, married, the last I heard, to some guy who was expecting big things from Simpson-Sears or The Bay, hell, who could remember? Dear Cissy, I wrote, I just thought I would get in touch after all these years and tell you that I have been thinking of you today for the first time since our graduation dance when you cried on my shoulder and told me you had decided to marry this business administration guy because you really loved him and you knew I'd be hurt but it was probably best for all concerned and how you walked with me out to the car and got in the back seat with me and how even as I was undressing you it came over me that I had not the slightest interest in having you naked under me so I said crap on this and flung you out and drove away and have not thought again of you until this very day when mostly all I want to say is how are you Cissy, how has your life been though I can't really say I care one way or another and I know I'll never give you another thought once I seal this letter.

I sealed it and it was the goddamn truth, poor Cissy, probably a good thing I didn't know where to send it.

But it was pretty boring about that time, I wasn't sleepy, so I made another copy and sent one to the head office of Sears in Toronto and another to the Vancouver Bay because I wasn't up to searching out their master quarters, it didn't matter that much to me one way or the other.

I finished off the cheque-writing chores, writing a letter for each cheque, telling B.C. Telephone and Hydro and the like how much I valued their services and hoped we could continue now with a good relationship, that I wasn't one of those who believed for a minute that their profits were excessive, that they were money-grabbers and impolite and sticking it to their customers wherever they could.

I fell asleep pretty soon after that, must have, because about twelve I was wakened by the telephone, I was asleep on the sofa in my clothes when this great jangle came, and it was June of course calling me an S.O.B. prick and a lot of other things and she hoped I was enjoying myself, who did I have with me, she wasn't surprised, naturally I had never thought one minute of her, I was a selfindulgent prig without any feelings for anyone else and she had always known it would come to this — and I let her talk on, it didn't seem worth it to interrupt, I was even enjoying it in a mild way and appreciating June because normally she is such a steady person, level-headed, routine, somewhat ordinary, I guess, never saying much, taking life easy, you wouldn't think she was the type to have a thought in her head nor much emotion either.

"I'll kill you, kill you, kill you, you bastard!" she screamed that several times and I shrugged more or less, I asked if there was anything specific I had done to enrage her, to compel her to leave, that I'd be happy to apologize if that would make her feel better, that I'd promise to change, do better, try harder, if that would help her cope any easier with the situation. But she of course just continued to scream, not even using words any longer, the rare one like "Pig" or "S.O.B." but mostly just scream scream scream as though someone was slicing down her back with a butcher knife and finally her mother took the phone away from her and said Jake you've got to come over here, I can't do any more with her, and I sighed around a bit, I complained and tried to find excuses, said I had a lot to do, a lot of chores, but June's mother is an insistent woman and eventually I agreed I'd come over and do what I could.

That's how it happened that I came across Jack and his old glum-chum wife Alice another time. They were sitting outside my house in their car, just sitting there watching my door as if they thought it might suddenly burst into flames.

I opened the door on Alice's side and asked what they had on their minds. I don't know, it seemed to me that once I saw them there, it was as if I had expected it or should have, I wasn't very surprised.

So hello, Jack, hello, Alice, have you been here long, what's on your minds?

Alice, in the past I've felt some sorrow for Alice, she has always seemed so miserable, so glum, but always without a reason, no explanation for what's troubling her, that's just the way she is, glum and miserable, as if poor Jack has never kissed her and she had never wanted him to, as if nothing has ever happened to her and why should it, the truth is that Alice hasn't any imagination or interest, I suppose if she goes through her day and finds time to wash her hair or sweep the floor then that has been a pretty good day for her, nothing to complain about, about what she expected from the day, in fact it occurred to me as I opened her door that here was the first time 1 hadn't found Alice with her hair in rollers and now it had happened twice today so something very strange must be going on here.

They didn't say anything right away so I told them that I hoped they hadn't been brooding about Jack's comments to me, that truthfully I didn't mind a bit and Jack was absolutely right in telling me I was developing into a first-rate cipher, that I didn't mind in the least and was only just mildly surprised that anyone had noticed any difference in me, I certainly didn't intend to go around as if I had some sign hung on me saying NOTHING BOTHERS ME.

"Jake, Jake, Jake," Jack moaned at last, "Get in, let's drive around a while."

I thought he had in mind going down to the S&W drive-in for maybe a hamburger and coke, because we do that together sometimes with Alice and June and the kid along, so I had to tell them I didn't think I could make it, I'd received an urgent telephone call a moment ago and had to get across town fast.

"From June?" asked Alice, and I admitted that was the case.

She hugged me then, quite suddenly, I didn't so much as see her arms reaching out for me, she simply pulled me to her with the strength of a wild beast and pressed my head against her neck, thumping me on the back and repeating "Poor Jake, Poor Jake, oh you poor man, oh let us help you, I'm sure you will feel better if you'll only talk about it."

It was Jack who had to make her let me go, who pried her arms from around me. "For God's sake, Alice," he said, "how can he talk with you strangling him?" and she sat back quietly after that, sulking, biting her lips like a retarded child because she doesn't like him speaking to her in those tones, I guess.

"Now the reason we are parked in front of your house like this," he explained, "is because June called us, she was worried about YOU."

Worried? I said, and he said, "Yes, she was afraid you might do something to yourself."

Like what? I asked.

"Something criminal," said Jack, "and June said she would never forgive herself for it."

"She figured she'd be to blame," said Alice, "that she wouldn't be able to look at herself in the mirror ever again if you went and did something stupid to yourself like slicing your wrist, oh Jake you know she worships the ground you walk on, if only you weren't so peculiar!"

They continued to talk in that vein for some time, I couldn't say anything to calm them down. Finally I said, "Look, I thought you understood me, I don't care about any of this, suicide is the last thought from my mind, you don't need to worry about me."

Alice gave me a consoling look, she kept reaching for my hand or my face or my leg and I kept trying to move out of her reach, lately I have just not liked at all her wanting to touch whoever she's talking to. "So look," I said and it seemed to me my calm ought to have been blissfully penetrating — "Look, why don't the two of you toot along and look after your own lives, I'm fine, and I'm confident June and I can handle this without your help."

But they wouldn't accept it, they were offended, they insisted I get in the car and they'd drive me over to June's mother's house, June needed their help now even if I refused it and they wouldn't dream of walking out on a friend.

I got in the car, what the hell.

During the ride I tried to relax, not lose sight of this new life I'd found for myself. The truth is I couldn't help feeling some resentment, a guy comes along who isn't bothered by anything and right away everyone starts losing their wigs.

"Who was that man who came by your house earlier?" asked Alice, and I told her it was Mr. Zooker from the insurance company, and I saw them exchange glances and a moment later Alice broke into tears, she was quite nasty, how stupid, she said, and how mindless and vindictive and self-centred suicides were, they never thought of other people, of wives and children left behind, what would happen for instance to poor little Cherise who had never done anything to anybody? She'd hate me forever, she said, if I killed myself, that would really show me up for the kind of jerk I was, and I could tell Jack pretty much shared her feelings, he looked like he wanted to punch me, kept staring at me in the rearview mirror as if I might do it right there in the back seat of his station-wagon with its smell of dog.

All the lights were on at the house, I saw that as we turned the corner. All the doors were wide open and even as Jack made his slow approach I could see someone running out into the yard and back in again every third second, run out and pull her hair and yell and then run in again. Naturally it was June, in her housecoat, in her stocking feet, her hair stringy, a thousand lines in her face that I had never seen before. She looked a mess but the truth is I hardly noticed. Before the car came to a stop she was already coming at me with her fingernails, spitting and clawing and screaming, punching me around until everyone except her was satisfied. Her mother is a genteel lady, she hates scenes, she appeared at last and pulled June off of me and led her back inside.

"Don't think you don't deserve it," Alice told me, and Jack added that I'd better not try anything, he was watching me. They all went into the living room to look after June and June's mother came out to pat my arm and lead me upstairs to where the kid was.

"She couldn't sleep, poor child," she said, "she was calling you and finally June got angry and locked her in the closet but I managed to find a spare key and get her out, be kind to her, Jake, she doesn't understand."

I smiled and told her I would do the best I could and she patted me again and returned downstairs.

I entered the room, usually a guest room but hardly ever used now because June's mother says she's tired of people, and the kid was seated in a child's rocker that was much too little for her rocking in the dark, not saying anything. She was cute, I was touched in a distant way, I really didn't feel much of anything, no more than the simple aesthetic response to a child's silhouette in a tiny tot's chair.

"Is that you, Daddy?" she asked, and I replied it was, and she said, "don't turn on the light, please."

I asked why, had her mother been pinching her again.

"Not much," she said, "on my legs and on my stomach some but it doesn't hurt very much."

I turned on the lights. She had a few welts on her skin, a zig-zag of purple wounds down her legs, nothing to get upset about.

"Everything was fine," she said, "once I was locked in the closet, I hope you haven't been worried."

I told her I wasn't, I knew she could take care of herself. I noticed her hair was wet and asked her how that had happened. She told me her mother had made her take a bath but she hadn't wanted to and so June had held her under the water.

I'm glad you didn't drown, I told her, and she said she was glad too but that someone still had to clean up the bathroom because June had gone through the room pulling everything out of the cupboards and the medicine cabinet and throwing it all in the bathwater, she really had made a wreck of the place.

I told her not to mind, someone would see to it, that June probably bad got confused and thought she was at home because normally she was spic and span and especially in her mother's house.

The kid said she didn't mind, she'd tried to clean it up herself but June had kept pinching her. "But are we really leaving you, Daddy?" she asked, "June says we are and that you don't mind, that you're itching to be alone."

I asked her how she felt about it.

"I don't ever want to be alone," she said, "but I can manage if I have to."

She had a blanket around her shoulders and was shivering, it seemed somewhere between the bath and the closet she'd lost her clothes.

I stepped out of the room to look for them and found June snarling at the foot of the stairs, restrained by Jack and Alice and her mother, furious to get upstairs and sink her teeth into me.

Let her go, I told them, and after a moment or two they released her. She charged forward, taking about five or six steps before her breath gave out and she gasped down on the carpet, sobbing. Now take her back to the sitting room, I told them, and Jack came up and got her and led her back down.

There comes a time in your life, you start giving orders and no one in the world will stop to question them.

I found the kid's clothes in the bath water and wrung them out. I drained the tub and put to one side those things that hadn't been ruined.

I could hear Jack and Alice talking downstairs, though June and her mother were silent and there seemed to be some sort of fight developing between Jack and Alice. No one had thought to close the doors and the house was under a distinct chill.

No go, I told the kid, you're going to have to make do with a blanket.

She turned her face away, hoping I wouldn't notice that her cheeks were swollen.

I crossed the room and slid up the window. It looked clean outside, brisk, an open sky, a hatful of stars — a fairly regular scene for this time of the year.

"I'm going to cut out now, kid," I told her.

She sniffed a bit and hugged the blanket tight around her.

I climbed over the sill and felt for the fire escape rung and started down.

The kid came down behind me. I looked up and she was all naked above me, distorted like a dummy, the blanket flapping us.

"My shoes," she said, when we were on the ground.

The ground was cold, even icy. I stooped and she climbed on my back. We ran across the yard, jogged under the trees. Her knees wrapped tight around my waist, one hand gripped my shoulder she rode light and handsome as an apple.

How far can you go with a kid on your back? I don't know. After a while she began giggling, I giggled too. After a time, you don't feel anything, a slow giggle is good for you, the giggles give you wings.

"How far do we go, Daddy?"

Not far. We spent the night here: a fairly routine, a fairly ordinary place. Not much happens here. We can get along. Tomorrow — maybe the next day — we'll go out, ring up her mother, run a quick check on our affairs. But there's no hurry. There never is. Our lives are routine, normal: you won't find much that bothers US.

ANNE BERNARD (a.k.a. Ann Copeland) was born in Hartford, Connecticut and was an Ursuline nun for 13 years before moving with her family to New Brunswick in 1971. Her publications include *Season of Apples, The Back Room, Earthen Vessels,* and *The Golden Thread,* which was nominated for the Governor General's Award for Fiction. She now lives in Salem, Oregon and teaches at Willamette University. This story first appeared in CFM No. 18 in 1975.

Siblings

ANNE BERNARD

IT CONTINUED TO BOTHER SISTER REGINALD that she and Sister Thomas had argued. It had been more than a friendly disagreement; she had felt that. In the space behind their words she had felt depths of conviction threatened. It had been one of those human encounters when words seem the shield rather than the expression of some much deeper conflict, sometimes unknown even to the speakers. And though she had been vaguely aware of that disturbing disparity between what they said and what it meant, she had felt her own inadequacy to clarify. In such moments inexperience was a burden.

"But I just don't believe that's the way to handle students," Sister Thomas had insisted. They were walking at recreation the evening before, picking up the discussion that had begun after lunch. In the heat of their exchange, Sister Thomas' strides got longer and longer with each emphasis, and she swung her skirt and veil decisively around when they reached the end of the end of the drive and started back toward the house. "You've *got* to establish yourself on a different level from the students. I learned that the hard way." The thin lines between her light eyebrows deepened slightly. "They squirm and they push and yell; you've got to speak with authority." She pulled at her cincture absentmindedly as they walked.

"This isn't elementary school, though," Sister Reginald countered. She was suddenly tired from her effort to convey what she felt as a certainty about their girls. "After all, the girls have been through that. They come to high school looking for a challenge. They don't want, in fact, they can't stand" — here, she passed a quick look sideways to see how Sister Thomas would take that, for she wanted only to emphasize, not wound — "seeing us like a group of marshalls, wielding our power, playing the old role of strict nun. And I really do believe your class will shape up without that."

Sister Thomas drew herself up. It was a well known gesture of hers, imitated both within and outside the cloister — Sister Thomas drawing herself up. She was tall and very straight, tall enough that when the community lined up for solemn processions you could easily spot her head above the rest. Her angular features, thoughtful, a trifle stern even in repose, were tamed by immaculate white starched linens. She looked Sister Reginald full in the face. They were good friends. The younger sister felt again the force of that directness and affection and strength that had made her instinctively turn to Sister Thomas when she had come, new, to this community two years ago. She was the youngest. She was well-educated — better, in fact, than her friend. She was glad to have come to what all recognized as one of the happiest communities in the province. She was lucky and she knew it. The high school was new, and there was enthusiasm and generosity of spirit behind it. And after years of preparing to teach (for the province had upgraded its professional requirements) it had been a distinct relief for her to step into the classroom where she could face human beings as equals, in some way, and begin. She had yet to experience real fatigue with the whole endeavor. When she caught glimpses of that in others, it saddened her.

"It isn't that I don't appreciate my position, you know," said Sister Thomas. "I know how the girls feel. They know perfectly well that I've been teaching art in the lower school for ten years here. They know that I'm just filling in for the last two months of the school year in a subject about which I know nothing. Think of yourself in that position."

She did. It was hard to imagine. Hard to imagine years of phonics and sums, trips to the washrooms, patrolling the cafeteria, wiping the noses, drilling the heads, reassuring the parents, meeting the spirits of dozens and dozens of little people. In their blue and white uniforms. Gold stars on their papers. Blue ribbons for Especially Good Conduct. And then, overnight, with no time to prepare the material, to be sent into the high school for one class only: economic geography. Still on the lower school faculty, but exported one hour a day to the high school to teach sophomores. It made her burn that people were put in this position. Sister Thomas had gone, obediently. But she was aware of her vulnerability, and she wasn't used to being vulnerable in exactly that way. She had her strengths and she knew them.

"I do know how you must feel." Sister Reginald heard her response ring hollow. Did she? Armed with her M.A., her enthusiasm, and her permission to revamp the provincial English syllabus. So that her girls had the feeling, at least, that what they were doing was new. Who else among their friends outside had a clue about sentence patterns? Or phonemes? She felt her own competence briefly and wondered if she could imagine how it felt to be Sister Thomas, facing tenth graders day after day, burning the midnight oil to master the next ten pages before tomorrow's class, and then branded by careless sophomores as just an incompetent filler from the lower school.

"I know it's hard," she persisted doggedly. "But you don't have to resort to drill to win them." She thought of her juniors coming back after lunch snickering among themselves about Sister Thomas' latest tactic.

All the nuns were matter for comparison and gossip in the cafeteria. That she knew. But at times she wished her own girls would scruple about passing on their tidbits to her. She believed in loyalty and did not want to betray her friend. On the other hand, she valued having the girls' confidence.

"You know what Mother Thomas is doing, Mother?" Gloria, frizzy-haired and wide-eyed, had confided to her as they cleaned up after school. "She's posting her girls' papers. Posting! And the one who improves most in neatness gets a prize at the end of the month!"

Her insides had contracted but she could feel her facial expression remaining placid, matter-of-fact. Wishing they knew the same Sister Thomas she did, and loved.

"Oh, Gloria." Minimizing it. "That's nothing. Mother Thomas is a terrific teacher. You just wait. By June, you girls will have mastered the material. *Then* you'll appreciate it!" Slamming the last window with the long pole. "Draw the shades this afternoon, would you please? The sun gets in before we do in the morning, and it's hot."

They were always hanging around. She liked it and she didn't. That day she didn't. Here was one more comment to add to her collection of student negatives about Sister Thomas. The remarks bothered her, collecting in her memory and festering until, reluctantly, she thought maybe she should talk to Sister Thomas herself. It should be between them only. That was the strength of their relationship. It could be. Some nuns would have run right to the principal or even to Reverend Mother. They were friends. But it was delicate. She was younger, some fifteen years. She might be educated, even capable, but she was sensitive to her own position. Nonetheless, it was right to speak.

So she did. She had sought out Sister Thomas after lunch yesterday, had nudged her silently off the line heading for recreation, and taken her out behind the new convent where the noon hour was full of sun, freshly turned soil, and robins looking for worms. They stood near the long rows of dark, moist earth in the humid heart of midday, and she tried to explain her feelings.

"You *know* you can teach. You know you can maintain discipline, even under trying circumstances. Why not see if you can reach them with a bit lighter hand?" The sun directly behind Sister Thomas was blinding her, and she felt the disadvantage of having to squint. She was hot and awkward. Who was she to be doing this? But it should be said. Who else would? Sister Thomas was too fine to be the butt of their giggles. Or was she exaggerating?

"I just can't see it!" Sister Thomas towered in the sunshine. Her response was utterly impersonal. Sister Reginald seemed to have struck unwittingly at a matter of principle. She secretly admired her friend's detachment, even as it frustrated her. "Discipline is a problem everywhere. It's hard for you to have a perspective on it, perhaps." She generously included Sister Reginald and continued emphatically, "There *is* something to be said for making them toe the line."

It depends on the line, thought Sister Reginald, but stood quietly in the sun, trying to hear. She could feel moisture forming on her shoulders under the habit.

"Let the girls talk. The fact is that I've been left with a class that had been let slide all year, and they've got to learn something before the semester is over. I *owe* it to them."

"But don't you see, it makes your task all the harder. If you're trying to teach students who are laughing at you, or looking down at you, how can you get them ever to do their best work?"

"But you yourself know they need a firm hand. There's absolutely no way this could be a discussion class, at this point. I know perfectly well that's what the girls thrive on — and waste a lot of time at." She moved her figure over to shade the other's squinting eyes. "I barely learn the material before they do."

Sister Reginald, appreciating the shade, sensed the deeper focus of her friend's complaint: her assignment, her own lack of preparation, her felt inadequacy to adapt that quickly to a whole new situation. The odds were against her. She regretted having spoken and wished they were back at school, out of this beastly sun and the discomfort of impotence.

But they had continued, back and forth, for the few minutes of noon recreation, until the bell had rung a welcome silence on their unresolved exchange. Perhaps it was simply in the nature of things. The dangling question had hung between them all afternoon as they went their separate ways: classes, duties in the house, Office. It was not until after supper that they could talk again, and then was just as futile.

"I can't change now. The whole situation is too far gone, me included." Sister Thomas smiled, ruefully. She had evidently thought over their remarks during her afternoon. Her strides gained speed as they walked. "I like the girls. They'll come to know that. And I want them to learn that material. Their parents are paying good money to send their children to us."

Children. The word chafed Sister Reginald. Her juniors were closer to her age than Sister Thomas was. She suppressed a comment. She knew that a difference of opinion, even a basic one, would not substantially alter her friend's steady openness. Still, she longed to share, not just to tolerate, a point of view. She felt herself cut off from it for good — a combination of age, experience, and temperament, perhaps.

"Well, if you think that's the only way for you, I guess it is." They turned toward the chapel. The bell was about to ring.

"Never mind." Sister Thomas smiled. Her humor was not electric, but simply born of the insight that much of life, including her own, was fundamentally comic. Her companion felt her own over-seriousness. "Don't you worry. In two months it will all be over. And who knows what next year may bring? Maybe they'll send me to the missions! I've lived through far worse than these two months!"

Sister Reginald felt small. She followed Sister Thomas into the cool chapel feeling appreciated but put down. She had been presumptuous. It better not to have spoken. Sister Thomas was no fool. She was obviously managing her own vulnerable situation with strategies time had proven effective. Perhaps she was right. Student cruelties were, after all, passing and — she felt it as she walked down the nave to genuflect in the front — the world of school was far off from this world of worship and fidelity.

She took her place in the choir stall near the front, reaching automatically for her liber. The vermicular intoned.

"Jube domne, benedicere."

She opened at Compline.

"Noctem quietem et finem perfectam concedat nobis Dominus omnipotens."

The brilliant mid-April sunshine of the next afternoon was irresistible. Sister Reginald was out the door of her homeroom the moment the last student had left. One free period! Today she would waste it luxuriating in the sun. She needed fresh air. The fourth class in one week on *Great Expectations* — that would tire anyone. And the whole afternoon would be given to the Glee Club, trying to control fidgeting bodies and whip them into singing shape for the concert, two short weeks away. All outdoors — at least the luscious outdoors around the school in suburban Maryland — beckoned. As she stepped out of the school corridor into the sunshine, her feeling of release was intense.

The magnolia tree at the end of the walk was in full bloom. The border along the gravel drive to the new convent spilled with color: daffodils, tulips, jonquils, even a few crocuses still left. It was hot enough that the black serge felt heavy on her wrists as she stooped to look more closely at the tulip near the hedge just outside the school door. And she could feel beads of perspiration already forming under her plastic headband. Yesterday, her templets had been soaked by the end of the school day. When she put her hand up to her cheek where it was usually indented by the starched white pieces, she could feel their limp dampness taking the shape of her cheek instead of cutting into it. Summer was surely here — and still two months of school to go.

Despite the splendor of her surroundings, she carried within a slightly lumpish feeling, one blight on her own inner landscape. It was the memory of her minutes yesterday with Sister Thomas, blurred now by succeeding hours of prayer and teaching, the routine chores of getting through twenty-four hours. There was nothing to do, she knew, but live with it. The lump would dissolve. She longed for a more active way to dissipate it.

The last period facing her when she returned to school would be Guidance. The girls would be restless. A session on parenthood. She swiftly suppressed the anticipation, opening herself instead to the luscious warmth on her face as she slowly dawdled up the path in the direction of the convent.

She thought of her juniors with vague affection. They were her best class in two years of teaching. Louise, in the first row, overdone eye-shadow, toothy grin, whose forbidden nail polish they tacitly agreed to ignore in the interest of larger gains.

"But why are you called *Mother? I* could see it with some of the other nuns, the older ones, but with you it just doesn't feel right."

"We're *all* called Mother, Louise. It's the tradition of the Order. Some nuns in other Orders are trying to establish a sisterly relationship with their students. But we think of ourselves as spiritual mothers."

Louise had looked unconvinced. "But you call each other Sister. What do you call your superior? Is she Mother?"

The forsythia gleamed. She broke off one tiny bloom and it lay, yellow and fresh, in her hand. She should, perhaps, make her meditation now. There was no other time this whole afternoon, from after school until supper. The chapel would be cool. But dark. And indoors. She could feel the flagstones under her heels. Right now she wanted to be vague, not focussed. The freshly cut grass smelled faintly and pervasively sweet. Maybe after night prayer, during study hour, she could bring out a lawn chair and meditate then. The outside world would be still. It was her favorite time of day. The world inside the house would be enveloped by Great Silence: older nuns padding about in their slippers, quietly preparing for bed, younger nuns trying to get their work done for the next day of school. Tomorrow looked lighter for her. *Great Expectations* was well in hand. Perhaps tonight she could get a decent night's sleep.

"Now, Sister"— she felt her insides tighten as Reverend Mother had spoken to her last week in what was intended as an understanding tone — "I know you have a heavy class load and teaching English involves lots of papers. But it still does seem to me that you could get your prayers in and be in bed at a decent hour. I don't want you sick. I've seen the light under your door around midnight for three nights in a row now." Firm, uncomprehending, flicking a speck of dust from her immaculate desk blotter. She really *wanted* to help. Then, leaning forward earnestly, one hand fiddling with the Sacred Heart paperweight near her telephone . . .

Sister Reginald kicked a pebble with desultory energy. It rolled into the rut by the side of the drive. Just up the slope before her stood the new convent. Light under the door! Here at least she had a door — instead of the old dormitory curtain — and *could* stay up past retiring hour to get work done without disturbing others.

"Yes, Reverend Mother." Looking up at the old, kindly but firm, oh so firm, face. And certain. That was what got to her. Living in a world untouched by her dilemmas. They did not share one, not one dilemma. No, that was exaggerating. But how could she tell a sixty-year-old veteran of the world of third graders and obedient subjects, who lived by the book and spoke with authority from it, that students asked questions she couldn't answer, that authority had its distinct limits, and that even the world of sophomore English knew grammatical concepts she had never heard of. Suprasegmental contours . . .

Sister Thomas would soon be starting her economic geography class.

The sun warmed the crown of her head. At moments, having

something on her head really bothered her. Looking straight ahead was no problem. But try to turn to left or right: limited vision, plus stiff obstructions. First the headpiece — a plastic and starched vise — over it the starched vise — over it the starched strip, finally the veil. She struggled to be patient and relax in the sun.

Languidly, she moved up the path, past the shell of the old white frame house they had called their home for so many years, toward the new convent. It was handsome in a modern efficient way. Stone-yellowish pink. Two stories. The visitors said they liked it, and then looked nostalgically toward the old frame house, now almost totally demolished. She shared some of their nostalgia, but for different reasons.

Coming into that house two years ago had been for her an initiation. She had come fresh from the best preparation the Order could give: five years of rigorous training, plus graduate study in English. Everything had been done to turn them out ready. Five years of assigned tasks, sometimes difficult, and the expectation of perfection. She had grown almost inured to the everpresent feeling of falling short. That burden of queasiness in the stomach had seemed part of the vocation.

Then Profession — "forever" — and the assignment to this house. A world of thirty women, of all ages, mostly old, with ailments. Some of them nasty ailments. Only gradually had she discovered their charity in its eccentricities. Sister Clotilda in the kitchen, one of the few lay sisters left in the Order, cantankerous and lame. Hobbling about, grouching over every potato she peeled. But working, always, thinking of what would please. Sending special "homemade sticky buns" into the refectory for your breakfast when it was your birthday. If she liked you. Otherwise, no sticky. Just homemade buns. Sister de Porres, sixty if she was a day, ageless behind her wrinkles, wizened and bent, pushing mounds of white linen through the ancient wringer and drying them in the sun. Or hauling them in by the furnace. She couldn't put her own headdress together. Sister Reginald had won that office, a compliment, and then assembled it, whispering, after night prayer on Saturday nights. Sister Mercy, senile, unfailingly gracious when you met her in the hall heading the wrong way.

"Sister dear, could you show me the way to chapel?" She might be in her underwear, or less. Always with her glasses on, smiling benignly.

Dribbling egg at breakfast onto the napkin her neighbour tucked in under her whiskered chin. She loved to read the newspaper in chapel, invariably upside down. Somehow she always arrived at meals, steered by whatever member of the community happened by.

Gradually, Sister Reginald had come to see the possibilities of individual give and take within this community. It had been hard at first, but the older nuns here (everyone in the province knew it) were extraordinary. They had been schooled by a poverty she had never known. And they were grateful for new blood in the high school. It meant a future rising from their toil. Now they had a new convent to grow old and die in.

They had individual cells, large bathrooms in each wing, and quiet floors — unlike the boards of the old house that had echoed every footstep. The older nuns could go from cell to refectory to chapel and never climb a stair. They deserved it. A sink in each cell, too. Their life, on the face of it, was less cluttered, more orderly. The new chapel was a real chapel: stone floors and walls, austerely beautiful sanctuary, choir stalls of oak, a real pipe organ, and even large bells out in front for the midday and evening Angelus. No more chanting Office in a made-over parlor with a wheezy pedal organ that went dead above A.

The sun felt warmer on the crown of her head. How much time had she left? She paused absentmindedly in front of the shell of the old convent. It stood shadowed by the new.

They could not demolish it until the new one was complete. So now, day after day, the tidy stone convent stood solidly watching the demolition of its former self. Today she could see one or two elderly nuns watching, too. They had carried their lawn chairs to a discreet distance from the demolition site and sat meditating. Watching. Or perhaps just dozing in the sun.

Beyond them, small children from the lower school swarmed on the playground for their twenty minute afternoon break. Screams. Swings. A blue and white blur of running and falling and skipping rope. In the sunshine the sounds were happy, disasters muffled by distance and early summer.

Sister Thomas would be meeting her class.

She stopped in front of the ghost of a convent. Most of the white frame had been carted away. Pieces of porch remained, and two jagged steps one had to climb over to get inside the shell. The wall between the old long chapel and the visitors' parlor was still standing. This had been the front of the house, where seculars were allowed. She thought, with some warmth, of the refectory and community room downstairs, which cloister kept from public view: the sloping floors covered in old, curling linoleum that had been her Saturday morning job to scrub and polish before chapter; the low ceiling, pipes running around what was actually a basement so that when dinner was served by any but the shorter nuns, they had to bend strategically so as not to spill the soup. For Sister Thomas it had been a disaster. The community room right there, too: just two long tables under another set of lights, where she had spent so many desperate hours trying to study and prepare classes under flickering fluorescence and groaning pipes that announced each time the plumbing was used as the older nuns upstairs prepared for bed. Above all, the jostle: elbow to elbow. All trying to study under the same light. Poverty.

She paused on the first porch step, half tempted to make the pilgrimage, not of nostalgia but of irreverent curiosity to see how the places that had held the old daily order might now look, room by room, emptied, torn down, and whispering with ants. The large crew of workers had left yesterday. She could hear only one steady thud, thud, thud — like the sound of a pickaxe against resisting ground — dull, not brassy, against something sullenly unyielding. The wielder was invisible.

She stopped in and moved slightly forward to the spot where the community had lined up in anticipatory silence for solemn entrance into chapel on First Class Feast Days. She could hear muffled grunts.

"Uh. Uh."

As though someone were straining terribly, struggling with something heavy, pushing a boulder perhaps.

"You Goddam sonofabitch bastard! Damn ya! Damn ya!"

The shout cut the sunlight. A large dark shadow came flinging out of the old chapel through the frame door. He was big. The muscular body, contorted in frenzy, glistened with sweat. A tiny piece of metal gleamed against his heaving chest, the silver chain that held it swinging slightly.

One thing held her, horrified. Blood. It poured from his head. From his upper arm. And from one spot just below his knee. He hurtled forward flinging legs and huge hands frantically, looking instinctively for something to clutch to break his inevitable fall. Uncontrollable momentum, like the mindless course of a powerful log swirling downstream in heaving sweeping currents past branches, inlets, rocks, rapids, on, on, toward the unknown harbor that must ultimately appear.

She backed away. There was no chance he could or would grab her, but even though a good twenty feet separated them, she felt the nerves along her spine tighten in fear. He was oblivious of her. A few feet behind him, through the same door, staggered a man of about equal size holding a length of pipe murderously. Swinging it. Advancing. Swinging it.

She turned and ran.

There were no screams. Why were there no screams? She ran furiously. Down the driveway, toward the entrance of the school. Was the first man about to die? Was he beyond protesting? He was bleeding badly. Past the flower border she ran, holding her skirt up to her knees with both hands. Faster. Finally, into the school. Past the red velour Holy Spirit on the front bulletin board, bordered by the Honor Roll. *Veni Pater Pauperum.* April, 1962. Sister Thomas' work.

She was running for Sister Thomas. It was an instinctive choice. The girls were changing classes. They would have to start Guidance without her.

Would he die? Was he, even now, up there on the ground inside the house, being beaten silently to a pulp as, in the distance, the older nuns meditated and thanked God for their new home? Dozing gratefully in the sun. She pushed past lines of girls that seemed suddenly thick and uncooperative. Unyielding bodies full of hair and notebooks.

Sister Thomas would just be starting class. Was his head bashed in? Had he found a piece of pipe for his own defense? Was he fighting back? Who was he — up there in the hulk of their house, invading and destroying? Dear God, let him live.

"Up there," she gulped breathlessly, urgently, at the classroom door. "In the old convent. Come! One man is killing another."

Sister Thomas was ahead of her out the door. For a moment she glimpsed the students gaping at them as they rushed away. Happy reprieve. Extra sunshine in their day.

Sister Thomas tore up the path. Her legs were longer. She didn't have to run. Her strides made Sister Reginald, panting to keep up, breathless as she explained.

"The first one was bleeding. From the face. He looked as if he'd die." She tried to ease off the stitch in her side. Sister Thomas' chiselled profile headed into the sunlight, up the hill, toward the shell, bent forward in concentration. In front of the old convent she stopped.

Only one man was visible. They could hear slow groans. The other must be lying on the ground, too low for their line of vision unless they should enter the house itself.

The second man held high over his head the pipe. He panted. He too was tired, deadly tired, they could see. He paused there, eyes down, raising the pipe high in the clear warm air, a glistening colossus. He brought it down, Thud.

"See here! You stop that immediately!" A staccato handclap broke the sunshine. Stopped the pipe. The hand upraised.

"Stop that immediately. This is no place for such behavior. Stop that and come out here!"

Sister Thomas stood, firmly quiet. She glared. She waited. She waited in the patience of a lifetime. Years of standing in hot sun, in rawedged wind, of clapping sternly, of managing play-yards with hordes of squirming, screaming children tearing their uniforms. She commanded. The standing man looked at her, dazed. Out of that world swirling through blood and beating, the mingling of sunshine and children's recess, the quiet distant eyes of meditating prayer, he seemed to recognize her. A faint gleam lighted in his crazed eyes and he paused, weaving slightly, for one long second in the sun.

The pipe fell. Thud.

Sister Reginald felt her backbone go slack. Was the other man dead? Should they go forward and look? Her own uncertainties and terrors were held and relieved in the simple depth of her friend who stood there looking stern, expecting obedience. Was she frightened? There was no trace of it.

Sister Thomas moved forward steadily, over the step and into the shell of the parlor where seculars had sat on Visiting Sundays in winter, sipping tea and talking softly. In a few strides she was over to the man. He waited wordlessly, panting, long drawn breaths rasping in ragged rhythm from his chest. At his feet lay the other man moving slightly from side to side, groaning and bleeding. The dirt around his head was red and soft and one eye had swollen shut. He held the other closed.

"What do you mean by this?" she demanded. "What is going on? This is no place to be fighting. You should know better!" She stooped to examine the prone man.

Sister Reginald, close behind her, recognized the rhetoric. It was the perfect rhetoric to which there could be no answer. It got lines out of school on time, kept lunch-time mayhem under control, sent short legs running to retrieve a forgotten tablet. It was the rhetoric her girls hated as they bristled with sullen resentment or cruel superiority at expectations so simple and clear. She recognized in those words the tone of a lifetime spent making small order out of small chaos, trying to live the order it understood. Its truth penetrated the unfamiliar chaos in which they stood: demolition indecipherable. Its clarity brought her momentary relief.

Then she saw that the standing man wept. Large tears that welled up slowly from the bloodshot whites of his eyes and ran down his creased checks to disappear in the shining beads of perspiration lining his upper lip. He stood there dumbly, feet apart, long arms hanging heavily by his sides. His bared chest heaved slowly, in fury or grief.

"Sister! Go call the ambulance and the police. Use the house phone." Sister Thomas did not look up. Her voice was muffled but decisive as she bent lower to put her large white handkerchief, folded into a thick square, on the forehead wound. It melted, a limp crimson.

For the second time in that hour Sister Reginald ran from the old convent parlor, from that house — now not to the high school, but quickly to the front door of the nearby convent. It was unlocked.

The front hall was quiet and cool, antiseptically clean. No one was about, not even the portress. Behind the heavy inner doors, in the cloistered sections of the house, she could imagine what was going on. The older nuns would be resting, or meditating, or making their spiritual reading. Sister de Porres was in the laundry working steadily in the dry heat of the blowers, trying to keep up with the daily demand for crisp linens in this humidity. Sister Clothilda was shuffling about the kitchen cursing her new oven.

She quickly found the list for emergency calls on the telephone stand.

"Please. Immediately. Yes, just outside the new convent. Yes, you will need a stretcher. Thank you."

Then the police. They would know exactly where to come, for vandalism had been a problem during the days of demolition.

"Yes, the old convent. The man is very badly hurt. Thank you."

Done. She went through the heavy doors to find Reverend Mother. She should be warned that police car and ambulance would be on the promises shortly.

"He cried all the time, even getting into the police car," said Sister Thomas as they walked together that evening. When they had stood in a circle after supper waiting for recreation to start, Reverend Mother had told the community about the afternoon's drama. She prodded for details, but Sister Thomas resisted the pressure to elaborate the Intention they would all remember at tomorrow's Mass. She was almost laconic in her narration.

This was the first moment Sister Reginald had had a chance to question her alone. They walked down the driveway toward the school.

"He had difficulty speaking. And then I myself had a hard time making out what he was saying. I couldn't give him my undivided attention, the other man was in too much pain. But somehow, between groans and tears, he made himself fairly clear."

They turned around in the drive and headed back toward the convent. The forsythia was drooping slightly under evening. Around them the air was warm and still, broken only by the murmur of nuns' voices and occasional laughter. In small groups of two or three they walked about the grounds, grateful for this spring release from winter evenings of recreation over sewing in the stuffy community room. The grass was still faintly fragrant. Sounds of the daytime world had receded. Play-yards were empty, school windows shut tight for the night. Ahead of them was the old convent shell, open and vulnerable. Mute. In a day or two even that would be gone.

There was a quiet intensity about Sister Thomas as she finished her story. "They were brothers. He was stricken with grief at what he'd done. I could see that. His fury was spent and there was no way he could exorcise his grief. The damage was done." She adjusted her cincture. "They both loved the same woman. Perhaps it was either kill the brother or her. That part was never clear. Anyway, he wanted to talk. Who knows when he'll have another chance. He couldn't get it all out. They'd been working on the demolition crew here for weeks and were hired to stay on today to finish some smaller jobs. It was to be their last day working together. Somehow their disagreement came to a head and they began to fight. Who knows what triggered it?" She paused, breathing deeply the soft early summer air folding evening about them. "Misunderstanding is always a mystery."

They were passing the old convent. The bell for the end of recreation rang. No more time for words; the back door of chapel was open. One by one, older first, the nuns filed in for Compline. With a nod, Sister Thomas took her place in rank, disappearing silently in the chain of black forms entering chapel. Sister Reginald waited for the end of the line. Then she noiselessly closed the door behind them all.

Great Silence had begun.

W.P. KINSELLA was born in Alberta and now lives in White Rock, British Columbia. His publications include *If Wishes Were Horses, Dance Me Outside, Born Indian,* and *Shoeless Joe,* upon which the movie *Field of Dreams* was based. This story first appeared in CFM No. 20 in 1976.

Illianna Comes Home

W.P. KINSELLA

MY NAME IS SILAS ERMINESKIN. I am eighteen years old. Me and Frank Fence-post and a couple of other guys are taking a course that the government offers on how to be mechanics. I fix things pretty good and our instructor, Mr. Nichols, says he thinks he can get me an apprentice job with a tractor company in Wetaskiwin when I finish.

One part of the course I don't like is that I got to write an essay. I'm lucky I can write. Frank Fence-post can write most of his name, but he is faking everything else since the course started. Mr. Nichols says I got a funny sense of humor, so I should just write about the funniest thing that ever happened to me.

I been thinking about that, and I think the funniest thing that ever happened to me was when my sister Illianna came home to the reserve with her white man husband.

Illianna she smart. She stayed at school until grade eight and then went all the way to Calgary to work. She worked too. Waited tables at the New Zenith Cafe and she don't drink and do bad things like Suzie Calf-robe and some of the other girls who go to the city. Illianna she pretty, and she proud she pretty. She said to me in one of her letters she not going to do nothing to spoil herself, like drink and fight.

Eathen Firstrider, he sure is mad when she up and goes away, because he been her boyfriend ever since she was twelve, and he figure they would get married. Eathen he won fifty dollars in the calf roping contest at the Ponoka Stampede last summer. When he do, he buy a record of Buffy St.-Marie, even though he ain't got no record player, because he say she look like Illianna. He got the record picture on the wall of his cabin. He still figures that he gonna marry with Illianna some day.

Then Illianna writes home that she married with a white man. Mrs. Robert McGregor McVey is what we should call her now. Her husband is a businessman. He's old too, twenty-five, and even been for one year to the university somewhere. Illianna she don't work no more and they got an apartment in one of the big buildings in Calgary.

Ma, she has bad feelings that our Illianna married with a white man. But she not half as mad as Eathen Firstrider when I tell him. Eathen, he polishes the big blade of his hunting knife on his jeans and talks about taking scalps. Frank Fence-post, he laugh and say, "We don't do that no more."

"It's time we started again," says Eathen. Then he throws the knife right through the one-by-four side of the kindling box. Eathen he's already twenty and all us guys look up to him. He rides in the rodeos and knows all about girls and cars. Two years ago he was outrider on the chuckwagon races at the Calgary Stampede. He spent twenty-five dollars of his wages on a white girl down at the Queen's Hotel, and she taught him all kinds of things that he wasn't too sure about. When he got back he told us guys about it for two hours and how he was gonna do all these things to and with Illianna. And he weren't lying to us. He don't know, but me and Frank and Charlie Fence-post was hanging off the roof of the cabin looking in the window.

Eathen sure figured that he was going to marry illianna, but it wasn't long after she went away to Calgary. Eathen still figures all them things he taught her made her able to catch a white man, and he gets mad every time he thinks about it. But I bet Illianna being tall and slim and pretty helped some too.

Anyway, Illianna was married a year when she says in a letter she coming home for a long weekend with her white man husband.

They pull into the yard in a new car, one with chrome wheels and white and blue racing stripes. A car so big and new that it looks like it belongs to a finance man.

The car stops and the kids come creeping out from behind the cabins like the deer do sometimes when they think there is no one around. The kids walk with their necks out and like they haven't got any toes. Eathen Firstrider is standing cross-legged against the wall of his cabin, smoking a roll-yer-own that is about as long and thin as he is.

If Illianna wasn't my sister, I wouldn't have known her. She let her hair grow real long and she was wearing a white coat, and a white suit, and white boots. I think while I'm walking up to her that Illianna, she going to be a white woman one way or another.

Then her husband he get out, and he look like one of them pictures out of the Eaton's catalogue. He got a hat with a funny little brim, an overcoat, and a suit and tie. He got shiny black shoes with toe rubbers too.

He shakes hands with me, and Ma too. Ma ignores him, and she don't speak so much on Illianna. Ma's wearing her good speckled dress and her purple kerchief. She looks in the back of the car, not walking over to it but just by rolling her eyes. Then she looks hard on Illianna's tummy and says, "Where your babies?"

"Ma," Illianna says, giving her a real harsh look.

"Well, where your babies?"

"We haven't got any babies."

"How come? You been married most a year. When I been married a year I had you and Joseph already, and Silas in my stomach."

"Really Ma. We just don't want children yet." Illianna, by her voice, lets Ma know she wishes she would shut up. Ma just nods knowingly and continues right on.

"What's with don't want? You get a good man you get lots of babies. What's wrong with him?" She nods toward McVey who has been standing like he frozen, one hand still stuck out in front like maybe he going to shake hands on someone else. About this time Eathen Firstrider strolls across the yard, walking very slow.

"Hello Illianna," he says. Then he say some very personal things to her in our language. Now I know why Ma and Eathen have been holding council in our cabin for the last three days. That white man, he'd take his hand back quick if he knew what Eathen was saying. Illianna's cheeks get bright pink and she looks sharp on her McVey, but he is not interested in Eathen.

McVey has moved in on Ma, and he is trying to make himself useful by explaining his financial position and telling her that it will be two more years before they can afford babies. He assures Ma that Illianna and him will have kids when they want them, only I'm sure I hear him say something about papooses. Ma she just looks blank and rolls her eyes like when she have too much moonshine. Illianna she got one hand on McVey's sleeve kind of pulling him back, but she listening too, only to Eathen Firstrider, who says things that make everyone blush, except McVey, who don't know anyone but him is talking.

When McVey stops for breath, Ma, she just goes on from where she left off before.

"Louis Coyote, he blind," she say, "he lost his leg when the tractor run over him, but he still make babies. Edith Coyote pop any day now with their fifteenth."

McVey he just kind of shake his head, then he explain things to Ma again. Only this time he tells it like he was talking to a little kid. When he is finished Ma speaks in our language to Illianna.

"What's she say?" McVey asks Illianna.

"She wants me to tell her what you said."

"But you said she understands English . . ."

Ma interrupted him again to speak to Illianna.

"She says she only understands English when an Indian speaks it," says Illianna.

"That's impossible," says McVey, who is about a foot shorter than Eathen, even with his fancy hat on.

"I'm sorry, Bob," Illianna says, "let's go inside. I'll have a talk with Ma later." Then she gives Eathen a funny smile, and me the same, like she was saying the thing for her to do was get into the fancy car and drive back to the city. Instead, we all go into the cabin where Ma is mumbling in our language about, "Money don't have nothing to do with make babies."

"I'll bring in your suitcase," I say to McVey.

He looks hard on Illianna, but she smiles on me.

"That would be very nice, Silas," she says.

McVey gives me the keys to his car, but very slowly like it is part of his hand he is passing to me.

"You be careful you don't scratch nothing, Si," he says to me. Si, I ain't never been called Si in my whole life.

There must be fifteen kids gathered around the car with their faces pressed against the windows. They are just looking at the white upholstery and touching the shiny paint. Frank Fence-post is there running the aerial up and down. I get the suitcase out of the back seat and one of the younger kids lugs it into the cabin. My girlfriend, Sadie One-wound, has arrived.

"Boy, that's some big car," she says, "Will you buy us one like this when you get a job?"

"First pay cheque," I promised.

"Can I sit in it, Silas?"

"Well, I don't know." But Frank already has the door open and about a dozen kids are climbing in the back. I get behind the wheel, just to keep Frank from sitting there, and Sadie crawls over me and squeezes in next to Frank. Margaret Standing-at-the-door has just crawled through the passenger window and is sitting on Frank's lap.

"Start it up," yells Sadie, and the kids in the back cheer. I figure it won't do no harm to start the motor, so I give the key a turn and boy do it ever start fast.

Up to this time I ain't drove so much. I used to sit in the One-wound's Studebaker with no wheels and shift gears until the finance men came and towed it away.

About ten seconds after I start the car my brother-in-law charges out of the cabin, and he's coming for me with a not nice look on his face.

"Get going," yells Frank. Then he pulls the gear shift into drive, reaches over and stomps my foot on the gas pedal so hard that the car nearly stands on its hind legs. The car sprays dirt and gravel and from the terrible yell I hear, I guess that McVey was behind the car. We shoot straight ahead, miss the corner of One-wound's cabin by only a little bit, and lose Charlie Fence-post who was too late to get in the car, but was sitting on the hood.

"Steer," yells Sadie above everyone else. But I just watch what is happening, which is when we drive over part of an old land disc, a tire goes bang and we swing to the left and straight into the slough behind Wolfchild's cabin. V-room, v-room, the car goes, and shoots mud and water back a long way, which is far enough to spray McVey and Charlie

Fence-post who are coming after us. The kids in the back are all cheering. Sadie One-wound hugs my arm, and the car still goes v-room, v-room.

McVey runs into the water, opens the door and pulls out the keys. He uses cuss words on me that I never heard before, so I guess there are still things that we can learn from the white man. Me and Frank are busy saying how we'll get Louis Coyote's pick-up and pull the car right out. McVey is busy clearing the kids out of the back of the car and telling me to shut to hell up, and he'll call the A.M.A., whatever that is. I hope it ain't nothing to do with the R.C.M.P.

It turns out that the A.M.A. is the tow truck up at Wetaskiwin, which is about twenty-five miles away. McVey he say he don't need no help from us, but after he walks all the way to Hobbema Crossing to use the phone at the service station, with us and the little kids walking a respectable distance behind him, it seems that the tow truck won't come out to the reserve for nobody no matter how white he is. So we all go and get Louis Coyote's pick-up and with McVey directing, pull the car out and change the tire. Illianna is really mad with us, because mainly of McVey's suit which she says cost two hundred dollars, and the fact, she says, that he catches cold so easy.

We all try to talk soft on him after that. I take him for a walk around the reserve, along the way we pick up the Fence-post boys and a few others. I show him my collection of car parts. Frank, he talks lots about how we strip down cars when we know the finance men coming to take them away, and how we changed plates and painted Louis Coyote's pick-up so that even the finance men don't know it no more.

"It been most a year since anyone been looking for that truck," says Frank, and tells about how when we hear the finance men is coming we quick tear up the culvert by the slough so they got to walk instead of drive around the reserve.

"I am employed by a finance company," says my brother-in-law.

"Hey, partner, I been lying to you," says Frank thinking real fast.

McVey gives us a talk like they do down to the technical school, and he uses the same voice he used on Ma a while ago. He tells us how it's not nice to strip down cars and hide trucks and how other people have to pay for it when we do things like that, and how if we'd only pay our bills there wouldn't be no trouble.

Frank, he says it sure is nice for them other people to pay and all, because he always been worried that the R.C.M.P. come around looking for something else but moonshine. Brother Bob, he just shake his head and kick little rocks with his toe rubbers.

"You think we should let him get away?" Frank says to me in our language. "You can bet the finance man's gonna come back after Louis' pick-up, and maybe even the R.C.M.P. after our car parts."

"We could drown him over in Muskrat Lake," says Charlie Fencepost. "Illianna, she don't miss him after a couple of days, and I bet nobody else would."

"Or we could just sort of lose him, leave him out in the dark for Eathen Firstrider to find," says Frank.

"I have a better idea," I say. "We don't do nothing to him. Ma and Mad Etta and Eathen, they got something planned. Better we shouldn' do nothing to upset it."

"What are you guys talking about," says McVey.

"We sure do like your little rubber shoes, partner," Frank tells him.

It sure is bad that McVey should be a finance man. This makes him to us like the cavalry must have been to the old-time Indian. He is also like magpie, whenever his mouth open bad sounds come out. When I tell him my girlfriend Sadie One-wound has fifteen brothers and sisters, McVey, he say with a laugh, "No wonder they call you guys fucking Indians." No one laugh and McVey he sure wish he is back in the big city.

Ma been holding council with Mad Etta over to her cabin. Mad Etta is sort of a mid-wife around the reserve, but if we still had medicine men she would be one. Mad Etta is so big she got a tree-trunk chair over at her cabin, because ordinary chairs they crack up when she sits on them. I've seen them bulldog smaller steers at the rodeos. Everyone know her over at the Alice Hotel in Wetaskiwin, they got two chairs wired together and braced with two-by-fours so Mad Etta can drink beer and not bust up the furniture.

It is next morning before I find out what Ma and Mad Etta are planning. The night before, we give Illianna and her husband the other bed in the cabin, so me and the kids sleep on the floor. I lie awake and listen while Illianna teases McVey, in a nice way, about they should try to make a baby.

"Good God, no," says McVey. "Why there must be ten other people all around us."

Illianna laugh her pretty laugh and say that they won't hear nothing that they haven't heard before. And I bet she thinking of the fun she used to have with Eathen Firstrider back when she lived here and that used to be her bed.

I can tell by the way the cabin creaks that Frank Fence-post is on the roof, hanging over the edge and looking in on Illianna and her white man. He may as well go to sleep like I do.

At breakfast, Ma talks away in our language.

"You got to get him out for the evening, me and Mad Etta and somebody else we got a nice surprise for Illianna." By her tone of voice nobody would know she wasn't talking about the porridge she is stirring up. The him she talks about is of course McVey, but she refers to him in our language as, "he who has no balls."

Illianna lights into Ma after that, and McVey must figure nobody speaks English no more as he sits polishing his spoon and knife on his tie.

Ma, she don't back away one bit. What she says to Illianna is pretty hard to translate into English but it amount to, "You may love your white man for the fancy things he can give you but you still got hot pants for Eathen Firstrider."

Illianna, she laugh and throw up her hands. Then she say to McVey in English, "You wear your warm coat today. You know how easy you take cold."

After breakfast, I say to McVey, "Brother Bob, we is really sorry about what we do to the car and for all the trouble we cause. We want you should enjoy your visit here, so tonight me and Frank and some of the boys, we make party for you. Show you good time. We going to make you an honorary Indian, just like when the Premier come down here to get us to vote for him."

You had better believe that I had to do some tall talking to get the boys to agree to that. I say, "Look, we make him a blood brother, he won't go sending the other finance men snooping around here and he don't send the R.C.M.P. after our car parts. It a lot better than killing him. Besides, I think he would like to be nice to us but he don't know how."

"We should drown him in Muskrat Lake," says Frank Fence-post.

McVey look at me up and down like maybe I want to borrow money from him. Then he say he guesses it would be o.k. we have the party. We say fine, and start to make plans that we take him to the ceremonial clearing which is way back in the hills a half mile, and which we just decide is going to be ceremonial clearing.

We send Frank Fence-post down to the Chief's cabin to borrow the ceremonial war bonnet, the same one we tie on the premier and some French hockey player who claimed he was a quarter Assinoboine. But word travels fast on the reserve, and the Chief he say among other things that no white finance man ever going to wear the tribal war bonnet. So instead of war bonnet, Frank he come back with a five gallon cream-can full of dandelion wine that he borrow without asking.

Most of the day McVey, he stay pretty close to Illianna and to his fancy car. About supper time, me and the boys go over to Mad Etta's. She been three days boiling up some strong medicine for Eathen Firstrider. Mad Etta she make the medicine out of tiger lilies, paintbrush, pig bristles, and many things that only she know about. It smell so strong that it hurt my nose from outside the cabin. We have to make fun on Eathen so that he brave to go in. The medicine was boiling on the back of the stove in an open enamel pan, and it look like an oil change down at the Texaco garage.

Eathen is now not nearly so brave or so tall as he has been.

"How I going to drink pig bristles?" he wants to know.

"You drink," say Mad Etta, "or Etta sit on you and make you drink."

We all make some more fun on Eathen so he has to drink or look like he afraid. So he drink.

"You make many babies now," says Mad Etta, "Anybody you lie down with have many babies, even Etta." Then she laugh and laugh, shaking on her tree-trunk chair.

"Etta could have babies and nobody would know," she say, and laugh and laugh, patting her five-flour-sack dress.

My girlfriend, Sadie One-wound stops me on the way home from Mad Etta's and wants to know who pulled most of the feathers out of the turkey that her father keeps in a pen behind their house. I don't know.

But I find out when all us guys get to the clearing about nine that evening. Frank and Charlie got a good fire going and they already been sampling the wine that they borrowed. Frank, he got a long piece of paper with turkey feathers glued down each side, and he fastens this on Brother Bob's head as soon as we get there.

"We is sorry we can't get the tribal war bonnet from the Chief," he say, "but this we make ourselves."

"It is very nice," Brother Bob say, but he look around funny like maybe he wish he have some other finance men there to keep him company.

Frank gets a big water dipper full of wine and gives it to McVey. "That don't taste like wine," my brother-in-law say, "it's too sweet." "Plenty honey in it," says Frank.

"It's the frogs that give it the sweet taste," says Charlie.

Brother Bob kind of chokes a little, but then he sees that we are just making fun on him. McVey goes to put down the dipper, but Frank lifts his arm back up.

"You gonna be Indian, you drink like Indian."

So Brother Bob finishes the dipper and Frank fills it again.

"I didn't mean to say it wasn't good," he say, and he smile on us for the first time since he come home with Illianna.

Illianna make me promise to look after McVey and see that he don't catch no cold. I figure that plenty of wine keep him warm and also make him nice to know. We all know that home-made wine kick harder than bucking horse. But McVey he don't know that.

After a while we all have lots of wine and we make noises and dance around the way we think a white man would expect us to. Then we put our hands on his hands and name him Robert Fire-chief our blood brother. Fire-chief is a name that Frank got from down at the Hobbema Texaco garage.

Like I promised Illianna, I try to look after our new Indian, but after the wine starts him to glow, he runs around making what he thinks are war whoops, and singing one little, two little, three little Indians, and stomping around in a circle like a movie Indian.

McVey thinks that the name Fire-chief makes him a chief. So he leads us whooping around the clearing and then down the trail a ways. He is yelling something about Tonto and silver bullets. What he don't know is that we coming to a pretty deep creek. I remember what I promise Illianna and am just about to tell him watch out, when a little by himself and with a little help from Frank Fence-post he falls head first into the water. He comes up looking like a calf in a mud hole.

He is one wet Indian. We herd him back to Wolfchild's cabin which is the closest one to where we are. He is sneezing already, and boy do I know Illianna is going to be mad on me. We set McVey on the floor in front of the stove which Frank and me is filling with cut pine. Then we dig up an old pair of Eddy Wolfchild's jeans and a shirt that belong to his sister.

"That's mighty white of you guys," say my brother-in-law.

While we are wiping off the mud and trying to warm up our new Indian, Charlie Fence-post comes running back from our cabin where he has gone to check on how Eathen is doing. He pull me off to one side.

"Eathen over there all right," he say, "but it no wonder she ain't got no babies. Even I know they don't get no babies from what they doing to each other."

"Give Eathen time," I say, "he got to do first all the tricks that white girl in Calgary showed him. Eathen he know how babies made, but with Mad Etta's medicine in him, he get babies any way he do it."

Edith Wolfchild comes home while we all sitting around. She looks at Brother Bob shivering on the floor.

"You cold, huh?" she say to him, and then cuddles up close.

Frank Fence-post, he makes a bad face, but I say pointing at McVey, "He blood brother now, if Edith likes him that her business."

I don't think Edith so much likes McVey as she don't like Illianna, which is a long time story, so guess she figures to get even on Illianna for whatever wrong she done her. Edith puts her fat little arms around McVey and kisses him lots. He comes to life and touch her back some. She lead him over to the bed and start taking off the clothes that we just put on him.

"Go away, you guys," she says to us, but we don't.

They get under the covers. Edith is doing a lot of moving around. but I think I can hear Brother Bob's teeth still chattering. Before long Edith gets out of bed and starts putting on her clothes. McVey, looking very sick, wraps a blanket around himself and sits on the oven door. The cabin gets a little warm by now.

Eathen comes running into the cabin. He is about a foot taller than he was over at Mad Etta's, so I know without asking that all has gone pretty good over at our place. He smiles a lot on Robert Fire-chief.

"We are blood brothers, now," he tells him a few times.

Eathen sure feels big to tell him this. Fire-chief just sits stupid on the oven door. He has eyes like a dead owl and burps a lot.

Next morning, McVey is very pale, even for a white man, very quiet and look some smaller than when he come. He also has cold for which Illianna is very mad on me and the boys. Me and the Fence-post boys say good-bye to him in his Indian name and he seem some pleased.

"Fire-water plenty bad," he say, and try to laugh, but we can see it hurts his head to do that. Eathen saunters by and smiles on Illianna. He tells Illianna personal things again.

"Next time you come bring lots of babies," says Ma.

They is all ready to go but the fancy car won't start. McVey looks under the hood and wants to know who the hell took off with the distributor. But we still say we don't know much about cars, and maybe the kids been playing with it or something.

We borrow Louis Coyote's pick-up again and drive them to catch the bus at Hobbema Crossing. Illianna, she real quiet and look at us like we cow chips or something. McVey, he say Wounded Knee gonna look like a picnic when he gets through with us. I think he even say he gonna write his M.P.

Next morning a whole string of cars comes up the road into the reserve. There is the big white tow truck from Wetaskiwin, a car full of R.C.M.P. and about eight guys in suits and hats who look just like Brother Bob. They move right along and we barely have time to tear the culvert out by the slough so they have to walk up to the houses.

Eathen, he with the fancy car, about eight miles back in the hills. It funny, but all of a sudden, today, none of us speak English very much. We never heard of anybody named Eathen Firstrider, and the Ermineskins all moved away a long time ago, to Calgary, maybe.

Cars? No. We ain't got no cars. One old pick-up truck around sometimes, but it down to the rodeo at Drumheller for a week or so. They all finally go away shaking their heads and saying how dumb we are.

Illianna writes to us to say we better send back the car or she never have anything to do with us again. But we know she don't stay mad with us forever.

She writes again in a few months to say she gonna have a baby. You think that don't get a celebration. Ma and Eathen borrow the truck, load Mad Etta in the back and go to Wetaskiwin. We set Etta on her two chairs together at the Alice Hotel and buy her lots of beer.

Illianna sends us a little white card when the baby come. A boy, they call him Robert Ermineskin McVey. He looks like Ma, say illianna.

Everybody counts their fingers and sure enough it's within about a week of when she was home. We have another celebration. Everybody, they shake hands with Eathen Firstrider, and give drinks to Mad Etta. Everyone is very much proud that Illianna have an Indian Baby.

All us guys learned to drive on the fancy car. It got the muffler torn off and pretty well shot to hell by now, but Eathen still drives everybody around the reserve in it.

I'm not so sure anymore that it is such a funny thing that I have written about, but if it gets me a job with the tractor company, then I guess it is o.k.

MAVIS GALLANT was born in Montreal, Quebec and now lives in Paris, France. Her publications include *The Other Paris, Green Water, Green Sky, The Pegnitz Junction,* and *From the Fifteenth District.* This story first appeared in a special volume of CFM devoted to Mavis Gallant, No. 28 in 1978.

With A Capital T

MAVIS GALLANT

For Madeleine and Jean-Paul Lemieux

IN WARTIME, in Montreal, I applied to work on a newspaper. Its name was *The Lantern*, and its motto, "My light shall shine," carried a Wesleyan ring of veracity and plain dealing. I chose it because I thought it was a place where I would be given a lot of different things to do. I said to the man who consented to see me, "But not the women's pages. Nothing like that." I was eighteen. He heard me out and suggested I come back at twenty-one, which was a soft way of getting rid of me. In the meantime I was to acquire experience; he did not say of what kind. On the stroke of twenty-one I returned and told my story to a different person. I was immediately accepted; I had expected to be. I still believed, then, that most people meant what they said. I supposed that the man I had seen that first time had left a memorandum in the files: "To whom it may concern — Three years from this date, Miss Linnet Muir will join the editorial staff." But after I'd been working for a short time I heard one of the editors say, "If it hadn't been for the god-damned war we would never have hired even one of the god-damned women," and so I knew.

In the meantime I had acquired experience by getting married. I was no longer a Miss Muir, but a Mrs. Blanchard. My husband was overseas. I had longed for emancipation and independence, but I was learning that women's autonomy is like a small inheritance paid out a penny at a time. In a journal I kept, I scrupulously noted everything that came into my head about this, and about God, and about politics. I took it for granted that our victory over Fascism would be followed by a sunburst of revolution — I thought that was what the war was about. I wondered if going to work for the capitalist press was entirely moral. "Whatever happens," I wrote, "it will be the Truth, nothing half-hearted, the Truth with a Capital T."

The first thing I had to do was write what goes under the pictures.

There is no trick to it. You just repeat what the picture has told you like this:

"Boy eats bun as bear looks on."

The reason why anything has to go under the picture at all is that a reader might wonder, "Is that a bear looking on?" It looks like a bear, but that is not enough reason for saying so. Pasted across the back of the photo you have been given is a strip of paper on which you can read: "Saskatoon, Sask. 23 Nov. Boy eats bun as bear looks on." Whoever composed this knows two things more than you do — a place and a time.

You have a space to fill in which the words must come out even. The space may be tight; in that case, you can remove "as" and substitute a comma, though that makes the kind of terse statement to which your reader is apt to reply, "So what?" Most of the time, the Truth with a Capital T is a matter of elongation: "Blond boy eats small bun as large bear looks on."

"Blond boy eats buttered bun," is livelier, but unscrupulous. You have been given no information about the butter. "Boy eats bun as hungry bear looks on," has the beginnings of a plot, but it may inspire your reader to protest: "That boy must be a mean sort of kid if he won't share his food with a starving creature." Child-lovers, though less prone to fits of anguish than animal-lovers, may be distressed by the word "hungry" for a different reason, believing "boy" subject to attack from "bear." You must not lose your head and type, "Blond bear eats large boy as hungry bun looks on," because your reader may notice, and write a letter saying, "Some of you guys around there think you're pretty smart, don't you?" while another will try to enrich your caption with, "Re your bun write-up, my wife has taken better pictures than that in the very area you mention."

At the back of your mind, because your mentors have placed it there, is an obstruction called "the policy factor." Your paper supports a political party. You try to discover what this party has had to say about buns and bears, how it intends to approach them in the future. Your editor, at golf with a member of parliament, will not want to have his game upset by: "It's not that I want to interfere, but some of that bun stuff seems pretty negative to me." The young and vulnerable reporter would just as soon not pick up the phone to be told, "I'm ashamed of your defeatist attitude. Why, I knew your father! He must be spinning in his grave!" or, more effectively, "I'm telling you this for your own good — I think you're subversive without knowing it."

Negative, defeatist and subversive are three of the things you have been cautioned not to be. The others are seditious, obscene, obscure, ironic, intellectual and impulsive.

You gather up the photo and three pages of failed captions, and knock at the frosted glass of a senior door. You sit down and are given a view of boot soles. You say that the whole matter comes down to an ethical question concerning information and redundancy; unless "reader" is blotto, can't he see for himself that this is about a boy, a bun, and a bear?

Your senior person is in shirtsleeves, hands clasped behind his neck. He thinks this over, staring at the ceiling; swings his feet to the floor; reads your variations on the bear-and-bun theme; turns the photo upside-down. He tells you patiently, that it is not the business of "reader" to draw conclusions. Our subscribers are not dreamers or smart alecks; when they see a situation in a picture, they want that situation confirmed. He reminds you about negativism and obscuration; advises you to go sit in the library and acquire a sense of values by reading the back issues of *Life*.

The back numbers of *Life* are tatty and incomplete, owing to staff habits of tearing out whatever they wish to examine at leisure. A few captions, still intact, allow you to admire a contribution to pictorial journalism, the word "note:"

"American flag flies over new post office. Note stars on flag."

"GI waves happily from captured Italian tank. Note helmet on head."

So, "Boy eats bun as bear looks on. Note fur on bear." All that can happen now will be a letter asking, "Are you sure it was a bun?"

From behind frosted-glass doors, as from a leaking intellectual bath, flow instructions about style, spelling, caution, libel, brevity, and something called "the ground rules." A few of these rules have been established for the convenience of the wives of senior persons and reflect their tastes and interests, their inhibitions and fears, their desire to see close friends' pictures when they open to the social page, their fragile attention span. Other rules demand that we pretend to be independent of British Foreign policy and American commerce otherwise our readers, discouraged, will give up caring who wins the war. (Soon after victory British foreign policy will cease to exist; as for American commerce, the first grumbling will be heard when a factory in Buffalo is suspected of having flooded the country with defective twelve-inch pie tins.) Ground rules maintain that you must not be flippant about the Crown — an umbrella term covering a number of high-class subjects, from the Royal Family to the nation's judicial system — or about our war effort or, indeed, our reasons for making any effort about anything. Religions, in particular those observed by decent Christians, are not up for debate. We may however, describe and denounce marginal sects whose puritanical learnings are even more dizzily slanted than our own. The Jehovah's Witnesses, banned as seditious, continue to issue inflammatory pamphlets about Jesus; patriotic outrage abounds over this. The children of Witnesses are beaten up in public schools for refusing to draw Easter bunnies. An education officer, interviewed, declares that the children's obstinate observance of the Second Commandment is helping Hitler. Everyone knows that the Easter bunny, along with God and Santa Claus, is on our side.

To argue a case for the children is defeatist; to advance reasons against their persecution is obscure. Besides, your version of the bunny conflict may be unreliable. Behind frosted-glass doors lurk male fears of female mischief. Women, having no inborn sense of history, are known to invent absurd stories. Celebrated newspaper hoaxes (perpetrated by men, as it happens) are described to you, examples of irresponsible writing that have brought down trusting editors. A few of these stories have been swimming, like old sea turtles, for years now, crawling ashore wherever British possessions are still tinted red on the map. "As the niece of the Governor-General rose from a deep curtsy, the Prince, with the boyish smile that has made him the darling of five continents, picked up a bronze bust of his grandmother and battered Lady Adeline to death" is one version of a perennial favourite.

Privately, you think you could do better. You will never get the chance. The umpires of ground rules are nervous and watchful behind those doors. Wartime security hangs heavy. So does the fear that the end of hostilities will see them turfed out to make way for war correspondents wearing nonchalant mustaches, battered caps, carelessly-knotted white scarves, raincoats with shoulder tabs, punctuating their accounts of Hunnish atrocities perceived at Claridges and the Savoy with "Roger!" and "Jolly-oh!" and "Over to you!"

Awaiting this dreadful invasion the umpires sit, in shirt-sleeves and braces, scribbling initials with thick blue pencils. "NDG" stands for "No Damned Good." (Clairvoyant, you will begin to write "NBF" in your journal meaning "No Bloody Future.") As a creeping, climbing wash of conflicting and contradictory instructions threatens to smother you, you discover the possibilities of the quiet, or lesser hoax. Obeying every warning and precept, you will write, turn in, and get away with, "Dressed in shoes, stockings and hat appropriate to the season, Mrs. Horatio Bantam, the former Felicity Duckpond, grasped the bottle of champagne in her white-gloved hand and sent it swinging against the end of HMCS *Makeweight* that was nearest the official party, after which, swaying slightly, she slid down the ways and headed for open waters."

As soon as I realized that I was paid about half the salary men were earning, I decided to do half the work. I had spent much of my adolescence as a resourceful truant, evolving the good escape dodges that would serve one way and another all my life. At *The Lantern* I used reliable school methods. I would knock on a glass door — a door that had nothing to do with me.

"Well, Blanchard, what do you want?"

"Oh, Mr. Watchmaster — it's just to tell you I'm going out to look something up."

"What for?"

"An assignment."

"Don't tell me. Tell Amstutz."

"He's organizing fire-drill in case of air-raids."

"Tell Cranach. He can tell Amstutz."

"Mr. Cranach has gone to stop the art department from striking."

"Striking? Don't those buggers know there's a war on? I'd like to see Accounting try that. What do they want now?"

"Conditions. They're asking for conditions. Is it all right if I go now, Mr. Watchmaster?"

"You know what we need around here, don't you? One German regiment. Regiment? What am I saying? Platoon. That'd take the mickey out of 'em. Teach them something about hard work. Loving your country. Your duty. Give me one trained German sergeant. I'd lead him in. 'O.K. — you've been asking for this!' Ratatatat. You wouldn't hear any more guff about conditions. What's your assignment?"

"The Old Presbyterians. They've decided they're against killing people because of something God said to Moses."

"Seditious bastards. Put 'em in work camps, the whole damned lot. All right, Blanchard, carry on."

I would go home, wash my hair, listen to Billie Holiday records.

"Say, Blanchard, where the hell were you yesterday? Seventy-nine people were poisoned by ham sandwiches at a wedding party on Durocher Street. The sidewalk was like a morgue."

"Actually, I just happened to be in Mr. Watchmaster's office. But only for a minute."

"Watchmaster's got no right to ask you to do anything. One of these days I'm going to close in on him. I can't right now — there's a war on. The only good men we ever had in this country were killed in the last one. Look, next time Watchmaster gets you to run his errands, refer it to Cranach. Got that? All right, Blanchard, on your way."

No good dodge works forever.

"Oh, Mr. Watchmaster, I just wanted to tell you I'm going out for an hour or two. I have to look something up. Mr. Cranach's got his door locked, and Mr. Amstutz had to go home to see why his wife was crying."

"Christ, what an outfit. What do you have to look up?"

"What Mussolini did to the Red Cross dogs. It's for the 'Whither Italy?' supplement."

"You don't need to leave the building for that. You can get all you want by phone. You highbrows don't even know what a phone is. Drop around Advertising some time and I'll show you down-to-earth people using phones as working instruments. All you have to do is call the Red Cross, a veterinarian, an Italian priest, maybe an Italian restaurant, and a kennel. They'll tell you all you need to know. Remember what Churchill said about Mussolini, eh? That he was a fine Christian gentleman. If you want my opinion, whatever those dogs got they deserved."

Interviews were useful: you could get out and ride around in taxis and waste hours in hotel lobbies reading the new American magazines, which were increasingly difficult to find.

"I'm just checking something for *The Lantern* — do you mind?"

"Just so long as you don't mar the merchandise. I've only got five *Time*, three *Look*, four *Photoplay* and two *Ladies Home*. Don't wander away with the *Esquire*. There's a war on."

Once I was sent to interview my own godmother. Nobody knew I knew her, and I didn't say. She was president of a committee that sent bundles to prisoners-of-war. The committee was launching an appeal for funds; that was the reason for the interview. I took down her name as if I had never heard it before: Miss Edna May Henderson. My parents had called her "Georgie," though I don't know why.

I had not seen my godmother since I was eight. My father had died, and I had been dragged away to be brought up in different cities. At eighteen, I had summoned her to a telephone: "It's Linnet," I said. "I'm here, in Montreal. I've come back to stay."

"Linnet," she said, "Good gracious me." Her chain-smoker's voice made me homesick, though it could not have been for a place — I was in it. Her voice, and her particular Montreal accent, were like the unexpected signatures that underwrite the past: If this much is true, you will tell yourself, then so is all the rest I have remembered.

She was too busy with her personal war drive to see me then, though she did ask for my phone number. She did not enquire where I had been since my father's death, or if I had anything here to come back to. It is true that she and my mother had quarrelled years before; still, it was Georgie who had once renounced in my name, "the devil and all his works, the vain pomp and glory of the world, with all covetous desires of the same, and carnal desires of the flesh." She might have been curious to see the result of her bizarre undertaking, but a native canny Anglo-Montreal prudence held her still.

I was calling from a drugstore; I lived in one room of a cold-water flat in the east end. I said, "I'm completely on my own, and entirely self-supporting." That was so Georgie would understand I was not looking for help; at all events, for nothing material.

I realize now how irregular, how fishy even, this must have sounded. Everybody has a phone, she was probably thinking. What is the girl trying to hide?

"Nothing" would have been the answer. There seemed no way to connect. She asked me to call her again in about a month's time, but of course I never did.

My godmother spent most of her life in a block of granite designed to look like a fortress. Within the fortress were sprawling apartments, drawn to an Edwardian pattern of high ceilings, dark corridors, and enormous kitchens full of pipes. Churches and schools, banks and prisons, dwellings and railway stations were part of an imperial convallation that wound round the globe, designed to impress on the minds of indigenous populations that the builders had come to stay. In Georgie's redoubt, the doorman was shabby and lame; he limped beside me along a gloomy passage as far as the elevator, where only one of the sconce lights fixed to the panelling still worked. I had expected someone else to answer my ring, but it was Georgie who let me in, took my coat, and indicated with a brusque gesture, as if I did not know any English, the mat where I was to leave my wet snowboots. It had not occurred to me to bring shoes. Padding into her drawing room on stockinged feet, I saw the flash photograph her memory would file as further evidence of Muir incompetence; for I believe to this day that she recognized me at once. I was the final product, the last living specimen of a strain of people whose imprudence, lack of foresight, and refusal to take anything seriously had left one generation after another unprepared and stranded, obliged to build life from the ground up, fashioning new materials every time.

My godmother was tall, though not so tall as I remembered. Her face was wide and flat. Her eyes were small, deep-set, slightly tilted, as if two invisible thumbs were pulling at her temples. Her skin was as coarse and lined as a farm woman's; indifference to personal appearance of that kind used to be a matter of pride.

Her drawing room was white, and dingy and worn-looking. Curtains and armchairs needed attention, but that may have been on account of the war: it had been a good four years since anyone had bothered to paint or paper or have slipcovers made. The lamps were blue and white, and on this winter day already lighted. The room smelled of the metallic central heating of old apartment buildings, and of my godmother's Virginia cigarettes. We sat on worn white sofas, facing each other, with a table in between.

My godmother gave me Scotch in a heavy tumbler and pushed a dish of peanuts towards me, remarking in that harsh evocative voice, "Peanuts are harder to find than Scotch now." Actually, Scotch was off the map for most people; it was a civilian casualty, expensive and rare.

We were alone except for a Yorkshire terrier, who lay on a chair in the senile sleep that is part of dying.

"I would like it if Minnie could hang on until the end of the war," Georgie said. "I'm sure she'd like the victory parades and the bands. But she's thirteen, so I don't know."

That was the way she and my parents and their friends had talked to each other. The duller, the more earnest, the more literal generation I stood for seemed to crowd the worn white room, and to darken it further.

I thought I had better tell her straightaway who I was, though I imagined she knew. I did not intend to be friendly beyond that, unless she smiled. And even there, the quality of the smile would matter. Some smiles are instruments of repression.

Telling my new name, explaining that I had married, that I was now working for a newspaper, gave an accounting only up to a point. A deserted continent stretched between us, cracked and fissured with bottomless pits over which Georgie stepped easily. How do you deal with life? her particular Canadian catechism asked. By ignoring its claims on feeling. Any curiosity she may have felt about such mysteries as coincidence and continuity (my father was said to have been the love of her life; I was said to resemble him) had been abandoned, like a game that was once the rage. She may have been unlucky with games, which would explain the committee work; it may be dull, but you can be fairly sure of the outcome. I often came across women like her, then, who had no sons or lovers or husbands to worry about, and who adopted the principle of the absent, endangered male. A difference between us was that, to me, the absence and danger had to be taken for granted; another was that what I thought of as men, Georgie referred to as "boys." The rest was beyond my reach. Being a poor judge of probabilities, she had expected my father to divorce. I was another woman's child, foolish and vulnerable because I had lost my dignity along with my boots; paid to take down her words in a notebook; working not for a lark but for a living, which was unforgivable even then within the shabby fortress. I might have said, "I am innocent," but she already knew that.

My godmother was dressed in a jaunty blue jacket with a double row of brass buttons, and a pleated skirt. I supposed this must be the costume she and her committee wore when they were packing soap and cigarettes and second-hand cheery novels for their boys over there in the coop. She told me the names of the committee women, and said, "Are you getting everything down all right?" People who ask that are not used to being interviewed. "They told me there'd be a picture," she complained. That explained the uniform.

"I'm sorry. He should be here now."

"Do you want me to spell those names for you?"

"No. I'm sure I have them."

"You're not writing much."

"I don't need to," I said. "Not as a rule."

"You must have quite a memory."

She seemed to be trying to recall where my knack of remembering came from, if it was inherited, wondering whether memory is of any use to anyone except to store up reasons for discord.

We gave up waiting for the photographer. I stood stork-like in the passage, pulling on a boot. Georgie leaned on the wall, and I saw that she was slightly tight.

"I have four godchildren," she said. "People chose me because I was an old maid, and they thought I had money to leave. Well, I haven't. There'll be nothing for the boys. All my godchildren were boys. I never liked girls."

She had probably been drinking for much of the day, on and off; and of course there was all the excitement of being interviewed, and the shock of seeing me: still, it was a poor thing to say. Supposing, just supposing, that Georgie had been all I had left? My parents had been perfectly indifferent to money — almost pathologically so, I sometimes thought. The careless debts they had left strewn behind and that I kept picking up and trying to settle were not owed in currency.

Why didn't I come straight out with that? Because you can't — not in that world. No one can have the last retort, not even when there is truth to it. Hints and reminders flutter to the ground in overheated winter rooms, lie stunned for a season, are reborn as everlasting grudges.

"Goodbye, Linnet," she said.

"Goodbye."

"Do you still not have a telephone?" No answer. "When will it come out?" She meant the interview.

"On Saturday."

"I'll be looking for it." On her face was a look I took to mean anxiety over the picture, and that I now see to have been mortal terror. I never met her again, not even by accident. The true account I wrote of her committee and its need for public generosity put us at a final remove from each other.

I did not forget her, but I forgot about her. Her life seemed silent and slow and choked with wrack, while mine moved all in a rush, dislodging every obstacle it encountered. Then mine slowed too; stopped flooding its banks. The noise of it abated and I could hear the past. She had died by then — thick-skinned, chain-smoking survivor of the regiment holding the fort.

I saw us in the decaying winter room, saw the lamps blazing coldly on the dark window panes; I heard our voices: "Peanuts are harder to find than Scotch now." "Do you send parcels to Asia, or just to Germany?"

What a dull girl she is, Georgie must have thought; for I see, now, that I was seamless, and as smooth as brass; that I gave her no opening.

When she died, the godsons mentioned in her will swarmed around for a while, but after a certain amount of scuffling with trustees they gave up all claim, which was more dignified for them than standing forlorn and hungry-looking before a cupboard containing nothing. Nobody spoke up for the one legacy the trustees would have relinquished: a dog named Minnie, who was by then the equivalent of one hundred and nineteen years old in human time, and who persisted so unreasonably in her right to outlive the rest of us that she had to be put down without mercy.

GUY VANDERHAEGHE was born in Saskatchewan, where he still lives. His publications include *Man Descending*, for which he received the Governor General's Award for Fiction in 1982, and *The Englishman's Boy*, for which he received the same award in 1996. This story first appeared in CFM No. 34/35 in 1980.

The Watcher

GUY VANDERHAEGHE

I SUPPOSE it was having a bad chest that turned me into an observer, a Watcher, at an early age.

"Charlie has my chest," my mother often informed friends. "A real weakness there," she would add significantly, thumping her own wishbone soundly to further specify locality.

I suppose I did. Family lore had me narrowly escaping death from pneumonia at the age of four. It seems I spent an entire Sunday in delirium, soaking the sheets. Dr. Carlyle was off at the reservoir rowing in his little skiff and couldn't be reached — something for which my mother illogically refused to forgive him. She was a woman who nursed and tenaciously held to dark grudges. Forever after that incident the doctor was slightly and coldly dismissed in conversation as a "man who betrayed the public's trust."

Following that spell of pneumonia, I regularly suffered from bouts of bronchitis which often landed me in hospital in Fortune, forty miles away. Compared to the oxygen tent and whacking great needles that were buried in my skinny rump there, being invalided at home was a piece of cake. Coughing and hacking, I would leaf through catalogues and read comic books until my head swam with print-fatigue. My diet was largely of my own whimsical choosing — hot chocolate and graham wafers were staples. They were supplemented by sticky sweet cough drops which I downed one after another until my stomach could take no more, revolted and tossed up the whole mess.

With the first signs of improvement in my condition my mother moved her baby to the living-room chesterfield where she and the radio could keep me company. The electric kettle followed me and was soon burbling in the corner, jetting steam into the air to keep my lungs moist and pliable. Neither quite sick nor quite well, these were the best days of my illnesses. My stay at home hadn't yet made me bored and restless, my chest no longer hurt when I breathed, and that loose pocket of rattling phlegm meant I didn't have to worry about going back to school just yet. So I luxuriated in this steamy equatorial climate, this jungle mugginess, tended by a doting mother as if I were a rare tropical orchid.

My parents didn't own a television and so my curiosity and attention were focussed on my surroundings during my illnesses. I tried to squeeze every bit of juice out of them. Sooner than most children I learned that if you kept quiet and still and didn't insist on drawing attention to yourself as many kids did, that adults were inclined to regard you as being one with the furniture, as significant and sentient as a hassock. By keeping mum I was treated to illuminating glances into an adult world of convention, miseries and scandals. I wasn't sure at the age of six what a miscarriage was, but I knew that Ida Thompson had had one and that now her plumbing was buggered.

And watching old lady Kuznetzky hang her washing through a living room window trickling with condensed kettle steam I was able to confirm for myself the rumour that the old girl scorned panties. As she bent down to rummage in her laundry basket I caught a brief glimpse of huge, white buttocks that shimmered in the pale spring sunshine.

I also soon knew (how I don't remember exactly) that Norma Ruggs had business with the Liquor Board Store when she shuffled by our window every day at exactly 10:50 A.M. She was always at the store door at 11:00 when they unlocked and opened up for business. At 11:15 she trudged home again, a pint of ice cream in one hand, a brown paper bag disguising a bottle of fortified wine in the other, and her blotchy complexion painted a high colour with shame.

"Poor old girl," my mother would say, whenever she caught sight of Norma passing by in her shabby coat and sloppy man's overshoes. They had been in high school together, and Norma had been class brain and valedictorian. She had been an obliging dutiful girl and still was. For the wine wasn't Norma's — the ice cream was her only vice. The booze was her husband's, a vet who had come back from the war badly crippled.

Neither sleet, nor snow, nor pregnancy kept Norma from her appointed rounds. She was like Kant, you could set your watch by her.

All this careful study of adults may have made me old before my time. In any case it seemed to mark me in some recognizable way as being "different" or "queer for a kid." When I went to live with my grandmother in July of 1959 she spotted it right away. Of course, she was only stating the obvious when she declared me skinny and delicate, but she also noted in her vinegary voice that my eyes had a bad habit of never letting her go, and that I was the worst case of little pitchers having big ears that she had ever come across.

I ended up at my grandmother's because in May of that year my mother's bad chest finally caught up with her, much to her and everyone else's surprise. It had been pretty generally agreed by all her acquaintances that Mabel Bradley's defects in that regard were largely imagined. Not so. A government sponsored x-ray program discovered tuberculosis, and she was packed off, pale and drawn with worry for a stay in the sanitorium at Fort Qu'Appelle.

For roughly a month, until the school year ended, my father took charge of me and the house. He was a desolate, lanky, drooping weed of a man who had married late in life but nevertheless had been easily domesticated. I didn't like him much.

My father was badly wrenched by my mother's sickness and absence. He scrawled her long, untidy letters with a stub of gnawed pencil, and once he got shut of me, visited her every weekend. He was a soft and sentimental man whose eyes ran to water at the drop of a hat, or more accurately, death of a cat. Unlike his mother, my Grandma Bradley, he hadn't a scrap of flint or hard-headed common sense in him.

But then neither did any of his many brothers and sisters. It was as if the old girl had unflinchingly withheld the genetic code for responsibility and practicality from her pinheaded offspring. Life for her children was a series of thundering defeats, whirlwind calamities, or at best, hurried strategic retreats. Businesses crashed and marriages failed, for they had — my father excepted — a taste for the unstable in partners marital and fiscal.

My mother saw no redeeming qualities in any of them. By and large they drank too much, talked too loudly, and raised ill-mannered children; monsters of depravity whose rudeness provided my mother with endless illustrations of what she feared I might become. "You're eating just like a pig," she would say, "exactly like your cousin Elvin." Or to my father. "You're neglecting the belt. He's starting to get as lippy as that little snot, Muriel."

And in the midst, in the very eye of this familial cyclone of mishap and discontent stood Grandma Bradley, as firm as a rock. Troubles of all kinds were laid on her doorstep. When my cousin Criselda suddenly turned big tummied at sixteen and it proved difficult to ascertain with any exactitude the father, or even point a finger of general blame in the direction of a putative sire, she was shipped off to Grandma Bradley until she had delivered. Uncle Ernie dried out on Grandma's farm and Uncle Ed hid there from several people he had sold prefab, assemble-yourself, cropduster airplanes to.

So it was only family tradition that I should be deposited there. When domestic duties finally overwhelmed him, and I complained too loudly about fried egg sandwiches for dinner again, my father left the bacon rinds hardening and curling grotesquely on unwashed plates, the slut's wool eddying along the floor in the currents of a draft, and drove the one hundred and fifty miles to the farm, *right then and there.*

My father, a dangerous man behind the wheel, took any extended trip seriously, believing the highways narrow, unnavigatable ribbons of carnage. This trip loomed so dangerously in his mind that rather than tear a hand from the wheel, or an eye from the road, he had me, *chronic sufferer of lung disorders,* light his cigarettes and place them carefully in his dry lips. My mother would have killed him.

"You'll love it at Grandma's," he kept saying unconvincingly, "you'll have a real boy's summer on the farm. It'll build you up, the chores and all that. And good fun too. You don't know it now, but you are living the best days of your life right now. What I wouldn't give to be a kid again. You'll love it there. There's chickens and everything."

It wasn't exactly a lie. There were chickens. But the everything — as broad and overwhelming and suggestive of possibilities as my father tried to make it sound — didn't cover much. It certainly didn't comprehend a pony or a dog as I had hoped — chickens being the only livestock on the place.

It turned out that my grandmother, although she had spent most of her life on that particular piece of ground and eventually died there, hadn't cared much for the farm and was entirely out of sympathy with most varieties of animal life. She did keep chickens for the eggs, although she admitted that her spirits lifted considerably in the fall when it came time to butcher the hens.

Her flock was a garrulous, scraggly crew which spent their days having dust baths in the front yard, hiding their eggs, and, fleet and ferocious as hunting cheetahs, running down scuttling lizards which they trampled and pecked to death while their shiny expressionless eyes shifted dizzily in their stupid heads. The only one of these birds I felt any compassion for was Stanley the rooster, a bedraggled male who spent his days tethered to a stake by a piece of bailer twine looped around his leg. Poor Stanley crowed heart-rendingly in his captivity, his comb drooped pathetically, he was utterly crest-fallen as he lecherously eyed his bantam beauties daintily scavenging. Grandma kept him in this unnatural bondage to keep him from fertilizing the eggs and producing blood spots in the yolks. Being a finicky eater I approved this policy, but nevertheless felt some guilt over Stanley.

No, the old Bradley homestead, all that encompassed by my father's everything, wasn't very impressive. The two story house, though big and solid, needed paint and shingles. A track had been worn in the kitchen linoleum clean through to the floorboards and a long rent in the screen door had been stitched shut with waxed thread. The yard was little more than a tangle of thigh-high ragweed and sowthistle that the chickens repaired to for shade. A windbreak of spruce on the north side of the house was dying from lack of water and the competition from scotch thistle. The evergreens were no longer green, their sere needles fell away from the branches at the touch of a hand.

The abandoned barn out back was flanked by two mountainous rotted piles of manure which I remember sprouting button mushrooms after every warm soaker of a rain. That pile of shit was the only useful thing in a yard full of junk: wrecked cars, old wagon wheels, collapsing sheds. The barn itself was mightily decayed. The paint had been stripped from its planks by rain, hall and dry blistering winds, and the roof sagged like a tired nag's back. For a small boy it was an ominous place on a summer day. The air was still and dark and heavy with heat. At the sound of footsteps rats squeaked and scrabbled in the empty mangers, and the sparrows which had spattered the rafters white with their dung whirred about and fluted cries which sounded less bird-like than ghostly.

No bucolic splendor to speak of there certainly. Pretty nondescript and run down. Which brings me to my grandmother who wasn't either. Nondescript or run down that is.

In 1959 Grandma Bradley would have been sixty-nine which made her a child of the last century's gay nineties, although the supposed gaiety of that age didn't seem to have had much impress on the development of her character. Physically she was an imposing woman. Easily six feet tall she carried a hundred and eighty pounds on her generous frame without prompting speculation as to what she had against girdles. She could touch the floor effortlessly with the flat of her palms and pack an eighty pound sack of chicken feed on her shoulder. She dyed her hair auburn in defiance of local mores and never went to town to play bridge, whist, or canasta without wearing a hat and getting dressed to the teeth. Grandma loved card games of all varieties and considered anyone who didn't as a mental defective.

A cigarette always smoldered in her trap. She smoked sixty a day and rolled them as thin as knitting needles in an effort at economy. These cigarettes were so wispy and delicate they tended to get lost between her swollen fingers.

And above all she believed in plain speaking. She let me know that as my father's maroon Meteor pulled out of the yard while we stood waving goodbye on the front steps.

"Let's get things straight from the beginning," she said without taking her eyes off the car as it bumped toward the grid road. "I don't chew my words twice. If you're like any of the rest of them I've had here, you've been raised as wild as a goddamn Indian. Not one of my grandchildren have been brought up to mind. Well you'll mind around here. I don't jaw and blow hot air to jaw and blow hot air. I belted your father when he needed it, and make no mistake I'll belt you. Is that understood?"

"Yes," I said with a sinking feeling as I watched my father's car disappear down the road, swaying from side to side as its suspension was buffeted by potholes.

"These bloody bugs are eating me alive," she said slapping her arm. "I'm going in."

I trailed after her as she slopped back into the house in a pair of badly mauled, laceless sneakers. The house was filled with a half-light that changed its texture with every room. The venetian blinds were drawn in the parlour and some flies carved immelmanns in the dark air that smelled of cellar damp. Others battered their bullet bodies tip tap, tip tap against the window panes.

In the kitchen my grandmother put the kettle on the stove to boil for tea. After she had lit one of her matchstick smokes, she inquired through a blue haze if I was hungry.

"People aren't supposed to smoke around me," I informed her. "Because of my chest. Dad can't even smoke in our house."

"That so?" she said genially. Her cheeks collapsed as she drew on her butt. I had a hint there, if I'd only known it, of how she'd look in her coffin. "You won't like it here then," she said. "I smoke all the time."

I tried a few unconvincing coughs. I was ignored. She didn't respond to the same signals as my mother.

"My mother has a bad chest, too," I said. "She's in a TB sanitorium."

"So I heard," my grandmother said, getting up to fetch the whistling kettle. "Oh I suspect she'll be right as rain in no time with a little rest. TB isn't what it used to be. Not with all these new drugs." She considered. "That's not to say though that your father'll ever hear the end of it. Mabel was always a silly little shit that way."

I almost fell off my chair. I had never thought I'd live to hear the day my mother was called a silly little shit.

"Drink tea?" asked Grandma Bradley, pouring boiling water into a brown tea pot.

I shook my head.

"How old are you anyway?" she asked.

"Eleven."

"You're old enough then," she said taking down a cup from the shelf. "Tea gets the kidneys moving and carries off the poisons in the blood. That's why all the Chinese live to be so old. They all live to be a hundred."

"I don't know if my mother would like it," I said. "Me drinking tea."

"You worry a lot for a kid," she said, "don't you?"

I didn't know how to answer that. It wasn't a question I had ever considered. I tried to shift the conversation.

"What's there for a kid to do around here?" I said in an unnaturally inquisitive voice.

"Well, we could play cribbage," she said.

"I don't know how to play cribbage."

She was genuinely shocked. "What!" she exclaimed. "Why you're eleven years old! Your father could count a cribbage hand when he was five. I taught all my kids to."

"I never learned how," I said. "We don't even have a deck of cards at our house. My father hates cards. Says he had too much of them as a boy."

At this my grandmother arched her eyebrows. "Is that a fact? Well hoity toity."

"So since I don't play cards," I continued in a strained manner I imagined was polite, "what could I do — I mean for fun?"

"Make your own fun," she said. "I never considered fun such a problem. Use your imagination. Take a broomstick and make like Nimrod."

"Who's Nimrod?" I asked.

"Pig ignorant," she said under her breath, and then louder, directly to me, "ask me no questions and I'll tell you no lies. Drink your tea." And that, for the time being, was that.

It's all very well to tell someone to make their own fun. It's the making of it that is the problem. In a short time I was a very bored kid. There was no one to play with, no horse to ride, no gun to shoot gophers, no dog for company. There was nothing to read except the *Country Guide* and *Western Producer*. There was nothing or nobody interesting to watch. I went through my grandmother's drawers but found nothing as surprising there as I had discovered in my parents!

Most days it was so hot that the very idea of fun boiled out of me and evaporated. I moped and dragged myself listlessly around the house in the loose-jointed, water-boned way kids have when they can't stand anything, not even their precious selves.

On my better days I tried to take up with Stanley the rooster. Scant chance of that. Tremors of panic ran through his body at my approach. He tugged desperately on the twine until he jerked his free leg out from under himself and collapsed in the dust, his heart bumping the tiny crimson scallops of his breast feathers, the black pellets of his eyes glistening, all the while shitting copiously. Finally in the last extremis of chicken terror he would allow me to stroke his yellow beak and finger his comb.

I felt sorry for the captive Stanley and several times tried to take him for a walk, to give him a chance to take the air and broaden his limited horizons. But this prospect alarmed him so much that I was always forced to return him to his stake in disgust, while he fluttered, squawked and flopped.

So fun was a commodity in short supply. That is, until something interesting turned up during the first week of August. Grandma Bradley was dredging little watering canals with a hoe among the corn stalks on a bright blue Monday morning, and I was shelling peas into a collander on the front stoop, when a black car nosed diffidently up the road and into the yard. Then it stopped a good twenty yards short of the house as if its occupants weren't sure of their welcome. After some time, the doors opened and a man and woman got carefully out.

The woman wore turquoise-blue pedal pushers, a sloppy black turtleneck sweater, and a gash of scarlet lipstick swiped across her white vivid face. This was my father's youngest sister, Aunt Evelyn.

The man took her gently and courteously by the elbow and balanced her as she edged up the front yard in her high heels, careful to avoid turning an ankle on a loose stone, or in an old tire track.

The thing which immediately struck me about the man was his beard, the first I had ever seen grace a face. Beards weren't popular in 1959 — not in our part of the world. His was a randy, jutting, little goat's beard that would have looked wicked on any other face but his. He was very tall and his considerable height was accented by a lack of corresponding breadth to his body. He appeared to have been racked and stretched against his will into an exceptional and unnatural anatomy. As he walked and talked animatedly his free hand fluttered in front of my aunt. It sailed, twirled and gambolled on the air. Like a butterfly enticing a child, it seemed to lead her hypnotized across a yard fraught with perils for city shod feet.

My grandmother laid down her hoe and called sharply to her daughter. "Evvie!" she called. "Over here, Evvie!"

At the sound of her mother's voice my aunt's head snapped around and she began to wave jerkily and stiffly, striving to maintain a tottering balance on her high-heeled shoes. It wasn't hard to see that there was something not quite right with her. By the time my grandmother and I reached the pair, Aunt Evelyn was in tears, sobbing hollowly and jamming the heel of her palm into her front teeth.

The man was speaking calmly to her. "Control. Control. Deep steady breaths. Think sea. Control. Control. Control. Think sea, Evelyn. Deep. Deep. Deep," he muttered.

"What the hell is the matter, Evelyn?" my grandmother asked sharply. "And who is *he?*"

"Evelyn is a little upset," the man said, keeping his attention focused on my aunt. "She's having one of her anxiety attacks. If you'd just give us a moment we'll clear this up. She's got to learn to handle stressful situations." He inclined his head in a priestly manner and said, "Be with the sea, Evelyn. Deep. Deep. Sink in the sea."

"It's her damn nerves again," said my grandmother.

"Yes," the man said benignly with a smile of blinding condescension. "Sort of."

"She's been as nervous as a cut cat all her life," said my grandmother, mostly to herself.

"Momma," said Evelyn weeping. "Momma."

"Slide beneath the waves, Evelyn. Down, down, down to the beautiful pearls," the man chanted softly. This was really something.

My grandmother took Aunt Evelyn by her free elbow, shook it, and said sharply, "Evelyn, shut up!" Then she began to drag her briskly towards the house. For a moment the man looked as if he had it in mind to protest, but in the end he meekly acted as a flanking escort for Aunt Evelyn as she was marched into the house. When I tried to follow, my grandmother gave me one of her looks and said definitely, "You find something to do out *here.*"

I did. I waited a few minutes and then duck-walked my way under the parlour window. There I squatted with my knobby shoulder blades pressed against the siding and the sun beating into my face.

My grandmother obviously hadn't wasted any time with the social niceties. They were fairly into it.

"Lovers?" said my grandmother. "Is that what it's called now? Shackup you mean."

"Oh, momma," said Evelyn, and she was crying, "it's all right. We're going to get married."

"You believe that?" said my grandmother. "You believe that geek is going to marry you?"

"Thompson," said the geek, "my name is Thompson, Robert Thompson, and we'll marry as soon as I get my divorce. Although Lord only knows when that'll be."

"That's right," said my Grandmother, "Lord only knows." Then to her daughter. "You got another one. A real prize off the midway didn't you? Evelyn, you're a certifiable lunatic."

"I didn't expect this," said Thompson. "We came here because Evelyn has had a bad time of it recently. She hasn't been eating or sleeping properly and consequently she's got herself run down. She finds it difficult to control her emotions, don't you, darling?"

I thought I heard a mild yes.

"So," said Thompson continuing, "we decided Evelyn needs some peace and quiet before I go back to school in September."

"School," said my grandmother. "Don't tell me you're some kind of teacher?" She seemed stunned by the very idea.

"No," said Aunt Evelyn and there was a tremor of pride in her voice that testified to her amazement that she had been capable of landing such a rare and remarkable fish. "Not a teacher. Robert's a graduate student of American Literature at the University of British Columbia."

"Hoity toity," said Grandmother. "A graduate student. A graduate student of American Literature."

"Doctoral program," said Robert.

"And did you ever ask yourself, Evelyn, what the hell this genius is doing with you? Or is it just the same old problem with your elevator panties? Some guy comes along and pushes the button. Up, down. Up, down."

The image this created in my mind made me squeeze my knees together deliciously and stifle a giggle.

"Mother," said Evelyn continuing to bawl.

"Guys like this don't marry barmaids," said my grandmother.

"Cocktail hostess," corrected Evelyn. "I'm a cocktail hostess."

"You don't have to make any excuses, dear," said Thompson pompously. "Remember what I told you. You're past the age of being judged."

"What the hell is that supposed to mean?" said my grandmother. "And by the way, don't start handing out orders in my house. You won't be around long enough to make them stick."

"That remains to be seen," said Thompson.

"Let's go, Robert," said Evelyn nervously.

"Go on upstairs, Evelyn, I want to talk to your mother."

"You don't have to go anywhere," said my Grandmother. "You can stay put."

"Evelyn go upstairs." There was a pause and then I heard the sound of a chair creaking, then footsteps.

"Well," said my Grandmother at last, "round one. Now for round two, get the hell out of my house."

"Can't do that."

"Why the hell not?"

"It's very difficult to explain," he said.

"Try."

"As you can see for yourself Evelyn isn't well. She is very highly strung at the moment. I believe she is on the verge of profound personality adjustment, a breakthrough." He paused dramatically, "Or breakdown."

"It's times like this that I wished I had a dog on the place to run off undesirables."

"The way I read it," said Thompson unperturbed, "is that at the moment two people bulk very large in Evelyn's life. You and me. She needs the support and love of us both. You're not doing your share."

"I ought to slap your face."

"She has come home to try and get a hold of herself. We have to bury our dislikes for the moment. She needs to be handled very carefully."

"You make her sound like a trained bear. Handled. What that girl needs is a good talking to, and I am perfectly capable of giving her that."

"No, Mrs. Bradley," Thompson said firmly in that maddeningly self-assured tone of his. "If you don't mind me saying so, I think that's part of her problem. It's important now for you to let Evelyn just *be.*"

"Get out of my house," said my Grandmother at the end of her tether.

"I know it's difficult for you to understand," he said smoothly, "but if you understood the psychology of this you would see it's impossible for me to go, or for that matter, for Evelyn to go. If we leave she'll feel that at last you've rejected her. If I go at your wishes, she'll feel *I've* rejected her. It can't be done. We're faced with a real psychological balancing act here."

"Now I've heard everything," said my Grandmother. "Are you telling me you'd have the gall to move into a house where you're not wanted and just . . . just *stay there?*"

"Yes," said Thompson. "And I think you'll find me quite stubborn on this particular point."

"My God," said my Grandmother. I could tell by her tone of voice that she had never come across anyone like Mr. Thompson before. At a loss for a suitable reply, she simply reiterated, "My God."

"I'm going upstairs now," said Thompson. "Maybe you could get the boy to bring in our bags while I see how Evelyn is doing. The car isn't locked." The second time he spoke his voice came from further away; I imagined him paused in the doorway. "Mrs. Bradley, please let's make this stay pleasant for Evelyn's sake."

She didn't bother answering him.

When I barged into the house sometime later with conspicuous noisiness, I found my Grandmother standing at the bottom of the stairs staring up the steps. "Well I'll be damned," she said under her breath. "I've never seen anything like that. Goddamn freak." She even repeated it several times under her breath. "Goddamn freak. Goddamn freak."

Who could blame me, if after a boring summer I felt my chest tighten with anticipation. Adults could be immensely interesting and entertaining if you knew what to watch for.

But at first things were disappointingly quiet. Aunt Evelyn seldom set forth outside the door of the room she and her man inhabited by squatters' right. There was an argument, short and sharp, between Thompson and Grandmother over this. The professor claimed no one had any business prying into what Evelyn did up there. She was an adult and had the right to her privacy and her own thoughts. My grandmother claimed *she* had a right to know what was going on up there, if nobody else thought she did.

I could have satisfied her curiosity on that point. Not much was going on up there. Several squints through the keyhole had revealed Aunt Evelyn lolling about the bedspread in a blue housecoat, eating soda crackers and sardines, and reading a stack of movie magazines she had had me lug out of the trunk of the car.

Food, you see, was beginning to become something of a problem for our young lovers. Grandma rather pointedly set only three places for meals, and Evelyn, out of loyalty to her boyfriend, couldn't very well sit down and break bread with us. Not that Thompson didn't take such things in his stride. He sauntered casually and conspicuously about the house as if he owned it, even going so far as to poke his head in the fridge and rummage in it like some pale hairless bear. At times like that my grandmother was capable of looking through him as if he didn't exist, or just as a dog circling a pole, regard him with an eye for the spot most suitable to relieve itself upon.

On the second day of his stay Thompson took up with me, which was all right as far as I was concerned. I had no objection. Why he decided to do this I'm not sure exactly. Perhaps he was looking for some kind of an ally, no matter how weak. Most likely he wanted to get under the old lady's skin. Or maybe he just couldn't bear not having anyone to tell how wonderful he was. Thompson was that kind of a guy.

I was certainly let in on the secret. He was a remarkable fellow. He dwelt at great length on those things which made him such an extraordinary human being. I may have gotten the order of precedence all wrong, but if I remember correctly there were three things which made Thompson very special and different from all the other people

I would ever meet, no matter how long or hard I lived.

First, he was going to write a book about a poet called Allen Ginsberg which was going to knock the socks off everybody who counted. It turned out he had actually met this Ginsberg the summer before in San Francisco and asked him if he could write a book about him and Ginsberg had said, "Sure, why the hell not?" The way Thompson described what it would be like when he published this book left me with the impression that he was going to spend most of the rest of his life riding around on people's shoulders and being cheered by a multitude of admirers.

Second, he confessed to knowing a tremendous amount about what made other people tick and how to adjust their mainsprings when they went kaflooey. He knew all this because at one time his own mainspring had gotten a little out of sorts. But now he was a fully integrated personality with a highly creative mind and strong intuitive sense. That's why he was so much help to Aunt Evelyn in her time of troubles.

Third, he was a Buddhist.

The only one of these things which impressed me at the time was the bit about being a Buddhist. However, I was confused because in the *Picture Book of the World's Great Religions* which we had at home, all the Buddhists were bald, and Thompson had a hell of a lot of hair, more than I had ever seen on a man. But even though he wasn't bald he had an idol. A little bronze statue with a whimsical smile and slightly crossed eyes which he identified as Padma-sambhva. He told me that it was a Tibetan antique he had bought in San Francisco as an object of veneration and an aid to his meditations. I asked him what a meditation was and he offered to teach me one. So I learned to recite with great seriousness and flexible intonation one of his Tibetan meditations while my grandmother glared across her quintessentially Western parlour with disbelieving eyes.

I could soon deliver, "A king must go when his time has come. His wealth, his friends and his relatives cannot go with him. Wherever men go, wherever they stay, the effect of their past acts follows them like a shadow. Those who are in the grip of desire, the grip of existence, the grip of ignorance, move helplessly round through the spheres of life, as men or gods or as wretches in the lower regions."

Not that an eleven year old could make much of any of *that*.

Which is not to say that even an eleven year old could be fooled by Robert Thompson. In his stubbornness, egoism and blindness he was transparently un-Buddhalike. To watch him and my Grandmother snarl and snap their teeth over that poor, dry bone, Evelyn, was evidence enough of how firmly bound we all are to the wretched wheel of life and its stumbling desires.

No, even his most effective weapon, his cool benevolence, that patina of patience and forbearance which Thompson displayed to Grandmother, could crack.

One windy day when he had coaxed Aunt Evelyn out for a walk I followed them at a distance. They passed the windbreak of spruce, and at the sagging barbed-wire fence, he gallantly manipulated the wires while my aunt floundered over them in an impractical dress and crinoline. It was the kind of dippy thing she would decide to wear on a hike.

Thompson strode along through the rippling grass like a wading heron, his baggy pant legs flapping and billowing in the wind. My aunt moved along gingerly behind him, one hand modestly pinning down her windteased dress in the front, the other hand plastering the back of it to her behind.

It was only when they stopped and faced each other that I realized that all the time they had been traversing the field they had been arguing. A certain vaguely communicated agitation in the attitude of her figure, the way his arm stabbed at the featureless wash of sky implied a dispute. She turned toward the house and he caught her by the arm and jerked it. In a Fifties' calendar fantasy her dress lifted in the wind exposing her panties. I sank in the grass until their seed tassels trembled against my chin. I wasn't going to miss watching this for the world.

She snapped and twisted on the end of his arm like a fish on a line. Her head was flung back in an exaggerated, antique display of despair; her head rolled grotesquely from side to side as if her neck were broken.

Suddenly Thompson began striking awkwardly at her exposed buttocks and thighs with the flat of his hand. The long gangly arm slashed like a flail as she scampered around him, the radius of her escape limited by the distance of their linked arms.

From where I knelt in the grass I could hear nothing. I was too far off. As far as I was concerned there were no cries and no pleading. The whole scene, as I remember it, was shorn of any of the personal idiosyncrasies which manifest themselves in violence. It appeared a simple case of karmic retribution.

That night, for the first time, my aunt came down to supper and claimed her place at the table with queenly graciousness. She wore shorts too for the first time, and gave a fine display of mottled, discoloured thighs which reminded me of bruised fruit. She made sure, almost as if by accident, that my grandmother had a good hard look at them.

Right out of the blue my grandmother said, "I don't want you hanging around that man anymore. You stay away from him."

"Why?" I asked rather sulkily. He was the only company I had. Since my aunt's arrival Grandmother had paid no attention to me whatsoever.

It was late afternoon and we were sitting on the porch watching Evelyn squeal as she swung in the tire swing Thompson had rigged up for me in the barn. He had thrown a length of stray rope over the runner for the sliding door and hung a tire from it. I hadn't the heart to tell him I was too old for tire swings.

Aunt Evelyn seemed to be enjoying it though. She was screaming and girlishly kicking up her legs. Thompson couldn't be seen. He was deep in the settled darkness of the barn, pushing her back and forth. She disappeared and reappeared according to the arc which she travelled through. Into the barn, out in the sun. Light, darkness. Light, darkness.

She ignored my question. "Goddamn freak," she said scratching a match on the porch rail and lighting one of her rollies. "Wait and see, he'll get his wagon fixed."

"Aunt Evelyn likes him," I noted pleasantly, just to stir things up a bit.

"Your Aunt Evelyn's screws are loose," she said sourly. "And he's the son of a bitch who owns the screwdriver that loosened them."

"He must be an awful smart fellow to be studying to be a professor at a university," I commented. It was the last dig I could chance.

"One thing I know for sure," snapped my grandmother. "He isn't smart enough to lift the toilet seat when he pees. There's evidence enough for that."

After hearing that, I took to leaving a few conspicuous droplets of my own as a matter of course on each visit. Every little bit might help things along.

I stood in his doorway and watched Thompson meditate. And don't think that, drenched in *satori* as he was, he didn't know it. He put on quite a performance sitting on the floor in his underpants. When he came out of his trance he pretended to be surprised to see me. While he dressed we struck up a conversation.

"You know, Charlie," he said while he put on his sandals (I'd never seen another grown man wear sandals in my entire life), "you remind me of my little Padma-sambhva," he said nodding to the idol squatting on his dresser. "For a while you know I thought it was the smile, but it isn't. It's the eyes."

"It's eyes are crossed," I said, none too flattered at the comparison.

"No they're not," he said good-naturedly. He tucked his shirttail into his pants. "The artist, the maker of that image, set them fairly close together to suggest — aesthetically speaking — the intensity of inner vision, its concentration." He picked up the idol and looking at it said, "These are very watchful eyes, very knowing eyes. Your eyes are something like that. From your eyes I could tell you're an intelligent boy." He paused, set Padma-sambhva back on the dresser and asked, "Are you?"

I shrugged.

"Don't be afraid to say it if you are," he said. "False modesty can be as corrupting as vanity. It took me twenty-five years to learn that."

"I usually get all A's on my report card," I volunteered.

"Well that's something," he said looking around the room for his belt. He picked a sweater off a chair and peered under it. "Then you see what's going on around here, don't you?" he asked. "You see what your grandmother is mistakenly trying to do?"

I nodded.

"That's right," he said. "You're a smart boy." He sat down on the bed. "Come here."

I went over to him. He took hold of me by the arms and looked into my eyes with all the sincerity he could muster. "You know, being intelligent means responsibilities. It means doing something worthwhile with your life. For instance, have you given any thought as to what you would like to be when you grow up?"

"A spy," I said.

The silly bugger laughed.

* * *

It was the persistent rhythmic thud that first woke me, and once wakened, I picked up the undercurrent of muted clamour, of stifled struggle. The noise seeped through the beaverboard wall of the adjoining bedroom into my own, a storm of hectic urgency and violence. The floorboards of the old house squeaked; I heard what sounded like a strangled curse and moan, then a fleshy, meaty concussion which I took to be a slap. Was he killing her at last? Choking her with the silent, poisonous care necessary to escape detection?

I remembered Thompson's arm flashing frenziedly in the sunlight. My aunt's discoloured thighs. My heart creaked in my chest with fear. And after killing her? Would the madman stop? Or would he do us all in, one by one?

I got out of bed on unsteady legs. The muffled commotion was growing louder, more distinct. I padded into the hallway. The door to their bedroom was partially open, and a light showed. Terror made me feel hollow; the pit of my stomach ached.

They were both naked, something which I hadn't expected, and which came as quite a shock. What was perhaps even more shocking, was the fact that they seemed not only oblivious to me, but to each other as well. She was slung around so that her head was propped on a pillow resting on the footboard of the bed. One smooth leg was draped over the edge of the bed and her heel was beating time on the floorboards (the thud which woke me) as accompaniment to Thompson's plunging body and the soft, liquid grunts of expelled air which he made with every lunge. One of her hands gripped the footboard and her knuckles were white with strain.

I watched until the critical moment, right through the growing frenzy and ardour. They groaned and panted and heaved and shuddered and didn't know themselves. At the very last he lifted his bony, hatchet face with the jutting beard to the ceiling and closed his eyes; for a moment I thought he was praying as his lips moved soundlessly. But then he began to whimper and his mouth fell open and he looked stupider and weaker than any human being I had ever seen before in my life.

"Like pigs at the trough," my grandmother said at breakfast. "With the boy up there too."

My aunt turned a deep red, and then flushed again so violently that her thin lips appeared to turn blue.

I kept my head down and went on shovelling porridge. Thompson still wasn't invited to the table. He was leaning against the kitchen counter, his bony legs crossed at the ankles, eating an apple he had helped himself to.

"He didn't hear anything," my aunt said uncertainly. She half whispered this conspiratorially across the table to Grandmother. "Not at that hour. He'd been asleep for hours."

I thought it wise, even though it meant drawing attention to myself, to establish my ignorance. "Hear what?" I inquired innocently.

"It wouldn't do any harm if he had," said Thompson, calmly biting and chewing the temptress' fruit.

"You wouldn't see it, would you?" said Grandma Bradley. "It wouldn't matter to you what he heard? You'd think that was manly."

"Manly has nothing to do with it. Doesn't enter into it," said Thompson in that cool way he had. "It's a fact of life, something he'll have to find out about sooner or later."

Aunt Evelyn began to cry. "Nobody is ever pleased with me," she said matter of factly. "I'm going crazy trying to please you both. I can't do it." She began to pull nervously at her hair. "He made me," she said finally in a confessional, humble tone to her mother.

"Evelyn," said my grandmother, "you have a place here. I would never send you away. I want you here. But he has to go. I want him to go. If he is going to rub my nose in it that way he has to go. I won't have that man under my roof."

"Evelyn isn't apologizing for anything," Thompson said. "And she isn't running away either. You can't force her to choose. It isn't healthy or fair."

"There have been other ones before you," said Grandma, "this isn't anything new for Evelyn."

"Momma!"

"I'm aware of that," he said stiffly, and his face vibrated with the effort to smile. "Provincial mores have never held much water with me. I like to think I'm above all that." Suddenly my grandmother spotted me. "What are you gawking at!" she shouted. "Get on out of here!"

I didn't budge an inch.

"Leave him alone," said Thompson.

"You'll be out of here within a week," said Grandmother. "I swear."

"No," he said smiling. "When I'm ready."

"You'll go home and go with your tail between your legs. Last night was the last straw," she said. And by God you could tell she meant it.

Thompson gave her his beatific Buddha-grin and shook his head from side to side, very, very slowly.

* * *

A thunder storm was brewing. The sky was a stew of dark swollen cloud and a strange apple-green light. The temperature stood in the mid-nineties, not a breath of breeze stirred, my skin crawled and my head pounded above my eyes and through the bridge of my nose. There wasn't a thing to do except sit on the bottom step of the porch, keep from picking up a sliver in your ass, and scratch in the dirt with a stick. My grandmother had put her hat on and driven into town on some unexplained business. The professor and my aunt were upstairs in their bedroom, sunk in a stuporous, sweaty afternoon's sleep.

Like my aunt and Thompson, all the chickens had gone to roost to wait for rain. The desertion of his harem had thrown the rooster into a slap. Stanley trotted neurotically around his tethering post, stopping every few circuits to beat his bedraggled pinions and crow lustily in masculine outrage. I watched him for a bit without much curiosity, and then climbed off the step and walked toward him, listlessly dragging my stick in my trail.

"Here Stanley, Stanley," I called, not entirely sure how to summon a rooster, or instill in him confidence and friendliness.

I did neither. My approach only further unhinged Stanley. His stride lengthened, the tempo of his pace increased, and his head began to dart abruptly from side to side in furtive despair. Finally, in a last desperate attempt to escape, Stanley upset himself trying to fly. He landed in a heap of disarranged, stiff, glistening feathers. I put my foot on his string and pinned him to the ground.

"Nice pretty, pretty Stanley," I said coaxingly, adopting the tone that a neighbour used with her budgie, since I wasn't sure how one talked to a bird. I slowly extended my thumb to stroke his bright red neck feathers. Darting angrily he struck the ball of my thumb with a snappish peck and simultaneously hit my wrist with his heel spur. He didn't hurt me, but he did startle me badly. So badly I gave a little yelp. Which made me feel very foolish and more than a little cowardly.

"You son of a bitch," I said, reaching down slowly and staring into one unblinking glassy eye in which I could see my face looming larger and larger. I caught the rooster's legs and held them firmly together. Stanley crowed defiantly and showed me his wicked little tongue.

"Now, Stanley," I said, "relax, I'm just going to stroke you. I'm just going to pet Stanley."

No deal. He struck furiously again with a snake-like agility, and bounded in my hand, wings beating his poultry smell into my face. A real fighting cock at last. Maybe it was the weather. Perhaps his chicken pride and patience would suffer no more indignities.

The heat, the sultry menace of the gathering storm made me feel prickly, edgy. I flicked my middle finger smartly against his tiny chicken skull, hard enough to rattle his pea-sized brain. "You like that, buster?" I asked, and snapped him another one for good measure. He struck back again, his comb red, crested, and rubbery with fury.

I was angry myself. I turned him upside down and left him dangling, his wings drumming against the legs of my jeans. Then I righted him abruptly; he looked dishevelled, seedy and dazed.

"Okay Stanley," I said, feeling the intoxication of power, something which kids seldom have the opportunity to exercise. I had this son of a bitch. "I'm boss here, and you behave." There was a gleeful edge to my voice, which surprised me a little. I realized I was hoping this confrontation would escalate. Wishing that he would provoke me into something.

Some strange images came into my head: the bruises on my aunt's legs; Thompson's face drained of life, lifted like an empty receptacle toward the ceiling, waiting to be filled, the tendons of his neck stark and rigid with anticipation.

I was filled with anxiety, the heat seemed to stretch me, to tug at my nerves and my skin. Two drops of sweat, as large and perfectly formed as tears, rolled out of my hairline and splashed on to the rubber toes of my runners.

"Easy, Stanley," I breathed to him, "easy," and my hand crept deliberately towards him. This time he pecked me in such a way, directly on the knuckle, that it actually hurt. I took up my stick and rapped him on the beak curtly, the prim admonishment of a schoolmarm. I didn't hit him very hard, but it was hard enough to split the length of his beak with a narrow crack. The beak fissured like the nib of a fountain pen. Stanley squawked, opened and closed his beak spasmodically, bewildered by the pain. A bright jewel of blood bubbled out of the split and gathered to a trembling bead.

"There," I said excitedly, "now you've done it. How are you going to eat with a broken beak? You can't eat anything with a broken beak. You'll starve you stupid goddamn chicken."

A wind that smelled of rain had sprung up. It ruffled his feathers until they moved with a barely discernible crackle.

"Poor Stanley," I said, and at last, numbed by the pain, he allowed me to stroke the gloss of his lacquer feathers.

I wasn't strong enough or practiced enough to do a clean and efficient job of wringing his neck, but I succeeded in finishing him off after two clumsy attempts. Then because I wanted to leave the impression that a skunk had made off with him, I punched a couple of holes in his breast with my jack knife and tried to dribble some blood on the ground. Poor Stanley produced only a few meagre spots; this corpse refused to bleed in the presence of its murderer. I scattered a handful of his feathers on the ground and buried him in the larger of the two manure piles beside the barn.

"I don't think any skunk got that rooster," my grandmother said suspiciously, nudging at a feather with the toe of her boot until, finally disturbed, it was wafted away by the breeze.

Something squeezed my heart. How did she know?

"Skunks hunt at night," she said. "Must have been somebody's barn cat."

"You come along with me," my grandmother said. She was standing in front of the full length hall mirror, settling on her hat, a deadly looking hat pin poised above her skull. "We'll go into town and you can buy a comic book at the drugstore."

It was Friday and Friday was shopping day. But Grandma didn't wheel her battered De Soto to the curb in front of the Brite Spot Grocery, she parked it in front of Maynard & Pritchard, Barristers and Solicitors.

"What are we doing here?" I asked.

Grandma was fumbling nervously with her purse. Small town people don't like to be seen going to the lawyer's. "Come along with me. Hurry up."

"Why do I have to come?"

"Because I don't want you making a spectacle of yourself for the halfwits and loungers to gawk at," she said. "Let's not give them too much to wonder about."

Maynard & Pritchard, Barristers and Solicitors smelled of wax and varnish and probity. My grandmother was shown into an office with a frosted pane of glass in the door and neat gilt lettering that announced it was occupied by D.F. Maynard, Q.C. I was ordered to occupy a hard chair, which I did, battering my heels on the rungs briskly enough to annoy the secretary into telling me to stop it.

My grandmother wasn't closeted long with her Queen's Counsel until the door opened and he glided after her into the passageway. Lawyer Maynard was the neatest man I had ever seen in my life. His suit fit him like a glove.

"The best I can do," he said, "is send him a registered letter telling him to remove himself from the premises, but it all comes to the same thing. If that doesn't scare him off, you'll have to have recourse to the police. That's all there is to it. I told you that yesterday and you haven't told me anything new today, Edith, that would make me change my mind. Just let him know you won't put up with him any more."

"No police," she said. "I don't want the police digging in my family's business and Evelyn giving one of her grand performances for some baby skinned constable straight out of the depot. All I need is to get her away from him for a little while, then I could tune her in. I could get through to her in no time at all."

"Well," said Maynard shrugging, "we could try the letter, but I don't think it would do any good. He has the status of a guest in your home, just tell him to go."

My grandmother was showing signs of exasperation. "But he *doesn't* go. That's the point. I've told him and told him. But he won't."

"Mrs. Bradley," said the lawyer emphatically, "Edith, as a friend, don't waste your time. The police."

"I'm through wasting my time," she said.

Pulling away from the lawyer's office my grandmother began a spirited conversation with herself. A wisp of hair had escaped from under her hat, and the dye winked a metallic red light as it jiggled up and down in the hot sunshine.

"I've told him and told him. But he won't listen. The goddamn freak thinks we're involved in a christly debating society. He thinks I don't mean business. But I mean business. I do. There's more than one way to skin a cat or scratch a dog's ass. We'll take the wheels off his little red wagon and see how she pulls."

"What about my comic book?" I said, as we drove past the Rexall.

"Shut up."

Grandma drove the De Soto to the edge of town and stopped it at the Ogden's place. It was a service station, or rather had been until the B.A. company had taken out their pumps and yanked the franchise, or whatever you call it, on the two brothers. Since then everything had gone steadily downhill. Cracks in the windowpanes had been taped with masking tape, and the roof had been patched with flattened tin cans and old license plates. The building itself was surrounded by an acre of wrecks, sulking hulks rotten with rust, the guts of their upholstery spilled and gnawed by rats and mice.

But the Ogden brothers still carried on a business after a fashion. They stripped their wrecks for parts and were reputed to be decent enough mechanics whenever they were sober enough to turn a wrench or thread a bolt. People brought work to them whenever they couldn't avoid it, and the rest of the year gave them a wide berth.

The Ogdens were famous for two things: their meanness and their profligacy as breeders. The place was always aswarm with kids who never seemed to wear pants except in the most severe weather and tottered about the premises, their legs smeared with grease, shit or various combinations of both.

"Wait here," my grandmother said, slamming the car door loudly enough to bring the two brothers out of their shop. Through the open door I saw a motor suspended on an intricate system of chains and pulleys.

The Ogdens stood with their hands in the pockets of their bib overalls while my grandmother talked to them. They were quite a sight. They didn't have a dozen teeth in their heads between them, even though the oldest brother couldn't have been more than forty. They just stood there, one sucking on a cigarette, the other on a coke. Neither one moved or changed his expression, except once, when a tow-headed youngster piddled too close to Grandma. He was lazily and casually slapped on the side of the head by the nearest brother and ran away screaming, his stream cavorting wildly in front of him.

At last their business concluded the boys walked my grandmother back to the car.

"You'll get to that soon?" she said, sliding behind the wheel.

"Tomorrow all right?" said one. His words sounded all slack and chewed, issuing from his shrunken, old man's mouth.

"The sooner the better. I want that seen to, Bert."

"What seen to?" I asked.

"Bert and his brother Elwood are going to fix that rattle that's been plaguing me."

"Sure thing," said Elwood. "Nothing but clear sailing."

"What rattle?" I said.

"What rattle? What rattle? The one in the glove compartment," she said, banging it with the heel of her hand. "That rattle. You hear it?"

* * *

Thompson could get very edgy some days. "I should be working on my dissertation," he said, coiled in the big chair. "I shouldn't be wasting my time in this shithole. I should be working!"

"So why aren't you?" said Evelyn. She was spool knitting. That and reading movie magazines was the only things she ever did.

"How the christ do I work without a library? You see a goddamn library within a hundred miles of this place?"

"Why do you need a library?" she said calmly. "Can't you write?"

"Write," he said looking at the ceiling. "Write, she says. What the hell do you know about it? What the hell do you know about it?"

"I can't see why you can't write."

"Before you write you research. That's what you do, you *research.*"

"So bite my head off. It wasn't my idea to come here."

"It wasn't me that lost her goddamn job. How the hell were we supposed to pay the rent?"

"You could have got a job."

"I'm a student. Anyway, I told you, if I get a job my wife gets her hooks into me for support. I'll starve to death before I support that bitch."

"We could go back."

"How many times does it have to be explained to you? I don't get my scholarship cheque until the first of September. We happen to be broke. Absolutely. In fact, you're going to have to hit the old lady up for gas and eating money to get us back to the coast. We're stuck here. Get that into your empty fucking head. The Lord Buddha might have been able to subsist on a single bean a day, I can't."

My grandmother came into the room. The conversation stopped.

"Do you think," she said to Thompson, "I could ask you to do me a favour?"

"Why Mrs. Bradley," he said smiling, "whatever do you mean?"

"I was wondering whether you could take my car into town to Ogden's to get it fixed."

"Oh," said Thompson, "I don't know where it is. I don't think I'm your man."

"Ask anyone where it is. They can tell you. It isn't hard to find."

"Why would you ask me to do you a favour, Mrs. Bradley?" inquired Thompson complacently. Watching him operate was like listening to someone drag their nails down a blackboard.

"Well you can be goddamn sure I wouldn't," said Grandma trying to keep a hold on herself, "except that I'm right in the middle of doing my pickling and canning. I thought you might be willing to move your lazy carcass to do something around here. Every time I turn around I seem to be falling over those legs of yours." She's looked at the limbs in question as if she might like to dock them somewhere in the vicinity of the knee.

"No, I don't think I can," said Thompson easily, stroking his goat beard.

"And why the hell can't you?"

"Oh, let's just say I don't trust you, Mrs. Bradley. I don't like to leave you alone with Evelyn. Lord knows what ideas you might put in her head."

"Or take out."

"That's right. Or take out," said Thompson with satisfaction. "You can't imagine the trouble it took me to get them in there." He turned to Evelyn, "She can't imagine the trouble can she, dear?"

Evelyn threw her spool knitting on the floor and walked out of the room.

"Evelyn's mad and I'm glad," shouted Thompson at her back. "And I know how to tease her!"

"Charlie come here," said Grandma. I went over to her. She took me firmly by the shoulder. "From now on," said my Grandma, "my family is off limits to you. I don't want to see you talking to Charlie here, or to come within sniffing distance of Evelyn."

"What do you think of that idea, Charlie?" said Thompson. "Are you still my friend or what?"

I gave him a wink my Grandma couldn't see. He thought that was great; he laughed like a madman. "Superb," he said. "Superb. There's no flies on Charlie. What a diplomat."

"What the hell is the matter with you, Mr. Beatnik?" asked Grandma, annoyed beyond hearing. "What's so goddamn funny."

"Ha! Ha!" roared Thompson. "What a charming notion! Me a beatnik!"

* * *

Grandma Bradley held the mouthpiece of the phone very close to her lips as she spoke into it. "No, it can't be brought in. You'll have to come out here to do the job."

She listened with an intent expression on her face. Spotting me pretending to look in the fridge she waved me out of the kitchen with her hand. I dragged myself out and stood quietly in the hallway.

"This is a party line," she said, "remember that."

Another pause while she listened.

"Okay," she said and hung up.

* * *

I spent some of my happiest hours squatting in the corn patch. I was completely hidden there. Even when I stood, the maturing stalks reached a foot or more above my head. It was a good place. On the hottest days it was relatively cool in that thicket of green where the shade was dark and deep and the leaves rustled and scraped and sawed dryly overhead.

Nobody ever thought to look for me there. They could bellow their bloody lungs out for me and I could just sit and watch them getting uglier and uglier about it all. There was some satisfaction in that. I'd just reach up and pluck myself a cob. I loved raw corn. The newly formed kernels were tiny pale pearls of sweetness that gushed juice. I'd munch and munch and smile and smile and think, why don't you drop dead?

It was my secret place, my sanctuary, where I couldn't be found or touched by them. But all the same, if I didn't let them intrude on me — that didn't mean I didn't want to keep tabs on things.

At the time I was watching Thompson stealing peas at the other end of the garden. He was like some primitive man who lived in a gathering culture. My Grandma kept him so hungry he was constantly prowling for food: digging in cupboards, rifling the refrigerator, scrounging in the garden.

Clad only in Bermuda shorts he was a sorry sight. His bones threatened to rupture his skin and jut out every which way. He sported a scrub-board chest with two old pennies for nipples and a wispy garland of hair decorated his sunken breastbone. His legs looked particularly rackety, all gristle, knobs and sinew.

We both heard the truck at the same time. It came bucking up the approach, spurting gravel behind it. Thompson turned around, shaded his eyes and peered at it. He wasn't much interested. He couldn't get very curious about the natives.

The truck stopped and a man stepped out on to the runningboard of the '51 IHC. He gazed around him, obviously looking for something or someone. This character had a blue handkerchief sprinkled with white polka dots tied in a triangle over his face. Exactly like an outlaw in an Audie Murphy western. A genuine goddamn Jesse James.

He soon spotted Thompson standing half-naked in the garden, staring stupidly at this strange sight, his mouth bulging with peas. The outlaw ducked his head back into the cab of the truck, said something to the driver, and pointed. The driver then stepped out on to his runningboard and standing on tippy-toe peered over the roof of the cab at Thompson. He too wore a handkerchief tied over his mug, but his was red.

Then they both got down from the truck and began to walk very quickly towards Thompson with long menacing strides.

"Fellows?" said Thompson.

At the sound of his voice the two men broke into a stiff-legged trot, and the one with the red handkerchief, while still moving, stooped down smoothly and snatched up the hoe that lay at the edge of the garden.

"What the hell is going on here boys?" said Thompson, his voice pitched high with concern.

The man with the blue mask reached Thompson first. One long arm, a dirty clutch of fingers on its end, snaked out and caught him by the hair and jerked his head down. Then he kicked him in the pit of the stomach with his work boots.

"Okay fucker," he shouted, "too fucking smart to take a fucking hint?" and he punched him on the side of the face with several short, snapping blows that actually tore Thompson's head out of his grip. Thompson toppled over clumsily and fell in the dirt. "Get fucking lost," blue mask said more quietly.

"Evelyn!" yelled Thompson to the house. "Jesus Christ, Evelyn!"

I crouched lower in the corn patch and began to tremble. I was certain they were going to kill him.

"Shut up," said the man with the hoe. He glanced at the blade for a second, considered, then rotated the handle in his hands and hit Thompson a quick chop on the head with the blunt side. "Shut your fucking yap," he repeated.

"Evelyn! Evelyn! Oh God!" hollered Thompson, "I'm being murdered! For God's sake, somebody help me!" The side of his face was slick with blood.

"I told you shut up, cock sucker," said red mask, and kicked him in the ribs several times. Thompson groaned and hugged himself in the dust.

"Now you get lost fucker," said the one with the hoe, "because if you don't stop bothering nice people we'll drive a spike in your skull."

"Somebody help me!" the professor yelled at the house.

"Nobody there is going to help you," the blue mask said. "You're all on your own, smart arse."

"You bastards," said the professor, and spat ineffectually in their direction.

For his defiance he got struck a couple of chopping blows with the hoe. The last one skittered off his collar bone with a sickening crunch.

"That's enough," said red mask, catching the handle of the hoe. "Come on."

The two sauntered back towards the truck laughing. They weren't in any hurry to get out of there. Thompson lay on his side staring at their retreating backs. He was crying. His face was wet with tears and blood.

The man with the red mask looked back over his shoulder and wiggled his ass at the professor in an implausible imitation of effeminacy. "Was it worth it, tiger?" he shouted. "Getting your ashes hauled don't come cheap do it?"

This set them off again. Passing me they pulled off their masks and stuffed them in their pockets. They didn't have to worry about Thompson when they had their backs to him; he couldn't see their faces. But I could. No surprise. They were the Ogden boys.

When the truck pulled out of the yard its gears grinding, I burst out of my hiding place and ran to Thompson who had got to his knees and was trying to stop the flow of blood from his scalp with his fingers. He was crying. Another first for Thompson. He was the first man I'd seen sport a beard, or wear sandals. Now he was the first man I'd seen cry. It made me uncomfortable.

"The sons of bitches broke my ribs," he said panting with shallow breaths. "God, I hope they didn't puncture a lung."

"Can you walk?" I asked.

"Don't think I don't know who isn't behind this," he said, getting carefully to his feet. His face was white. "You saw them," he said. "You saw their faces from the corn patch. We got the bastards."

He leaned a little on me as we made our way to the house. The front door was locked. We knocked. No answer. "Let me in, you old bitch!" shouted Thompson.

"Evelyn, open the goddamn door!" Silence. I couldn't hear a thing move in the house. It was as if they were all dead in there. It frightened me.

He started to kick the door. A panel splintered. "Open this door! Let me in you old slut or I'll kill you!"

Nothing.

"You better go," I said nervously. I didn't like this one little bit. "Those guys might come back and kill you."

"Evelyn!" he bellowed. "Evelyn!"

He kept it up for a good five minutes, alternately hammering and kicking the door, pleading with and threatening the occupants. By the end of that time he was sweating with exertion and pain. He went slowly down the steps sobbing — beaten. "You saw them," he said, "we have the bastards dead to rights."

He winced when he eased his bare flesh on to the hot seat covers of the car.

"I'll be back," he said starting the motor of the car. "This isn't the end of this."

When Grandma was sure he had gone, the front door was unlocked and I was let in. I noticed my grandmother's hands trembled a touch when she lit her cigarette.

"You can't stay away from him, can you?" she said testily.

"You didn't have to do that," I said. "He was hurt. You ought to have let him in."

"I ought to have poisoned him a week ago. And don't talk about things you don't know anything about."

"Sometimes," I said, "all of you get on my nerves."

"Kids don't have nerves. Adults have nerves. They're the only ones entitled to them. And don't think I care a plugged nickel what does, or doesn't, get on your nerves."

"Where's Aunt Evelyn?"

"Your Aunt Evelyn is taken care of," she replied.

"Why wouldn't she come to the door?"

"She had her own road to Damascus. She has seen the light. Everything has been straightened out," she said. "Everything is back to normal."

* * *

He looked foolish huddled in the back of the police car later that evening. When the sun began to dip, the temperature dropped rapidly, and he was obviously cold dressed only in his Bermuda shorts. Thompson sat all hunched up to relieve the strain on his ribs, his hands pressed between his knees, shivering.

My grandmother, who had been expecting the visit, went out to meet the constable before he reached the house. I followed her, at a safe distance, down the steps.

My grandmother and the constable spoke quietly by the car for some time; occasionally Thompson poked his head out the car window and said something. By the look on the constable's face when he spoke to Thompson, it was obvious he didn't care for him too much. Thompson had that kind of effect on people. Several times during the course of the discussion the constable glanced my way.

I edged a little closer so I could hear what they were saying.

"He's mad as a hatter," said my grandmother. "I don't know anything about any two men. If you ask me, all this had something to do with drugs. My daughter says that this man takes drugs. He's some kind of beatnik."

"Christ," said Thompson, drawing his knees up as if to scrunch himself into a smaller, less noticeable package, "the woman is insane."

"One thing at a time, Mrs. Bradley," said the R.C.M.P. constable.

"My daughter is finished with him," she said. "He beats her you know. I want him kept off my property."

"I want to speak to Evelyn," Thompson said. He looked bedraggled and frightened. "Evelyn and I will leave this minute if this woman wants. But I've got to talk to Evelyn."

"My daughter doesn't want to see you, mister. She's finished with you," said Grandma Bradley, shifting her weight from side to side. She turned her attention to the constable. "He beats her," she said, "bruises all over her. Can you imagine?"

"The boy knows," said Thompson desperately. "He saw them. How many times do I have to tell you?" He piped his voice to me, "Didn't you, Charlie? You saw them, didn't you?"

"Charlie?" said my grandmother. This was news to her.

I stood very still.

"Come here, son," said the constable.

I walked slowly over to them.

"Did you see the faces of the men?" the constable asked, putting a hand on my shoulder. "Do you know the men? Are they from around here?"

"How would he know?" said my grandmother. "He's a stranger."

"He knows them. At least he saw them," said Thompson. "My little Padma-sambhva never misses a trick," he said, trying to jolly me. "You see everything don't you, Charlie? You remember everything don't you?"

I looked at my grandmother who stood so calmly and commandingly, waiting.

"Hey, don't look to her for the answers," said Thompson nervously. "Don't be afraid of her. You remember everything don't you?"

He had no business begging me. I had watched their game from the sidelines long enough to know the rules. At one time he had imagined himself a winner. And now he was asking me to save him, to take a risk when I was more completely in her clutches than he ever would be. He forgot I was a child. I depended on her.

Thompson, I saw, was weak. He couldn't protect me. God, I remembered more than he dreamed. I remembered how his lips had moved soundlessly, his face pleading with the ceiling, his face blotted of everything but abject urgency. Praying to a simpering, cross-eyed idol. His arm flashing as he struck my aunt's bare legs. Crawling in the dirt covered with blood.

He had taught me that, "Those who are in the grip of desire, the

GUY VANDERHAEGHE

grip of existence, the grip of ignorance, move helplessly round through the spheres of life, as men or gods or as wretches in the lower regions."

Well, he was helpless now. But he insisted on fighting back and hurting the rest of us. The weak ones like Evelyn and me.

I thought of Stanley the rooster and how it had felt when the tendons separated, the gristle parted and the bones crunched under my twisting hands.

"I don't know what he's talking about," I said to the constable softly. "I didn't see anybody."

"Clear out," said my grandmother triumphantly. "Beat it."

"You dirty little son of a bitch," he said to me. "You mean little bugger."

He didn't understand much. He had forced me into the game; and now that I was a player and no longer a watcher he didn't like it. The thing was that I was good at the game. But he being a loser couldn't appreciate that.

Then suddenly he said, "Evelyn." He pointed to the upstairs window of the house and tried to get out of the backseat of the police car. But of course he couldn't. They take the handles off the back doors. Nobody can get out unless they are let out.

"Goddamn it!" he shouted. "Let me out! She's waving to me! She wants me!"

I admit that the figure was hard to make out at that distance. But any damn fool could see she was only waving goodbye.

JANE URQUHART was born in Little Long Lac, Ontario and now lives in Wellesley, Ontario. Her publications include *Changing Heaven, Storm Glass, Whirlpool*, and *Away*. This story first appeared in CFM No. 39 in 1981.

Five Wheelchairs

JANE URQUHART

1
Shoes

LATER THAT EVENING he took off his shoes. He tossed them casually under the grand piano and began dancing. Although he began dancing he did not stop drinking. He was capable of balancing a full glass of wine on his forehead. He did that now; balancing and drinking, balancing and drinking. The removal of the shoes helped him with the balancing. It also helped him with the dancing. He didn't need any help with the drinking.

The carpet was a soft grey colour and was made of pure wool. Wine from unbalanced glasses had formed permanent scarlet pools across its surface. But they were mementos of another time, before he had become polished, practised, professional; before he had learned all there was to know about balance and before he had learned the little that he knew about dancing. He hadn't spilled a drop for months now, except into the cavity of his mouth. What was more, he had become able, by a simple bending of the knees, to refill his glass without removing it from his forehead. A master indeed!

She watched him, with some embarrassment, from her wheelchair in the corner. She thought he looked ridiculous, then she thought he looked charming, then she thought he looked ridiculous again. She wondered if balancing acts like this one were part of the awesome responsibility one assumed when able to move about of one's own accord; that is to say without the chair. She thought of balancing her teacup on her own forehead but realized that dancing was a necessary, and for her impossible, part of the routine. Besides, she was nervous and unskilled and did not want to add a brown spot to the numerous red ones already on her carpet. She preferred, as it were, to keep the colour scheme consistent.

Ah, but he was charming dancing there in her living room, moving precariously from step to step like a Niagara daredevil. But oh, there was such tension when he lurched forward or backward in order to prevent a tumble or spill. After a full evening of it she would be exhausted for days; lacking the strength to play show tunes on her piano, lacking the strength to whistle. In fact, she dreaded these performances which caused her emotions to swing wildly from pleasure to tension and back again. And yet she was somehow addicted and, perhaps because she felt inwardly that no one should be without one, he danced for her often. And balanced too.

Although his neck was beginning to ache, he moved cautiously across the room to the shelf where the records were kept. The third album on the left towards the bottom was the original cast recording of "Annie Get Your Gun." He admitted the music was dated and silly but he liked it none the less. There was, after all, "no business like show business." He was living proof of that. He executed an awkward pirouette, took a healthy swallow of wine, and felt for the record like a blind man reading braille. He fumbled with the cover and then with the machine. A few minutes later he was moving his arms in time to the tune as if to imitate enthusiastic singing. He did not remove the glass from his forehead.

She was beginning to find the sight of his adam's apple a bit disconcerting but, positioned as she was, in a room with stair cases at every possible exit, she was unable to remove herself from the somewhat uncomfortable scene. She wondered if turning her wheelchair to face the wall would be interpreted as a violent gesture. She decided that, at the very least, it would appear discourteous. She began instead to sing halfheartedly along with the song. "Your favorite uncle died at dawn," she sang quietly. "Top of that /your Ma and Pa have parted/ you're broken hearted /but you go on," she continued. And as she continued, his acrobatics seemed charming again, even the lurches. Such is the mysterious power of even the mildest form of participation.

He thought about the ceiling. When he was balancing it filled the entire sphere of his peripheral vision. The ceiling, he decided, was to him now what the floor had been at dancing school; the floor where he had watched his shoes collide with the patent leather attached to the feet of the girls in the class. They who were so much more graceful than he, they who were so much taller. From then on he attributed most of his problems with women to an inability to keep his feet in places where patent leather wasn't. It had soured every relationship and chipped away at his confidence until he had avoided dancing girls altogether. And then, one day he had discovered the lady in the wheelchair, and slowly he had begun to dance again, and not only to dance but to balance.

She thought about the hospital and how there was no music there; just the public address system constantly uttering the monotonous names of Doctors. There weren't any balancers either. Not unless you took into consideration those few, unsteady individuals who had recently been released from crutches. They had practised a kind of delicate, fumbling dance, as if their very bodies were as fragile as the glass this man carried on his forehead. They should have had some music she concluded, in retrospect, while listening to the tune of her own vocal chords increase in volume.

He began to hear her song above the strings and trumpets of the recording. It sounded small and feeble but it was there none the less. "My goodness, she knows the words," he thought as he performed another lurching pirouette. He bent his knees beside the table, refilled his glass, quickly drank the contents, and filled it again. "There's no people like show people" he heard her warble in a voice that seemed to be getting stronger and then, "they smile when they are low." He cracked his knuckles once or twice to show her that balancing wasn't the only thing that he did well.

By now there was no doubt in her mind that she liked the song. There was also no doubt in her mind that she liked singing the song.

Even his adam's apple was no longer an unpleasant sight when she was singing. In fact, it began to resemble the cheerful bouncing ball of a sing along film. "Even with a turkey that you know will fold, you might be stranded out in the cold" she sang with great vitality. As her mind discovered rhythm her hands beat time on the leather arm rests of her wheelchair. She moved everything she could; her mouth, her forehead, her shoulders, her eyebrows, her arms, her stomach. She thought it was a shame that she couldn't tap her patent leather shoes. Just after she had shouted "next day on your dressing room they've hung a star" and was about to bellow "let's go on with the show," his glass fell to the floor.

The next morning he was gone. This was no surprise to her. He was always gone the next morning. Gone, gone, gone. She counted the stains on her one hundred percent wool rug . . . ten . . . no, eleven now. The most recent pool was a deeper, richer crimson than the rest having not had the benefit of time to soften it. She was unable to understand why he had wept when his glass had tumbled to the floor the previous evening. Surely not out of consideration for the carpet. Compositionally, in fact, this particular spill was rather well placed and enhanced the general scheme. He'll get over it, she decided. He always did, and as far as she could gather, he always would.

Then she noticed the shoes. He was gone but his shoes were not. They lay, under the piano, where he had so casually tossed them just before he started balancing. You could tell that they had been abandoned. The laces looked tangled, confused, miserable. The tongues lolled obscenely like those of hanged men. One shoe lay on its side and looked as injured and pathetic as an animal that has recently been struck by a car. The other sat bolt upright as if listening for its master's voice. "How on earth did he ever get home?" she wondered.

Beyond her window lay a fresh, consistent inch of snow. It must have fallen while she was sleeping. It covered the lawns and the sidewalks. It covered the roofs and the roads. Although it was a cloudy day, reflected white light created the illusion of sunshine and brightened the interior of her home. It added a cheerful overtone to the spectacle of the deserted shoes.

His car had made tracks in the snow. The tracks moved out of the driveway, arced briefly, and advanced toward the end of the street. The long scars they made on the white surface of the road allowed bits of the asphalt to show through — indicating that this was not a cold, definite snow, but one that was likely to disappear by mid afternoon. She thought that, perhaps, its only function was to remind her of the season and to illustrate the fact of the man's departure; the empirical proof of something she had learned long ago through experience. A kind of resignation settled over her spirit.

Then, as she was about to turn from the window to begin her day, something familiar caught her eye. Pressed into the snow, which lay on the pathway leading from her door to her driveway, were two, long, continuous lines. They might have been made by two children riding bicycles side by side in the snow. They might have been made by a sled. They might even have been made by a baby carriage. But she knew, as surely as she had walked across the room to the window, that they had been made, early that morning, by a departing wheelchair.

She pirouetted once on her patent leather shoes. Then she danced joyfully into the kitchen to make her breakfast. Later that day she would skip to the supermarket to buy a spray can filled with rug shampoo. But not until she'd taken his shoes to the Salvation Army.

2
Dreams

AS MIGHT BE expected, her wedding night dreams were both weird and eventful, taking her in and out of countries that she didn't even know existed. She would later attribute these flights of fancy to the after effects of the food served at the reception. But that night the dreams gave her no time to ponder the reasons for their arrival. They just kept happening, one after another, until the one about the wheelchairs woke her up, shouting.

But not in fear, or at least not from any worry about her own safety. She had felt in fact, during the course of the dream, remarkably detached, as if she had been watching a play in which she had only one line; a line that was spoken from the wings. But when it came time for her to speak that line she was aware, even in the dream, that it came from some other, surer, part of her brain, from those same heretofore unrecognized countries.

"Don't forget your seatbelts! Don't forget your seatbelts!" she cried, awaking both John and herself.

"Seatbelts." he said, "What seat belts?"

She confessed her dream. All the men she had known in her relatively short life had been presented to her in series, like credits at the end of a film. They were all in wheelchairs, but such wheelchairs! Suspended from thin strong rope they gave their occupants the opportunity to swing back and forth against a clear blue sky. The men involved had looked to her like strange trapeze artists or happy preschool children on playground swings. They were having, it appeared, a wonderful time. Then for reasons unknown, even to herself, the cautionary business of the seatbelts had grabbed her vocal chords.

Having no personal use for interpretation of any kind John pronounced the dream absurd and therefore boring. She agreed, they laughed, and fell easily back to sleep.

The next morning they jogged two miles along the beach. She was always surprised by the response that the sight of a naked pair of male legs awoke in her. It was honest visual pleasure combined with admiration for a supple functioning form bereft of excess. Male excess was distributed elsewhere, in the face, around the middle, but rarely in the legs. They were holy territory, uninhabited by fat cells. They were perfectly fabricated systems designed, perhaps, to carry primitive hunters, quietly and swiftly through some complicated forest. Now they carried John across the sand, through the wind, and along the frothy edges of the sea. Later, in the city, they would carry him through the labyrinth of street and subway to an office every weekday for the rest of his life. She watched the large muscle at the back of his thigh flex and relax with the rhythm of running.

Over lunch, which was served on the terrace of the hotel, they discussed the gifts they had received and divided them into three categories: lovely, passable, and impossible. Yellow was her favourite colour so all of the yellow paraphernalia slipped easily into the "lovely" category. The steadily increasing profusion of yellow objects had been, in fact, a great comfort to her in the week or so preceding the wedding.

She imagined the one bedroom apartment they had chosen filling up with radiant sunlight like the gold leaf backgrounds she had seen in old paintings. She pictured herself bent over a sewing machine stitching yellow gingham curtains while stew bubbled in the yellow enamel pot on the stove. There was also in this picture an image of John, threading his way through the subway system, coming home, on his long lithe legs, to her. At night, she imagined, they would rub themselves all over with the gift of giant yellow bath towels, just before they slipped between the gift of flowered yellow stay press sheets.

She thought of John's legs rising without a ripple from the yellow bath mat at his feet.

Into the category of impossible they placed such items as blue mountain pottery and salt and peppershakers with the words salty and peppy burned into them.

Into "Passable" they placed such items as electric frying pans and waffle irons.

This kind of classification game was one they played often. It had the two-fold positive effect of supplying them with conversational material and providing them with a well ordered private universe. Where categories were concerned they agreed on everything: from music to cocktails, from politics to comic strips, from airports to laundromats. Their value systems were as assured and as tidy as the Holiday Inn at which they were staying. It was all very comforting.

Games not withstanding, they were neither of them children. He had practised law for a full five years and had, just recently, been offered a partnership in the firm. In his usual practical, deliberate way he had waited a week or so before saying 'yes' to the proposition. It was the same week that she had handed in her resignation to the paper, marriage her excuse. She felt little regret at the prospect of abandoning her career. Although it had been the job she wanted, the job she had studied for, much like most of her affairs, it had quickly passed through a phase of novelty and into the hazy realm of habit. A few days before she left the girls in the office held a small shower for her. A lot of the accumulated yellow objects were a result of this event.

A combination of the beer they had consumed with lunch and their first morning of strong sunshine had made them feel sleepy. They decided to return to the room for a rest. The desk clerk smiled benignly as they passed through the lobby, his face altering to the odd grimace of a man barely able to suppress a wink. He was aware of their honeymoon status. She remembered passing through similar lobbies of similar hotels with men she had not been married to. The desk clerks there had remained tactfully aloof, the situation being so less easy to classify.

After they made love John rolled over and lit a cigarette. Some of the smoke became trapped in the few beams of sun that had worked their way through the heavy curtains.

"Why wheelchairs?" he asked. "Why were they in wheelchairs?"

"Who?" she replied drowsily from the other side of the bed.

"Your boyfriends, your boyfriends in the dream."

"Who knows?" she said, falling asleep, "Who ever knows in dreams?"

Later in the afternoon, when they awakened from their nap, John would decide to go for a swim. She would decide to sit on the balcony and write thankyou notes to her friends, the generous donors of "the lovely, the passable, and the impossible." "Dear Lillian," she would begin. Then something would capture her attention. It would be the sight of John walking down across the beach towards the water, walking on his beautiful spare legs. With his back turned he would be unaware that she was watching him. He would become smaller and smaller until, at last, he would collapse into the water. She would study the predictable repetitious motions of the waves surrounding him until, with a kind of slow horror, she would realize that the organized behavior of the Atlantic was what the rest of her life would be, one week following another, expectations fulfilled in easy categories, and the hypnotic monotony of predictable responses.

O my God, she would think briefly, Why does he seem to be having such a good time?

Then she would dismiss this and all other related thoughts from her mind forever and continue her thankyou note.

"Dear Lillian" she would write, "John and I just love Blue Mountain Pottery."

3

Charity

WHEN SHE ARRIVED at the hospital they put her in a wheelchair. Under the circumstances this seemed somewhat absurd. Certainly there was something wrong with her. Yes, something was definitely wrong with her. But nothing, as far as she knew, was wrong with her legs. At least not yet. But then she remembered. In hospitals they always put you in a wheelchair. Regardless of what the problem was, if you could still sit up they put you in a wheelchair. Probably to assure you that you were sick, even if you weren't.

But she was sick. Just that morning she had announced to him, between sobs, "Harold, I'm sick," and then, when he didn't respond, "I'm SICK Harold. Put me in the hospital!"

After that he had sighed, put down the newspaper, and walked across the room to the telephone. She had continued to sob, her face buried in her hands, but she had left a tiny crack between her fingers so that she could see what he was doing. He was fumbling through his address book looking for the phone number of the doctor.

"God he's slow!" she mumbled to no one in particular.

Eventually, and on the kindly advice of the family physician, he had taken her to the hospital. But, let it be noted that he took his sweet time about it. It seemed to her that they had driven around each block six times before advancing to the next. She was probably right. He often played little tricks like this when he was taking her to the hospital. He hated taking her to the hospital. He thought it was ridiculous. She was perfectly aware of his feelings but she was also aware that they got there none the less. So there she sat in the wheelchair and there he stood at the admitting desk yawning over the same old tedious forms. She gathered together all the loathing she could muster and aimed it at the indentation just beneath his skull and in the center of his shaved neck. To her amusement he brought his left hand up and scratched that very spot, just as he might have had an insect landed there.

She didn't like him much and that was the truth. He didn't like her much either; but then, what did he like? Certainly not his job at the Kleaning Cloth factory which was boring and repetitious, certainly not his children who had, mercifully, all grown up and moved away, certainly not his dog who bit him daily on his departure to, and his arrival from, the Kleaning Cloth factory, and certainly not these idiotic forms he had to fill out every single time he brought her to the hospital. He also didn't like the itchy feeling he got at the base of his neck each time he turned his back in her presence. The terrible truth about all these things was that they were, in his eyes, ridiculous. And there was no doubt in his mind that his wife was ridiculous as well. Not only was she ridiculous but everything connected to her was ridiculous: her tears were ridiculous, her meals were ridiculous, and whatever the hell was wrong with her was ridiculous. Her ridiculous doctors, in their ridiculous, kindly wisdom, could not bring themselves to tell him what was, in fact, wrong with her. Finally he stopped asking, and the minute he stopped asking he stopped caring.

Her suitcase, he knew, was filled with ridiculous negligees which she had ordered over the years from the back sections of movie magazines and comic books and which she kept especially for her hospital experiences. He handed this precious cargo to a nurse who had appeared, like a long awaited taxi, from around the corner. Then he turned to leave. Just as he was about to enter the revolving glass doors he heard the nurse chirp to his wife, "And how are we today?" He thought this was a ridiculous question to ask anyone who sat sobbing in a wheelchair.

When she was certain that he had gone she stopped sobbing. Soon she was gliding through green halls, in and out of elevators, past rooms filled with fragrant flowers. She looked forward, with great pleasure, to her lunch which she knew would arrive on silent rubber wheels and would include florescent pink jello topped with dream whip. Once in her room she picked out a florescent pink negligée to wear, knowing that it would match the jello. Then she slipped between the delicious, starched white sheets and relaxed against the smooth, firm fibre of the hospital mattress. 'Let the bastard pack his own twinkies' she said to herself just before she fell into a deep and dreamless sleep.

She awoke an hour later to the arrival of her anticipated lunch. It was everything that she had hoped for and she devoured it with relish, right down to the last, tiny, quivering mouthful. Then she reached into the night table drawer for the two wonderful books that she had stuffed into her suitcase along with the negligées. One of these books was entitled "Lovelier After Forty" and the other "How to Develop Your Personality, A New You!" Both had been written by an ex-heavyweight champion with whom she was, of course, in love. She could never hope to meet him but she was in love with him anyway. Contact was incidental. It was the tone of his words that attracted her. They were easy words; words that made her feel warm and comfortable in a way that Harold never had. During her frequent stays at the hospital she would often spend her afternoons imagining "the champion" (as she secretly called him) bending over her like a parasol of rippling muscles and shining skin, breathing easy words into her ears.

"Many a homely younger woman has, through persistence, turned herself into a beautiful, lovable, older woman," he would whisper, and then, "You are not alone. There are order and truth and eternal reality in the universe."

And when she danced with him upon the shores of her imagination he crooned exotic instructions into the microphone of her brain.

"Draw hips slightly forward then flick backwards quickly as if to strike imaginary wall with buttocks . . .," he would sigh. Then she would sigh and chant along with his ballroom litanies, while her stark, private room turned from institution to palace, to mysterious night club, to the starlight lounge, to Hernando's Hideaway.

During this particular stay at the hospital dancing took up some of her time, but the greatest portion of her energy was devoted to personal development; that is, the development of her NEW SELF, a self that would necessarily be lovelier after forty. There were, she knew, seven success secrets and the champion had assured her that the mastery of these would result in a young and magnetic personality. SECFIMP was the key, seven was the number:

1   S Sincerity
2   E Enthusiasm
3   C Charity
4   F Friendliness
5   I Initiative
6   M Memory
7   P Persistence

And the greatest of these was charity.

How kind she was to the champion; sewing imaginary buttons on his skin tight clothing and cooking up imaginary feasts in her brain. She allowed him to read newspapers or watch ball games all night and she never complained. She ironed his imaginary socks. She kept his imaginary house spotlessly clean and she never burdened him with her own insignificant problems. She showed a definite interest in his career, encouraging him to confess to her those tiny nagging moments of self doubt that afflict every man at one stage or another. But most importantly, she wore her negligées constantly in an effort to keep herself as young and attractive as she was the day she first imagined him.

He was pleased but not entirely satisfied. He introduced her to his greatest beauty secret — a three week plan to beautify her bust contour. He assured her that no one was more interested in helping her with this delicate problem than he. He sympathised. He understood. Hadn't he once been a ninety pound weakling, who through persistent effort had raised himself to the very heights of power and personal magnetism? Hadn't he counselled countless other women who were suffering from the misery and self consciousness brought about by the fact that they possessed an unattractive bosom? Didn't he know everything there was to know about the growth and tone of pectoral muscles? Of course he did. Of course he had. And he would help her by setting forth a rigid schedule of exercises that she could begin that very day.

The weeks rolled by both in illusion and in reality. Nurses glided in and out of her makeshift gym. They tread softly on squeaky shoes. They carried their trays of jello and dream whip with courtly precision. They wrote mysterious messages on the chart at the foot of her bed. They gathered in huddles and murmured outside her door. They brought in fresh white slabs of clean starched sheets. They distributed pills and tiny paper cups filled with luke warm water. They administered enemas. Their wedding bands glowed on their smooth white hands. And they tactfully ignored the presence of the champion, to all intents and purposes they didn't see him at all. And so, of course, they couldn't notice how, when the wheelchair, which would take their patient back to the lobby where Harold was waiting, appeared at the door, a man in skin tight clothing put down his barbells and scratched the back of his neck, just as he might have had an insect landed there.

4
Gift

MONSIEUR DELACOUR was certain that it was spring. 'Spring is here,' he announced, silently, to himself. The thought rattled in the rafters of his brain, avoiding altogether the area phrenologists label *voice*. Monsieur Delacour hadn't had a voice for years. Some mysterious being or event had snatched it away from him, and the truth was, Monsieur Delacour couldn't have cared less.

He also didn't care about his left side. Whoever or whatever had snatched away the voice part of his brain had also made off with the area which controls the left arm and leg. And so Monsieur Delacour got around with the aid of a wooden crutch and his wonderful talent for hopping. A long, thin man, who had always resembled a large wading bird, Monsieur Delacour had adjusted, years ago, to his one legged method of transportation. It suited him just fine. Later a doctor would actually remove the non functioning left leg. But, at the moment, it was still attached to Monsieur Delacour. Still, he didn't care about it. Not one bit.

He did, however, care about spring, and now, despite the winter chill that still hung in the air, he knew it was spring. His stubborn belief was based on the fact that today, for the first time in six months, a tiny feeble ray of sun had entered the damp octagonal square where Monsieur Delacour's house occupied a corner. The sunbeam had paused briefly on a moldy stone wall and then had quickly disappeared as if it were in a hurry to visit more attractive places; places where grasses, or even weeds, were a conceivable possibility.

But sun, you say, can enter enclosed spaces even in winter. Not these spaces, not those winters. The sun had barely the strength to drag itself above the horizon, never mind the bravery to invade the narrow twisting streets and the slimy paved piazzas of Monsieur Delacour's home town. Tall mossy walls everywhere, grey-green vegetation of the parasitic variety, everyone relocated or dead of the plague in the year 1527; that's what it was like. We tourists love places like this. We think they look like the environments of fairy tales. We have never lived there.

But Monsieur Delacour loved it too — because it was his home town and because it provided him with a corner in which to live. Here he did what he could with his chickens and rabbits, did what he could with the stone bench outside his door, and did what he could with his wife. It had become apparent, early in his relationship with her, that whoever or whatever had snatched away the parts of his brain labelled *voice, left arm,* and *left leg,* had decided to leave the area marked privates totally unaltered. Hence Monsieur Delacour could do a great deal with his wife. And at the moment that we find him watching the sun on the wall he had eight children. And there would be more.

Monsieur Delacour's wife was a handful. "She's a handful," said Monsieur Delacour, silently. Then he chuckled to himself. Like everything else the chuckle rattled in the rafters of his brain, refused, as it was, the release of vocal chords. A large woman, whose remaining teeth had been seriously eroded by a constant assault of chocolate, Madame Delacour was the friendliest person in town. And the most talkative. She talked about everything: from weather to underwear, from school to defecation, from witches to astronauts, from politics to wheelchairs. And she would talk to anyone; to you or me or dogs or cats or chickens or the Mayor or the Curé. It was all the same to her.

It was winter that made her a handful. In a town where nothing happens in the summer, less than nothing happens in the winter and Madame Delacour became bored. Nothing helped; not the television which, by virtue of its size, blocked the only window in the house, not the kids whose collective naughty imagination would keep the most blasé among us on our toes, not the constant supply of chocolate which was made possible by cheques from the state that arrived at the door. Winter bored her, absolutely and completely, and nothing helped. Nothing, that is, except death.

Madame Delacour was fervently drawn to the drama and ceremony connected with death. Not her own, of course. That was, as she wisely knew, a party she could not attend. But anyone else's fascinated her. She appeared at all the funerals she could, dressed appropriately for the occasion in her vast purple dress and with lipstick smeared all over her wide mouth and sparse teeth. She mourned with the mourners and eulogized with the eulogizers. Often her sadness was sincere but, more often, the excitement that death causes in a small town cancelled all but the most fleeting of sorrows. Madame Delacour at a funeral was like a child at a birthday party, and the corpse involved like a brand new recently unwrapped gift.

But there was a small problem. There were simply not enough deaths to keep her occupied. The tiny population of the town could only produce a certain number each year, and although most of these occurred, conveniently, in the darkest, and most boring, part of the winter, Madame Delacour became restless and dissatisfied. Boredom waited for her on the street after each funeral. She began to invent deaths.

And so it came to be that, after a few long dark winters, almost everyone in the town had been reported dead three or four times before they, in fact, expired. Madame Delacour became, as Monsieur Delacour soapily, and so silently put it, a handful. Even the dogs and the chickens avoided her chatter. Everyone likes to discuss the actual death of a neighbour, but invented death is something else. It's foolish to weep and bemoan the fate of a friend who, at that very moment, is buying two tins of pate and a grosse baguette in the local Epicerie. And it's most embarrassing if and when the friend in question finds out about your outburst of emotion. And so, as Madame Delacour found fewer and fewer people with whom to discuss imaginary death she turned more and more to her husband.

Monsieur Delacour loved his wife. And it wasn't that he was against death either. He just didn't care about it one bit. Someone or something could come and snatch it away for all the difference it would make to him. He was far more interested in the children, chickens and rabbits who all fit nicely, if a little snugly, into his small corner in the square. He liked to watch their numbers increase. It was something he could count on. He wished his wife had something she could count on too, for Monsieur Delacour was as certain as could be that all of the important deaths had already happened.

Because he could not speak Monsieur Delacour's thoughts consisted mostly of observations and explanations which he put to himself in the form of announcements. Questions were, you might say, out of the question since they could not be articulated. And only occasionally did he make decisions; only when it was absolutely necessary. He felt it was necessary now.

"Spring is here," he announced, silently, to himself. "In spring Mme Delacour visits the larger square near the church and watches the tourists come and go. Then she makes up stories about the people she has seen there; movie stars and counts and earls, thieves and convicted murderers, millionaires and soccer players, queens and presidents all stream into her imagination and the power of death subsides. She would be perfectly happy watching this parade of strangers that lasted through the summer and on into the fall. But then the fanciful funerals would begin again. Something had to be done about her."

And, oddly enough, just that morning Social Services had decided that they must do something about Monsieur Delacour. Around nine o'clock a plump, cheerful man had leapt out of a white van. Then he had dragged a brand new wheelchair into Monsieur Delacour's kitchen. He had sat in it himself in order to demonstrate its safety and efficiency. He had shown Monsieur Delacour how to work the gears and manipulate the wheels. It had shone in the grimy kitchen as brightly as a diamond tiara. It was like a carriage for a king. And Monsieur Delacour didn't care about it at all. It seemed to him to be just one more contraption that might be snatched away at any minute. So, as soon as the white van had pulled away, Monsieur Delacour hopped outside to his stone bench in order to watch for spring.

It was the combination of the change of the season and the appearance of the wheelchair that gave him the idea and that brought about the decision.

He would give Madame Delacour the wheelchair for the winter. He didn't, after all, care about it one bit and, unlike the use of his voice, his left arm and left leg, he could be sure that he had donated it to a worthy cause. With a little goat's bell attached to it, and a colourful cushion placed in the seat, it would be the perfect vehicle for her imagination. She could spend the winter months inventing the illnesses that had forced her into the chair; illnesses that were awe inspiring but not fatal — a party she could attend. She would turn her attentions away from other people's deaths and towards her own diseases.

Monsieur Delacour leaned back against the cold stone wall behind him. Anticipation rattled happily through his brain. First he anticipated the summer afternoons when the sun would warm (though never dry) the stones around his corner. Then he anticipated the seven pink petunias Madame Delacour would place in a box outside the single window that the television blocked. Then he thought about his own death, which he didn't care about in the least, but which would be the greatest of his gifts to Madame Delacour. And finally, with a definite smile he thought about Madame Delacour1

herself, and how she would look in her winter wheelchair, moving through the streets of town, accompanied by the distant voice of a tiny bell. Freed from the clutches of boredom her face, he decided, would reflect a combination of invented pain and immeasurable happiness.

5
The Drawing Master

ALL BUT ONE of his students were drawing the canopied bed. Eleven of them were fixed, with a furious attention, on the object, puzzling out the perspective and gritting their teeth over the intricate folds provided by the drapery of its rather dirty, velvet curtains. Pencils in hand, they twitched, scratched heads, scratched paper and erased. Individually, they studied their neighbour's work and vowed to give up drawing altogether. Collectively, they laboured with a singleness of purpose worthy of great frescoed ceilings and large blocks of marble. All for the rendering of a rather tatty piece of furniture where someone, long forgotten, had no doubt slept and maybe died.

He walked silently behind the group, noting how the object shrank, swelled, attained monumentality, or became deformed from notebook to notebook. What, he wondered, brought them to this? In a building full of displayed objects, why this automatic attraction to the funereal cast of velvet and dark wood? This must be the bed that the child in all of them longed to possess; to draw the dusty curtains round and suffocate in the magic of contained privacy. It would be as cosy and frilly and mysterious as the darkened spaces underneath the fabric of their mother's skirts. The womb, he concluded, moves them like a magnet in all or any of its symbolic disguises.

The twelfth of the bunch was drawing a stuffed bird. Mottled by time and distorted by the glass bell that covered it, it pretended, without much credibility, to be singing its heart out on the end of a dry twig. Its former colours, whatever they may have been, were now reduced to something approaching grey. The face of the young man, who had chosen to reproduce this bundle of feathers, was reflected once in the glass bell and again, rather larger, in the display case and was also approaching grey. The drawing master glanced quickly over the young man's shoulder and discovered, as he had expected, a great deal of nothing. Fifteen years in the profession had taught him to read all signs with cynicism. A student situated apart from the crowd, the choice of alternate subject matter was, to his mind, the result of a social rather than a creative decision.

"You must like birds Roger," he commented wryly, and then, "There are some who seem to prefer beds."

The young man's face acquired a spot of colour, but in no other way did he respond to the remark.

The drawing master moved on. At this point there was little he could do for them except leave them alone. And furthermore, this was usually the case once he had taught them the rules. He believed, in the thick of it all, that the rules were the bones of the work. Within the structure they provided, great experiments could be performed, giant steps could be taken. And so his students suffered through weeks of colour theory, months of perspective. They reduced great paintings to the geometry of compositional analysis. Like kindergarten children, they arranged triangles and squares on construction paper. Then, after a written test where the acquired basics were transcribed to paper, he hired a small bus and drove them to this old, provincial museum where he allowed them to choose their own subject matter. Year after year, the drawing master searched in vain for the student who would make the giant step, who would perform the great experiment, just as year after year, he looked for evidence of the same experiment, the same step in his own work.

The drawing master moved on and now he was looking for his own subject matter. For he had brought with him a small bottle of ink and a tin box in which he kept his straight pen and his nibs. He could feel this paltry equipment weighing down his right hand pocket, altering somewhat the appearance of the cut of his jacket. Aware of this, he often rearranged the tools giving himself the look of a man with an abundance of coins that he liked to jingle. Then he shifted his shoulders back and mentally convinced himself that a slight bulge at the hip could not alter a look of dignity so long in the making. There was still, after all, the faultless cravat, and the leather pants, the well trimmed beard speckled with grey.

And now he began to move past display cases; one filled with butter presses, another with spinning wheels. Still another contained miniature interiors of pioneer dwellings complete with tiny hooked rugs and patchwork quilts. He paused briefly before the collection of early Canadian cruets, interested in the delicate lines of twisted silver. But they turned to drawings so quickly in his mind that the actual execution on paper seemed futile and boring and he walked away from them. Past blacksmith's tools and tomahawks, past moccasins and arrowheads and beadwork, past churns and pressed glass, past century old pottery from Quebec and early models of long silent telephones, past ridiculously modern mannequins clothed in the nineteenth century, until he found himself looking through the glass of a window and out into the fields.

And then he thought of the drive through the countryside to this small county museum which had been situated, with the intention of pleasing both, between the two major towns of the surrounding vicinity. The students, nervous and silent in such close quarters with their teacher, had offered little interference to the flow of his consciousness and he had almost become absorbed by the rush of the landscape as it flashed past the windows of the van. A strong wind had confused the angle of fields of tall grass and had set the normally well organized trees lurching against the sky. Laundry had become desperate splashes of colour let loose in farm yards. Even the predictable black and white of docile cows seemed temporary, as if they might be sent spiralling towards fence wire like so much tumbleweed. The restlessness of this insistent motion, this constant churning hyperactivity, had distracted the drawing master, but he had felt the strong, hard edged responsibility of the highway to such an extent that even now, when he observed the landscape through the safe confined space of the window frame, he was somehow unable to grasp it. And he turned back towards the interior of the museum.

Here he sketched, for his own amusement, and possibly for the amusement of his children at home, two or three elderly puppets that hung dejectedly from strings attached to flat wooden crosses. Completing, with a few well chosen lines, the moronic wide-eyed stare of the last one, he cleaned the nib of his pen with a rag that he carried with him for that purpose and prepared to return to his class. Then his eye was caught by a large white partition set back against the left hand corner of the room. He walked over to it with a kind of idle curiosity and peered around its edge.

There, awaiting either repair or display case, and hopelessly stacked together like tumbling hydro towers, were five Victorian wicker wheelchairs. A few had lost, either through over use or neglect, the acceptable curve of their shape and sagged over their wheels like fat women. One had retained its shape but the woven grid of its back was interrupted by large gaping holes. The small front wheels of another had become permanently locked into a pigeon toed position through decades of lack of oil. All in all they appeared to be at least as crippled as their absent occupants must have been — as if by some magic process each individual's handicap had been mysteriously transferred to their particular chair. The drawing master was fascinated. He had found his subject matter.

An hour later he had completed five small drawings. They were, as he knew, his best. The crazy twisted personality of each chair distributed itself with care across the surface of the paper. Expressed in his fine line their abandoned condition became wistfully personal, as sad as forsaken toys in the attic or tricycles in the basement, childless for years. Vacant coffins, open graves, funeral wreaths — they were all there, competing with a feeling of go-carts and red wagons. The drawing master carefully placed his precious drawings inside the interior of his jacket pocket. When he arrived home that evening he would mat and frame them and put them under glass. But now he would stroll casually over to his pupils, who had dispersed, and were wandering around the room gazing absently into display cases.

Except for the one young man who seemed to be still involved in the rendering of the dead bird. The drawing master approached him and bent over his shoulder in order to offer his usual words of quiet criticism, perhaps a few words about light and shade, or something about texture. He drew back, however, astonished. There, before, him on the paper, was a perfectly drawn skeleton of a bird and surrounding that, and sometimes covering it or being covered by it in a kind of crazy spacial ambiguity, drawn in by the student with the blunt ends of a pocket full of crayons, was the mad, turbulent landscape. It shuddered and heaved and appeared to be germinating from the motionless structure of the bird whose bones the young man has sensed beneath dust and feathers. And it needed no glass to protect it, no frame to confine it. And it was as confused and disordered and wonderful as everything the drawing master had chosen to ignore.

KEATH FRASER was born in Vancouver, British Columbia, where he still lives. His publications include *Taking Cover, Foreign Affairs,* and *Bad Trips.* This story first appeared in CFM No. 40/41 in 1981.

This Is What You Were Born For

KEATH FRASER

TANNED AND LOOKING FIT, full of plans for races and even overnight voyages aboard *Inside Out,* Patrick knew nothing of his own congestive heart. Later on Axel kept dreaming of his friend's wrist bent unnaturally upon the dew, palm clutching the Cordline grip, his cheek at rest against the iron's cold blade. It was an ignominious death. A morning of hooks, topped shots, mulligans — Axel could only hope Patrick had died the instant his two-iron met the ball, to have saved him the last embarrassment of a shot that squirted fifty yards. (He could not have known, nor did it matter now, the ball was not his own.) The arresting thing to Axel was how life went on. Birdsong in the alders, the hemlocks in sunlight, golfers playing through. He had no choice but to wave them through. His own foursome stuck gamely together in its tragic clump while the high school phys-ed teacher did all the mouth-to-mouth resuscitation, chest-banging, and temple-slapping that the deceased Patrick endured. The pressing question had been who should go for help. The plainclothes priest, who along with the teacher rounded out their impromptu foursome, declined to leave Patrick's side, and Axel didn't feel at his age he could run all the way back to the clubhouse himself. Luckily, a student cutting the green to which they had all aspired (the sixth) answered their shouts. By the time the inhalator arrived, Patrick's pants were soaked through at the knee. No one wanted to close his eyes. No one, except the firemen, was sure he was dead. They rolled him onto a stretcher and pulled a white blanket over his balding scalp. At his temples were little wet spots of Extreme Unction.

That evening Lucy left Axel alone to ponder man's fragility. A final contortion, some mud on your cheek, a red inhalator making tracks across an April fairway: nothing unique. There were golf courses from Uplands to Westchester, Jasper to the Florida Keys. And among the men who haunted them — in flight from stress, fat, genetics — heart disease was rife. Ball-wallopers, most of them (like Patrick), overweight and seldom in harmony with the little spheres they set, sometimes, whizzing in air.

After an appropriate interval, though no sailor himself, Axel offered what he considered a fair price for *Inside Out*, but Jane Bishop said he could have it for a song, in honour of the fraternal time he and Patrick had enjoyed aboard it. She didn't actually say a song. She just named an absurdly low sum and Axel, who was not convinced he really wanted the sloop, felt like singing. When she broke down and asked him if he knew that Patrick had cheated on her once — had another woman, she was not sure where — Axel told her rubbish. He knew Patrick like a brother; her husband had been among the loyalest men he knew. This cheered her up. He kissed her hair. They were all in this together he said. In the end, promising to take her for sails, he forgot she hated boats.

Of course they both knew that Patrick had acquired *Inside Out* just two weeks before his death. Not long after, in fact, the Bishops' return from Maui. Fact seeped into myth, however. And on the rare occasions when she saw the Smarts thereafter, Jane Bishop would recall the loyalty and even passion the retired Patrick had poured into his boat, which made Axel (nodding sympathetically) wonder if such a myth had not also become the way she'd chosen to remember her marriage. She was a shy woman, and instead of flowering into widowhood, as was sometimes the case with widows, she drooped. Lucy tried to interest her in the opera, bridge, Spanish cooking; but Jane would not or could not pull out of it and was finally left to seed. Lucy's patience went only so far.

Certainly Axel's proposal to buy Patrick's sailboat tried her patience. He'd been out in the thing *once*. Had he any guarantee sailing wouldn't give him ennui the way carpentry did fifteen years ago — ennui and saws he couldn't sell? He should recognize his own whimsy by now. But to Axel owning a sailboat had begun to seem like an investment in himself. How often, after all, did a retired man get the chance to buy something new in his life? How often, for that matter, did any man? If Lucy could see little sense in deliberately tempting fate, heeling over on a windy gulf, so much the better. She could stay home. She could take her chances on his returning home, full of himself.

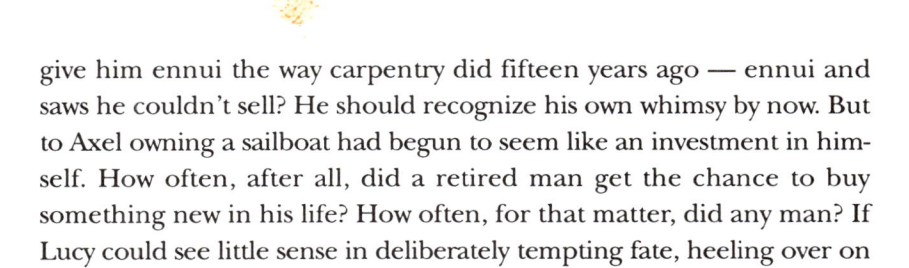

Sailor home from the sea, smug Odysseus. He wondered if Brad, their son, felt exhilarated returning from the skies. Brad was a man of action, led a life of adventure, with sirens from the galley bringing coffee to his cockpit on transoceanic flights.

If Axel had it to do over, an adventurer is what he too would become. Rather than a desk-rooted senior geologist responsible for noting the slender profiles and irregular occurrences of oil and gas traps in glaucoilite sands. Patrick had been an adventurer. Had surprised everyone by hopping into bed with Petro-Canada, when that company was just starting up and already the pariah of the oil patch. When this buccaneer announced he was bailing out of the free-enterprise system, as he put it, to climb aboard the socialist rig of the Liberal government, it was to be his last hurrah, doing something for the country by helping to prevent international companies like Axel's from swallowing up Canada. Axel came to admire his friend's courageous move, foolish and even threatening as it was, and began to realize that action was central to one's life. While Axel had carried on at the same old life, Patrick, a world-class engineer, went on to commit regular adultery in the office pool right or wrong, he'd been someone who knew where centre was.

"I was approached by this young woman with a foxy bottom, who wanted, when all was said and done, to swizzle my stick. The rewards at home were venial, so I let her."

Embarking on your own meant harder work and maybe no status at all. An adventurer was somebody, an entrepreneur, who assumed risks, ran risks, organized risks for venture. The entrepreneur was a breed apart. Indeed, when Axel was planning *his* indiscretion — his early retirement, hadn't he experienced something of the single-mindedness of an entrepreneur? And when he eventually submitted his letter of resignation, a little recklessly (felt Lucy) before looking into how much pension he'd lose by retiring seven years early, didn't he suddenly shed (figuratively, for literally it took longer) the belt of pudge he could once roll with his fingers? Paying the price of his way out: that had been a champagne day.

Like the day he and Patrick went sailing, sails snapping, jackets billowing, thinning hair salt-blown and growing, it felt, out of their crowns' refurbished skins. With more authority than skill they'd tacked past Kitsilatio, Jericho, Locarno (where they narrowly missed a wet-suited windsurfer skimming past their bow), Spanish Banks — all the beaches — to the chiming bell-buoy off Point Grey.

"Sheet!" called Patrick, whenever the telltales drooped. And Axel had cranked the writer, to tighten their foresail.

The wind had picked up, and Patrick had to figure out how to reef the mainsail by reading his manual. He reefed and Axel took the helm. Neither of them felt very balanced. They were sailing as close to the wind as they knew how, heedless of any desire to take cover, chuckling and giddy at their angle of heel. By fiddling with the traveller Patrick had managed, with a shove, to bring back the boat to fifteen degrees of centre.

Yes, they'd been pleased with themselves that day, to be sailors with so little practice. No practice. Sailing downwind off the mountainous shore of Stearman Beach, Patrick struggled to set up the spinnaker pole with Axel at the tiller. Then Patrick came back to the cockpit to pull the chute clear of the turtle. That done he dropped the foresail, took the helm, and Axel flew the spinnaker. Patrick worked the pole. Together they would soon have been crack enough to enter races.

"Gybe!" cried Patrick. "No," he said. "Let's hoist the Genoa and drop the chute."

Off Sunset Beach where the city's skyline soared above, they dropped their sails and motored back up False Creek to the marina. Patrick had touched his friend's arm and said cheerfully, "Listen, we'll do this again, eh? In another week or two? I'll look into racing."

"You bet," said Axel.

And wanting to do something in return, Axel made up his mind — how he came to regret his propriety — that he would book a game of golf one Saturday morning soon.

Still in bed he could hear a sound he hadn't heard since retiring to the West Coast: a snow shovel scraping concrete. Was it? In May? He realized he was dreaming and so let the shovel scrape his inner ear like the rough tongue of a morning lover. But the memory of her unappealing breath and porky thighs woke him up. He reassured himself that Alberta (province, not lover) was hundreds of miles and several mountain ranges distant.

He heard nothing.

Since coming out to the Coast last fall he and Lucy hadn't stopped congratulating themselves on their early retirement from winter temperatures that could crack sidewalks. Axel had wanted to return here to live ever since the war, when his squadron had received its basic training at Jericho. Then he moved over to Pat Bay on the Island and from there (unluckily) north to the Skeena Valley, and finally Alaska. Lucy's big thrill was to look up the daily extremes of their native province, where they'd lived in a comfortable neighbourhood overlooking the Bow River and Rockies, seventy miles away. Her newspaper vigil had been a tart reminder of prairie temperatures, like one's tongue momentarily stuck to the blade of a snow shovel. Axel could remember his father digging them out of their farmhouse in Pincher Creek one winter, half a century ago, when the snow had drifted to the eaves, and then quietly dropping his shovel to complain of creeping paralysis in his arms. He thought of Patrick in the soft, unfrozen humus. He thought of his stiff, congealed father. Had the sound in his dream, like Chekov's broken string, portended some loss? Well, that was a bit inane, since coming to live in a rain forest wasn't like losing an orchard at all. The reverse, if anything.

He scratched his beard, got up, drew back the curtain and saw the sun high on the mountains. A crowd of joggers pattered by like rain.

The winter had been mild and everything stayed green, instead of going yellow then white under cold that covered the prairie like a snowman's lung. Bamboo, salal, rhododendron, laurel, grass: green green green. From their condominium the Smarts looked out over the Lagoon. Out there in the Park, encircled by sea, were a thousand acres of forest and miles of trails. Axel spent the fall and winter gazing in wonder at the hundreds of joggers who trotted by into the Park. None seemed the least ashamed of his body, not even the sway-bummed ladies Lucy's age who were proud, *alive* to the world. Roller skaters swished by, fell against the curb and split open their heads, jived past dressed in overalls and coloured laces, headphones stuck in their ears. There were black men sometimes, up from Washington, often balding men, and men with dogs and other men.

This morning one very fat girl was crumpled up like a centipede on the sidewalk trying to right herself; her wheels kept skidding off sideways making sparks. He watched. *He* preferred to gaze on some lovely young thing poised above a bike's saddle, her jeans cut off so high up as to make moons of her buttocks.

Through ancient cedars, firs, and thigh-high sword ferns growing out of the rank earth, he and Lucy were in the habit of walking in the forest every afternoon. It was she who pointed out, in a swampy hollow near Beaver Lake, what Alberta must have been like millions of years ago before all the organic matter settled to the bottom of a sea or was carried there by ancient rivers. He, whose job it had been to evaluate anticlines, faults, traps — the geological structures of sedimentary basins indicating where oil might be found — was surprised. She was right, of course. He'd never thought by moving west he had also been moving backwards. It made him feel younger — definitely.

And so in February had come the camellia, magnolia, plum, azalea, and hyacinth blossoms. The variety of life! Every night Lucy claimed to hear quarrelling upon the black waters beyond their window — duffleheads, canada geese, wood ducks. Along the shoreline of the Park they spotted grebes and harlequins, goldeneyes and oystercatchers. Anchored farther out in the Bay were the freighters that tooted at midnight to call back their exotic crews from the fleshpots downtown. Indonesian, Chinese, Indian, Ceylonese. . . .

Axel stood in his pajamas watching the fat girl spinning her wheels, unable to rise. She'd given up and was undoing the laces on her skates. Dressed in white, which made her look fatter, she was perspiring with heat and exertion. He went into the bathroom to shave. "Poor thing," he muttered. She had kneecaps the size of grapefruit.

To him the appealing bodies belonged to High School kids lying in the sand with skin so new it wanted rubbing. Since Patrick's death he had taken to walking the 5 1/2-mile seawall around the Park every morning before lunch. The sunbathers were out along Second and Third Beaches oiling themselves with sweet-smelling cocoa butter. He wondered, as he walked, if his own adrenaline-enriched feeling — wasn't the way the young felt all the time; you couldn't go wrong being centred in the chest. The young lived like they were flying, which required a good deal more effort than they ever received credit for.

When he came home he discovered Lucy had gone out leaving his lunch on the table. Probably visiting the latest refugees. But there was a note to say this was her day to go see *Bufferfly* in Seattle — she'd forgotten chartered bus back late, did he mind, not to worry she'd take a cab home from the station.

So Axel walked downtown to the art gallery, into a clean, cosmopolitan city, the streets free of dust blown in off the plains and laid down in clouds. It reminded him of Swiss cities he and Lucy had visited on a Cook's tour of five countries seven years ago: mountains fast by, the ocean a bonus.

The exhibition at the gallery shocked him. He had expected to see the permanent collection of Emily Carrs — swirling rain forests, totem poles, the sky like an eye in the canvas. Hung instead was a series of eighty prints by Goya called *Los Desastres de la Guerra*. War, famine, persecution pictures of Spain's War of Independence against Bonaparte between 1808 and 1814.

Plate 12, a small etching, struck him on the head like a bag of nails. Up close to it he watched a man vomiting over corpses on the ground: he was falling forward, his palms outspread, hair on end, vomit descending in a stream like blood. *Was* it blood? Only one of the corpses had a face, it man with his limbs twisted against the earth. Axel thought of Patrick. This was the besieged town of Zaragoza, said the catalogue, where cholera bad broken out in 1809, and 350 people a day were dying because neither medicine nor food was reaching them. He tried to read into this etching, but *Para Eso Habeis Nacido* offered up only a dark ominous cloud, very still over everything, like smoke.

It wasn't Art. Around Art he usually got an aching back. The Tate had nearly finished him one day in high summer two years ago, crowds pushing, — Turner overwhelming, Lucy relentless with observations derived from her History of Art course. No, this was different. For one thing he was alone. Even the Pinkerton guard was in another room.

He floated from image to image, light-headed. He stood, peered at, entered into . . . what? Naked corpses being dumped into black, yawning pits? A man hanging upside down and naked being sliced in half by a sword? Armless men impaled on tree stumps? A torso bound to branches, its separated arms tied up by the wrists, its head impaled on a bough? In all of these he heard no cries, nothing. Only the hum of conditioned air. There were pictures of beggars in despair, wolves waiting, monks defecating as they ate, vampires gorging on the blood of collapsed Spaniards. One of the final prints showed Truth — a woman surrounded by clergy and mourners — dead. Axel was impressed. The last print of her asked *Si Resucitara?* It was all so lugubrious he had to wonder why it didn't depress him beyond words. He thought of the war and the dying and the diseased. Stretched, like the skin of a balloon, he walked back to the West End feeling calmer, lighter than he had in years.

A week later, walking the seawall, he met a woman of thirty-five who sold life insurance. She was sitting on a bench with a notebook, and when he went past she looked up and said hello.

Her name was Elspeth Stiles, and she was looking (no strings attached) for someone suitable to father the child she was planning to bear. Now that she had risen close to the top of her profession she could, it seems, afford to take an extended leave of absence. She was on the lookout for a stranger, because there were no friends whom she wished to sacrifice to the vanishing kind of paternitys she had in mind. As these details emerged over the next few weeks, their effect on Axel was to break the rhythm of his life.

He found himself making up excuses not to accompany Lucy on the walks past age-old ravines, over Primeval bogs, or through trees alive in the time of Cabot. She made him feel heavy. In the evening they discontinued her reading Russian literature aloud because he found it necessary, so he said, to be reading on his own at the library downtown. (He told her he was planning to write a short history of the oil boom in Alberta, beginning with the Leduc strike in 1947, and was doing research among rare monographs he couldn't bring home.)

And so Lucy was left to read the Russians alone, along with books on cooking Malaysian style, Canadian history, horticulture, the Onassis fortune, thalidomide adults, Barbara Walters's tips on how to talk to anybody, what gays want, the Australian outback, cholesterol-free diets, contract bridge, antique fry pans, guiltless marriage without children (a present from their daughter), back roads of the southern Okanagan, Diaghalev, slipped discs, miscegetiation, enjoying your canary, paranormal life after death (what to expect), Albania, a history of Boeing (a present from their son), Canada through Hollywood's eyes, three difficult solutions for the Boat People, Rattenbury, parole by reason of doubt, article-writing for Profit, and others. As the spring wore on and Axel's research became more involved, more refined, her library grew. She would finger facts like worry heads. Axel found the books she was reading a nuisance because there was diminishing space on the coffee table to rest his leg when he read the morning paper and sipped tea,

By now he was sailing every day. Lucy disliked sailing, or the idea of sailing, as much as Jane Bishop. So Axel was able to learn the ropes by himself without guilt over taking ages to get anywhere had his wife been aboard. Sometimes he just sat in a hole offshore, drifting on the tide, trying to pick out Elspeth's office building, the sun on his back. If they were going to meet that evening in their usual lounge at the Sylvia, he would make up his mind what to take her (flowers, a bottle of liqueur, mints) and wonder how to persuade her to come sailing. For they were still in the courtship stage, and she did not wish to rush into anything, including boats, without a proper assessment of Axel's qualities. She would ask him, for example, to bring along snaps of his children at different ages (that he'd had both a boy and a girl counted in his favour, for Elspeth liked balance.) On another occasion she might require him to do little tests concerning his emotional security and innate intelligence, tests that she had cut out of *Family Circle* and *Chatelaine* or, failing the energy to demand more, she might just settle back with her Singapore Sling and ask him to tell her about his 'life experience.' Flattered, Axel would urge her to come sailing as a way of widening her own life. Didn't she know there was nothing more relaxing, after an arduous day in the office, than a sunset sail? But no, she (they) had other fish to fry. As the results of his little tests emerged, she grew increasingly more solicitous, affectionate, loving. He surrendered his suspicion that perhaps she hated boats and began to relax in the knowledge that his own attractiveness would be enough to win her aboard, with no need to harp.

On Saturday mornings they would sit on the covered veranda of the pavilion in the park and drink tea, converse endlessly and eat bran muffins. They talked of oil and politics, inflation, and children.

"Genes as in g," said Elspeth, "are a lot like jeans as in j. I've thought about this. Really, you don't go out and buy any pair like you used to. I mean you can, but you like to shop around for a snug fit instead of just an okay fit for wearing around the house. People out for dinner read your label to compare their own pair. I've watched them. You wear jeans like you used to wear pearls. It's really a revolution what's happened to jeans . . . from togs for blue bloods right down to butch denim. There's nothing the matter with bargain hunting — but it's not long before a truly rock-bottom pair of jeans shrinks and gets old. The right jeans can take you a good swatch of time just to find, if you're looking for quality."

Showers fell, robins pecked worms in the geranium beds, gibbons whooped in the zoo. Although Axel still felt in no more control of their friendship than before, he had begun to feel the tide slowly swinging in his favor. He was, he felt it safe to suppose, on the making tack.

After three weeks she allowed him to visit her at home for the first time. She too lived in the West End, a couple of blocks from the Smarts, in a rented two-bedroom apartment overlooking the sea and tennis courts, twelve floors up.

"Yes, a child for the second bedroom," said Elspeth, "is what I've decided."

Axel was standing in the doorway of a sun-flooded room.

"First I redecorated. This wallpaper and the white brocade curtains." There were yellow ducks and white sails covering the walls. "And this cradle, I had to scrape and paint it. The rockers squeaked so I oiled them. As you can see, I don't have any toys." (He made a mental note to bring her some.) "I don't like clutter."

They sat together on her balcony watching the sunset and sipping mint tea on ice. It was a hot humid evening in late May, full of glare and smelling heavily of salt. She repeated how she'd been looking for someone content to father a child but indifferent to any future rights as husband or father. Someone who would pretty much agree, after providing the service, to beat it.

"Period," she said, refilling her glass.

Axel recoiled slightly. But she had a way of wrinkling her brow when she spoke that seemed to assume his compliance as well as understanding. She said she used to wonder how on earth she was going to find the right man.

She would take along a memo pad from her office and sit on the seawall watching men jog, bicycle, stroll, and roller-skate by her bench as she noted down characteristics that struck her as chic.

"LEAN HIPS," she wrote.

Under hips, "BLACK HAIR."

She showed him her pad. She had crossed out "BLACK" and written "BLOND." Then apparently had decided brown went better with auburn (the color of her own hair) so crossed out blond.

"BUT NOT UNGAINLY."

Then, "GOOD TEETH."

Underneath, "BUT HOW TO KNOW THEY'RE HIS OWN?"

Axel owned up to having had two molars crowned, no big deal he suggested, since the rest were his. "As teeth go," he said, "they're not bad."

Elspeth told him she had quite a list, after just two walks. A typical page of her memo pad was full of crossed-out fancies (as she called them), qualified fancies, or fancies substituted for others in blue ballpoint ink.

All Axel was allowed to see on one page were "CLEFT" and "RAZOR BUM" — both crossed out. She didn't want a hairy child so had taken chests and legs into account. Nor a quitter so she had looked to see at what stage of physical exhaustion joggers and skaters were by the time they reached her bench on the seawall — over four miles from the Rowing Club where most men set out. For some reason, men with sloping shoulders seemed freshest.

"GORDIE HOWE" she'd jotted on the top corner of one page.

On the porch of the Tennis Hut, alone over coffee, she had sat down to take stock. What she'd wanted was there deep inside her, she knew: the insuperable happiness of fulfillment, or at least the potential for such. She had breathed the indescribable (at least to her) spring air and written,

"NOSE: SENSE OF SMELL." The tennis players at their game in the soft, heavy air conjured up words like "OLIVE-SKINNED" and "GRACEFUL" — the first so her child would tan instead of burn, the second so it would have coordination for sports. She disliked sports herself but would never discourage a child.

Axel wondered how a retired man like himself, walking unremarkably along the seawall, could have appealed to a woman seeking such physical perfection. He thought he had long ago run out of whatever attributes she appeared to consider important. Her log read like fragments gathered from the observation of men in motion — in transit backwards, it seemed, to a time when their bodies were not yet sliding into decay. He felt young, yes, but knew he looked his age — or close to it

Was it her whimsical sense of humour? She flipped the page and showed him a little poem she'd composed in an idle moment for straight men to hang around their necks. (This growing out of the rhetorical query, "IS HOMOSEXUALITY INHERITED/ LEARNED/ OR BOTH?" She had little patience with sailors, say, who did not live up to her model requiring them to have women in every port.)

THIS MAN IS REGULAR
MACHO, STRAIGHT
PLEASE DO NOT PESTER
UNLESS YOU ARE A WOMAN
THEN ONLY IF BEAUTIFUL
OR OF NOBBY MIND
THE PARK IS FULL OF OPPORTUNITY
TRY THE LAGOON

Underneath this was some information from the tennis pro about stringing racquets — to the effect that "GUT" cost more than "FIBRE."

She confessed she had never played tennis in her life. She had, however, been loved. For a while. Her first (and only) husband still called her up for dinner on occasion and liked to hint that he for one wouldn't mind picking up the pieces; a corporation man, he liked the tidiness of clichés. He also liked, when they argued, to slap her face with his socks — which is why she left him, partly. Mainly it was because she didn't feel like giving up her career to provide the family that he thought he needed to appear up and coming. She was spoiling for a fight, he said, and he resented her for wanting to carry the can herself. He nagged her so often she finally left him to carry his oil can. All this twelve years ago. Since then she had sold more policies than anyone else in her company; she had been good for life insurance. Now she wanted something for herself.

Me, thought Axel.

But how exactly did he come into the picture? "What is it you think I have you'd like to pass on?"

He was willing to risk pressing the point in order to gain whatever control of the situation he might, as a result of his fascination, deserve: a hand on the tiller, as it were, in a phrase her husband would have appreciated. It was true his own children were reasonably intelligent, even handsome. But if that was what she was after, he said, a reasonably successful man with children of proven soundness, why one with children her own age?

"I decided looks weren't so important," said Elspeth, "as temperament. Equilibrium."

She showed him the page she was doodling on the day she spoke to him on the seawall. It was empty except for a little stickman at the bottom of a vast, white sky. "He was symbolic," she said, "of the patient stranger." She poured herself another glass of tea. "Here was somebody who'd give me time to assess his genes. You were the first man to come along who looked like my stickman. You were walking along very tragically."

"I was feeling very buoyant."

"That's what I mean," she said. "You had an actor's walk."

"Really?"

"I felt you'd be a good listener. You are a good listener."

"I wish you'd tell my wife. She says I need Yoga."

Elspeth put down her memo pad and placed her hand in his. "I'd rather tell you"

The time had come for them to make love and, so Elspeth hoped, a baby. She confided that she had looked into the possibility of having one with Down's syndrome and found out that her chances of that at thirty-five were only one in two hundred and eighty. Besides, there were now modern techniques like amniocentesis to spot warped chromosomes in the fetus. Had he heard of ultra sound — or ritodrine, the new drug that helped prevent premature labour? The whole field, she had discovered, was opening up. She looked at him with a twinkle. Forty-five per cent of all women having regular intercourse without contraceptives, she said, got pregnant within six months; eighty-five per cent within a year. At her age, however, only fifty per cent of women got pregnant within a year, and only a quarter within six months.

"So you see, my dear sir, you have your work cut out."

They finally got down to it after tea, affectionately, and with a good deal of thoughtfulness for one another's anxiety. Elspeth put on a record. She had a classical collection. Axel hadn't felt this way since the days he and Lucy launched themselves in the backseat of a Chevrolet, almost forty years ago, on the summer banks of the Bow. (The water flowing past them on those sweet, poplar nights had long ago passed east into Hudson Bay and farther, he was sad to reflect, into the oceans of the world.) He kept wondering how long he could savour this smell, this touch, this moment — before his sails collapsed and he needed to wander into the bathroom to check himself for telltale marks in the mirror. Need he remind himself that pride in the patience and control of a mature man could be broached by a loose neck?

After making love they would walk by one end of the lagoon in the dusk where willows trailed their leaves in the tributary gliding there under a stone bridge. Their affair was reinforced by the proximity of ducklings, goslings in the rushes and weeds. Flushed, she would gaze resolutely upon this new life and take him home to try once more. Daylight Saving Time expanded their evenings and the lingering light in the West added to Axel's enchantment. Sometimes, instead of the Lagoon, they walked on the seawall and watched an old Japanese woman in gossamer skirts picking seaweed off the rocks. Elspeth liked to go down to the rocks herself and uncover finger limpets, hermit crabs, periwinkles. She appeared enterprisingly suited to a life of and by the sea. It was June now, and watching her, Axel felt full of thrust and purpose and joy. It was absurd his joy, wild, at his command. He sketched little portraits for her, of men in the Air Force he'd known, of men in tire oil business, of Patrick. She seemed to enjoy hearing him create their lives out of air. He had a firm voice and sang, she was willing to bet, like Placido Domingo. When they conversed she learned which side to avoid because of his bad ear. She also learned the importance of keeping highly sophisticated seismic explorations secret. Wildcatting was a serious and competitive business. To him it seemed farcical, their relationship, so incongruous was their abandon. So *fierce*. By trying to catch her cycle at its ripest, life at least was moving through a new orchard of experience. His capacity for pleasure grew. He was beginning to fall in love.

In drawing closer to Elspeth he overcame feelings of heaviness around Lucy. They resumed their daily walks in the Park.

"Did you know Osoyoos has the only desert in Canada?" she would ask.

"Havelock Ellis," she might report, "was an urlagniac. He liked to watch women pee."

These were facts she was sure of, unlike the fact of Axel, who was beginning to act oddly by cooking lunch, giving her neck massages, and buying her little gifts like oregano — not gifts, really, surprises. Lately, life seemed full of surprises. (Like the black-haired book-stealer who, when she confronted him in a store, started stuttering — his gratitude, it turned out — and told her he was studying oriental magic. Anyhow, she told the manager.) Axel made her peasant omelettes and afterwards listened while she read him Gogol. Not that he was listening to Gogol; he would smoke a cigarillo and think of Goya. How fortunate to be living in an age free of marauding armies, epidemics, persecution. He didn't know what men were born for — Goya's world or his own. Sometimes his own world, full of his wife's strong uninflected voice, could be cut by the chop of a passing helicopter.

All along he continued to sail with increasing skill. When, with the solstice, the winds died and made afternoon sailing less rompish, he liked to lie out on the foredeck and let the sun tan his skin. In some ways retirement was a suspension of belief in one's vulnerability. But by making him aware of success, Elspeth was to be treasured because she made him conscious of failure, too. Like Patrick, she reminded him of death. He now realized that there were other ways of being dead than just rotting in the earth. Nature's way, he decided, was to lull organisms to death. Rare was it for decaying brain cells to be woken up by sexual love and required to cut back across the wake of Time.

Thus it was mainly the young who were aware of dying: Brad, his son, who worried more about going down in a plane than a pilot should ever admit; his daughter Delia, who'd devoted her life to uncovering ancient villages in the Sudan because of her discovery one summer of a Blackfoot shard along the banks of Old Man River, which made her cry, and her mother say, handing her an egg sandwich, that she must have got her lachrymation from Axel.

And Elspeth. Who, in plain fear of getting too old to perform a woman's unique function, had decided to overcome the bigger fear of actually having a child, which in her unmarried state took more than ordinary courage.

Fear of death, in whatever form, was responsible for your living more passionately. He only had to hear Elsbeth grunting and whimpering in his arms to know how much she wanted a child. It was comical, this desperate need on both their parts, to risk so much in the presence of a stranger. Wasn't it the very young, the teenagers just out of the sea, who, if they knew less about spiritual intimacy, knew more about facing decay? Even lying in the sand they worked harder at staying alive. For the older you got, the more others seemed strangers. Among the voting, friendship and spontaneity were natural, as among any group of strangers facing a crisis. With age and the disappearing crisis of survival, you lost your fear of dying and got self-centred. Experience taught you ways of fabricating illusion, forgetfulness. Only in choosing, thought Axel, did you stay alive. Choosing to give up your house, friends, city — to come and live on the West coast; or Elspeth, taxonomer of men, choosing to sit on a park bench with her pen in search of a mate. Even Lucy, buying books off a rack to feed her mind against the increasingly frequent loss of her husband to his research at the close of the day.

"Did you know," she asked, "that Francis Chichester was full of cancer the last time he tried to cross the Atlantic?"

But he could not be held long — any more than a teenager — by such knowledge unconnected to his chest. She did, however, trick him into staying home one evening by asking over guests and not telling him till he came in off his boat to expect Dan Ceiling for dinner.

A disaster. Not only because Axel felt anxious when he had no opportunity to go out and telephone Elspeth about his absence at *her* place. But too because Ethel Ceiling (Jane Bishop's sister) was, it turned out, so maniacally bitter about everyone including her adult children, that she made an ass of herself and a debacle of dinner. Lucy finally asked Dan to take her home. The Smarts couldn't understand how he tolerated her. Nor could Jane, who said if it wasn't for Ethel he would have been offered the chairmanship of Westcoast Pipeline long ago. After the Ceilings disappeared Axel said he needed a walk, excused himself, and went out to telephone Elspeth from a booth at 1.00 p.m.

"If you want," offered Axel, "I can come over all night tonight."

With summer Elspeth had grown a little distant, even impatient. Once in jest she told him he was just like her husband. Satisfying her, he recognized, wasn't at all a straightforward affair. For one thing it involved the conception of a fetus. For another, Elspeth's odd perception of their love-making — she liked to whisper in his ear how she was beyond him,

"As if I'm sitting on the other side of the room, watching you both."

Already she was wondering why she wasn't pregnant. And she hadn't yet been out in his sloop.

"Elspeth?"

If she was serious about conceiving, he said, she'd let him come for the night. He'd phone Lucy and tell her he was going to sleep over on his boat to get an early start in the morning to Collingwood Channel.

"We'll be in clover," he promised. "At war against the Grim Reaper."

There was a short pause before she hung tip, telling him O.K.

For no apparent reason Axel began to dream about Patrick. These nightmares went on for exactly a week. They were mainly of Patrick on the golf course dying, or already dead. Ants on his tongue, a crow up his nose; the plainclothes priest giving him the kiss of life (in the ear), at the same time slinging a golf ball in his stole toward the green. But the green, like the rest of the course, was covered in snow. He failed to shake these images, even around Elspeth, and woke up groggy with pictures on the brain of his friend's grotesque and decomposing body, its arteries lacing the torso like wires. At other times the corpse was blue and frozen. Seven mornings after the first dream he woke up at home refreshed and blank of any images of Patrick. This was the morning his world fell still.

At first he failed to notice the stillness. That is, he noticed it, but attributed it to the calm he was feeling from his unruffled sleep. The night before, he'd come home late from Elspeth's and gone straight to bed, exhausted. Lucy blamed this exhaustion on straining his eyes at the library and informed him with more hope than confidence that he wasn't to do any research for a week. Had he forgotten what happened to Patrick? When she came into the bedroom with this tea that morning he told her he was feeling wonderfully rested.

His words enjoyed neither weight nor effect. Nor did her own lips as they moved make any sound to challenge the faint white hum he was hearing. Like a loquacious mime she set down the tray. He asked her to speak up. She was moving her lips and saying — what was she saying? There was nothing in her voice.

According to the specialist she took him to Axel was deaf ("As in stone?" asked Lucy). No amount of reassurance about her husband's capacity yesterday to hear normally — well, fairly normally — would convince the doctor that she was telling him the truth. And the incomprehensible distortions that escaped from Axel's mouth only suggested to the doctor that Axel had suffered some sort of stroke, although his reflexes, apart from his tongue's seemed exemplary.

Men didn't go deaf overnight, he explained. Had this ever happened before? Had Axel experienced any dizziness, headaches, loud explosions recently?

Axel could only liken his sudden affliction to waking up in the morning full of the blackness that temporarily follows the rubbing of eyes. He needed more time to refocus, as it were, retune. Meanwhile the doctor, himself an older man, sat him down in a little soundproof booth, which reminded Axel of a plastic bubble, and fitted him with a pair of pilot's headphones through which he heard nothing, and that made him feel sick. Afterwards the doctor put him in a dentist's chair and struck a tuning fork next to his head. Hearing nothing, Axel concluded, was nauseous. A hearing-aid did nothing to diminish or increase what he was hearing; it only made him feel whoozier. Lucy put the hearing-aid and an extra battery in her purse.

That evening when he insisted on going to the library, it was Lucy's turn not to believe her ears. She could make out his stumpy sounds enough to realize he'd gone mad. She remonstrated. About his not hearing cars approaching intersections, maybe, or the fire alarm in the library. Lightheaded and buoyed up, he kissed her forehead, smiled, told her not to worry. "What?" she said. He was drifting imperceptibly away from her now. Apart from his ears, if she only knew, he felt quite well, though his balance was still off, as if he'd been confined to bed for drinking cheap vodka and had just got up.

The problem was explaining all this to Elspeth. Convinced he was drunk — he sounded so incoherent — she wanted him to leave. Axel removed an empty notebook from the briefcase he carried every evening and began to fill it with explanations at the coffee table. At first, because she refused to believe he couldn't understand her, he wrote, "NOT GOOD AT LIP-READING." Adding, "PLEASE WRITE."

So she took his notebook. "THIS IS VERY AFFECTED," she wrote.
"I KNOW. SO'S TALKING."
"CAN'T YOU HEAR AT ALL?"
"A HUM I THINK." He wanted her to relax, laugh it Off. "JUST TEMPORARY. DON'T BE IMPATIENT."
"What do you mean?" she said out loud.
"BACK TO SCRATCH IN NO TIME," he wrote. "I'LL MAKE IT IN DUE COURSE." Then remembered this was probably the kind of language her husband had used.

She seemed unconvinced, uneasy, even unhappy. He wanted to take her in his arms, smell her hair, nibble the hollow in her neck, but she spurned him. just sat there. Wasn't it her who should be comforting him? She was preoccupied, brooding. Nuts to her, thought Axel, if that's all the sympathy I get I might as well wait out my recovery with Lucy.

There was an uncomfortable fencing of pens against the coffee table. At last she picked up his notebook and wrote simply, "I'M PREGNANT."

He could have burst into song. "CONGRATULATIONS!"

She wasn't ready for the swiftness of his response. She appeared put off by it and withdrew. Was it his hearing? Was she worried about a congenital defect he might have passed on to the fetus, hardening of the arteries, say, or whatever caused deafness?

"PERIOD" she wrote cryptically

Her period did she mean? "NOT HAD YOUR PERIOD?" he wrote. "SURE SIGN."

Elspeth shook her head. "FINISHED," she wrote. "REMEMBER? YOU AND ME."

As if he had misheard instead of misread her, Axel inclined his once better ear slightly forward seeking clarification.

She mouthed the words distinctly. "That's it. Finished. Us."

Was it, he wondered, that he didn't *want* to hear? It seemed they'd only just met — what? eight, nine weeks ago? — begun to make love, and for Axel to feel as if he were flying again. He was angry.

"I WANT TO GO ON SEEING YOU," he wrote.

"I'm sorry."

"What?"

"I DON'T WANT ANY COMPLICATIONS," she wrote. "YOU KNEW THE CONTRACT."

"WHAT COMPLICATIONS? LIKE A FATHER?"

"Yes."

"I *AM* THE FATHER."

"BUT NOT MY HUSBAND."

"LOVER!"

"Well, not anymore."

"What?"

"IMPOSSIBLE NOW. CAN'T YOU UNDERSTAND? IT WAS A CONTRACT — YOU AGREED TO TAKE OFF WHEN I GOT PREGNANT. YOU GOT YOUR (here she'd scratched out a word) PAYMENT. AND I GOT MINE. O.K.?" She added, "I'M SORRY ABOUT YOUR EARS. I REALLY AM."

She sounded like a tart. Had their weeks together meant nothing more to her than the means to this end? He tried to talk.

"God Almighty?" he began. "I think I'm in love with you!" By the look of pity on her face he wasn't sure if she understood. "I *feel* like I'm in love with you," he said. "Don't you understand?" He refused to paper talk anymore. He spread his arms tragically. "I never agreed never to see you again. Not once. The child is yours, right. But so am I."

This declaration, however, that he could neither hear nor measure the soundness of by the amount of air being pushed by his larynx (a lot it seemed), served only to replace the pity on her face with blankness. Wonder, really. What was the matter with him that he sounded like a lunatic? A stroke? Why hadn't dumbness struck him along with his deafness? No, he'd failed to communicate any of this tenderness, and now he was losing her. Standing there with his mouth bleeding sound in a senseless stream. Yet where did he belong if it wasn't here, at peace instead of war, in the West with a woman who could make him fly?

"I CAN'T UNDERSTAND YOU," she wrote. "SORRY."

"You should!" he shouted. "Oh, you should!"

He thought he actually heard these words. But it was only snow falling, flattening all sound, except for the faint hum coming .... So unused to hearing nothing, which was not the same as silence, he was sure it must sound like something. For a moment he was back in the Art Gallery listening to the air circulating endlessly through vents. Elspeth was standing in the middle of the room with her arms crossed. She looked forbearing. He felt sorry for her feeling sorry for him; he shouldn't have come over till his hearing came back.

He wrote, "I'LL CALL YOU. I'LL BE BETTER SOON." But instead of showing her these words, he changed his mind, turned to a fresh page and printed. He tore out the page and folded it, touching her cheek.

The note, when she opened it, said —

But at the door he suddenly lost his balance on her shiny goatskin rug and fell forward on his face.

Of course calling her on the telephone was fruitless, and when he went over to her apartment building he could never tell whether or not she was answering the telecom. On three occasions he was able to slip into the building behind some other people (who may have questioned him, he couldn't be sure), but when he knocked on her door no one answered. His letters received no reply, In late August a letter he had addressed to Elspeth came back unopened, and Lucy, who went down for the mail that morning, asked who this woman was he'd written to close by. Although Axel had had little to do with his research lately, he made up a lie about the rare book librarian having given him the name to contact for a copy of a pamphlet on fossil fuels published by a small Edmonton press in 1948.

"WHAT'S THIS WOMAN TO DO WITH THAT?" wrote Lucy (who now had her own memo pad).

"DAUGHTER OF EDITOR," he answered. "APPARENTLY."

He destroyed the letter unopened and went sailing. Instead of driving to the marina, he now took the bus. Lucy insisted on the bus. She also insisted on his staying home where she could keep an eye on his "PROGRESS" (sometimes she forgot and called it his "BURDEN"). When he did stay home she would try to knock some sound into his head by fiddling for hours, it seemed, with the hearing-aid in his eardrum. She rubbed and massaged his ear but it felt permanently numb. To him they'd begun to seem like an old couple in the pavilion squeezing their teabag, outside on the veranda, to the bitter end. They went to another specialist and Axel underwent new tests (the same tests).

Lucy moped. One day Axel discovered a list on the kitchen table:

CHROMATIC SCALE SHOULD BE PRACTISED WITH THE THUMB, FOREFINGER, AND MIDDLE FINGER.

"LISTEN TO GREAT SINGERS." FROM THEM YOU WILL LEARN HOW TO PHRASE. "BEAUTIFUL SOUND" IS THE SECRET.

A CLEAN, EVEN *STACCATO* HELPS TO DEVELOP A CLEAN, EVEN *LEGATO*.

"INTERPRET YOUR OWN WAY, AS LONG AS YOU DON'T CHANGE WHAT IS WRITTEN."

They didn't even own a piano. It was signed, in Lucy's hand, CHOPIN.

Only aboard *Inside Out* did Axel seem to regain some of the balance his loss of hearing had upset. Rubbing his face the wind reminded him of a smooth bonelike pressure on his forehead he sometimes remembered, or thought he remembered, from fevers as a child. He loved it when Lucy rubbed his face with her palms, when Elspeth had stroked his forehead with the back of her hand, like a mother her child. Feeling pressure like a mask on his face was liberating. He concluded that it was not his mother so much as himself he was remembering. Himself rowing, it felt away from his mother. In fact, he had heard of people who claimed to remember their births. Not Patrick, mind you. Patrick made no claims to any sort of music of the spheres, though it was he who had named his boat so patly, if unwittingly, for his rebirth as a retired man. His plain ambition had been to sail through the Strait of Juan de Fuca, and, finally, across the Pacific to Hawaii.

Poor Patrick, thought Axel, as he cruised the Bay. To have died in war, in the inevitable grip of head-hunting and the daily grind, would have been less absurd than dying after peace was signed, sealed, and delivered in his Pension Notice. What was retirement but illusion anyway? Patrick's heart hadn't benefited from retirement. An illusion, yes, like this hum. What was it, his hum, if nothing at all? Had the dying Patrick heard it, too — going on and on like some falling in time? For Patrick's poor heart, used to flushing out the cholesterol inside it like a boat pump, retirement had been a jejune peace. Was he, Axel, simple for believing that a new self, lighter body, was even credible anymore?

In the face of a header off the Gulf he tacked.

No, he would never give up his boat to listen to snow shovels again, but he might have to surrender the youthful illusion that he was still vulnerable. It frightened him that he might have begun *not* to fear death. He began to hear such thoughts like the knell of a bell-buoy, the sailor's church.

He began to make up voyages. Alone in his sloop he crossed the Pacific as old Goya had crossed the Pyrenees deaf and alone at seventy-eight. More down to earth was the sail he took with the Safeway girl in late September. The sun set in their eyes, and in the windows of the city, and against the dull orange hulls of the anchored freighters from Asia. An easterly was blowing and the water sibilated past. *She* had no trouble understanding him.

He told her of the mountains he himself had crossed, for which he was still ashamed though never exposed. Mountains he had never even told Lucy about. He'd been flying his Hurricane on Dusk Patrol back to Terrace in 1944. Down the mountainous Skeena Valley, down . . . She had to remember, he told this girl, that men without war invented war: on parade, in training, on patrol. For instance, they used to practise target shooting on timber wolves, diving down upon packs of them dogtrotting across the ice of alpine lakes or feeding on moose carcasses in meadows, opening up with their wing-mounted 30 millimeter cannons, scattering and maiming and killing. In those days the myth of the wolf as an unwelcome predator died hard; there was no shame in killing wolves; all the pilots with no combat experience overseas, against eighter Krauts or Japs, painted wolf ears on their fuselages instead of stars.

Well, one spring evening, he explained to her, the Devil had entered his soul. Below to starboard, he (Axel) had spotted the long black outline of a freight train winding down the Valley, a snake with a powerful beacon in its forehead, and the almost invisible coal smoke marking its spine. He radioed Hickey in the other Hurricane to circle and watch him, and circling himself, like a kite, to line the snake up, he dove ardently to the tracks and levelled off. Switching on only one of his landing lights, the starboard light, he approached the locomotive dead ahead in the gloom.

Not until he awoke next morning did he hear what had happened when he pulled up his nose. His deception had worked too well. The engineer, tugging like mad on his emergency brake to avoid a head-on collision with the other train, had managed to turn his own on end, falling inside his cab down a long embankment still covered in snow, pursued by the rest of his accordioned train. He did not survive the fall. Returning with Hickey to base, Axel never dreamed of such an accident. When he found out over breakfast, he despaired. Another man was lying broken-backed, dead on his account, in a smoking wreck. He himself deserved to be exposed and court-martialled, but cajoled by Hickey the squadron swore to keep his secret. Nothing (nothing more) was said. Soon as an agreement between the RCAF and USAF, they were all relocated to Annette Island to help train American pilots for duty in the Aleutians. Axel wanted out of this squadron of men; he burned to go to Japan. Instead he was assigned to fly another model, the Canso Flying Boat, on submarine patrol off Alaska for what turned out to be the last year of the war.

Maybe because she seemed too young for censure, or because she was a stranger, he willingly exposed himself in his worst light. Talking to this girl helped to lift his mind weighted down with age and failure. Talking was cathartic. She was sympathetic, reticent. She could have been thinking that if he was off his head a bit, maybe the hum inside it came from his long hours of patrol inside the Flying Boats.

Was his child, Elspeth's child, hearing the same hum inside the womb right now? When did it begin and when end?

Still out after dark, phosphorescence churning up in the ocean behind them, they watched an immense red moon rise over the city while their spinnaker ballooned above. Underneath it he felt like some figure in a cartoon. Running with the wind they discovered themselves in the middle of a race and other boats beating back up to a finish line somewhere astern. Who, he wanted to know, really knew where he was going? He told her where to switch on the running lights. His fat orange spinnaker floated above them as thin as skin, a second harvest moon. All the other yachts, he presumed, had rounded the turning mark that he couldn't see yet. What he did see was the girl in her white T-shirt and white jeans, emerging from the cabin, luminous with contentment.

Following his last doctor's appointment, Lucy had driven him to the supermarket where he caught sight of a wanderer in Produce, who was gathering grapefruit into plastic bags, and then just spilling them back into their bin. She was maybe eighteen or twenty. Axel had studied her till he could see her, it seemed, without having to look — young firm skin, short thick hair, fuller than usual lips — a picture. Blond hair, no hips, no makeup at all. She had glided down long aisles in pants and a cotton shirt he could glimpse her shoulders through.

He watched her across women's hands hefting pork picnics (Lucy's hands among them), beyond women peering into egg cartons for breakage, eyeing — who was she eyeing? The tall sanguine clerk piling corn niblets in a can pyramid? Axel had tried to catch her eye across cartons and cartons of cigarettes at the checkout.

"Come sailing!" he wanted to sing out (did sing out, only no one understood his cacophony, and he pitied them their worlds made fearful by unfathomed sound). Out in the parking lot where she was placing a small bag of groceries in the front seat of her car, he had approached her in the strong September sun with his shirt unbuttoned on his chest . . . .

It remained unbuttoned now as he stood in the cockpit with his hand on the tiller heading west. The gallery was full of tea, honey bars, rum, lamb chops, cans of sweet corn. He listened to their wake gurgling up like cream. The large rubber turning mark that loomed out of darkness he confronted like an explorer coming across his first iceberg off Newfoundland. Impulsively, but with no intention of rounding it himself nor of blundering against its yellow sloping sides, he swung closer for a better look.

In an instant his rudder was hung up on the anchor line and his spinnaker was pulling them nowhere. Hung up in the wine-dark sea, chute full of wind, travelling . . . and untravelling. Why did they not broach?

Glowing, she re-emerged through the hatch to say — oh yes, he *heard* her say — "Axel, may I call you Axel? Where's the corkscrew?"

And he told her, with a smile, she didn't need one.

"Unwire the cork and ease it out. Love."

The explosion, when she did, went foaming out across the sea.

MATT COHEN was born in Kingston, Ontario and now divides his time among Verona, Ontario, Toronto, and the south of France. His publications include *Last Seen, Emotional Arithmetic, Freud: The Paris Notebooks,* and *The Sweet Second Summer of Kitty Malone.* This story first appeared in CFM No. 43 in 1982.

The Sins Of Tomas Benares

MATT COHEN

A NARROW THREE-STOREY house near College Street had been the home of the Benares family since it arrived in Toronto in 1936. Beside the front door, bolted to the brick, was a brass name-plate that was kept polished and bright. DR. TOMAS BENARES, it read.

Benares had brought the name-plate — and little else — with him when he and his wife fled Spain in 1936. For twenty years it had resided on the brick beside the doorway. And then, after various happinesses and tragedies — the tragedies being unfortunately more numerous — it had been replaced triumphantly by a name-plate — DR. GABRIEL BENARES. This son, Gabriel, was his only child to have survived those twenty years.

He had lost, not only siblings, but also his mother. The day Gabriel Benares' nameplate was proudly mounted in place of father's, Tomas could at least say to himself that perhaps his string of bad fortune had finally been cut, for despite everything he now had a son who was a Doctor, like himself, and who was married with two children.

In the year of 1960 the Benares household was still a prosperous one. True, the Benares family had not moved north in the city like many other immigrants who had made money, but during the era of DR. GABRIEL BENARES nameplate, the household reached a certain peak of efficiency. The adjoining house was purchased to give space for an expanded office and to provide an investment for Gabriel Benares' swelling income as a famous internist. The back yards of both houses were combined into one elegant pavilion that was tended twice a week by a professional gardener, an old Russian Jew who Tomas Benares had met first as a patient, then at the synagogue, and who spent most of his time drinking tea and muttering about the injustices that had been brought upon his people, while Tomas himself, by this time retired, toothless and bent of back, crawled around the flower beds on his knees, wearing the discarded rubber dishwashing gloves of his son's extraordinarily beautiful wife.

A few years after the birth of his only daughter, Gabriel Benares was walking with her down to College Street, as he did every Saturday, to buy a newspaper and a bag of apples, when a black Ford car left the street and continued its uncontrolled progress along the sidewalk where Gabriel was walking.

Instinctively, Gabriel scooped Margaret into his arms, but the car was upon him before he could move; Gabriel Benares, forty-one years old and the former holder of the city intercollegiate record for the one hundred yard dash, had time only to throw his daughter onto the adjacent lawn while the car mowed him down.

The next year, 1961, the name-plate on the door changed again: DR. TOMAS BENARES reappeared. There had been no insurance policy and the old man, now 74 years of age but still a licensed physician, recommenced the practice of medicine. He got the useless gardener to re-divide the yard with a new fence, sold the house next door to pay his son's debts, and took over the task of providing for his daughter-in-law and his two grandchildren.

Before re-opening his practice Tomas Benares got new false teeth and two new suits. He spent six months reading his old medical textbooks and walked several miles every morning to sweep the cobwebs out of his brain. He also, while walking, made it a point of honour never to look over his shoulder. On the eve of his 94th birthday, Tomas Benares was sixty-two inches tall and weighed one hundred and twelve pounds. These facts he noted carefully in a small diary. Each year, sitting in his third-floor bedroom study, Tomas Benares entered his height and weight into the pages of this diary. He also summarized any medical problems he had experienced during the year past, his prognosis for the coming year. In addition, there had once been an essay-like annual entry in which he confessed the outstanding sins and moral omissions of his previous year and outlined how he could correct or at least repent them in the year to follow. These essays had commenced when Tomas was a medical student, and had continued well past the year in which his wife died. But when he retired the first time from practicing medicine, and had the time to read carefully over fifty years of entries, he had noticed that his sins grew progressively more boring with age. And so, after that, he simply recorded the number of times he had enjoyed sexual intercourse that year.

Now, almost 94, Tomas Benares couldn't help seeing that even this simple statistic had been absent for almost a decade. His diary, it seemed, was getting shorter while his life was getting longer. Flipping backwards he could see that his last statistic had been when he was eighty-six — one time; the year before — none at all — but in his 84th there had been a dozen transgressions. Transgressions! — they should have been marked as victories. Tomas brushed back the wisps of white hair that still adorned his skull. He couldn't remember feeling guilty or triumphant, couldn't remember any detail at all of the supposed events. Perhaps he had even been lying. According to the entry, his height during that erotic year had been sixty-four inches and his weight exactly twice that — a hundred and twenty-eight. In the year 1956, when he had begun compiling the statistics, there had been only one admission of intercourse, but his height had been sixty-five inches and his weight a hundred and forty.

Suddenly Tomas had a vision of himself as an old-fashioned movie — in each frame he was a different size, lived a different life — only accelerating the reel could make him crowd into one person.

He was sitting in an armchair, an old blue armchair that was in the living room when Margarita was still alive. There he used to read aloud in English to her, trying to get his accent right, while she in the adjacent kitchen washed up the dinner dishes and called out his mistakes. Now he imagined pulling himself out of the armchair, walking to the window to see if his grandson Daniel's car was parked on the street below. He hooked his fingers, permanently curved, into the arms of his chair. And then he pulled. But the chair was a vacuum sucking him down with the gravity of age. Beside him was a glass of sherry. He brought it to his lips, wet the tip of his tongue. He was on that daily two hour voyage between the departure of his day nurse and the arrival of Daniel. Eventually, perhaps soon, before his weight and height had entirely shrunk away and there were no statistics at all to enter into his diary, he would die. He wanted to die with the house empty. That was the last wish of Tomas Benares.

But even while his 94th birthday approached, Tomas Benares was not worrying about dying. To be sure he had gotten smaller with each year, and the prospect of worthwhile sin had almost disappeared; but despite the day nurse and iron gravity of his chair, Tomas Benares was no invalid. Every morning this whole summer, save the week he had the flu, his nurse whose name was Elizabeth Rankin had helped him down the stairs and into the yard where, on his knees, he tended his gardens; so that while the front of the house had been let go by his careless grandson Daniel, at least the back was preserved in the splendour it had known for almost fifty years, and bordering the carefully painted picket fence that surrounded the small yard were banks of flowers, the old strawberry patch, and in one corner a small stand of raspberry canes that were covered by netting to keep away the plague of thieving sparrows.

This morning, too, the morning of his birthday, Elizabeth Rankin helped him down the stairs. And sipping at his glass of home-made raspberry wine, Tomas tried to recreate in his nostrils the force of the warm summer he had felt as Elizabeth led him into the humid air.

Elizabeth Rankin had strong arms, but although he could hardly walk down the three flights of stairs by himself — let alone climb back up — he could think of his own father, who had lived to 123, and of his grandfather Benares who had lived to the same age: there was, in fact, no doubt that this enormous number was fate's stamp on the brow of the Benares men, though even fate could not always cope with automobiles.

But, as his own father had told Tomas, the Benares were to consider themselves blessed because fate seemed to pick them out more frequently than other people. For example, Tomas' father Antonio was born in 1820 had waited through two wives to have children, and when one was finally born, a boy, he died of an unknown disease that winter brought to the Jewish quarter of Kiev. So frightened had he been by this show of God's spite, that he had sold the family lumbering business and rushed his wife back to the cradle of his ancestor, Spain, where she bore Tomas in 1884. Tomas' grandfather had, of course, been hale and hearty at the time: 104 years old he had lived on the top floor of the house just as Tomas now lived on the top floor of his own grandson's house.

That old man's face, Tomas' grandfather's, had been round brown, baked-apple dry by the sun and surrounded by a creamy white fringe of beard. He had been born in 1780 and Tomas, bemoaning his diary on the occasion of his oncoming 94th, realized suddenly that he was holding two hundred years in his mind. Yes, that was it, his father had warned him: the Benares men were long-lived relics whose mind sent arrows back into the swamp of the past, so deep into the swamp that the lives they remembered were clamped together in a formless gasping mass, waiting to be shaped by those who remembered. The women were more peripheral: stately and beautiful they were easily killed perhaps bored to death, by the small round-headed stubborn men who made up the Benares tribe.

"We were always Spaniards," the old man told Tomas, "stubborn as donkeys." "Stubborn as a donkey," the child Tobias had whispered. Had his mother not already screamed this at him? And he imagined ancient Spain: a vast sandy expanse where the Jews had been persecuted and in revenge had hidden their religion under prayer shawls and been stubborn as donkeys.

And they hadn't changed, Tomas thought gleefully, they hadn't changed at all; filled with sudden enthusiasm and the image of himself as a white-haired virile donkey, he pulled himself easily out of his chair and crossed the room to the window where he looked down for Daniel's car. The room was huge, the whole third floor of the house save for an alcove walled off as a bathroom. Yet even in the afternoon the room was dark as a cave, shadowed by its clutter of objects that included everything from his marriage bed to the stand-up scale with the weights and sliding rule that he used to assess himself for his yearly entry.

From the window he saw that his grandson's car had yet to arrive. On the sidewalk instead were children travelling back and forth on tricycles, shouting to each other in a fractured mixture of Portuguese and English. As always, when he saw children on the sidewalk, he had to resist opening the window and warning them to watch out for cars. It had been Margaret, only four years old, who had run back to the house to say that "Papa is sick," and then had insisted on going back down the street with Tomas.

Two hundred years: would Margaret live long enough to sit frozen in a chair and feel her mind groping from one century to the next? Last year, on his birthday, she had given him the bottle of raspberry wine he was now drinking. "Every raspberry is a blessing," she had said. She had a flowery tongue, like her brother, and when she played music Tomas could sense her passion whirling like a ghost through the room. What would she remember? Her mother who had run away, her grandmother whom she had never known, her father covered by a sheet by the time she and Tomas had arrived, blood from his crushed skull seeping into the white liner.

They had come a long way, the Benares, from the new Jerusalem in Toledo through France and Italy to two centuries in Kiev only to be frightened back to Spain before fleeing again — this time to a prosperous city in the New World. But nothing had changed, Tomas thought, even the bitterness over his son's death still knifed through him exactly as it had when he saw Margaret's eyes at the door, when Daniel, at the funeral, broke into a long keening howl.

Stubborn as a donkey. Tomas straightened his back and walked easily from the window towards his chair. He would soon be 94 years old; and if fate was to be trusted, which it wasn't, there were to be thirty more years of anniversaries. During the next year, he thought, he had better put some effort into improving his statistics.

He picked up his diary again, flipped backwards, fell into a doze before he could start reading.

On his 94th birthday Tomas slept in. This meant not waking until after eight o'clock; and then lying in bed and thinking about his dreams. In the extra hours of sleep, Tomas had dreamt that he was a young man again, that he was married, living in Madrid, and that at noon the bright sun was warm as he walked the streets from office to the cafe where he took lunch with his cronies. But in this dream he was not a doctor but a philosopher; for some strange reason it had been given to him to spend his entire life thinking about oak trees, and while strolling the broad leafy streets it was precisely this subject that held his mind. He had also the duty, of course, of supervising various graduate students, all of whom were writing learned dissertations on the wonders of the oak; and it often, in this dream, pleased him to spend the afternoon with these bright and beautiful young people, drinking wine and saying what needed to be said.

In the bathroom Tomas shaved himself with the electric razor that had been a gift from Daniel. Even on his own birthday he no longer trusted his hand with the straight razor that still hung, with its leather strop, from a nail in the wall. This, he suddenly thought, was the kind of detail that should also be noted in his annual diary — the texture of his shrinking world. Soon everything would be forbidden to him and he would he left with only the space his own huddled skeleton could occupy. After shaving Tomas washed his face, noting the exertion that was necessary just to open and close the cold water tap, and then he went back to the main room where he began slowly to dress.

It was true, he was willing to admit, that these days he often thought about his own death; but such thoughts did not disturb him. In fact, during hours when he felt weak and sat in his chair breathing slowly, as if each weak breath might be his last, he often felt Death sitting with him. A quiet friend, Death; one that was frightening at first but now was a familiar companion, an invisible brother waiting for him to come home.

But home, for Tomas Benares, was still the world of the living. When Elizabeth Rankin came to check on him, she found Tomas dressed and brushed. And a few minutes later he was sitting in his own garden, drinking espresso coffee and listening to the birds fuss in the flowering hedges that surrounded his patio. There Tomas, at peace, let the hot sun soak into his face. Death was with him in the garden, in the seductive buzz of insects, the comforting sound of water running in the nearby kitchen. The unaccustomed long sleep only gave Tomas the taste for more. He could feel himself drifting off, noted with interest that he had no desire to resist, felt Death pull his chair closer, his breath disguised as raspberries and mimosa.

At seventy-four years of age, also on his birthday, Tomas Benares had gone out to his front steps, unscrewed his son's nameplate and re-affixed his own. In the previous weeks he had restored the house to the arrangement it had known before his original retirement.

The front hall was the waiting room. On either side were long wooden benches, the varnished oak polished by a generation of patients.

This front hall opened into a small parlour that looked onto the street. In that room was a desk, more chairs for waiting, and the doctor's files. At first his wife ran that parlour; after her death Tomas had hired a nurse.

Behind the parlour was the smallest room of all. It had space for an examination table, a glass cabinet with a few books and several drawers of instruments, and a single uncomfortable chair. On the ceiling was a fluorescent light and the window was protected by venetian blinds made of heavy plastic.

After Gabriel's death, his widow Bella and the children had stayed on in the Benares household, and so on the morning of the reopening Tomas had gone into the kitchen to find Bella making coffee and feeding breakfast to Daniel and Margaret. He sat down wordlessly at the kitchen table while Bella brought him coffee and toast, and he was still reading the front section of the morning paper when the doorbell rang. Daniel leapt from the table and ran down the hall. Tomas was at that moment examining the advertisement he had placed to announce the recommencement of his practice.

"Finish your coffee," said Bella. "Let her wait. She's the one who needs the job."

But Tomas was already on his feet. Slowly he walked down the hall to the front parlour. He could hear Daniel chatting with the woman, and was conscious of trying to keep his back straight. He was wearing, for his new practice, a suit newly tailored. His former tailor had died, and it was his son who had measured Tomas with the cloth tape, letting his glasses slide down to rest on the tip of his nose in exactly the same way his father had.

The tailor's son had written Daniel Benares down in his order book and Tomas hadn't had the heart to correct him. Now in his new blue suit, a matching tie, and one of the linen shirts that Marguerita had made for him, Tomas stood in his front parlour.

"Dr. Benares, I am Elizabeth Rankin; I answered your advertisement for a nurse."

"I am pleased to meet you, Mrs. Rankin."

"Miss Rankin." Elizabeth Rankin was then a young woman entering middle age. She had brown hair, which was parted in the middle and then pulled back in a bun behind her neck, eyes of a darker brown in which Tomas saw a mixture of fear and sympathy. She was wearing a skirt and a jacket, but had with her a small suitcase in case it was necessary for her to start work right away.

"Would you like to see my papers, Dr. Benares?"

"Yes, if you like. Please sit down."

Daniel was still in the room and Tomas let him watch as Elizabeth Rankin pulled out her diploma proving that she had graduated from McGill University in the biological sciences, and another diploma showing that she had received her R.N. from the same university.

"I have letters of reference, Dr. Benares." Daniel, please get a cup of coffee for Miss Rankin. Do you —

"Just black, Daniel."

They sat in silence until Daniel arrived with the coffee, and then Tomas asked him to leave and closed the door behind him.

"I'm sorry," Elizabeth Rankin said. "I saw the advertisement and . . ."

She trailed off. It was six months since Tomas had seen her, but he recognized her right away; she was the woman who had been driving the car that had killed his son. At the scene of the accident she had shivered in shock until the ambulance arrived. Tomas had even offered her some sleeping pills. Then she had re-appeared to hover at the edge of the mourners at Gabriel's funeral.

"You're a very brave woman, Miss Rankin."

"No, I —" Her eyes clouded over. Tomas, behind the desk, watched her struggle. When he had seen her in the hall, his first reaction had been anger.

"I thought I should do something," she said. "I don't need a salary, of course and I am a qualified nurse."

"I see that," Tomas said drily.

"You must hate me," Elizabeth Rankin said.

Tomas shrugged. Daniel came back in the house and stood beside Elizabeth Rankin. She put her hand on his shoulder, and the boy leaned against her.

"You mustn't bother Miss Rankin," Tomas said, but even as he spoke he could see Elizabeth's hand tightening on the boy's shoulder.

"Call Margaret," Tomas said to Daniel, and then asked himself why indeed he should forgive Elizabeth Rankin. No reason came to mind, and while Daniel ran through the house, searching for his sister, Tomas sat in his reception room and looked carefully at the face of Elizabeth Rankin. The skin below her eyes was dark, perhaps she had trouble sleeping; and though her expression was maternal she had a tightly drawn quality that was just below the surface, as though the softness was simply a costume.

He remembered a friend who had been beaten by a gang of Franco's men, saying he felt sorry for them. When Tomas' turn came, he had felt no pity for his assailants. And although what Elizabeth Rankin had done was an accident, not a malicious act, she was still the guilty party. Tomas wondered if she knew what he was thinking, wondered how she could not. She was sitting with one leg crossed over the other, her eyes on the door through which the sounds of the children's feet came. And then Margaret, shy, sidled into the room. Tomas made a formal introduction. He was thinking, as he watched Margaret's face, how strange it was that the victims must always console their oppressors.

Margaret, four years old, curtsied and then held out her hand. There was no horrified scream, no flicker of recognition.

"Miss Rankin will be coming every morning," Tomas announced. "She will help me in my office."

"You are very kind, Dr. Benares."

"We will see," Tomas said. It was then that he had an extraordinary thought, or at least a thought that was extraordinary for him. It occurred that Elizabeth Rankin didn't simply want to atone, or to be consoled. What she wanted was to be taken advantage of.

Tomas waited until the children had left the room, after which he closed the door. He stood in front of Elizabeth Rankin until she, too, got to her feet.

"Pig," Tomas Benares hissed; and he spat at her face. The saliva missed its target and landed instead on the skin covering her right collarbone. There it glistened, surrounded by tiny beads, before gliding down the open V of her blouse.

The eyes of Elizabeth Rankin contracted briefly. Then their expression returned to a flat calm. Tomas, enraged, turned on his heel and walked quickly out of the room. When he came back fifteen minutes later, Elizabeth Rankin had changed into her white uniform and was sorting through the files of his son.

Bella said it wasn't right.

"That you should have her in the house," she said. "It's disgusting."

"She has a diploma," Tomas said.

"And how are you going to pay her? You don't have any patients."

This discussion took place in the second floor sitting room after the children were asleep. By this time Tomas had already taken up residence on the third floor, and the sitting room on the second floor had been where Bella and Gabriel could go to have their privacy.

"At first I thought maybe you didn't recognize her," Bella started again, "and so I said to myself, What sort of a joke is this? Maybe she didn't get enough the first time, maybe she has to come back for more."

"It was an accident," Tomas said.

"So you forgive her?" Bella challenged. She had a strong, bell-like voice which, when she and Gabriel were first married, had been a family joke, one even she would laugh at; but since his death the tone had grown rusty and sepulchral.

Tomas shrugged.

"I don't forgive her," Bella said.

"It was an accident," Tomas said. "She likes to work it out of her system."

"What about me? How am I going to work it out of my system?"

At thirty Bella was more beautiful than when she had been married. The children had made her heavy but grief had carved away the excess flesh. She had jet black hair and olive skin that her children had both inherited. Now she began to cry and Tomas, as always during these nightly outbursts of tears, went to stand by the window.

"Well," Bella insisted, "What do you expect me to do?"

When she had asked this question before, Tomas advised her to go to sleep with the aid of a pill. But now he hesitated. For how many months, for how many years could he tell her to obliterate her evenings in sleeping pills.

"You're the saint," Bella said. "You never wanted anyone after Marguerita."

"I was lucky," Tomas said. "I had a family."

"I have a family."

"I was older," Tomas said.

"So," Bella repeated dully, "you never did want anyone else."

Tomas was silent. When Gabriel brought her home he had asked Tomas what he thought of her. "She's very beautiful," Tomas had said. Gabriel had happily agreed. Now she was more beautiful but, Tomas thought, also more stupid.

"It is very hard," Tomas said, "for a man my age to fall in love."

"Your wife died many years ago . . ."

Tomas shrugged. "I always felt old," he said, "ever since we came to Canada." All this time he had been standing at the window and now he made sure his back was turned so that she wouldn't see his own tears. The day Gabriel was killed, he had cried with her. Since then, even at the funeral, he had refused to let her see his tears. Why? He didn't know. The sight of her, even the smell of her walking into a room, seemed to freeze his heart.

"If there was —" Bella started. She stopped. Tomas knew that he should help her, that she shouldn't have to fight Gabriel's ghost *and* his father, but he couldn't bring himself to reach out. It was like watching an ant trying to struggle its way out of a pot of honey.

"If there was someone else," Bella said. "Even a job."

"What can you do?" Tomas asked, but the question was rhetorical; Bella had married Gabriel the year after she had finished high school. She couldn't even type.

"I could be your receptionist, instead of her."

"Nurse," Tomas interrupted. "I need a nurse, Bella."

"I can put a thermometer in someone's mouth," Bella said. "Are people going to die while you're next door in the office?"

"A doctor needs a nurse," Tomas said. "I didn't invent the rules."

"There's a rule?"

"It's a custom, Bella."

"And anyway," Bella said, "who's going to take care of the children?"

"That's right, the children need a mother."

"We need Bella in the kitchen making three meals a day so at night she can cry herself to sleep, while the murderer is working off her guilt so at night she can go out and play with the boys, her conscience clean."

"You don't know what she does at night."

"You're such a saint," Bella said suddenly. "You are such a saint the whole world admires you, do you know that?"

"Bella"

"The holy Doctor Benares, at seventy-four years of age he ends his retirement and begins work again to provide for his widowed daughter-in-law and his two orphaned grandchildren. Has the world ever seen such a man? At the shul they're talking about adding a sixth book to the Torah." She looked at Tomas and Tomas, seeing her out of control, could only stand and watch; she is like an ant, he was thinking now. The ant is at the lip of the pot. It may fall back in the honey, in which, case it will drown, or it may escape after all.

"You're such a saint," Bella said in her knife-edge voice, "you're such a saint that you think poor Bella just wants to go out and get laid." She was teetering on the edge now, Tomas thought.

"You should see your face now," Bella said. "*Adultery*, you're thinking. *Whore.*"

"It's perfectly normal for a healthy —"

"Oh healthy shit," Bella screamed. "I just want to go out. Out, out, *out.*"

She was standing in the doorway, her face beet-red, panting with her fury. Tomas, sitting still in his armchair, could feel his own answering blush searing the backs of his ears, surrounding his neck like a hot rope.

"Even the saint goes for a walk," Bella's voice had dropped again. "Even the saint can spend the afternoon over at Herman Levine's apartment playing cards and drinking beer."

Tomas could feel his whole body burning and chafing inside the suit he was still wearing. *The saint*, she was calling him. And what had he done to her? Offered her and her family a home when they needed it. "Did I make Gabriel stay here?" Tomas asked. And then realized, to his shame, that he had said the words aloud.

Now he saw Bella in the doorway open her mouth until it looked like the muzzle of a cannon. Her lips struggled and convulsed, the room filled with unspoken obscenities.

Tomas reached a hand to touch the veins in his neck. They were so gorged with blood he was choking. He tore at his tie, forced his collar open.

"Oh God," Bella moaned.

Tomas was coughing, trying to free his throat and chest. Bella was in the corner of his hazed vision, staring at him in the semi-detached way he had watched her only a few moments before.

The saint, Tomas was thinking, she calls me the saint. *Icho de la granda putan.* For a moment he could think in neither English nor Spanish. There was just a rising tide of hatred and resentment, a dozen garbled sentences of self-justification.

In the small hours of the morning, Tomas Benares was lying in the centre of his marriage bed, looking up at the ceiling of the bedroom and tracing the shadows with his tired eyes. These shadows: cast by the streetlights they were as much a part of his furniture as was the big oak bed, or the matching dresser that presided on either side — still waiting, it seemed, for the miraculous return of Marguerita.

As always he was wearing pajamas, another of Marguerita's sewing talents, and like the rest of his clothes they had been cleaned and ironed by the same Bella who had stood in the doorway of the second floor living room and bellowed and panted at him like an animal gone mad.

The languages that had deserted Tomas in that moment had since returned. For hours he had been lying on his back, staring up at the shadows and letting the carefully formed sentences run through his head. The windows were opened and while he argued with himself Tomas could feel the July night trying to cool his skin, soothe him. But he didn't want to be soothed, and every half hour or so he raised himself on one elbow and reached for a cigarette, flaring the light in the darkness and feeling for a second the distant twin of the young man who had lived in Madrid forty years ago, the young man who had taken lovers, all of them beautiful in retrospect, whispered romantic promises, all of them ridiculous, and then had the good fortune to fall in love with and marry a woman so beautiful and devoted even his dreams could never have imagined her. And yet it was true, as he had told Bella, that when he came to Canada his life had ended.

Even lying with Marguerita in this bed he had often been unable to sleep, had often with this very gesture lit up a small space in the night in order to feel close to the young man who had been deserted in Spain.

Return? Yes, it had occurred to him after the war was finished. Of course Franco was still in power then, but it was his country and there were others who had returned. And yet, what would have been the life of an exile returned? The life of a man keeping his lips perpetually sealed, his thoughts to himself; the life of a man who had hid his heart in order to have the sights and smells that were familiar.

Now, Tomas told himself wryly, now he was an old man who had lost his heart for nothing at all. Somehow, over the years, it had simply disappeared, like a beam of wood that is being eaten from the inside, it had dropped away without him knowing it.

Tomas Benares on his seventy-fourth birthday had just put out a cigarette and lain back with his head on the white linen pillow to resume his study of the shadows when he heard the footsteps on the stairs up to his attic.

Then there was a creak of the door opening and Bella, in her nightgown and carrying a candle, tiptoed into the room.

Tomas closed his eyes.

The footsteps came closer, he felt the bed sag with her weight. He could hear her breathing in the night, it was soft and slow; and then as he realized he was holding his own breath, he felt Bella's hand come to rest on his forehead.

He opened his eyes. In the light of the candle her face was like stone, etched and lined with grief.

"I'm sorry," Tomas said.

"I'm the sorry one. And imagine, on your birthday."

"That's all right. We've been too closed in here, since —" Here he hesitated because for some reason the actual event was never spoken of — "Gabriel died."

Bella now took her hand away and Tomas was aware of how cool and soft it had been. Sometimes, decades ago, Marguerita had comforted him in this same way when he couldn't sleep. Her hand on his forehead, fingers stroking his cheeks, his eyes, soothing murmurs until finally he drifted away, a log face-down in the cool water.

"There are still lives to be lived," Bella was saying, "the children."

"The children," Tomas repeated. Not since Marguerita had a woman been in this room at night. For years he had locked the door, and even the rare times he was sick, he returned to locking the door again, in case someone — who? — should dare to come on a "mission of mercy."

"I get tired," Bella said. Her head drooped and Tomas could see, beyond the outline of her nightdress, the curve of her breasts, the fissure between. A beautiful woman, he had thought before; and nor was he as saintly as Bella imagined. On certain of the afternoons Bella thought he was at Herman Levine's, Tomas went to visit a different apartment, that of a widow who had once been his patient. She too knew what it was like to look at the shadows on the ceiling for one year after another, for one decade after another.

Now Tomas reached out for Bella's hand. Her skin was young and supple, not like the skin of the widow, or his own. There comes a time in every person's life, Tomas thought, when the inner soul takes a look at the body and says: enough, you've lost what little beauty you had and now you're just an embarrassment — I'll keep carrying you around but I refuse to take you seriously. Tomas, aside from some stray moments of vanity, had reached that point long ago; but Bella, he knew, was still in love with her body, still wore her own bones and skin and flesh as a proud inheritance and not an aging inconvenience. "Happy birthday," Bella said. She lifted Tomas' hand and pressed it to her mouth. At first what he felt was the wetness of her mouth. And then it was her tears that flowed in tiny warm streams around his fingers.

She blew out the candle at the same time that Tomas reached for her shoulder; and then he drew her down so she was lying beside him — her on top of the covers and him beneath, her thick jet hair folded into his neck and face, her perfume and the scent of her mourning skin wrapped around him like a garden. Chastely he cuddled her to him, her warm breath soothing as Marguerita's voice had once been. He felt himself drifting towards sleep, and he turned towards the perfume, the garden, turned towards Bella to hold her in his arms the way he used to hold Marguerita in that last exhausted moment of waking.

Bella shifted closer, herself breathing so slowly that Tomas thought she must be already asleep. He remembered, with relief, that his alarm was set for six o'clock; at least they would wake before the children. Then he felt his own hand, as if it had a life of its own, slide in a slow caress from Bella's shoulder to her elbow, touching in an accidental way her sleeping breast.

Sleep fled at once, and Tomas felt the sweat spring to his skin. Yet Bella only snuggled closer, breasts and hips flooding through the blanket like warm oceans. Tomas imagined reaching for and lighting a cigarette, the darkness parting once more. A short while ago he had been mourning his youth and now, he reflected, he was feeling as stupid as he ever had. Even with the widow there was no hesitation. Mostly on his visits they sat in her living room and drank tea; sometimes, by a ritual consent that was arrived at without discussion, they went to her bed and performed sex like a warm and comfortable bath. A bath, he muttered to himself, that was how he and Bella should become, chaste warm comforts to each other in the absence of Gabriel. It wasn't right, he now decided sleepily. To have frozen his heart to to this woman — his daughter-in-law after all; surely she had a right to love, to the warmth and affection due a member of the family.

Bella, he was ready to proclaim, you are the mother of my grandchildren, the chosen wife of my son. And if you couldn't apologize for shouting, at least you were willing to comfort me.

Tomas held Bella closer. Her lips, he became aware, were pressed against the hollow of his throat, moving slowly, kissing the skin and now sucking gently at the hairs that curled up from his chest. Tomas let his hand find the back of her neck. There was a delicate valley that led down from her skull; he had never seen *that*, past the thick black hair, would never have guessed she was built so finely.

Now Bella's weight lifted away for a moment, though her lips stayed glued to his throat, and then suddenly she was underneath the covers, her leg across his groin, her hand sliding up his chest.

Tomas felt something inside of him break. And then, as he raised himself on top of Bella the night too broke open; a giant black and dreamless mouth it swallowed them both. He kissed her, tore at her nightgown to suck at her breast, penetrated her so deeply that she gagged and yet though he touched and kissed her every private place, though they writhed on the bed and he felt the cool sweep of her lips as they searched out his every nerve; though he even opened his eyes to see the pleasure on her face, her black hair spread like dead butterflies over Marguerita's linen pillows, her mouth open with repeated climax, the night still swallowed them, obliterated everything as it happened, took them rushing down its hot and endless gorge until Tomas felt like Jonah in the belly of the whale; felt like Jonah trapped in endless flesh and his own flailing desire. And all he had to escape with was his own sex: like an old sword he brandished it in the blackness, pierced open tunnels, flailed it against the wet walls of his prison.

"Bella, Bella, Bella." He whispered her name silently. Every time he shaped his lips around her name, he was afraid the darkness of his inner eye would part, and Gabriel's face would appear before him. But it didn't happen. Even as he scratched Bella's back, bit her neck, penetrated her from behind, he taunted himself with the idea that somewhere in this giant night Gabriel must be waiting. His name was on Tomas' lips: Gabriel his son.

How many commandments was he breaking? Tomas, pressing Bella's breasts to his parched cheeks, couldn't even remember what they were.

Tomas felt his body, like a starved man at a banquet, go out of control. Kissing, screwing, holding, stroking: everything he did Bella wanted, did back, invented variations upon. For one brief second he thought that Marguerita had never been like this, then his mind turned on itself and he was convinced that this was Marguerita herself, back from the dead with God's blessing to make up, in a few hours, a quarter-century of lost time.

But as he kissed and cried over his lost Marguerita, the night began to lift and the first light drew a grey mask on the window.

By this time he and Bella were lying on their stomachs, side by side, too exhausted to move.

The gray mask began to glow, and as it did Tomas felt the dread rising in him. Surely God Himself would appear to take His revenge and with that thought Tomas realized he had forgotten his own name. He felt his tongue searching, fluttering between his teeth, tasting again his own sweat and Bella's fragrant juices. He must be, he thought, in hell. He had died and God, to drive his wicked soul crazy, had given him this dream of his own daughter-in-law, his dead son's wife.

"Thank you, Tomas."

No parting kiss, just soft steps across the carpet and then one creak as she descended the stairs. Finally the face of his son appeared. It was an infant's face, staring uncomprehendingly at its father.

Tomas sat up. His back was sore, his kidneys felt trampled, one arm ached, his genitals burned. He stood up to go to the bathroom and was so dizzy that for a few moments he had to cling to the bedpost with his eyes closed. Then, limping and groaning, he made the trip across the room. When he got back to the bed there was no sign that Bella had been there but the sheets were soaked as they sometimes were after a restless night.

He collapsed on the covers and slept dreamlessly until the alarm went off. When he opened his eyes his first thought was of Bella, and when he swung out of bed there was a sharp sting in his groin. But as he dressed he was beginning to wonder, even to hope that the whole episode was a dream.

A few minutes later, downstairs at breakfast, Tomas found the children sitting alone at the table. Between them was a sealed envelope addressed to "Dr. Tomas Benares, M.D."

"Dear Tomas," the letter read, "I have decided that it is time for me to seek my own life in another city. Miss Rankin has already agreed to take care of the children for as long as necessary. I hope you will all understand me and remember that I love you. As always, Bella Benares."

It was on his birthday that his garden always seemed to reach that explosive point which marked the height of summer. No matter what the weather, it was this garden that made up for all other deprivations, and the fact that his 94th birthday was gloriously warm and sunny made it doubly perfect for Tomas to spend the day outside.

Despite the perfect blessing of the sky, as Tomas opened his eyes from that long doze which had carried the sun straight into the afternoon he felt a chill in his blood, the knowledge that Death, that companion he'd grown used to, almost fond of, was starting to play his tricks. Because sitting in front of him, leaning towards him as if the worlds of waking and sleeping had been forced together, was Bella herself.

"Tomas, Tomas it's so good to see you. It's Bella."

"I know," Tomas said. His voice sounded weak and grumpy; he

coughed to clear his throat.

"Happy birthday Tomas."

He pushed his hand across his eyes to rid himself of this illusion.

"Tomas, you're looking so good."

Bella: her face was fuller now, but the lines were carved deeper, bracketing her full lips and corrugating her forehead. And yet she was still young, amazing, her movements were lithe and supple, her jet black hair was streaked but still fell thick and wavy to her shoulders, her eyes still burned, and when she leaned forward to take his hand between her own the smell of her, dreams and remembrances came flooding back.

"Tomas, are you glad to see me?"

"You look so young, Bella." This in a voice that was still weak, but Tomas' clearing cough was lost in the rich burst of Bella's laughter. Her laugh had always been her one redeeming feature and now Tomas, seeing her head thrown back and the flash of her strong teeth, could hardly believe that he, a doddering old man whose knees had been covered by a blanket in the middle of a summer had only a few years ago actually made love to this vibrant woman. Now she was like a racehorse in voracious maturity, while he was already shrunken into something too small for the glue factory.

"Bella, the children."

"I know Tomas. I telephoned Margaret, she's here. And I telephoned Daniel too. His secretary said he was at a meeting all afternoon, but that he was coming here for dinner."

"Bella, you're looking wonderful, truly wonderful." Tomas had his hand hooked in hers and, suddenly aware that he was half-lying in his chair, was using her weight to try to lever himself up.

Instantly Bella was on her feet, her arm solicitously around his back, pulling him into position. She handled his weight, Tomas thought, like the weight of a baby. He felt surrounded by her, overpowered by her smell, her vitality, her cheery good will. *Putan*, Tomas whispered to himself, what a revenge. Twenty years ago he had been her equal, and now, suddenly — what had happened? Death was in the garden; Tomas could feel his presence, the familiar visitor turned trickster. And then Tomas felt some of his strength returning, strength in the form of contempt for Bella, who had waited twenty years to come back to his house; contempt for Death who waited until a man was an ancient drooling husk to test his will.

"You're the marvel, Tomas. Elizabeth says you work every day in the garden. How do you do it?"

"I spit in Death's face," Tomas rasped. Now he was beginning to feel more himself again, and he saw that Bella was pouring him a cup of coffee. All night he had slept, and then again in the day, what a way to spend a birthday! But coffee would heat the blood, make it run faster. He realized that he was famished.

Bella had taken out a package of cigarettes now, and offered one to Tomas. He shook his head, thinking again how he had declined in these last years. Now Daniel wouldn't let him smoke in bed, even when he couldn't sleep. He was only allowed to smoke when there was someone else in the room, or when he was outside in the garden.

"Tomas. I hope you don't mind I came back. I wanted to see you again while — while we could still talk."

Tomas nodded. So the ant had escaped the honey pot after all, and ventured into the wide world. Now it was come back, wanting to tell its adventures to the ant who had stayed home. Perhaps they hadn't spent that strange night making love after all; perhaps in his bed they had been struggling at the edge of the pot, fighting to see who would fall back and who would be set free.

"So," Bella said. "It's been so long."

Tomas, watching her, refusing to speak, felt control slowly moving towards him again. He sat up straighter, brushed the blanket off his legs.

"Or maybe we could talk tomorrow," Bella said, "when you're feeling stronger."

"I feel strong." His voice surprised even himself — not the weak squawk it sometimes was now, a chicken's squeak hardly audible for over the telephone, but firm and definite, booming out of his chest the way it used to. Bella: she had woken him up once, perhaps she would once more.

He could see her moving back, hurt, but then she laughed again, her rich throaty laugh that Tomas used to hear echoing through the house when his son was still alive. He looked at her left hand; Gabriel's modest engagement ring was still in place, but beside it was a larger ring, a glowing bloodstone set in a fat gold band. "Tomas," Bella was saying, "you really are a marvel, I swear you're going to live to see a hundred."

"A hundred and twenty-three," Tomas said. "Almost all of the Benares men live to be a hundred and twenty-three."

For a moment the lines deepened again in Bella's face, and Tomas wished he could someday learn to hold his tongue. A bad habit that should have long ago been entered in his diary.

"You will," Bella finally said; her voice had the old edge. "Two hundred and twenty-three, you'll dance on all our graves."

"Bella."

"I shouldn't have come."

"The children —"

"They'll be glad to see me, Tomas, they always are."

"Always?"

"Of course. Did you think I'd desert my own children?"

Tomas shook his head.

"Oh I left, Tomas, I left. But I kept in touch. I sent them letters and they wrote me back. That woman helped me."

"Elizabeth?"

"I should never have called her a murderer, Tomas. It was an accident."

"They wrote you letters without telling me?"

Bella stood up. She was a powerful woman now, full-fleshed and in her prime; even Death had slunk away in the force of her presence. "I married again, Tomas. My husband and I lived in Seattle. When Daniel went to university there, he lived in my home."

"Daniel lived with you?"

"My husband's dead now Tomas, but I didn't come for your pity. Or your money. I just wanted you to know that I would be in Toronto again, seeing my own children, having a regular life."

"A regular life," Tomas repeated. He felt dazed, dangerously weakened. Death was in the garden again, he was standing behind Bella, peeking out from behind her shoulders and making faces. He struggled to his feet. Only Bella could save him now, and yet he could see the fear on her face as he reached for her.

"Tomas, I —"

"You couldn't kill me," Tomas roared. His lungs filled his chest like an eagle in flight. His flowering hedges, his roses, his carefully groomed patio snapped into focus. He stepped towards Bella, his balance perfect, his arm rising. He saw her mouth open, her lips begin to flutter. Beautiful but stupid, Tomas thought, some things never change. At his full height he was still tall enough to put his arm around her and lead her towards the house.

"It's my birthday," his voice booming, with the joke. "Let me offer you a drink to celebrate your happy return."

His hand had slid from her shoulder to her arm, the skin as smooth as warm silk. Her face turned towards his: puzzled, almost happy.

"Of course I forgive you," Tomas said.

Death was his constant companion, the one face that never turned away. Friend, trickster, shadow: but Death never spoke, never said how it would be to lose his grip on life and go sailing off into — where?

He rehearsed the last moment of his life, how it would be to die, the actual feeling of suddenly passing from life to death. He could imagine the first half of the transaction easily enough. Lying in bed, breathing quietly, the dimmed world would finally fade away, like drifting into sleep. But instead of it being sleep he drifted into, something else would be waiting.

But what? A nightmare tunnel full of terrors? A choir of heavenly angels dressed in robes of silk and honey? Black oblivion?

He'd had such a stranglehold on life that finally it was choking to death. Old since mixed with remembered dreams. There had been a boy he'd met in medical school, a young Jew who pushed his studies aside to drown himself in the Kabbala. "At the end of your life," the boy had said, "you will find yourself facing death and you will be terrified. You will say to yourself — Why did I waste all those decades when I should have been contemplating the only two things that really matter: my birth and my death."

But birth was too far away to be remembered. And surely there were better things to think about than that final moment when the cord was finally cut.

He lay on his back. Around him clustered people he hardly knew, suffocating him in a cloud of greed and desire, waiting for his final blessing.

"Gabriel. Gabriel, my son." He waited for a figure to detach itself, come forward.

"Take my blessing —" he began. He stopped. Death was his companion now. Death would travel with him when all others had deserted.

Tomas closed his eyes. He remembered going with his grandfather to the remains of the old Jewish cemetery in Madrid. He himself had still been young, his grandfather a century beyond youth, the graves so far gone that even the most intense and dazzling nights of their inhabitants could not be remembered, only invented. The old man had insisted on holding his hand. The old man's hand had been like that of a prehistoric creature, a dinosaur exhumed from millennia of protective muck. Now his own hand was old, the graves of the jews of Madrid had slipped one more century into the past.

"It's too late," he said. There was a hand on his forehead. Gentle fingers kissed his eyelids. The scent of Bella bloomed around him, her lips on his, her lips driving him deep into the waiting earth.

DOUGLAS GLOVER was born in Southwestern Ontario and now lives in Up-State New York. His publications include *Precious, Dog Attempts To Drown Man in Saskatoon*, and *A Guide To Animal Behavior*, which was nominated for the Governor General's Award for Fiction in 1991. This story first appeared in CFM No. 46 in 1983.

Dog Attempts to Drown Man In Saskatoon

DOUGLAS GLOVER

My wife and I decide to separate, and then suddenly we are almost happy together. The pathos of our situation, our private and unique tragedy, lends romance to each small act. We see everything in the round, the facets as opposed to the flat banality that was wedging us apart. When she asks me to go the the Mendel Art Gallery Sunday afternoon, I do not say no with the usual mounting irritation that drives me into myself. I say yes and some hardness within me seems to melt into a pleasant sadness. We look into each other's eyes and realize with a start that we are looking for the first time because it is the last. We are both thinking, "Who is this person to whom I have been married? What has been the meaning of our relationship?" These are questions we have never asked ourselves; we have been a blind couple groping with each other in the dark. Instead of saying to myself, "Not the art gallery again! What does she care about art? She has no education. She's merely bored and on Sunday afternoon in Saskatoon the only place you can go is the sausage-maker's mausoleum of art!" instead of putting up arguments, I think, "Poor, Lucy, pursued by the assassins unable to stay in on a Sunday afternoon." Somewhere that cretin Pascal says that all our problems stem from not being able to sit quietly in a room alone. If Pascal had had Lucy's mother, he would never have written anything so foolish. Also, at the age of nine, she saw her younger brother run over and killed by a highway roller. Faced with that, would Pascal have written anything? (Now I am defending my wife against Pascal! A month ago I would have used the same passage to bludgeon her.)

Note: Already this is not the story I wanted to tell. That is buried, gone, lost — its action fragmented and distorted by inexact recollection. Directly it was completed, it had disappeared, gone with the past into that strange realm of suspended animation, that coat rack of despair, wherein all our completed acts await, gathering dust, until we come for them again. I am trying to give you the truth, though I could try harder, only refrain because I know that that way leads to madness. So I offer an approximation, a shadow play, such as would excite children full of blind spots and irrelevant adumbrations, too little in parts; elsewhere too much. Alternately I will frustrate you and lead you astray. I can only say that, at the outset, my intention was otherwise; I sought only clarity and simple conclusions. Now I know the worst — that reasons are out of joint with actions, that my best explanation will be obscure, subtle and unsatisfying, and that the human mind is a tangle of unexplored pathways.

"My wife and I decide to separate, and then suddenly we are almost happy together." This is a sentence full of ironies and lies. For example, I call her my wife. Technically this is true. But now that I am leaving, the thought is in both our hearts: "Can a marriage of eleven months really be called a marriage?" Moreover, it was only a civil ceremony, a ten-minute formality performed at the City Hall by a man who, one could tell, had been drinking heavily over lunch. Perhaps if we had done it in a cathedral surrounded by robed priests intoning Latin benedictions we would not now be falling apart. As we put on our coats to go to the art gallery, I mention this idea to Lucy. "A year," she says. "With Latin we might have lasted a year." We laugh. This is the most courageous statement she has made since we became aware of our defeat, better than all her sour tears. Usually she is too self-conscious to make jokes. Seeing me smile, she blushes and becomes confused, happy to have pleased me, happy to be happy, in the final analysis, happy to be sad because the sadness frees her to be what she could never before. Like many people, we are both masters of beginnings and endings but founder in the middle of things. It takes a wise and mature individual to manage that which intervenes, the duration which is a necessary part of life and marriage. So there is a sense in which we are not married, though something *is* ending. And therein lies the greater irony. For in ending, in separating, we are finally and ineluctably together, locked as it were in a ritual recantation. We are going to the art gallery (I am guilty of over-determining the symbol) together.

It is winter in Saskatoon, to my mind the best of seasons because it is the most inimical to human existence. The weather forecaster gives the temperature, the wind chill factor and the number of seconds it takes to freeze exposed skin. Driving between towns one remembers to pack a winter survival kit (matches, candle, chocolate, flares, down sleeping-bag) in case of a breakdown. Earlier in the week just outside the city limits a man disappeared after setting out to walk a quarter of a mile from one farmhouse to another, swallowed up by the cold prairie night. (This is, I believe, a not unpleasant way to die once the initial period of discomfort has been passed.) Summer in Saskatoon is a collection of minor irritants: heat and dust, blackflies and tent caterpillars, the night-time electrical storms that leave the unpaved concession roads impassable troughs of gumbo mud. But winter has the beauty of a plausible finality. I drive out to the airport early in the morning to watch jets land in a pink haze of ice crystals. During the long nights the *aurora borealis* seems to touch the rooftops. But best of all is the city itself which takes on a kind of ghostliness, a dreamlike quality rising from the heated buildings to produce a mystery. Daily I tramp the paths along the riverbank, crossing and re-crossing the bridges, watching the way the city changes in the pale winter light. Beneath me the unfrozen town is a time of anxious waiting and endurance; all that beauty is alien, a constant threat. Many things do not endure. Our marriage, for example, was vernal, a product of the brief, sweet, prairie spring.

Neither Lucy nor I were born here; Mendel came from Russia. In fact there is feeling of the camp about Saskatoon, the temporary abode. At the university there are photographs of the town — in 1905 there were three frame buildings and a tent. In a bar I nearly came to blows with a man campaigning to preserve a movie theatre built in 1934. In Saskatoon that is ancient history, that is the cave painting at Lascaux. Lucy hails from an even newer settlement in the wild Peace River country where her father went to raise cattle and ended up a truck mechanic. Seven years ago she came to Saskatoon to work in a garment factory (her left hand bears a burn scar from a clothes press). Next fall she begins law school. Despite this evidence of intelligence, determination and ability, Lucy has no confidence in herself. In her mother's eyes she will never measure up and that is all that is important. I myself am a proud man, a gutter snob. I wear a ring in my left ear and my hair long. My parents migrated from a farm in Wisconsin to a farm in Saskatchewan in 1952 and still drive back every year to see the trees. I am two courses short of a degree in philosophy which I will never receive. I make my living at what comes to hand, house painting when I am wandering; since I settled with Lucy, I've worked as the lone overnight editor at the local newspaper. Against the bosses, I am a union man; against the union, I am an independent. When the publisher asked me to work days, I quit. That was a month ago. That was when Lucy knew I was leaving. Deep down she understands my nature. Mendel is another case: he was a butcher and a man who left traces. Now on the north bank of the river there are giant meat-packing plants spilling forth the odours of death, guts and excrement. Across the street are the holding pens for the cattle and the rail lines that bring them to slaughter. Before building his art gallery Mendel actually kept his paintings in this sprawling complex of buildings, inside the slaughterhouse. If you went to his office, you would sit in a waiting room with a Picasso or a Rouialt on the wall. Perhaps even a Van Gogh. The gallery is downriver at the opposite end of the city, very clean and modern. But whenever I go there I hear the panicky bellowing of the death-driven steers and see the streams of blood and the carcasses and smell the stench and imagine the poor beasts rolling their eyes at Gauguin's green and luscious leaves as the bolt entered their brains.

We have decided to separate. It is a wintry Sunday afternoon. We are going to the Mendel Art Gallery. Watching Lucy shake her hair out and tuck it into her knitted hat, I suddenly feel close to tears. Behind her are the framed photographs of weathered prairie farmhouses, the vigorous spider plants, the scarred child's school desk where she does her studying, the brick-and-board bookshelf with her meager library. (After eleven months there is still nothing of me that will remain.) This is an old song; there is no gesture of Lucy's that does not fill me instantly with pity, the child's hand held up to deflect the blow, her desperate attempts to conceal unworthiness. For her part she naturally sees me as the father who, in that earlier existence, proved so practised in evasion and flight. The fact that I am now leaving her only reinforces her intuition — it is as if she has expected it all along, almost as if she has been working toward it. This goes to show the force of initial impressions. For example, I will never forget the first time I saw Lucy. She was limping across Broadway, her feet swathed in bandages and jammed into her pumps, her face alternately distorted with agony and composed in dignity. I followed her for blocks — she was beautiful and wounded, the kind of woman I am always looking for to redeem me. Similarly, what she will always remember is that first night we spent together when all I did was hold her while she slept because, taking the bus home, she had seen a naked man masturbating in a window. Thus she had arrived at my door, laughing hysterically, afraid to stay at her own place alone, completely undone. At first she had played the temptress because she thought that was what I wanted. She kissed me hungrily and unfastened my shirt buttons. Then she ran into the bathroom and came out crying because she had dropped and broken the soap dish. That was when I put my arms around her and comforted her, which was what she had wanted from the beginning.

An apology for my style: I am not so much apologizing as invoking a tradition. Heraclitus whose philosophy may not have been written in fragments but certainly comes to us in that form. Kierkegaard who mocked Hegel's system-building by writing everything as if it were an afterthought, *The Unscientific Postscript*. Nietzsche who wrote in aphorisms or what he called "attempts," dry runs at the subject matter, even arguing contradictory points of view in order to see all sides.

Wittgenstein's *Investigations*, his fragmentary response to the architectonic of the earlier *Tractatus*. Traditional story writers compose a beginning, a middle and an end, stringing these together in continuity as if there was some whole which they represented. Whereas I am writing fragments and discursive circumlocutions about an object that may not be complete or may be infinite. "Dog Attempts to Drown Man in Saskatoon" is my title, cribbed from a facetious newspaper headline. Lucy and I were married because of her feet and because she glimpsed a man masturbating in a window as her bus took her home from work. I feel that in discussing these occurrences, these facts (our separation, the dog, the city, the weather, a trip to the art gallery) as constitutive of a non-system, I am peeling away some of the mystery of human life. I am also of the opinion that Mendel should have left the paintings in the slaughterhouse.

The discerning reader will by now have trapped me in a number of inconsistencies and doubtful statements. For example, we are not separating — I am leaving my wife and she has accepted that fact because it reaffirms her sense of herself as a person worthy of being left. Moreover it was wrong of me to pity her. Lucy is a quietly capable woman about to embark on what will inevitably be a successful career. She is not a waif nor could she ever redeem me with her suffering. Likewise she was wrong to view me as forever gentle and forbearing in the sexual department. And finally I suspect that there was more than coincidence in the fact that she spotted the man in his window on my night off from the newspaper. I do not doubt that she saw the man; he is a recurring nightmare of Lucy's. But whether she saw him that particular night, or some night in the past, or whether she made him up out of whole cloth and came to believe in him, I cannot say. About her feet, however, I have been truthful. That day she had just come from her doctor after having the stitches removed.

Lucy's clumsiness. Her clumsiness stems from the fact that she was born with six toes on each foot. This defect, I'm sure, had something to do with the way her mother mistreated her. Among uneducated folk there is often a feeling that physical anomalies reflect mental flaws. And as a kind of punishment for being born (and afterwards because her brother had died), Lucy's feet were never looked at by a competent doctor. It wasn't until she was twenty-six and beginning to enjoy a new life that she underwent a painful operation to have the vestigial digits excised. This surgery left her big toes all but powerless; now they flop like stubby, white worms at the ends of her feet. Where she had been a schoolgirl athlete with six toes, she became awkward and ungainly with five.

Her mother, Celeste, is one of those women who make feminism a *cause célèbre* — no, that is being glib. Truthfully, she was never any man's slave. I have the impression that after the first realization, the first inkling that she had married the wrong man, she entered into the role of submissive female with a strange, destructive gusto. She seems to have had an immoderate amount of hate in her, enough to spread its poison among many fishes. And the man, the father, was not so far as I can tell cruel, merely ineffectual, just the wrong man. Once years later Lucy and Celeste were riding on a bus together when Celeste pointed to a man sitting a few seats ahead and said, "That is the man I loved." That was all she ever said on the topic and the man himself was a balding, petit, functionary type, completely uninteresting except in terms of the exaggerated passion Celeste had invested in him over the years. Soon after Lucy's father married Celeste he realized he would never be able to live with her — he absconded for the army, abandoning her with the first child in a drover's shack on a cattle baron's estate. (From time to time Lucy attempts to write about her childhood — her stories always seem unbelievable — a world of infanticide, blood feuds and brutality. I can barely credit these tales seeing her so pure and composed, not prim but you know how she sits very straight in her chair and her hair is always in place and her clothes are expensive if not quite stylish and her manners are correct without being at all natural; Lucy is composed in the sense of being made up or put together out of pieces, not in the sense of being tranquil. But nevertheless she carries these *cauchemars* in her head: the dead babies found beneath the fencerow, blood on sheets, shotgun blasts in the night, her brother going under the highway roller, her mother's cruel silence. The father fled as I say. He sent them money orders, three-quarters of his pay, to that point he was responsible. Celeste never spoke of him and his infrequent visits home were always a surprise to the children; his visits and the locked bedroom door and the hot, breathy silence of what went on behind the door; Celeste's rising vexation and hysteria; the new pregnancy; the postmarks on the money orders. Then the boy died. Perhaps he was Celeste's favourite, a perfect one to hold over the tall, already beautiful, monster with six toes and (I conjecture again) her father's look. The boy died and the house went silent — Celeste had forbidden a word to be spoken — and this was the worst for Lucy, the cold parlour circumspection of Protestant mourning. They did not utter a redeeming sound, only replayed the image of the boy running, laughing, racing the machine, then tripping and going under, being sucked under — Lucy did not even see the body, and in an access of delayed grief almost two decades later she would tell me she had always assumed he just flattened out like a cartoon character. Celeste refused to weep; only her hatred grew like a heavy weight against her children. And in that vacuum, that terrible silence accorded all feeling and especially the mysteries of sex and death, the locked door of the bedroom and the shut coffin lid, the absent father and the absent brother, somehow became inextricably entwined in Lucy's mind; she was only ten, a most beautiful monster, surrounded by absent gods and a bitter worship. So that when she saw the naked man calmly masturbating in the upper storey window from her bus, framed as it were under the cornice of a Saskatoon rooming house, it was for her like a vision of the centre of the mystery, the scene behind the locked door, the corpse in its coffin, God, and she immediately imagined her mother waiting irritably in the shadow just out of sight with a towel to wipe the sperm from the windowpane, aroused, yet almost fainting at the grotesque denial of her female passion.

Do not, if you wish, believe any of the above. It is psychological jazz written *en marge*; I am a poet of marginalia. Some of what I write is utter crap and wishful thinking. Lucy is not "happy to be sad"; she is seething inside because I am betraying her. Her anger gives her the courage to make jokes; she blushed when I laughed because she still hopes that I will stay. Of course, my willingness to accompany her to the art gallery is inspired by guilt. She is completely aware of this fact. Her invitation is premeditated, manipulative. No gesture is lost; all our acts are linked and repeated. She is, after all, Celeste's daughter. Also do not believe for a moment that I hate that woman for what she was. That instant on the bus in a distant town when she pointed out the man she truly loved, she somehow redeemed herself for Lucy and for me, showing herself receptive of forgiveness and pity. Nor do I hate Lucy though I am leaving her.

My wife and I decide to separate, and then suddenly we are almost happy together. I repeat this crucial opening sentence for the purpose of reminding myself of my general intention. In a separate notebook next to me (vodka on ice sweating onto and blurring the ruled pages) I have a list of subjects to cover: 1) blindness (the man the dog led into the river was blind); 2) a man I know who was gored by a bison (real name to be withheld); 3) Susan the weaver and her little girl and the plan for us to live in Pelican Narrows; 4) the wolves at the icy zoo; 5) the battlefields of Batoche and Duck Lake; 6) bridge symbolism; 7) a fuller description of the death of Lucy's brother; 8) three photographs of Lucy in my possession; 9) my wish to have met Mendel (he is dead) and be his friend; 10) the story of the story of how the dog tried to drown the man in Saskatoon.

Call this a play. Call me Orestes. Call her mother Clytemnestra. Her father, the wandering warrior king. (When he died accidentally a year ago, they sent Lucy his diary. Every day of his life he had recorded the weather; that was all.) Like everyone else, we married because we thought we could change one another. I was the brother-friend come to slay the tyrant Celeste; Lucy was to teach me the meaning of suffering. But there is no meaning and in the labyrinth of Lucy's mind the spirit of her past eluded me. Take sex for instance. She is taller than I am; people sometimes think she must be a model. She is without a doubt the most beautiful woman I have been to bed with. Yet there is no passion, no arousal. Between the legs she is as dry as a prairie summer. I am tender, but tenderness is no substitute for biology. Penetration is always painful. She gasps, winces. She will not perform oral sex though sometimes she likes having it done to her, providing she can overcome her embarrassment. What she does love is for me to wrestle her to the living-room carpet and strip her clothes off in a mock rape. She squeals and protests and then scampers naked to the bedroom where she waits impatiently while I get undressed. Only once have I detected her orgasm — this while she sat on my lap fully clothed and I manipulated her with my fingers. It goes without saying she will not talk about these things. She protects herself from herself and there is never any feeling that we are together. When Lucy's periods began, Celeste told her she had cancer. More than once she was forced to eat garbage from a dog's dish. Sometimes her mother would simply lock her out of the house for the night. These stories are shocking; Celeste was undoubtedly mad. By hatred, mother and daughter are manacled together for eternity. "You can change," I say with all my heart. "A woman who only sees herself as a victim never gets wise to herself." "No," she says, touching my hand sadly. "Ah! Ah!" I think, between weeping and words. Nostalgia is form; hope is content. Lucy is an empty building, a frenzy of restlessness, a soul without a future. And I fling out in desperation, Orestes-like, seeking my own Athens and release.

More bunk! I'll let you know now that we are not going to the art gallery as I write this. Everything happened some time ago and I am living far away in another country. (Structuralists would characterize my style as "robbing the signifier of the signified." My opening sentence, my premise, is now practically destitute of meaning, or it means everything. Really, this is what happens when you try to tell the truth about something; you end up like the snake biting its own tail. There are a hundred reasons why I left Lucy. I don't want to seem shallow. I don't want to say, well, I was a meat-and-potatoes person and she was a vegetarian, or that I sometimes believe she simply orchestrated the whole fiasco, seduced me, married me, and then refused to be a wife — yes, I would prefer to think that I was guiltless, that I didn't just wander off fecklessly like her father. To explain this, or for that matter to explain why the dog led the man into the river, you have to explain the world, even God — if we accept Godel's theorem regarding the unjustifiability of systems from within. Everything is a symbol of everything else. Or everything is a symbol of death as Levi-Strauss says. In other words, there is no signified and life is nothing but a long haunting. Perhaps that is all that I am trying to say . . .) However, we *did* visit the art gallery one winter Sunday near the end of our eleven-month marriage. There were two temporary exhibitions and all of Mendel's slaughterhouse pictures had been stored in the basement. One wing was devoted to photographs of grain elevators, very phallic with their little overhanging roofs. We laughed about this together; Lucy was kittenish, pretending to be shocked. Then she walked across the hall alone to contemplate the acrylic prairie-scapes by local artists. I descended the stairs to drink coffee and watch the frozen river. This was downstream from the Idylwyld Bridge where the fellow went in (there is an open stretch of two or three hundred yards where a hot water outlet prevents the river from freezing over completely) and it occurred to me that if he had actually drowned, if the current had dragged him under the ice, they wouldn't have found his body until the spring breakup. And probably they would have discovered it hung up on the weir which I could see from the gallery window.

Forget it. A bad picture: Lucy upstairs "appreciating" art, me downstairs thinking of bodies under the ice. Any moment now she will come skipping toward me flushed with excitement after a successful cultural adventure. That is not what I meant to show you. That Lucy is not a person, she is a caricature. When legends are born, people die. Rather let us look at the place where all reasons converge. No. Let me tell you how Lucy is redeemed: preamble and anecdote. Her greatest fear is that she will turn into Celeste. Naturally, she is becoming more and more like her mother every day without noticing it. She has the financial independence Celeste no doubt craved, and she has been disappointed in love. Three times. The first man made himself into wandering rage with drugs. The second was an adulterer. Now me. Already she is acquiring an edge of bitterness, of why-me-ness. But, and this is an Everest of a but, the woman can dance! I don't mean at the disco or in a ballroom; I don't mean she studied ballet. We were strolling in Diefenbaker Park on summer day shortly after our wedding (this is on the bluffs overlooking Mendel's meatpacking plant) when we came upon a puppet show. It was some sort of children's fair: there were petting zoos, pony rides, candy stands, bicycles being given away as prizes, all that kind of thing in addition to the puppets. It was a famous troupe which had started in the sixties as part of the counterculture movement — I need not mention the names. The climax of the performance was a stately dance by two giant puppets perhaps thirty feet tall, a man and a woman, backwoods types. We arrived just in time to see the woman rise from the ground, supported by three puppeteers. She rises from the grass stiffly, then spreads her massive arms toward the man and an orchestra begins a reel. It is an astounding sight. I notice that the children in the audience are rapt. And suddenly I am aware of Lucy, her face aflame, this crazy grin and her eyes dazzled. She is looking straight up at the giant woman. The music, as I say, begins and the puppet sways and opens her arms towards her partner (they are both very stern, very grave), and Lucy begins to sway and spread her arms. She lifts her feet gently, one after the other, begins to turn, then swings back. She doesn't know what she is doing; is completely unselfconscious. There is only Lucy and the puppets and the dance. She is a child again and I am in awe of her innocence. It is a scene that brings a lump to my throat: the high, hot, summer sun, the children's faces like flowers in a sea of grass, the towering, swaying puppets, and Lucy lost in herself. Lucy, dancing. Probably, she no longer remembers this incident. At the time, or shortly after, she said, "Oh no! Did I really ? Tell me I didn't do that!" She was laughing, not really embarrassed. "Did anyone see me?" And when the puppeteers passed the hat at the end of their show, I turned out my pockets, I gave them everything I had.

I smoke Gitanes. I like to drink in an Indian bar on 20th Street near Eatons's. My nose was broken in a car accident when I was eighteen; it grew back crooked. I speak softly; sometimes I stutter. I don't like crowds. In my spare time, I paint large pictures of the city. Photographic realism is my style. I work on a pencil grid using egg tempera because it's better for detail. I do shopping centres, old movie theatres that are about to be torn down, slaughterhouses. While everyone else is looking out at the prairie, I peer inward and record what is entirely transitory, what is human. Artifice. Nature defeats me. I cannot paint ripples or a lake, or the movement of leaves, or a woman's face. Like most people, I suppose, my heart is broken because I cannot be what I wish to be. On the day in question, one of the coldest of the year, I hike down from the university along Saskatchewan Drive overlooking the old railway hotel, the modest office blocks, the ice-shrouded gardens of the city. I carry a camera, snapping end-of-the-world photos for a future canvas. At the Third Avenue Bridge I pause to admire the lattice of I-beams, black against the frozen mist swirling up from the river and the translucent exhaust plumes of the ghostly cars shuttling to and fro. Crossing the street, I descend the wooden steps into Rotary Park, taking two more shots of the bridge at a close angle before the film breaks from the cold. I swing round, focussing on the squat ugliness of the Idylwyld Bridge with its fat concrete piers obscuring the view upriver, and then suddenly an icy finger seems to touch my heart: out on the river, on the very edge of the snowy crust where the turgid waters from the outlet pipe churn and steam, a black dog is playing. I refocus. The dog scampers in a tight circle, races toward the brink, skids to a stop, barks furiously in the grey water. I stumble forward a step or two. Then I see the man, swept downstream, bobbing in the current, his arms flailing stiffly. In another instant, the dog leaps after him, disappears, almost as if I had dreamed it. I don't quite know what I am doing, you understand. The river is no man's land. First I am plunging through the knee-deep snow of the park. Then I lose my footing on the bank and find myself sliding on my seat onto the river ice. Before I have time to think, "There is a man in the river," I am sprinting to intercept him, struggling to untangle the camera from around my neck, stripping off my coat. I have forgotten momentarily how long it takes exposed skin to freeze and am lost in a frenzy of speculation upon the impossibility of existence in the river, the horror of the current dragging you under the ice at the end of the open water, the creeping numbness, again the impossibility, the alienness of the idea itself, the dog and the man immersed. I feel the ice rolling under me, throw myself flat, wrapped in a gentle terror, then inch forward again, spread-eagled, throwing my coat by a sleeve, screaming, "Catch it! Catch it!" to the man whirling toward me, scrabbling with bloody hands at the crumbling ledge. All this occupies less time than it takes to tell. He is a strange bearlike creature, huge in an old duffel coat with its hood up, steam rising around him, his face bloated and purple, his red hands clawing at the ice shelf, an inhuman "awing" sound emanating from his throat, his eyes rolling upwards. He makes no effort to reach the coat sleeve trailed before him as the current carries him by. Then the dog appears, paddling toward the man, straining to keep its head above the choppy surface. The dog barks, rests a paw on the man's shoulder, seems to drag him under a little, and then the man is striking out wildly, fighting the dog off, being twisted out into the open water by the eddies. I see the leather hand harness flapping from the dog's neck and suddenly the full horror of the situation assails me: the man is blind. Perhaps he understands nothing of what is happening to him, the world gone mad, this freezing hell. At the same moment, I feel strong hands grip my ankles and hear another's laboured breathing. I looked over my shoulder. There is a pink-cheeked policeman with a thin yellow moustache stretched on the ice behind me. Behind him, two teenage boys are in the act of dropping to all fours, making a chain of bodies. A fifth person, a young woman, is running toward us. "He's blind," I shout. The policeman nods: he seems to comprehend everything in an instant. The man in the water has come to rest against a jutting point of ice a few yards away. The dog is much nearer, but I make for the man, crawling on my hands and knees, forgetting my coat. There seems nothing to fear now. Our little chain of life reaching toward the blind drowning man seems sufficient against the infinity of forces which have culminated in this moment. The crust is rolling and bucking beneath us as I take his wrists. His fingers, hard as talons, lock into mine. Immediately he ceases to utter that terrible, unearthly bawling sound.

Inching backward, I somehow contrive to lever the deadweight of his body over the ice lip, then drag him on his belly like a sack away from the water. The cop turns him gently on his back; he is breathing in gasps, his eyes rolling frantically. "Tank you. Tank you," he whispers, his strength gone. The others quickly remove their coats and tuck them around the man who now looks like some strange beached fish, puffing and muttering in the snow. Then in the eery silence that follows, broken only by the shushing sound of traffic on the bridges, the distant whine of a siren coming nearer, the hissing river and my heart beating, I look into the smokey water once more and see that the dog is gone. I am dazed; I watch a drop of sweat freezing on the policeman's moustache. I stare into the grey flux where it slips quietly under the ice and disappears. One of the boys offers me a cigarette. The blind man moans; he says, "I go home now. Dog good. I all right. I walk home." The boys glance at each other. The woman is shivering. Everything seems empty and anticlimactic. We are shrouded in enigma. The policeman takes out a notebook, a tiny symbol of rationality, scribbled words against the void. As an ambulance crew skates a stretcher down the river bank, he begins to ask the usual questions, the usual, unanswerable questions.

This is not the story I wanted to tell. I repeat this *caveat* as a reminder that I am willful and wayward as a story-teller, not a good story-teller at all. The right story, the true story, had I been able to tell it, would have changed your life — but it is buried, gone, lost. The next day Lucy and I drive to the spot where I first saw the dog. The river is once more sanely empty and the water boils quietly where it has not yet frozen. Once more I tell her how it happened, but she prefers the public version, what she hears on the radio or reads in the newspaper, to my disjointed impressions. It is also true that she knows she is losing me and she is at the stage where it is necessary to deny strenuously all my values and perceptions. She wants to think that I am just like her father or that I always intended to humiliate her. The facts of the case are that the man and dog apparently set out to cross the Idylwyld Bridge but turned off along the approach and walked into the water, the man a little ahead of the dog. In the news account, the dog is accused of insanity, dereliction of duty and a strangely uncanine malevolence. "Dog Attempts to Drown Man," the headline reads. Libel law prevents speculation on the human victim's mental state, his intentions. The dog is dead, but the tone is jocular. *Dog Attempts to* Drown Man. All of which means that no one knows what happened from the time the man stumbled off the sidewalk on Idylwyld to the time he fell into the river and we are free to invent structures and symbols as we see fit. The man survives, it seems, his strange baptism, his trial by cold and water. I know in my own mind that he appeared exhausted, not merely from the experience of near-drowning, but from before, in spirit, while the dog seemed eager and alert. We know, or at least we can all agree to theorize, that a bridge is a symbol of change (one side to the other, hence death), of connection (the marriage of opposites), but also of separation from the river of life, a bridge is an object of culture. Perhaps man and dog chose together to walk through the pathless snows to the water's edge and throw themselves into uncertainty. The man was blind as are we all; perhaps he sought illumination in the frothing waste. Perhaps they went as old friends. Or perhaps the dog accompanied the man only reluctantly, the man forcing the dog to lead him across the ice. I saw the dog swim to him, saw the man fending the dog off. Perhaps the dog was trying to save its master, or perhaps it was only playing, not understanding in the least what was happening. Whatever's the case my allegiance is with the dog; the man is too human, too predictable. But man and dog together are emblematic — that is my impression at any rate — they are the mind and spirit, the one blind, the other dumb; one defeated, the other naive and hopeful, both forever going out. And I submit that after all the simplified explanations and crude jokes about the blind man and his dog, the act is full of a strange and terrible mystery, of beauty.

My wife and I decide to separate, and then suddenly we are almost happy together. But this was long ago, as was the visit to the Mendel Art Gallery and my time in Saskatoon. And though the moment when Lucy is shaking down her hair and tucking it into her knitted cap goes on endlessly in my head as does the reverberation of that other moment when the dog disappears under the ice, there is much that I have already forgotten. I left Lucy because she was too real, too hungry for love, while I am a dreamer. There are two kinds of courage: the courage that holds things together and the courage that throws them away. The first is more common; it is the cement of civilization; it is Lucy's. The second is the courage of drunks and suicides and mystics. My sign is impurity. By leaving, you understand, I proved that I was unworthy. I have tried to write Lucy since that winter — her only response has been to return my letters unopened. This is appropriate. She means for me to read them myself, those tired, clotted apologies. I am the writer of the words; she knows well enough they are not meant for her. But my words are sad companions and sometimes I remember . . . well . . . the icy water is up to my neck and I hear the ghost dog barking, she tried to warn me; yes, yes, I say, but I was blind.

PATRICK ROSCOE was born on the Spanish Island of Formentera in 1962 and has lived in Tanzania, England, Mexico, Paris, Madrid, and Canada. His publications include *The Lost Oasis, Love Is Starving for Itself, God's Peculiar Care,* and *Beneath the Western Slopes*. This story first appeared in CFM No. 50/51 in 1985, which was later published as the anthology *Moving Off the Map: From 'Story' to 'Fiction'*.

The Scent Of Young Girls Dying

PATRICK ROSCOE

a Petra jacobo de Lizama, con carino

AFTER CHONITA'S HUSBAND DIED, the old woman devoted her days to tending the flowers which grew in such profusion around her modern, white house. As she and Hector had lived in California for a number of years, returning to their home only just before the latter's painful death, the flower garden was gone quite wild. "The poor woman is trying to keep busy and forget her grief," said ladies of the town. Soon the scent of Chonita's roses became remarkably more pronounced and drifted entirely through the town, being strongest in the hours just after and before dark. "How pretty," said the town women, standing in their doorways with folded arms.

After the burial of Hector, Chonita was not heard to mention his name again. She showed no signs of sorrow and shrugged off any sympathy offered to her. For a time she was not observed visiting her late husband's grave.

This was not unusual. The graveyard was neglected. It lay on the edge of town behind a sagging barbed wire fence and beside a road on which many people walked every day. However, except on the infrequent occasions of burials, the townspeople seemed to forget about the graveyard. It was a lonely place and the plastic flowers faded in the sun. Grass grew thickly around the graves, obscuring them, and cement crosses cracked, then tumbled onto the ground. Occasionally one or two of the more civic-minded citizens, seeing it was becoming an eyesore, took an afternoon to slash at the brush. Their machetes glinted in the sun. Sometimes at night the townspeople were woken by wild dogs that came down from the hills to fight over graves.

Chonita seemed as unwilling to visit her fellow townspeople and former friends as she was the graveyard. Her years of absence in California had made her a stranger to her place of birth; it was decided she had acquired airs as well as money. The town ladies took offense and felt slighted by her seclusion.

Chonita's house was surrounded by a tall red iron fence, and no one was invited inside the yard. When the gate was briefly opened, people passing caught sight of masses of roses and witches' broom and japonestas. All day long they heard water splashing against leaves, running through flower beds, flowing into the earth. "Wasteful," commented the women of the town, who viewed ornamental gardening as an odd, and somewhat unwholesome, practise. "Chonita is trying to change God's seasons," the town ladies said. Very quickly their nerves became strained by the sound of water bubbling like a hidden spring behind the fence and the scent of roses wafting unavoidably into their houses.

One day the ladies realized, with a strange suddenness, that the old woman had been visiting the graveyard daily for a number of weeks. Although the visits were made with complete frankness, the town ladies felt that any action that for a time escaped their notice was suspect. They took pride in their keen powers of observation, and were irritated by any failure of them.

Every morning the iron gate clanged shut and Chonita walked through the streets. "Maria! Isabella! Veronica!" she called, and the twelve happiest and most beautiful little girls in town abandoned their mothers' mirrors and their jumping ropes and jacks to run to the old woman. Singing and laughing and clinging to her, the little girls frolicked around Chonita, forming a merry procession that passed to the graveyard. There the little girls skipped among headstones and crosses, and chased each other around and around. They looked like floating flowers, coming to light upon the long grass, then sinking into it in a circle around the old woman.

"Look around you," Chonita exclaimed. "Your grandmothers and aunts and sisters lie suffocating in the ground. I knew these women and girls; they died silently, though in great pain. Now they cry. Listen!" and the grass sighed and sobbed in the wind. "They want us to dig them out, pull the dirt off them, and allow them to breathe the open air again. They want to sit up and stretch themselves, they long to comb out their matted hair."

The little girls sat quietly, their faces made grave by the mournful sound of Chonita's voice. After a little while, they began to fidget. Then they scampered off to play again. The little girls hid behind gravestones, then jumped out at their friends, causing the air to ring with screams of joy and fear. The old woman took a green glass bottle from her bag and held it to her mouth. She spoke soothingly to the women lying beneath her. These sad and buried women called out to the little girls who danced above them. "Play" they cried. "Laugh and play! But remember us who listen beneath you."

Most mornings the town ladies gathered before Dona Lupita's store. They sewed and sat in little chairs on the sidewalk. Now and then the mothers of the girls who accompanied Chonita to the graveyard lifted their heads at the sounds of laughter floating down into the town. Initially these mothers were quite pleased their girls had been chosen by Chonita as her companions; they vaguely believed that somehow a part of the old woman's wealth would rub off on their babies. These hopes rapidly soured. The ladies took exception to the fact that while Chonita would hardly speak a civil word to them, she felt free to waltz off with their daughters whenever she pleased. Because they were somewhat in awe of the rich, proud woman, however, the town ladies were reluctant to confront her directly. They preferred to share their complaints among themselves.

"She should mind her flowers and leave our girls alone," stated a certain Senora Juarez.

"She'll kidnap our babies to the graveyard, yes, but would she deign to bring a single one of her million rosebuds to the Queen of Sapn's grave?"

"Oh, that strange, sweet smell," moaned Senora Aquino, pressing a hand to her brow. "It makes my head hurt so."

"Her precious, freakish flowers," snorted Senora Ortiz. "She grows them just to torment us with their smell, I swear."

"It's unhealthy," cried Senora Martinez, with emotion. "Our daughters will fall into old graves and break their necks. Our beautiful little girls will grow to be sick and sad, and they will wander pale and weeping in the moonlight. They will languish in their beds, and the scent of young girls dying will hang over our town like a dream."

Chonita sat beside a fallen angel and grieved, "Oh, what's become of you?" The angel had crashed down from heaven and lay face pressed into the earth. The old lady dug it out from the dying leaves and crumbled off caked dirt. She polished the white figure with her skirt, then kissed its smooth, blank eyes. The fat, smiling angel rested in her hand, arms floating in frozen flight.

Ravens swayed in the wild, old amapa tree with its arms that drooped down to the ground, its fingertips that brushed the waving grass. In the round house of the tree's shade Chonita sat stiffly, her legs stretched out straight before her, running shoes on her feet, a faded orange peasant dress crumpled around her knees.

Waves of emotion carved the old woman's face. She looked now at the angel, now at the golden-crowns nodding yellow heads nearby. "Oh, how could such a thing have happened?" she cried out suddenly, seeing broken Virgins in distress all around her. Mutilated, crippled, missing an arm, half a leg, their lower portions, they lay stretched helpless in the long grass.

Chonita trembled, listening to the breathing earth. "My daughters," she called, and a dozen heads bobbed over the tall grass toward her. Some were with plastic wreaths.

"Her husband's death unhinged her," said the town ladies. "She drove him into his grave, but she's still not happy. No, she must sit beside his grave, ranting and raving. No peaceful sleep for that poor man."

"But my little Maria says she doesn't even look at Hector's grave," commented Senora Alamena.

"No, she's too busy keeping an eye on the dead and buried women. She's afraid their ghosts will flirt with Hector."

"California changed her," remarked Senora Ortiz. "Since she's returned she thinks she's Susan Hayward, smoking and drinking and wearing slacks."

"Of course, Susan was a redhead," added Senora Obregon, and the other ladies nodded heads in interest.

Senora Martinez couldn't stand it. "Susan's dead!" she screamed. "Cancer took her. But our little girls are alive! Listen," she hissed. "I hear my Francesca whispering to her older and younger sisters, spreading the old woman's tales of tainted love. How will our babies find boys, homes, children?"

"Chonita is placing a curse upon our girls. She is jealous that God never gave her a daughter of her own. Our young girls toss and turn in their sleep, tormented by dreams of tragic love. They call out to be saved. Their hearts are withering before they've ever bloomed."

"Look! I've fallen!" laughed Chonita, lying helpless in the grass. The little girls flocked around her, heaving and pulling, their faces straining and ribbons falling from their hair. Chonita laughed breathlessly, and with the girls skipping around her she passed through weeds and grass and graves.

The old woman halted and tears flowed from her eyes. "Violetta Valquez. As white as a ghost and as pretty as a picture. Her long black hair was as heavy as the cross of Jesus. She died at seventeen. A fishing boy disappeared at sea, and she paced the shore for a hundred nights, her hair blowing in the wind, her nightdress soaked by the spray of crashing waves. Blood spilled from her broken heart, pouring out her throat like red wine upon the white pillow."

The little girls looked at one another in puzzlement, their eyes clouding with questions. When they started to cry they became frightened, because they did not know why they felt so sad. They screamed and wailed. "That's all right," said Chonita, bending over and patting first the grave, then the backs of the sobbing girls.

"Petra Esparza," she lamented, pointing to the ground, though no gravestone stood there. Wild flowers trailed across a slight hollow.

"She married a white-toothed charmer and it killed her, though it took her twenty years to find death. I would hear her screaming for death to come, but he wouldn't. He was as cold-hearted as the rest of them. They hear you crying for them night after night as they steal down dark streets. But they will not come for you." Chonita stood lost in thought, while around her the little girls screamed with high, piercing voices. Their eyes were closed and their faces tilted up to the sky. All at once they fell silent, then turned away as one. They ran through the long grass. Flashing red and yellow in the sun, they played hide and seek, and tag.

The little graveyard girls would not play with the other girls of the town. They walked in a cluster down the streets. Huddled together in the plaza, they threw glances at the men and boys around them. "Senor Marquez," the girls whispered loudly, pointing to an old man asleep on a bench. "He killed his wife. He drank and filled himself with poison. When his wife kissed him all the poison flowed into her. She died for him, while he walks around healthy and strong and looking at other women."

Their mothers heard these words and were filled with passions. Old scandals and secrets long buried were unearthed by this talk, and scenes occurred. "You Devil!" screamed the women. "We were like sisters until you came along. Murderer!"

The next day, their passions abated, the women ran into their houses at the sight of the accused man. "Look at this mess you've got me in!" they scolded their daughters. "I must now hide from my own neighbours. What is next?" they asked their little girls, who gazed raptly into mirrors.

It was a relief when the twelve girls grew old enough to attend school. Their mothers listened with satisfaction as chanted answers to unheard questions rang through the town. The girls would learn to read and write. They would learn that l-o-v-e spells baby and one plus one makes three.

The twelve little girls quickly worked charms upon their teacher, Senor Obesquo, a tall young man both romantic and single. They brought him armfuls of flowers from Chonita's garden every morning.

They sat closely around him, combing his hair, filing his nails, brushing his cheek with their warm breath. The perfume of the flowers and girls stole around Senor Obesquo. In a daze he watched them dance out the doorway of the school before classes had hardly begun, laughing shrilly as they ran hand in hand to the graveyard.

They always found the old woman there, although more and more she left off her sorrowful strolls and sat still beneath the amapa tree. "Clean off Senora Alonza, she is getting so dusty," Chonita implored. "And see how that big thistle is feeding off that slip of a girl over there? Oh, I'm getting too old to care for the dead."

On the other side of the graveyard the girls wandered among the cracked stones and crooked crosses, not seeing the words inscribed to speed young girls to heaven. Their skirts brushing the grass and grasshoppers flying in clouds around them, they discussed romance and love. Sometimes the words carried to the old woman, snatches of song mixing in with her dreams. If he is tall and strong and handsome, she heard. When he kisses you. His lips are soft. And his mouth tastes of honey, the young girls said blades of grass twirling in their mouths and hands. Love hurts, they said pacing, faces turned down to the ground, in prayer.

Isabella lifted her head quickly, like a deer, and saw the sea lying in the distance. They go out in boats. And they don't come back. Though you wait for them, she said a clear, calm voice, brushing her hair from her face.

With crushing feet the girls tramped trails. They made tunnels in the long grass, secret passages that closed behind them. Woken by their words, Chonita looked across the graveyard for the girls. Only tilted crosses rose from the sea of grass, and the graveyard appeared deserted.

At the meeting of the town junta one Sunday it was decided something must be done. "We are concerned," stated a group of women, and an eloquent speech was made on the topic of the sacred dead. The junta agreed that the girls must be kept from the graveyard, although it was not clear how this could be achieved: the town was famous for its headstrong girls and women. "Signs," proposed a Senor Lopez. "Playing In The Graveyard Is Prohibited. That should do the trick." Chonita's name was called out by someone at the back of the crowded Casino. "Which one of us will ask her to stay out of the graveyard?" another voice demanded. At this question the junta fell silent. "Mourning the dead is not a sin," muttered a third voice, before the junta quickly moved on to a new and unrelated topic.

At around this time the girls began going to the graveyard less frequently, although it was widely known that Senor Lopez's signs were not the reason. "Oh, yes, we tore down those stupid signs," laughed the young girls carelessly. They mostly came alone now, Veronica or Isabella or one of the others, walking quickly up to the amapa tree beneath which the old woman sat amid the falling poppies of February.

Upon hearing her name spoken, Chonita turned her head slowly and squinted up at the girl. "You have grown taller and more beautiful," she said musingly. "Yesterday you only wanted to run all the time. Breathlessly you ran with the other girls around and around the plaza. Now all at once you feel tired, too tired to lift your feet. You want to lie in bed all day and cry, though you feel no sadness. You sit in the doorway all night long, fanning yourself with a magazine and waiting to be caught."

The young girl looked quickly and guiltily away from the old lady's bright eyes, and she would not come alone to the graveyard again.

As with every passing season their daughters grew further from Chonita and closer to womanhood, the town ladies lost most of their awe of the old woman. They felt they had defeated her in a battle for their babies. Now when Chonita made the daily journey from her white house to the graveyard she was often accosted by the town ladies.

"Dona Chonita," they said. "You are not going all the way to the graveyard? It is far."

"California is far and Argentina is far," said Chonita. "But the graveyard is close."

"I must have told my Guadalupe to visit you a million times," simpered Senora Ortiz. "But you know how selfish and thoughtless these young girls are. Lupe is exactly the same as I was at her age, wild and boy-crazy as anything. I suppose you miss the girls."

"Old age, it happens," said the ladies, patting curls. "You must find it difficult to take proper care of your flower gardens now. Your roses don't seem to stink so much these days. They haven't died, have they!"

Chonita gave a small smile, then walked slowly on. Passing down the main street, she saw figures sitting motionless on straight-backed chairs, just inside open doorways. The rooms were dark, and the old women stared directly before themselves with blind, black eyes. Chonita remembered girls running through fields, hats with red ribbons falling from their hands. Wait for me, she had called to the older girls who ran in front of her. Next year I will be older and able to run as fast as you. Wait for me, she cried silently to the ghosts of girls dancing before her, beckoning her toward the graveyard.

Sometimes, turning a corner, Chonita found the sidewalk blocked by several of the girls who once had come singing and clinging to her. Now growing tall and curved, they wore uniforms and clutched books to their chests, like shields. They walked in twos or threes, long and shiny hair swinging to the same, secret beat. "Chonita," they said, their smiles sliding slyly past her.

The graveyard fell into a state of greater ruin and the paths worn by the girls became lost in waves of grass. Often the old woman fell asleep beneath the amapa tree in the afternoon heat. She lay there like a splash of red or purple paint. Yellow poppies fell upon her. When she awoke, suddenly, she sat up and in a voice of command called, "My daughters!" After a moment she called again. But no figures emerged from behind the headstones, and the graveyard was still.

One December the girls began to come calling at Chonita's gate in early evening. They passed through tangled flowers and shrubs, which crept closely around the white house, enfolding it. Inside they looked quickly at the glass and bottle on the table, the record turning on the record player. "You have so many things," they said in the blue light of Chonita's bedroom. Small, dust-covered flasks and jars and bottles lay scattered over the dressing table.

"They're all I brought with me from California, and now I can't think why I wanted them. Isn't that funny?" Chonita asked, looking up at the girls from where she sat on the edge of the bed. "Take them," she said, after a moment's silence, and the young girls picked over tubes of lipstick and pots of paint.

"And all these beautiful flowers growing wild. They just grow and die. Oh, Chonita, just one gardenia for my hair!" the girls implored. The old woman snipped the blossoms with scissors.

The girls ran away with their treasures. Chonita looked after them, the scent of gardenias bleeding in the dusk.

Like sleek, wild cats the twelve girls prowled around the plaza at night. Their eyes glittered cruelly, and their fingernails were long and sharp and pointed. Silver paint hooded their eyes, gold powder clung to their cheeks, red lipstick slashed their mouths. Gardenias grew in their hair. The girls wore strange dresses which they fashioned themselves while gathered together in the afternoons. Sparkling and glistening, phosphorescent in the dark, the gowns trailed carelessly across the ground. Plunging backs and necks exposed smooth, glowing skin. "And at their age!" cried old women, shocked.

"What can we do with them?" shrugged their mothers. "They blow cigarette smoke in our faces and laugh. They take after us. They're smart and know what they want, and how to get it, also."

The twelve girls swept like brush fire around the plaza, their mocking laughter and cigarette smoke burning the air. A heady, powerful scent surrounded them, and it caused the plaza to empty quickly. Choking and coughing, most of the townspeople stumbled away, in search of clearer, cooler air.

As evening drew on the laughter of the twelve circling girls became more wild and wicked. Their heavy perfume thickened. Still huddled where they had been all night, the boys of the town cast frightened glances at the smoking girls.

Chonita dreamed she was floating on a sea of scent to a place and time far away and unfamiliar. I don't like it here, she cried in her dream. Carry me back. But the scent died in the air, leaving her stranded.

She woke in complete darkness. The sound of abandoned laughter drifted down upon her. For a moment the old woman lay still, waiting for her familiar scent of her flowers to carry her back to the certainty that she was in her bed, her house, and not some other, distant place. But with the laughter came a strange, unfamiliar scent both deeper and darker than that produced by her flowers.

The old woman sat up and turned to the bedroom window. It was completely covered by leaves and blossoms of climbing rosebushes. Chonita pushed her face into the flowers and breathed deeply.

She went out in the hot, shiny night. Her candle bobbed through the back yard, around all sides of the house, and out on the road at front. By the flame Chonita saw her flowers reaching upward.

Other women, also woken by the reckless laughter, looked from bedroom windows and saw Chonita's candle dancing in the dark. What is that old woman looking for? they wondered. Their eyes passed to their daughters' empty beds, then turned in the direction of the graveyard, and to the lights weaving there.

As the solitary woman grew more alone, the gate to her yard was opened less often. However, the people of the town saw Chonita's rosebushes grow above the fence, then trail over it. Glad to be diverted from a growing anxiety over their girls, the town ladies for a time showed renewed interest in the old woman. "At last we see her famous flowers, but that's not enough," said the mothers of the twelve girls. "Visit Chonita and tell us: Is her house clean? are the bottles empty?"

"Oh, leave us alone," snapped the twelve girls. They sat long hours before mirrors, examining their beauty with troubled eyes. They were nervous and irritable, and spent the days in bed.

Aching heads made their mothers moan. "Perhaps," they suggested timidly, "you might wear a little less perfume. We can't even smell Chonita's roses anymore. Your scent is pretty, but it's too strong, darlings."

"I wear no perfume," cried each of the girls. "There goes Chonita now," they sobbed. They ran from windows and fell crying into chairs.

The road to the graveyard was becoming long. Once arrived there Chonita was too tired to walk among the stones and raise the fallen Virgins. Angels lay buried in the grass. Chonita sat in silence with the dead, her eyes wandering slowly from grave to grave.

When she took a few steps around the graveyard Chonita found bright, lost buttons, torn scraps of silk, broken bottles, wilted gardenia blossoms. She came upon places where the grass was flattened, as though graves large enough for two had been dug in it.

Now and then she stayed beneath the poppy tree until after dark. Upon returning to town, she found the main street brightly lit by streetlamps and music and calling children. It seemed she had been gone far away and for a long time, and the townspeople looked at her as they would at an unexpected and unwanted visitor.

When Maria died in childbirth at fifteen the ladies of the town shook their heads. "A woman's life is not easy," they said to one another. "Such is our lot." In the graveyard they wept and sang and prayed beneath dripping torches all through one night. Men smoked and drank, and empty bottles smashed against gravestones.

Isabella wandered out to sea one moonless night. Her filmy white dress floated around her in the dark water, covering her like a shroud as she sank.

The town was filled with tragedy as the twelve most beautiful girls died one by one. "Stay safe inside the house," mothers of the surviving girls implored. "Soon you will grow older, and the dangers will pass you by." However, the surviving girls would not understand their mothers words of caution. They did not appear to grieve for their dead friends, or even notice that they no longer were. Their finery grew finer, their smiles more cruel, their eyes more glittering. As they swept heedlessly around the plaza at night the air had an increasingly unbearable scent. The square was no longer the favourite place of relaxation for the townspeople, and even bats and owls deserted it.

Many people became frightened of the girls with their doomed laughter and poisoned kisses. Mothers warned sons. Yet the boys of the town were compellingly drawn to the condemned girls, and at night the plaza was crowded also with boys from neighbouring villages, and from even the capital city across the mountains. The dying young girls became famous throughout the entire state. The noises from the graveyard in the hours after midnight turned more wild and raucous, and in the town below people shuddered in their beds.

The young girls died quickly or slowly, and in all different ways. They fell suddenly in the plaza, toppling into gardenia bushes; they gasped and screamed for weeks in bed with strange chills and fevers. Several simply drifted off to sleep and never woke.

The town became immersed in the subject of young girls dying. Talk centered around diseases and accidents and details of funerals.

Mothers of girls still living accepted the inevitable and planned ahead for their attempts to outdo the others in terms of daughters' deaths. Each woman lavished mourning parties, sumptuous funeral feasts, and fashionable gowns of grief. Black became the most popular colour in town, and a mood of festivity prevailed.

A steady hammering sound descended from the graveyard during the daytime. Hearing it, the townspeople felt the pride of progress. At last their town was growing! The mothers of girls dead or dying sunk all available cash into the creation of splendid monuments to their babies' memories; most spent more than they could actually afford. "When you think about it, it's not so much," they reasoned. "Imagine how much it would have cost to feed and clothe and keep happy my poor darling for fifty years." The townspeople agreed with this logic one hundred per cent.

Chonita abandoned the graveyard to the carpenters and masons and mourning mothers, and remained almost always inside her red iron fence. In its excitement over the dying girls, the town had largely forgotten the old woman's existence. On the rare occasions when she ventured out into the streets, Chonita walked unnoticed as a ghost.

The light in her house was green and gloomy even on the brightest days. Leaves and blossoms pushed through the windows. As the rosebushes grew more thickly around her house, Chonita was drugged into drowsiness by their sweet, sickly smell. The uncontrolled growth was making it difficult to enter or leave the house.

Chonita listened to the screams of death and blows of hammers filtering through the plants which surrounded her. She began spending several hours daily pruning the rosebushes, and she halted the flow of water to their roots. It was quickly evident, however, that these actions did not stunt, but actually encouraged growth in her plants. Sometimes, after several drinks, Chonita staggered outside with an axe. She swung at the thick, twisted trunks of the rosebushes. But the wood was like iron, the old woman had grown too weak, and she dropped crying into the dark dirt littered with fallen petals.

At nights Chonita lay gasping for air. The wild roses trailed across her bedroom. The old woman had waking nightmares about vines growing like ropes around her and binding her forever. As she tossed in her bed, she often pierced herself upon thorns, staining the white sheets red. She felt the thick scent fill her, the way water must fill drowning lungs.

Nightly the cries from the graveyard sounded more loudly. Dragging herself from her bed of green leaves and red rose petals, Chonita pushed aside the thick growth blocking the window. The graveyard lay brightly in the distance. Music mixed with laughter and drunken shouts and cheers spilled down into the town. Another girl was being buried.

Chonita heard a furtive scuffling, a snipping sound, then footsteps fleeing. Going to the gate and opening it, she saw strangers running down the road, blossoms overflowing from their arms. Those flowers which bled over and hung outside her fence had been picked.

When she walked through the town the next day, Chonita could scarcely recognize it. Strangers in city clothes and carrying cameras about everywhere. Men stood at corners, with baskets of flowers at their feet. "Fifty pesos!" they shouted. "The scent of young girls dying! The most beautiful fragrance in the world! The blossoms that adorned the hair of the lovely Isabella Innocence! In memory of the glamorous Violetta Valquez!"

Women of the town knocked into Chonita, then hurried on. They ran up and down the crowded road, and in little circles. They wept out loud and wrung their hands. Falling upon strangers, they soaked shoulders with their tears. Then they lifted their faces, they became animated. "There are still three left, you know, but we have no hope. They say the governor himself will attend the funeral of the twelfth. Oh, it will be a grand affair. We have no hope, we have no hope!" they cried, running down the street.

When eleven of the doomed girls had died and only one remained, she was watched expectantly. As this last girl, Veronica, walked through the streets, people stared at her, called out to her, took her picture. At any moment it was assumed she would fall dead into the dirt. Sometimes she was shaken from sleep in the middle of the night when her anxious mother believed she had ceased breathing. There was an air of impatience in the town, which quickly turned to disappointment as time went by and Veronica would not die. Certain citizens felt the girl was thwarting their hopes deliberately and out of meanness; on one occasion a group of masked figures gathered in the dead of night before her family's house, chanting that she had an obligation and a duty to die.

Veronica grew to be as healthy as a horse. She turned into a dull and listless girl, prone to plumpness. Since all her girlfriends had died, she spent most of her time with her mother, pounding dough for tortillas, beating clothes clean in the sink. For a while curious strangers occasionally came to see "the last of the twelve," as she was called; but invariably they went away disappointed. Veronica had abandoned her finery and exotic ways, and little trace remained of the panther of a girl who had run wild in a pack of twelve. The flower vendors and city people melted into thin air, and for the most part the townspeople reverted back to their old habits of daily life. There was no more talk of a visit by the governor, and as months passed it was generally forgotten that Veronica had at one time been "one of the twelve."

She renewed her friendship with Chonita. Every afternoon she entered the iron gate, emerging some hours later with a flushed face. "We sit, we talk, we look at the flowers," was the girl's only answer to the questions of the town ladies. "I would like to marry now," Veronica announced one day, and in time her parents found her a nice, steady boy.

The graveyard was changed. It was now the favourite gathering place of the town ladies. They sat with their sewing and talked there through afternoons, often in neglect of household duties. The town junta elected several men to caretake the graveyard, and it became a neat and pretty place. Weeds were cut, grass trimmed, and fallen Virgins restored to a more fitting state. Several benches were installed.

The ladies always sat near one or another of the eleven magnificent graves which dwarfed over the site, and as they spoke their voices drifted down into the town. The eleven mothers of girls who had died young formed a kind of clique among the town ladies. "When my Rosario died," was the frequent beginning of conversations. "She was never more beautiful than at the last moment," it was averred. "It was the most fantastic sight! The cigarette fell, and in one second her dress became a ball of fire!" The ladies would shake their heads with sad pleasure, stitching and sewing while ravens swayed in the amapa tree above them. Now and then the ladies lifted their eyes from their handiwork. Breathing the clean, fresh air deeply, they looked at the graveyard. It was always so pretty when the sun began to set!

The house of flowers, they came to call Chonita's place. Roses and gardenias and japonestas grew more wildly in her yard, until they completely obscured the white dwelling. The old woman sat in her back yard, looking at the flowers and listening to water drip through the leaves. Veronica's babies tumbled over her. Dripping with sweat in the hot afternoon, the plump young matron wielded the machete. "They grow so quickly," marvelled the old woman, bouncing babies on her knees. "If you could just trim those bushes over there," she murmured, pointing. After Veronica and the babies left, Chonita burned the clippings in a fire beside her tall papaya tree. She stared raptly into the flames.

Sometimes she was startled by a woman's voice calling at her gate. "Dona Chonita, Dona Chonita, have you some roses for poor Guadalupe's grave?"

The old woman's face was inscrutable as she left the fire and cut an armful of blossoms. His scissors glinted in the sun. The mother of the young dead girl held the flowers to her face, then looked as though she had been tricked. "These blossoms have no scent! They used to make me dizzy a mile away! What happened?"

ROHINTON MISTRY was born in Bombay, India and now lives in Brampton, Ontario. His publications include *Tales from Firozsha Baag, Such a Long Journey,* for which he received the Governor General's Award for Fiction in 1991, and *A Fine Balance,* which was nominated for the Booker Prize. This story first appeared in CFM No. 50/51 in 1985, which was later published as the anthology *Moving Off the Map: From 'Story' to 'Fiction'.*

Condolence Visit

ROHINTON MISTRY

YESTERDAY had been the tenth day, *dusmoo,* after the funeral of Minocher Mirza. Dusmoo prayers were prayed at the fire-temple, and the widow Mirza awaited with apprehension the visitors who would troop into her house over the next few weeks. They would come to offer their condolences, share her grief, poke and pry into her life and Minocher's with a thousand questions. And to gratify them with answers she would have to relive the anguish of the most trying days of her life.

The more tactful ones would wait for the first month, maasiso, to elapse before besieging her with sympathy and comfort. But not the early birds; they would come flocking from today. It was open season, and Minocher Mirza had been well-known in the Parsi community of Bombay.

After a long and troubled illness, Minocher had suddenly eased into a condition resembling a state of convalescence. Minocher and Daulat had both quietly understood that it was only a spurious convalescence, there would be no real recovery. All the same, they were thankful his days and nights passed in relative comfort. Minocher had been able to wait for death freed from the agony which had racked his body for the past several months. And as it so often happens in such cases, along with relief from physical torment, the doubts and fears which had tortured his mind released their hold as well. He was at peace with his being which was soon to be snuffed out. Daulat, too, felt at peace because her one fervent prayer was being answered. Minocher would be allowed to die with dignity, without being reduced to something less than human; she would not have to witness any more of his suffering.

Thus Minocher had passed away in his sleep after six days spent in an inexplicable state of grace and tranquility. Daulat had cried for the briefest period; she felt it would be sinful to show anything but gladness when he had been so fortunate in his final days.

Now, however, the wretched practice of condolence visits would make her regurgitate months of endless pain, nights spent sleeplessly while she listened for his breath, his groans, his vocalization of the agony within. For bearers of condolences and sympathies she would have to answer questions about the illness, about doctors and hospitals, about nurses and medicines. She would be requested, tenderly but tenaciously, as though it was their entitlement, to recreate the hell her beloved Minocher had suffered, instead of being allowed to hold on to the memory of those final, blessed six days. The worst of it would be the repetition of details for different visitors at different hours on different days, until that intensely emotional time she had been through with Minocher would be reduced to a dry and dull lesson learned from a textbook which she would parrot like a schoolgirl.

Last year, Daulat's nephew, Sarosh, the Canadian immigrant who now answered to the name of Sid, had arrived from Montreal for a visit. He had brought her a portable cassette recorder, remembering her fondness for music, so she could tape her favourite songs from All-India-Radio's two Western music programmes: "Merry Go Round" and "Saturday Date." But Daulat had refused it, saying "I listen to music, and poor Minocher sick in bed? Never." She would not change her mind despite Sarosh-Sid's recounting of the problems he had had getting it through Bombay Customs.

Now she wished she had accepted the gift. It could be handy, she thought with bitterness, to tape the details, to squeeze all of her and Minocher's suffering inside the plastic case, and proffer it to the visitors who came propelled by custom and convention. When they held out their right hands in the condolence-handshake position (fingertips of left hand tragically supporting right elbow, as though the right arm, overcome with grief, could not make it on its own) she could thrust towards them the cassette and recorder: "You have come to ask about my life, my suffering, my sorrow? Here, take and listen. Listen on the machine, everything is there on tape. How my Minocher fell sick, where it started to pain, how much it hurt, what doctor said, what specialist said, what happened in hospital. This button? Is for Rewind. Some part you like, you can hear it again, hear it ten times if you want: how nurse gave wrong medicine but luckily my Minocher, sharp even in sickness, noticed different colour pills and told her to check; how wardboy always handled the bedpan savagely and shoved it underneath as if he was doing sick people a big favour; how Minocher was afraid when time came for sponge bath because they were so careless and rough — it felt like number three sandpaper on his bedsores, my brave Minocher would joke. What? This FF button? Means Fast Forward. If some part bores you, just press FF and tape will turn to something else: like how in hospital Minocher's bedsores became so terrible it would bring tears to my eyes to look, all filled with pus and a bad smell on him all the time, even after sponge bath, so that I begged of doctor to let me take him home; how at home I changed his dressing four times a day using sulfa ointment, and in two weeks bedsores were almost gone; how, as time went by and he got worse, his friends stopped coming when he needed them most, friends like you, now listening to this tape. Huh? This letter P? Stands for Pause. Press it if you want to shut off machine and ask more details of your friend Minocher's suffering . . ."

Daulat stopped herself. Ali, the bitter thoughts of a tired old woman. But of what use? It was better not to think of these visits which were as inevitable as Minocher's death. The only way out was to lock up the flat and live elsewhere for the next few weeks. Perhaps at a boarding house in Udwada, town of the most sacrosanct of all firetemples. But though her choice of place would be irreproachable, the timing of her trip would generate the most virulent gossip and criticism the community was capable of, to weather which she possessed neither the strength nor the audacity. The visits would have to be suffered, just as Minocher had suffered his sickness, with forbearance.

The doorbell startled Daulat. This early in the morning could not bring a condolence visitor. The clock was about to strike nine as she went to the door.

Her neighbour Najamai glided in, as fluidly as the smell of slightly rancid fat that always trailed her. Today it was supplemented by curry masala, Daulat realized, as the odours found and penetrated her nostrils. It was usually possible to tell what Najamai had been cooking; she carried a bit of her kitchen with her wherever she went.

Although about the same age as Daulat, widowhood had descended much earlier upon Najamai, turning her into an authority on the subject of religious-rituals-and-the-widowed-woman. This had never bothered Daulat before. But the death of Minocher offered Najamai unlimited scope and she had made the best of it, besetting and bombarding Daulat with advice on topics ranging from items she should pack in her valise for the four-day Towers of Silence vigil, to the recommended diet during the first ten days of mourning. Suddenly Najamai had metamorphosed into an unbearable nuisance. But her counseling service had to close shop with completion of the death rituals, and Daulat was again able to regard her in the old way, with a mixture of tolerance and mild dislike.

"Forgive me for ringing your bell so early in the morning but I wanted to let you know, if you need chairs or glasses, just ask me."

"Thanks, but no one will come — "

"No, no, you see, yesterday was *dusmoo*, I am counting carefully. How quickly ten days have gone! People will start visiting from today, believe me. Poor Minocher, so popular, he had so many friends, they will all visit — "

"Yes, they will," said Daulat, interrupting what threatened to turn into an early morning prologue to a condolence visit.

Najamai, meanwhile had spied Minocher' pugree.

"Oh, that's so nice, so shiny and black, in such good condition!" she rhapsodized.

It really was an elegant piece of headgear, and many years ago Minocher had purchased a glass display case for it. Daulat had brought it out into the living room this morning.

Najamai continued: "You know, pugrees are so hard to find these days, this one would bring a lot of money. But you must never sell it, never. It is your Minocher's, so always keep it." With these exhortatory words, she prepared to leave. Her eyes wandered around the flat for a last minute scrutiny, the sort that evoked mild dislike for her in Daulat.

"You must be very busy today, so I'll —" Najamai turned towards Minocher's bedroom and halted in mid-sentence, in consternation: "O *baap* ra! The lamp is still burning! Beside Minocher's bed — that's wrong, very wrong!"

"I forgot all about it," lied Daulat, feigning dismay. "I was so busy. Thanks for reminding. I'll put it out."

But she had no such intention. When Minocher had breathed his last, the family priest had been summoned, who gave her careful instructions on what was expected of her. The first and most important thing, the *dastoorji* had said, was to light a small oil lamp at the head of Minocher's bed; this lamp, he said, must burn for four days and nights, no more and no less, while prayers were performed at the Towers of Silence. But the little oil lamp became a source of comfort in a house grown quiet and empty for the lack of one silent feeble man, one shadow. She kept the lamp lit past the prescribed four days, replenishing it constantly with coconut oil.

"Didn't *dastoorji* tell you?" asked Najamai. "For the first four days the soul comes to visit here. The lamp is there to welcome the soul. But after four days, prayers are all complete, you know, and the soul must now quickly-quickly go to the next world. If the lamp is still burning the soul will be attracted to two different places — here, and the next world. You must put it out, you are confusing the soul," Najamai earnestly concluded.

Nothing can confuse my Minocher, thought Daulat, he will go where he has to go. Aloud she said, "I'll put it out right away."

"Good, good," said Najamal, "and oh, I almost forgot to tell you, I have lots of cold-drink bottles, Limca and Goldspot, if you need them."

What does she think, I'm giving a party the day after *dusmoo*? thought Daulat. In the bedroom she poured more oil in the glass, determined to keep the lamp lit as long as she felt the need. Only, the bedroom door must stay closed, so the tug-of-war between two worlds, with Minocher's soul in the middle, would not provide sport for visitors.

She sat in the armchair next to what had been Minocher's bed and watched the steady, unflickering flame of the oil-lamp. Like Minocher, she thought, reliable and always there; how lucky I was to have such a husband. No bad habits, did not drink, did not go to the racecourse, did not give me any trouble. Ali, but he made up for it when he fell sick. How much worry he caused me then, while he still had the strength to argue and fight back. Would not eat his food, would not take his medicine, would not let me help with anything.

In the lamp glass coconut oil, because it was of the unrefined type, rested golden-hued on water, a natant disc. With a pure, sootless flame the wick floated, a little raft upon the gold. And Daulat, looking for answers to difficult questions, stared at the flame. Slowly, across the months, borne upon the flame-raft, came the incident of the Ostermilk tin. It came without the anger and frustration she had known then, it came in a new light. And she could not help smiling as she remembered.

It had been the day of the monthly inspection for bedbugs. Due to the critical nature of this task, Daulat tackled it with a zeal unreserved for anything else. She worked side by side with the servant. Minocher had been made comfortable on the armchair and the mattress was turned over. The servant removed the slats, one by one, while Daulat, armed with a torch, examined every crack and corner. Then she was ready to spray the mixture of Flit and Tik-20, and pulled at the handle of the pump. But before plunging it in to poison every potential redoubt of *cimex lectularius,* she glimpsed, between the bedpost and the wall, a large tin of Ostermilk on the floor. The servant dived under to retrieve it. The tin was shut tight, she had to pry the lid open with a spoon. And as it came off, there rose a stench powerful enough to rip to shreds the hardy nostrils of a latrine-basket collector. She quickly replaced the lid, fanning the air vigorously with her hand. Minocher seemed to be dozing off, olfactory nerves unaffected. Was he trying to subdue a smile? The tin without its lid was placed outside the back door, in hopes that the smell would clear in a while.

The bedbug inspection was resumed and the Flitting finished without further interruption. Minocher's bed was soon ready, and he fell asleep in it.

The smell of the Ostermilk tin had now lost its former potency. Daulat squinted at the contents: a greyish mass of liquids and solids, no recognizable shapes or forms amongst them. With a stick she explored the gloppy, sloppy mess. Familiar objects began to emerge gradually, greatly transmogrified but retaining enough of their original state to agitate her. She was now able to discern a square of fried egg, exhume a piece of toast, fish up an orange pip. So! This is what he did with his food! How could he get better if he did not eat. Indignation drove her back to his bedroom. She refused to be responsible for him if he was going to behave in this way. Sickness or no sickness, I will have to tell him straight.

But Minocher was fast asleep, snoring gently. Like a child, she thought, and her anger had melted away. She did not have the heart to waken him; he had spent all night tossing and turning. Let him sleep. But from now on I will have to watch him carefully at mealtimes.

In the armchair beside the oil-lamp Daulat returned to the present. Talking to visitors of such things would not be difficult. But they would be made uncomfortable, not knowing whether to laugh or keep the condolence-visit-grimness upon their faces. The Ostermilk tin would have to remain their secret, hers and Minocher's. As would the oxtail soup, whose turn it now was to come sailing silently out of the past, on the golden discused flame-raft of Minocher's lamp.

At the meat market Daulat and Minocher had always argued about oxtail, which neither had ever eaten. Minocher wanted to try it, but she would say with a little shudder, "See how they hang like snakes. How can you even think of eating that? It will bring bad luck, I won't cook it."

He called her superstitious. But oxtail remained a dream deferred for Minocher. After his illness began, Daulat shopped alone, and at the butcher's she would remember Minocher's penchant for trying new things. She was often tempted to buy oxtail and surprise him — something different might revive his now almost-dead appetite. But the thought of bad luck associated with all things serpentine dissuaded her each time. Finally, when Minocher had entered the period of his pseudo-convalescence, he awakened on the second day after a peaceful night and said, "Do me a favour?" Daulat nodded, and he smiled wickedly. "Make oxtail soup." And that day, they lunched on what had made her cringe for years, the first hearty meal for both since the illness had commenced.

Daulat rose from the armchair. It was time now to carry out the idea she had had yesterday, walking past the Old-Age Home For Parsi Men on her way back from the fire-temple. If Minocher could, he would want her to give away his clothes, as he had often done. Many were the times he had gone through his wardrobe selecting things he did not need or wear anymore, wrapped them in brown paper and string, and carried them to the Home for distribution.

Beginning with the ordinary items of everyday wear, she started to sort his clothes: *sudras*, underwear, two spare *hustees*, sleeping suits, light cotton shirts for wearing around the house. She decided to make parcels right away — why wait for the prescribed year or six months or even a month and deny the need of the old men at the Home if she could (and Minocher certainly could) give today?

When the first heap of clothing took its place upon brown paper spread out on his bed, something wrenched inside her. The way it had wrenched when he had been pronounced dead by the doctor. Then it passed, as it had passed before. She concentrated on the clothes; one of each in every parcel: *sudra*, underpants, sleeping suit, shirt, would make it easier to distribute.

Bent over the bed, she worked unaware of her shadow on the wall, cast by the soft light of the oil-lamp. Though the curtainless window was open, the room was half-dark because the sun was on the other side of the flat. But half-dark was light enough in this room into which had been concentrated her entire universe for the duration of Minocher's and her ordeal. Every little detail in this room she knew intimately: the slivered edge of the first compartment of the chest of drawers where a *sudra* could snag, she knew to avoid; the little trick, to ease out the shirt-drawer which always stuck, she was familiar with; the special way to wiggle the key in the lock of the Godrej cupboard she had mastered a long time ago.

The Godrej steel cupboard Daulat tackled next. This was the difficult one, containing the "going-out" clothes: suits, ties, silk shirts, fashionable bush shirts, including some foreign ones given by her Canadian nephew, Sarosh-Sid, and the envy of Minocher's friends. This cupboard would be the hard one to empty out, with each garment holding memories of parties and New Year's Eve dances, weddings and *navjotes*. Strung out on the hangers and spread out on the shelves were the chronicles of their life together, beginning with the Parsi formal dress Minocher had worn on the day of their wedding: silk *dugli,* white silk shirt, and the magnificent pugree in its glass case in the living room.

She went to it now and opened the case. The pugree gleamed the way it had forty years ago. How grand he had looked then, with it splendidly seated on his head! There was only one other occasion when he had worn it since, on the wedding of Sarosh-Sid, who had been like a son to them. Sarosh's papers had arrived from the Canadian High Commission in New Delhi, and three months after the wedding he had emigrated with his brand new wife. Minocher had wanted Sarosh to wear the pugree who, however, had insisted, like so many modern young men, on an English styled doublebreasted suit. So Minocher had worn it instead. Pugree-making had become a lost art due to young men like Sarosh, but Minocher had known how to take care of his. Hence its mint condition.

Daulat took the pugree into the next room and looked for the advertisement she had clipped out of the Jame-jamshed. It had appeared six days ago, on the morning after she had returned from the Towers of Silence: "Wanted — a pugree in good condition. Phone no. —" Yesterday Daulat had called the number, the advertiser was still looking. He was coming today to inspect Minocher's pugree.

The doorbell rang. It was again Najamai from next door. In her wake followed her servant, Ramchandra, lugging four chairs of the stackable type. Her rancid-fat-curry-masala smell was embroidered by the attar of Ramchandra's hair oil, and the combination made Daulat wince.

"Forgive me for disturbing you again, I was just now leaving with Ramchandra, many-many things to do today. And there is no one at home if you need chairs so I brought them now only. That way you will . . ."

Daulat had stopped listening. Good thing the bedroom door was shut, or Najamai would have started another oil-lamp exegesis. Would this garrulous busybody never leave her alone? There were chairs in the diningroom which could be brought out.

With Sarosh-Sid's cassette recorder, she could have made a tape for Najamai too. It would be a simple one to make with many pauses during which Najamai did all the talking: Neighbour Najamai Take

One "Hullo, come in (long pause) ... hmm ... right (short pause) ... yes yes ... that's okay (long pause) ... right, right ..." It would be no trouble, compared to the tape for condolence visitors.

"... you are listening, no? So chairs you can keep as long as you like, don't worry, Ramchandra can bring them back after a month, two months, after friends and relatives stop coming. Come on, Ramu, come, we're getting late."

Daulat shut the door and withdrew into her flat. Into the silence of the flat where moments of life past and forgotten, moments lost, misplaced, hidden away, were waiting to be recovered. They were like the stubs of cinema tickets she came across in Minocher's trouser pockets or jacket, wrung through the laundry, crumpled and worn thin, but still decipherable. Or like the old programme for a concert at Scot's Kirk by the Max Mueller Society of Bombay, found in a purse fallen, like Scot's Kirk, into desuetude. On the evening of the concert, Minocher, with a touch of sarcasm, had quipped: Indian audience listens to Germans perform German music inside a church built by skirted men from Scotland — truly Bombay is a cosmopolitan city. The encore had been *Für Elise*. The music passed through her mind now, in the silent flat: the beginning in A minor, full of sadness and nostalgia and yearning for times gone by; then the modulation into C major, with its offer of hope and understanding. This music was like a person remembering — if you could hear the sound of the workings of memory, *Für Elise* is what it would sound like.

Remembering suddenly seemed extremely important, like some deep-seated need surfacing, manifesting itself in Daulat's flat. All her life those closest to her had reminisced about events from their lives; she, the audience, had listened, sometimes rapt, sometimes impatient. Grandmother would sit her down and tell stories from years gone by; the favourite one was about her marriage and the elaborate matchmaking that preceded it. Mother would talk about her Girl Guide days, with a faraway look in her eyes; she still had her dark blue Girl Guide satchel frayed and faded.

When grandmother had died no music was allowed in the house for three months. Even the neighbours had silenced their radios and gramophones for ten days. Daulat's brothers were forbidden to play cricket in the compound outside the building for a month, and they had taken it very hard. After sulking around the house for a while they tried to interest themselves in reading, the only activity that seemed suitable enough for a house in mourning. A few days passed and the two were captivated by the world of books, which was probably the best thing grandmother had done for her grandsons. During this time, Daulat's mother introduced her to kitchen and cooking — there was now room for one more in that part of the flat. With the exception of oxtail soup, Daulat had learned the various dishes. And when Minochers's belly, on his deathbed, craved oxtail soup, she quickly learned that dish as well.

Daulat had become strangers with her radio shortly after Minocher's illness had started. But the childhood proscription against music racked her with guilt whenever a strand of melody strayed into her room from the outside world. Minocher's favourite song was "At the Balalaika." During their courtship he had taken her to see *Balalaika*, starring Nelson Eddy, at a morning show. It was playing at the Eros Cinema, and Minocher had been surprised that she'd never seen it before. It was his fourth time. How did the song ... she hummed it, out of tune: At the Balalaika, one summer night a table laid for two, was just a private heaven made for two ...

The wick of the oil lamp crackled. It did this when the oil was low. She fetched the bottle and filled up the glass, shaking out the last drop, then placed the bottle on the windowsill: a reminder to replenish the oil.

Outside, the peripatetic vendors had started to arrive. The potato and onion man got louder as he approached: "Onions rupee a kilo, potatoes two rupees," faded as he went past, to the creaking obligato of his thirsty-for-lubrication cart. He was followed by the fishwalli, the eggman, the brato: biscuitwalla; and the ragman who sang with a sonorous vibrato:

Of old saris and old clothes I am collector
Of new plates and bowls in exchange I am giver ...

From time to time, B.E.S.T. buses thundered past and all sounds were drowned out. Finally came the one Daulat was waiting for. She waved the empty bottle at the oilwalla, purchased a quarter litre, and arranged with him to knock at her door every alternate day. She was not yet sure when she would be ready to let the lamp go out.

The clock showed half past four as she went in with the bottle. Minocher's clothes lay in neat brown paper packages, ready for the Old-Age Home. She shut the doors of the cupboards now almost empty, and thought, the clothes it takes a man a lifetime to wear and enjoy can be parcelled away in hours.

The man would soon arrive to see Minocher's pugree. She wondered what it was that had made him go to the trouble of advertising. Perhaps she should never have telephoned. Unless he had a good reason she was not going to part with it. Definitely not if he was just a collector.

The doorbell. Must be him, she thought, and looked through the peep-hole.

But standing outside were second cousin Moti and her two grandsons. Moti had not been at the funeral. Daulat did not open the door immediately. She could hear her admonishing the two little boys: "Now you better behave properly or I will not take you anywhere ever again. And if she gives you Goldspot or Vimto or something, be polite and leave some in the glass. Don't drink it all unless you want a pasting when you get home."

Daulat had heard enough. She opened the door and Moti, laden with eau-de-cologne, fell on her neck with woeful utterances and tragic tones. "O Daulat, Daulat! What an unfortunate thing to happen to you! O very wrong thing has come to pass! Poor Minocher gone! Forgive me for not coming to the funeral, but Peshotan's gout was so painful that day. Completely impossible. I said to Peshotan, least I can do now is visit you as soon as possible after *dusmoo.*"

Daulat nodded, tried to look grateful for the sympathy Moti was so desperate to offer. It was almost time to reach for her imaginary cassette player.

"Before you start thinking what a stupid woman I am to bring two little boys to a condolence visit, I must tell you there was no one at home they could stay with. And we never leave them alone. It is so dangerous. You heard about that vegetablewalla in Pherozeshah Baag? Broke into a flat, strangled a child, stole everything. Cleaned it out completely. *Parvar Daegar!* Save us from such wicked madmen!"

Daulat led the way into the living room, and Moti sat on the sofa. The two boys occupied Najamai's loaned chairs. The bedroom door was open just a crack, revealing the oil-lamp with its steady unwavering flame. Daulat shut it quickly lest Moti should notice and comment about the unorthodoxy of her source of comfort.

"Did he suffer much before the end? I heard from Rati — you know Rati, sister of Eruch Uncle's son-in-law Shapoor — she was at the funeral, she told me poor Minocher was in great pain the last few days."

Daulaut reached in her mind for the Start Switch of the cassette player but Moti continued: "Couldn't the doctors do something to help? From what we hear these days, they can do almost anything."

"Well," said Daulat, "Our doctor was very helpful, but it was a hopeless case, he told me."

"You know, I was reading in *Indian Express* last week that doctors in China were able to make" — here, Moti lowered her voice in case the grandsons were listening, shielded her mouth with one hand, and pointed to her lap with the other — "a man's Part. His girlfriend ran off with another man and he was very upset. So he chopped off" — in a whisper — "his own Part, in frustration, and flushed it down the toilet. Later he regretted it in hospital, and God knows how, but the doctors made for him" — in a whisper again — "a New Part, out of his own skin and all. They say it works and everything. Isn't that amazing?"

"Yes, very interesting," said Daulat, relieved that Moti had, at least temporarily, forsaken the prescribed condolence visit questioning.

The doorbell again. Must be the young man for the pugree this time.

But in stepped ever-solicitous Najamai. "Sorry, sorry. Very sorry, didn't know you had company. Just wanted to let you know I was back. In case you need anything." Then leaning closer conspiratorially, rancid-fat-curry-masala odours overwhelming Daulat, she whispered, "Good thing, no, I brought the extra chairs."

Daulat calculated quickly. If Najamai stayed, Moti would drift even further from the purpose of her visit. Najamai would also be pleased. So she invited her to sit. "Come in, please, meet my second cousin Moti. And these are her grandsons. Moti was just now telling me a very interesting case about doctors in China who made" — copying Moti's whisper — "a New Part for a man."

"A new part? But that's nothing new. They do it here also now, putting artificial arms-legs and little things inside heart to make blood pump properly."

"No no," said Moti. "Not a new part. This was" — in a whisper, dramatically pointing again to her lap for Najamai's benefit.

"And he can do everything with it. It works. Chinese doctors made it."

"Oh!" said Najamai, understanding everything. "A New Part!"

Daulat left the two women and went to the kitchen to open a bottle of Goldspot for the children. The kettle was ready and she poured three cups of tea. While she arranged the tray, the doorbell rang, for the third time. This had to be the young man. She was ready to abandon the tray and go to the door but Najamai called out, "It's all right, I'll open it, don't worry. Finish what you are doing."

Najamai said "Yes?" to the young man standing outside the door.

"Are you Mrs. Mirza?"

"No no, but come in. Daulat! There's a young man here asking for you."

Daulat settled the tray on the teapoy before the sofa and went to the door. "You're here to see the pugree. Please come in and sit." He took one of Najamai's loaned chairs.

Najamai and Moti exchanged glances. Come for the pugree? What was going on?

The young man felt obliged to say something. "Mrs. Mirza is selling Mr. Mirza's pugree to me. You see, my fiancee and I, we decided to do everything the proper traditional way at our wedding In correct Parsi dress and all."

Daulat heard him explain in the next room and felt relieved. It was going to be alright, parting with the pugree would not be difficult. The young man's reasons would have made Minocher exceedingly happy.

But Najamai and Moti were aghast. Minocher's pugree being sold and the man barely digested by vultures at the Towers of Silence! Najamai decided to take charge. She took a deep breath, tilted her chin pugnaciously. "Look here, *bawa,* it's very nice to see you want to do it the proper way. So many young men are doing it in suits and ties these days. Why, one wedding I went to, the boy was wearing a shiny black suit with lacey, frilly-frilly shirt and bow tie. Exactly like Dhobitalao Goan wedding of a Catholic it was looking! So we are happy about you." She paused, took another deep breath, and prepared for a fortissimo finale. "But this woman who is giving you the pugree, her husband's funeral was only ten days ago! Yesterday was *dusmoo*. And today you are taking away his pugree! It is not correct! Come back later!" With this, Najamai went after Daulat, and Moti followed.

The young man could see them go into a huddle from where he was, and could hear them as well. Moti was saying, "Your neighbour is right, this is not proper. Wait for a few days."

And Najamai was emboldened to the point of presenting one of her theories. "You see, with help of prayer the soul crosses over in four days. But sometimes the soul is very attached to this world and takes longer to make the crossing. And as long as the soul is here, everything like clothes, cupsaucer, brush-comb, all must be kept same way it was, exactly same. Or the soul becomes very unhappy."

The young man was feeling uncomfortable. He, of course, had not known that Daulat had been widowed as recently as ten days ago. Once again he felt obliged to say something. "Excuse me, maybe I should come back later for the pugree, the wedding is three months away."

"Yes! Yes!" said Najamai and Moti together; Najamai continued: "I don't want you thinking I'm stirring my ladle in your pot, but that would be much better. Come back next month, after *maasiso*. You can try it on today, see if it fits. In that there is no harm. Just don't take it away from the place where the soul expects it to be."

"I don't want to give any trouble," said the young man. "It's alright, I can try it later. I'm sure it will fit."

Daulat, with the pugree in her hands, approached the young man. "If you think it is bad luck to wear a recently dead man's pugree, and you are changing your mind, that is okay with me. But let me tell you, my Minocher would be happy to give it to you if he were here. He would rejoice to see someone get married in his pugree. So if you want it, take it today."

The young man looked at Moti and Najamai, at their flabbergasted countenances; then at Daulat who waited calmly for his decision. It was a tableau of four, frozen into inaction: two women slack-jawed with disbelief; another graced with poise and dignity, holding a handsome, black pugree; and in the middle an embarrassed young man pulled two ways, like Minocher's soul, in a tug-of-war between two worlds — a world governed by confused notions of decency and propriety on one side, and on the other, the world of a strong, determined woman guided by unfailing instincts, who would make her own rules from now on.

The young man broke the spell. He reached out for the pugree and gently took it from Daulat's hands.

"Come," she smiled, and led him into the bedroom, to the dressing table. He placed the pugree on his head and looked in the mirror.

"See, it fits perfectly," said Daulat.

"Yes," he answered, "it does fit perfectly." He took it off, caressed it for a moment, then hesitantly asked, "How much ... ?"

Daulat held up her hand. She had prepared for this moment; though she had dismissed very quickly the thought of selling it, she had considered asking for its return after the wedding. Now, however, she shook her head and took the pugree from the young man. Carefully, she placed it in the case and handed it back to him.

"It is yours, wear it in good health."

"Thank you," said the young man. "Thank you very much." He waited for a moment, then softly, shyly added, "And God bless you."

Daulat smiled, "If you have a son, maybe he will wear it too, on his wedding." The young man smiled back.

She saw him to the door and returned to the living room. Moti and Najamai were sipping halfheartedly at their tea, looking somewhat injured.

The children had finished their cold-drink. They were swishing the shrunken ice cubes around in the forbidden final quarter inch of liquid, left in their glasses as they'd been warned to, to attest to their good breeding. An irretrievably mixed-up and confusing bit of testimony.

A beggar was crying outside, "Firstfloorwalla balli! Take pity on the poor! Secondfloorwalla bai! Help the hungry!"

Presently, Najamai rose. "Have to leave now, Ramchandra must be ready with dinner." Moti took the opportunity to depart as well. "After a severe gout attack Peshotan hates to be left for too long."

Daulat was alone once more. Leaving the cups and glasses where they stood with their dregs of tea and Goldspot, she went into Minocher's room. It was dark except for the glow of the oil-lamp.

The oil was again low and she reached for the bottle, then changed her mind.

From under one of the cups in the living room she retrieved a saucer and returned to his room. For a moment she stood before the lamp, looking at the flame. Then she slid the saucer over it, covering up the glass, the way his face had been covered by a white sheet ten days ago.

In a few seconds the lamp was doused, snuffed out. The afterglow of the wick persisted; then it, too, was gone. The room was in full darkness.

Daulat sat in the armchair. The first round, at least, was definitely hers.

FRANCES ITANI was born in Belleville, Ontario and now lives in Ottawa. Her publications include *Man Without Face, Pack of Ice, Truth or Lies*, and *A Season of Mourning*. This story first appeared in CFM No. 56 in 1987.

After the Rain

FRANCES ITANI

"ONCE YOU GET THE HIDE SEPARATE, you'd think the worst'd be over, but oh no, Jesus no, it's pretty near a whole day's work."

Maybury was blood up to his armpits and though he wore rubber boots he felt something squish underfoot, didn't know what it was, probably a clot or a piece of belly gutted out.

"Ribs'll go to the hounds — I'll get the rest in back of the truck and Doc can run his tests. Though the magnet came through all right."

He rubbed his hands up and down the four-inch piece of metal noting its smoothness — not a bit of hardware attached, not a thing. So why did the cow die? He'd had it only six months.

He stood in the wind and raised one hand to scratch at the scalp under his cap, forgetting about what was on his hands, and then cursed and stood watching the two men down by the cabins. The wind kept the smell of cow from him, the sea wind — a real trap-breaker for the past three days.

"Take O-de-Cologne now," he said, and bent over the liver which he knew, even as he cut it free, was diseased, and a loop of bowel too, all inflamed.

"O-de-Cologne wouldn't know a cow from a pony and if he did he wouldn't be able to make up his mind to say out loud he knew which was which."

The hounds howled and moaned from the barn, knowing the ribs would soon be lying bloody in the pens, a full day's meat. If Maybury had a way to store the ribs he'd stretch out the supply. But there would be no room in the freezer now that the cow was nearly cut up and would be ground tomorrow for his foxes.

The North wind had been blowing three days and Maybury knew from the sky and from his skin that it was nearly blown out. The undertow sucking at the sand, the big waves settling, settling, nine hundred lobster traps strewn and broken for thirty miles up and down shore. From here he could barely see past the one high dune on his land to the sea, now all whitecaps but without the spume blowing high in the air. Just the waves, curled and battering one another into shore. And there was O-de-Cologne standing on the cliff, hands on hips, looking as if for once in his life he was about to make a decision. They were fighting, Maybury knew. O-de-Cologne and JJ were fighting. O had arrived in a surly mood. Him and Nora. And JJ agitating from the next cabin didn't help things, not one bit.

"I can get the rope up here," O said again. "I can get it up, no trouble at all."

"Like hell you can," said JJ. "You're fuckin crazy."

It was what Nora had said too; he'd winced when he heard her say it. "You're fuckin crazy," she'd said.

"Screw you, JJ," said O and turned a semicircle to grab at the post and lower himself over the cliff, edging his bare feet into notches that had blown full of sand. The whole face of the red cliff had altered with the storm, the sandy edge all cracked by the rain which had driven in horizontally from the sea for thirty-six hours, and the wind dried out and checked the flow of sand, stopping it mid-way, it seemed, up the cliff, though half the beach looked as if it had already blown up and over the dune and against the windows from inside, every bit of glass plastered over with muddy sand, glazed dark, deeper than the normal colour of red clay abundant everywhere on the island.

It was what Nora had said too. "You're fuckin crazy." She had rinsed her clothes in the bathroom sink and her underpants were hanging all around the shower to dry until the rain stopped and then she hung them on the line behind the cabin. High-waisted elastic-bound white cotton underpants.

O rooted backwards in his mind. He stamped his bare feet into the damp hard sand. "I'll get the fuckin lobster rope." And turned his head to see JJ at the top of the cliff, about to start down after him.

JJ had brought Minnie with him. Of all people, with Nora here. Sure as hell Nora'd go and shoot off her mouth back home but JJ said he didn't care. Things couldn't get any worse for him and he was damned he'd bring his wife one more time to the cabin when he was having his holiday. Though some holiday. Thirty-six hours of horizontal rain.

All one night I dreamed the water was seeping in under the floorboards and next morning sure enough the kitchen floor was covered in two inches of water. It had driven straight in across the boards of the veranda, in through the raised edge of linoleum right across the front window, the window that was dull and mud-splattered. Half inch of mud coated across the cliff posts, the veranda, the one broken lawn chair and any other thing that had its dwelling outside.

Minnie, he brings. Minnie who sells donuts and coffee and herself on the Ferry. I hear them through the cabin walls at night, even through the wind I hear them. Oh Jesus, I hear her high-pitched moan, even through the wind I hear her.

Maybury had the meat off all the bones. "One little knife, that's all it takes, a hunting knife but a good one. It's true. The ribs thrown up into the back of the truck, ribs first set aside for my hounds which are crying from three days of wind or the knowledge of this dead cow that I've got to finish." He threw the intestines up too and they splattered out the back end of the truck and he used both hands and threw them up again, and this time they stayed, the abdominal membrane still clinging to them transparently though one wide loop of bowel looked red and inflamed.

"What'll Doc say? I could set the ribs apart for the hounds but Doc will want to see all the parts. Just in case, I better drive all the parts to town." He threw the lungs up to the truck after he had split them open; they looked okay to him but who was he to tell? It was the liver he suspected and he fingered it with his big hands and then leaned over to wipe his hands on the grass and giggled to himself, "My cow probably died of cirrhosis, but how the hell did she get at the booze?"

Maybury felt the wind drop a little and the stench blocked his nostrils, a thick encompassing smell that caught him midway across the back of the throat so he couldn't breathe. He turned to look back towards the cliff. The sea was still high; anybody'd be a fool to go into her today. Not that he'd worry about JJ or O-de-Cologne. He'd seen them in the water only once and that time they'd been drunk. They'd been taking holidays for fourteen years in the two cabins though this was the first year JJ brought the woman from the Ferry — it was always the two wives before. And they had always left neat and orderly the day before tourist season and drove back to their homes before those fellows from Toronto showed up after the first of July. For sure Maybury never worried about the tourists. The farthest those pale men with their Toronto bellies ever got was from veranda to cliff-edge and back, a bottle of beer in hand. Back and forth, cliff to veranda, veranda to cliff, reaching for a new beer just about each time, all the while complaining about Maritime beer, peering down at the sea like it was a pair of dirty drawers. But O-de-Cologne and JJ turned up every year like old and faithful hounds, last week of June. They stayed until the thirtieth, last day of Lobster Season, and this year three days of wind and nine hundred Jesus traps had washed up along shore.

All the meat off the bones now. He had to get it up into the truck and to Doc's where it would be tested for parasites and the liver checked. The whole cow was there, it was a Jesus autopsy he was doing, the hell with the fox meat. He bet himself, there were three hundred pounds. He made a deal with himself that if there were three hundred or more he'd treat JJ and O-de-Cologne to a beer up at the house.

"It's buried that deep you wouldn't get it free with a ton of dynamite," JJ said.

O refused to believe this though he knew there was a good four thousand feet of rope and they both wanted it.

The storm has levelled the beach. Levelled it hard and smooth, everything ten inches higher because of the sand dropped by the sea. Not a ripple or ridge half-mile both ways and the rope sticking up out of the sand, a few loops here and there, I can sell all of her, if I can get her out I can sell her, every piece.

"What the hell would you do with it?" asked JJ. "Not that you'd ever get it free. You ever hear of a man fighting the sea with his bare fists?"

And he roared with laughter till the wind shook it up and up, up the cliffs where the swallows were frenzied after three days driven into the row of holes all along the clay face.

"What the hell are you — busting a gut laughing?" said O.

"You're jealous of Minnie," said JJ, "I know."

"That whore!"

"Whore be damned. She's a sight better than my old woman at home and Nora too for that matter, hanging her cotton bloomers to rattle in the wind."

"And whaddya pay her?" said O. "A week's wages off the Ferry?"

"She comes for free cause she's on vacation," said JJ.

And roared again while O looked down at tufts and loops of yellow rope and green, and measured with his eye the distance he'd have to drag her once he got her free of the ton of sand that sat on top of her.

"You'll never do it," said JJ. "All you got is your bare hands. I'm going up the cliff now to see if Minnie isn't waiting for me. And if you'd clear the Jesus mud off your windows I'd give your old Nora a wink too, when I go by."

"Leave her out of this," said O.

"She'll have her eye to the glass though, won't she," said JJ.

"And don't make so fuckin much noise at night. It's obscene."

"So that's it," said JJ, laughing again. "I knew you were jealous."

"When I take the feed to my foxes," said Maybury, "I mix a little ground fish with a little ground meat and some meal and stir it with a wide paddle and so help me the stench of it is worse than this cut-up cow. And my foxes crouch, hunched with quick eyes, crazed and bewildered as they fear my coming. Running the length of their cages, pulling their heads back the way that causes their necks to ripple and swell. With their sharp quick barks and elongated cries that never seem to come from them at all. And I have to get that she-fox tamed better, suckled though she was by the barncat, for she'd bite the hand off quick as look at me. I take the tongs leaning into the wire cage and clamp her cleanly round the neck, grabbing her by the tail as she thrashes wildly. And when she's been hung upside down a few times, tipped by the tail, she'll maybe learn not to snap when I go in with her feed. Great clumps of her pearly hair coming out in my hand when I let go of her tail."

Maybury lifted a great chunk of meat; it spilled out of his arms all directions, formless with the bones cut away as they were. The windpipe slashed neat and pale and open, gaping with the blood run out.

"When JJ and O-de-Cologne came this year I had them in to the house for a drink. Though it's impossible to know what a man like O-de-Cologne wants or likes; you'd have to follow him shelf to shelf at the liquor store to find out. For he hems and he haws and looks round the kitchen and says, 'Whaddever you're havin, it doesn't really matter,' and I keep sayin, 'You'd better say what you want, I can't decide for you.'

"He shifts from one foot to the other saying, 'Don't matter, I'll take what you're havin.' So I shove a drink of the strongest rum I've got into his fist. And by this time I know enough not to ask which cabin him and Nora want and which one JJ and Minnie will get, so I shove the key to Number 1 in the hand that's not holding the rum and JJ nods and says he'll take Number 2 then. Nora sittin out in the yard in one car and the one from the Ferry in the other. And neither of them will get out and come into the house."

So I up and borrow a spade from Maybury. He's on his knees in a heap of guts and hoofs and he looks up and says with a giggle, "Well now, O-de-Cologne, do you think you can make up your mind between the shovel and the spade?" Cowshit black and green spilling out of the bowels all around him. I grab the spade and bring it back and lower myself over the cliff and Nora, she's been watching from between the cracks in the mud on the window. She's wearing her railroad cap though she hasn't been out of the cabin once except to hang up her bloomers and an outfit that looks like a pair of men's striped pyjamas. I never knew anyone could be so sexless, I never knew it.

The sand fleas thick in the after-storm; they hit against my bare feet in sharp short flicks as I walk. Bouncing off the sand as though set in motion by underground spouts. Not hurting but multi-patterned and irritating because they are so inevitable and inescapable. And as I walk towards the rope where it's buried all a'tangle with the bashed-in traps, the crows fly up in screeching pairs, surprising, hidden as they are by the stinking heap of dulse rotting on the sand. Two people up coast shoveling dulse into bags, carting it off the beach.

So I go down the beach a way and start digging for my rope. A good twenty feet up from the water and I dig with Maybury's spade and it takes me forty minutes steady hard work pelting wet sand behind me before I really see what the job is I got ahead.

JJ sat on the step of cabin Number 2 and watched Minnie as she picked her way down the cliff to the sand below. She wore a mauve-coloured twopiece and had a white plastic purse over one arm and a faded towel over the other. The towel with a picture of a man who had a blimped-out middle and a black brush moustache, straw hat and a horizontal-striped bathing suit.

She gave herself a little shake when she got to the beach, the wind blowing ever so slightly now though the waves still high, and she set down her purse and began to arrange herself on the towel, the four corners of which she tried to keep from flipping up before she crouched and got herself stretched out flat.

JJ remembered last night, Minnie calling from the bedroom while he sat at the window with one bright light over the kitchen table, watching the huge soft-bellied moths as they hit the pane of glass, their double wings whirring up the pane as they climbed to the top then flung themselves out and down, only to start up the pane again.

After thirty-six hours of horizontal rain coming in from the sea, when a man couldn't open the door without a stinging blast of sand whipping his face through the screen, after thirty-six hours locked up with Minnie, he'd begun to have wild insane moments wishing this was like any other summer when he and Ada and O and Nora would come up, to Maybury's, last week of June.

He thought about last year when he and O had been drinking a case of beer on the cliff in front of the cabins, and the two women Nora and Ada sitting out on the veranda of Number 1. JJ wanted to teach O how to swim and they laughed and had a few beers while they thought it over and a few more to get into the proper mood. So they half-walked, half-ran to the cliff's edge where the sand was heaped soft from below. Daring each other to take a nose dive. First JJ took a dive straight down into dry sand, and after he climbed back up he helped O make up his mind by pushing him from behind. The women on the veranda shouting out into the air as if they weren't addressing anyone they knew, "Keep it up you damn fools, keep it up why don't you."

O raced out to the water first, splashing and stumbling as he ran, wet to his trunks and JJ right behind. So they got out to their waists and JJ tripped O in the water and bobbed his head under a few times, keeping him there to teach him how to hold his breath. O came up choking and laughing and they started tickling each other out there in the waves. They ran back in through the water and up the cliff pulling at each other's legs, half-sliding back on their bellies, finally rolling across the grass, covered by this time in red clay and mud, flipping the caps off their beer before they went back to the water for lesson number two. The women had gone inside but reappeared suddenly on the veranda shouting vaguely into the air again. "Do you know this man, Ada?" "No-oo, you've seen these two before, Nora?" Each holding a green plastic bucket of cold water and they let it fly saying, "You're no husbands of ours. We never seen you two before." O and JJ laughing so hard they cried, and ran out over the cliff without a thought to what was below. Flying with arms outstretched, too drunk to kill themselves. Then, back to the sea for lesson two while the women went inside to get their pails ready for another dousing and then sat on the veranda again.

So first I get it dug free and I see that the waves have dumped it in two clumps but joined, each weighing maybe three hundred pounds, some of it attached to pieces of trap and board, rusty nails sticking up through the sand. But I'm damned I'll cut the rope into two separate pieces — though that's how it falls naturally — because there are probably one or two main pieces, each maybe half-mile long. So I find an end and, start to backtrack on the rope, looping it through mud and cement and a tangle that's worse than a pot of spaghetti all of one piece. Each time I pull the end through I've got to find out where it goes deeper into the middle, following it as far as my arm will reach, my hands beginning to blister from the salt and sand and from the sheer work of it.

I go on like this another hour and I look back up the beach and see JJ sitting on top of the cliff, head down as if he's bored with it all, and Minnie on a towel below, and then Nora, in her railroad cap, kind of murmuring through the grass but sticking close to the cabin. And I see that if I'm to get the rope untangled before I budge her, it'll be dark before I get her half done. But if I can move the whole solid mass and drag her up the beach, I can work at her for the next six months in my own back yard if I want to. But

I can't, for the life of me, make up my mind what to do. Should I keep on back-looping, threading this now long loose end through? Or should I start to drag? Tide coming in now too, the waves getting closer each time I take another look at the grey undercurrents of the sea.

So, said JJ, I watch while O-de-Cologne digs in his heels and stands looking at the rope and walks circles around it, first one direction then the other. And after about ten minutes the poor bastard can't make up his mind what to do. Nora doing circles up here around the cabin, won't even speak to me she won't, because Minnie's down there with her plastic purse and Nora'll cut her dead if Minnie comes near so much as her veranda.

"There isn't an inch of truck not covered with meat; my foxes yapping in their pens," said Maybury. "When I get the word from Doc I'll drive back and though the sun has just come out — first time in three days — the meat is sure to be all right till I get it ground tomorrow. I'll close up the back of the truck and drive it into town. And I'll bet there's three hundred pounds or nothing, and if there's three hundred pounds I'll stand old JJ and O-de-Cologne to a beer."

The sky still partly grey from the storm though breaking up, the sun squeezing through here and there while the horizon, seen for the first time in three days, settles even and placid below the mass of cloud that has splintered overhead. I pull an easy loop of long yellow rope as thick as my thumb and I bend to it, crawling under, get it over my back and dig my heels into the sand. And I heave at her till I feel her budge and pull for all I'm worth and out she tears. And off I go dragging her backwards but just barely moving, and I get her maybe six inches up the beach in the first twenty minutes.

He looks like a dumb ox coming backwards up the beach with his heels dug in so I go down and stand beside him while he stops to catch his breath, and his eyes are glazed over like a beast of burden that will never see the end of its load. Digs his heels in again and lets out a moan through his teeth.

"Oh, JJ," he says, "why did ya have to go and bring Minnie on our holiday? Nora hasn't spoken to me for three days and we've been locked in that cabin for thirty-six hours of Jesus driving rain."

"It was a mistake to bring her, I agree, but do I run her out of the cabin now she's here?"

"I guess you have to live with your sins," he says.

And I say, "O, you'll never get this rope ten feet up the beach. Never in a week of Sundays will you get it up the beach."

"It would help if two men were pulling instead of one standing by flappin his lips," he says.

"I'm not breaking my back over that tangled mess. It'd take two days just to get one end free."

"I've already freed about sixty feet," he says.

"Cut it," I say. "Cut it now and have done with it. You'll be cutting it anyway the rate the tide's coming in. Unless you plan to work in the water waist deep in the dark."

I'll never cut it no. It's a beautiful piece of rope, probably a mile of it sitting at my feet, I'll never cut it no. I turn in a westerly direction up the coast and see that every object on the beach, every log, every stick of driftwood, every heap of dulse, every blade of marram grass has become a silhouette against the evening sky, and I figure it's about seven-thirty, tide rolling in fast. So I shift my back into the rope again and take one step and then another and don't bother looking at JJ who is standing with his mouth flapping as I pass him by.

"The liver is very suspicious," said Maybury. "I'll have to see what Doc has to say about the liver."

He climbed into the cab, stopping to look back at the dune and his land, stretched below him to the sea. O-de-Cologne was half-mile up the beach leaning backwards forty-five degrees into a loop of rope, and facing another ton of it on the sand. Minnie was pinned to the cliff working her way to the top on hands and knees, the arm that was stuck through the plastic purse waving frantically overhead, though every time she let go the face of the cliff she seemed to slip back a few inches. Old JJ prancing along like a boxer at O-de-Cologne's side. Nora not in sight though Maybury had caught a look of her earlier in some sort of railroad cap and a striped outfit while she was hanging her clothes on the line behind the cabin. It was the only time Maybury had seen her since that first night when she had refused to come into the house — though it had rained thirty-six hours in between — her in the one car, tight-lipped, and Minnie in the other, the two looking off in opposite directions.

"Well," said JJ, "I can't stand here watching you murder yourself." So he yanked at a separate loop of rope and ducked under it, standing beside O who had stopped again, puffing and blowing. The two, as though by some unspoken yet predetermined oath, digging in four heels and setting two backs to the sun, now heaving the enormous mass at a rate double that of O's though still not accomplishing anything at all.

"You think it's hopeless, don't you," said O.

"I'm only helping because you're too stupid to give up, not because I think we're going to do it before dark. And you haven't even thought how we'll get it up the cliff, have you?"

"Course I have. We get her to the bottom, I back the car to the cliff and we use the sixty feet I've already freed to pull her up."

"If we count to ten each time it might give us heart," said JJ.

"We'll try for ten then," said O. "And turnabout counting."

As we stop for our first breath, I turn. Just slightly so Nora won't know I'm looking and I see not Nora but Minnie, all dressed now, tearing out of Number 1 and running up the road after Maybury's truck. Maybury has stopped and waits for her, and after a minute or so backs up with the dust blowing out behind and before his truck in great red clouds. And now Nora comes out of Number 1 and stands on the edge of the cliff, her mouth moving in mocking shouts, the words tossed out into the wind, urgent and soundless. "She's gone," I say to JJ, ignoring Nora as I turn away. "I figured she'd go," he says. We set our backs to the sun again, and it's JJ's turn to count ten. And we shift the rope three, four feet though it nearly kills us to do so.

The sun had shown itself for a short time in the late afternoon and it broke free just before it was to set along the western line of the horizon. Clouds pulled back to reveal a long slit parallel to the waves and the large red flame flattened itself top and bottom and then a grey cloud swooped before it, and the flame fell out of sight.

Nora stood on the edge of the cliff for what seemed a very long time, watching the tide sweep in and the two men below, knowing by their movements they were hurting. She shouted again and again but was neither heard nor heeded. So she went back to the veranda, placed her railroad cap on the step beside her, and waited.

So when the men came up the cliff, defeated, she was able to tell them calmly from the veranda that all they had to do was slip the rope into the water. And as the waves had nearly surrounded it, this would not now be an onerous chore.

"O looks at her as though he's going to cry," said JJ. "And then we look at each other and go whooping down over the cliff, and it reminds me of that summer when I tried to teach O to swim and we nose-dived over the cliff, damn near killing ourselves at the bottom."

The tide is as high as it will ever be now. The rope slips in easily and is sucked up by one big wave and then another. We're wet to our waists, laughing and jumping the waves at the same time. The rope shifts, loosening and spreading out in the water, sand and mud sifting off the braid as we keep hold of our loops, not wrapped to our backs as before but easily now, in our hands. As JJ lets go to dive into a wave, clothes and all, I take the weight of the whole mass of rope in one finger, swishing it behind until we reach the spot below the cabins where Nora has the car already backed out on the cliff. "And why," I say to her, when we get the rope up and dragged to the veranda, "why in hell's name, Nora, didn't you tell us to put it in the water in the first place, instead of waiting till we damn near broke our backs in two."

"She talked all the way to town," said Maybury. "Upfront in the cab with me, and the cow parts in back. She'd talk the ear off a deadman. No wonder she and JJ got sick of each other after only three days."

And his grin stretched from one eyebrow to another as he thought of his foxes; for after dropping Minnie off and leaving Doc's he'd taken the meat late in the day to be weighed and ground because he couldn't wait until tomorrow.

"Cirrhosis," Doc had said.

"Cirrhosis of the liver? Hee hee hee."

"That's right. Your cow must have been in the ragweed some time or the other."

"Three hundred and three pounds of ground meat," said Maybury as his truck bumped over knots of red clay on the road. "Three hundred and three pounds of meat for my foxes."

SHARON BUTALA was born in Nipawin, Saskatchewan in 1940 and now lives near Eastend, Saskatchewan. Her publications include *The Fourth Archangel, Fever, Luna,* and *Queen of the Headaches,* for which she was nominated for the Governor General's Award for Fiction in 1986. This story first appeared in CFM No. 64 in 1988, a special issue on Saskatchewan writers.

The Prize

SHARON BUTALA

I CAN'T LOOK THROUGH THE window behind my desk to those hills to the west without thinking of the dinosaur skeleton that I know lies buried, a few bones exposed by the icy spring runoff, at the bottom of a decaying coulee, its grave a secret all the incomprehensible length of sixty-five million years. To see it I have only to walk a half-mile out onto the prairie, up a sage and cactus-strewn slope, around a thinly-grassed hill or two, retreating further and further from civilization into that gorge where only coyotes, deer and rabbits come, till I reach the place below an abandoned eagle's nest where the pieces of bone protrude from the yellowish clay.

When I was an obscure, barely-published writer filled with dreams of glory, I had made a solitary pilgrimage around the provinces to the few small towns and farms where writers of talent had once lived: to the homestead of the Icelandic poet, Stephan Stephansson in Alberta, to Margaret Laurence's family home in Manitoba, and in Saskatchewan I had searched for what had been the farm where Sinclair Ross was raised.

For a month I spoke to almost no one; I remember the feel of the steering wheel under my palms, day after day, the green countryside passing by the open car windows, the heat, the perpetual prairie wind, the undercurrent of loneliness that I could never quite shut off, and my determination that never wavered in spite of it. I felt propelled by some compulsion over which I had neither control nor desire for control. Was it only that I wanted to be close to the intimate, personal lives of writers who had achieved what I only aspired to? Not exactly that — I was searching for something I hadn't been able to name even to myself. Although I don't know why this happened, nor any reason for it, the truth is, I was in the grip of the conviction that I had been chosen for greatness.

In southern Saskatchewan I had found the village written about by an American writer who had lived there during his childhood. It was small, not more than seven hundred people lived there, but it was a pretty town, and the shallow river with its steep, grassy banks that wound its way through it, added to its charm. Rows of cottonwoods grew down the streets, probably planted by the first settlers at the beginning of the century, and they had grown so tall that their boughs met overhead to provide welcome shade in what I could see were summers so hot and dry they were barely endurable.

I remember I had no trouble finding the house. Knowledge of who its original owners were seemed to be part of the local folklore, and when I asked where it was, it was pointed out to me with a sort of casual pride that obviously didn't extend itself to concern about the house's preservation. It was in a sorry state of disrepair, but I could see that with its gables and its meticulously crafted wooden trim around the eaves, it had once been handsome. I remember that after I had seen its exterior — nobody answered when I knocked — I stopped to eat lunch in the town's only café, and then I drove on into Alberta.

Not long after that journey my first novel won the top literary prize in the country, and I was abruptly thrust from my impatient obscurity into a measure of fame. Where I had been ignored, I was suddenly in demand, the object of endless interest, of affection and jealousy. I was invited to give readings, lectures and workshops all across the country. I attended meetings, conferences, and parties where I talked too much and drank too much and took full advantage of any woman who showed interest in me.

But as the year after the prize passed, it grew harder and harder to find time to write; I began to feel more and more uneasy. I was afraid I liked the attention too much — people who had never said hello before the prize now hanging on my every word, everyone suddenly having time for me — I was ashamed, and a hollow was growing inside me. I was afraid I might not write again.

Now, lying in the morning in my rumpled, seldom-occupied bed, aching with dissatisfaction and the desire to go back to what I had been before the prize, I thought of that small, decaying house in that distant village. I thought, if only I could live far away from all this, be solitary, and remote from this craziness I'm mired in.

Eventually it came to me: I would use the advances I had received from the publishers of my novel in Britain and the United States to buy that house, I would restore it and I would make it my home. There, maybe, in the surroundings of the famous writer's childhood, where the great artist in him had surely been born, I would be able to finish my second novel. Maybe it would even be as good as everyone had said my first had been.

I got out of bed, I checked my calendar and then ignored it, I packed a suitcase, got into my car, and drove for five hours from Saskatoon south to the village where the house was. During that long drive my certainty grew that I was doing the right thing — the volume of work the man had produced well into his old age, the way that it echoed again and again, explicitly, implicitly, of his boyhood in that village he had made miraculous, the startling clarity of his vision, as though his puzzling, half-deprived, half-blessed childhood in that place had perfected in him a vein of prophecy even the best of us in our smoother lives had missed.

When I reached the village, I didn't pause on the short main street, but drove through puddles of melting ice down its length, made a turn, and pulled up in front of the writer's house, finding it as easily as if I went there every day. I parked, got out, and I marched up the sidewalk, the front door looked as though it hadn't been opened in years, to a door on the side, near the back of the house.

I knocked loudly, there was a thumping inside as though someone might have knocked over a chair or banged against a piece of furniture, and then the door opened.

"I want to buy your house," I said to the big, bulky old man who stood in the doorway blinking into the sunshine of the bright, biting, early spring day. He studied me for a minute out of deepset, small eyes.

"You come inside," he said, and stood back so I could pass into the house. I entered a small, cluttered room that smelled of bacon fat and grime.

"I pour you drink," he said. "Sit," indicating an old wooden chair with a burnt-wood design in the backrest. It was splattered with white paint, but the seat, where the paint hadn't touched it, was worn to a pale gold satin. I sat in it at the table in front of a window, he reached into a cupboard and brought out a whisky bottle and two small glasses. He filled the glasses with the thick, purple liquid from the bottle.

"Chokecherry wine," he said. "You got to get berries when just right," and he made a delicate, pinching gesture with his thick fingers. "My name Nick Esterhazy," he said. "You?" I told him my name, and silently resolved to wait for him to mention again the selling of the house.

He began to talk about his life, some roundabout way, maybe, to lead up to naming a price. He was a bachelor, a big, powerful man in no way broken by his years of hard labour as a section hand with the C.P.R., in a country that still remained, for him, foreign. He paused now and then in his telling to peer out the window where it was possible to see part of the sidewalk and the street. He all but slavered at the sight of the teenage girls, their books in their arms, passing by from the nearby high school. He waved his still muscular arms, his small, deep blue eyes gleaming darkly.

"Forty years," he whispered, leaning close to me so that I couldn't look away. "Forty years section hand. Work! I tell you we work." He held out his thick, gnarled hands as evidence. He made a fist, he bent his arm at the elbow and touched his bicep, looking meaningfully at me. He was about to go on, but someone knocked on the door. We had been so intent on each other that neither of us had noticed anyone passing the window. He rose hastily, his chair rocking noisily from his hand thrusting against its back as he stood, and opened the door.

A small, grey-bearded, slightly stooped old man peered up at Nick. He was dressed in a creased black suit that appeared to be made of a heavyweight cotton. The jacket had no collar and his plaid shirt was buttoned up tight against his wrinkled throat. He wore heavy black boots and a black hat too, and he was grinning, exposing a row of strong-looking, yellow teeth.

"So, Benjamin!" Nick boomed. "I not see you for long time! You sick?" I'm sure they heard him at the post office, two streets over.

"Want to buy chickens? I got good chickens," the old man said. Without waiting for Nick's answer, he turned to go back to the big van I could see idling at the curb, in front of my car. "I show you," he called over his shoulder.

"Make damn sure they got both leg!" Nick bellowed. I couldn't tell if he was teasing or not. "I don't want no more busted chicken!" The old man hurried down the narrow sidewalk, flapping one hand behind him as if to say, Don't be silly. Nick stood in the open door, his body blocking out all but a halo of light above his shoulders and around his head. The old man passed the window again. When he stopped, I could hear him panting.

When their transaction was finished, I watched Benjamin go back down the sidewalk and climb awkwardly into the van. As soon as he had shut the door it pulled away.

"Damn Hutterites," Nick muttered, but without rancour. He took the two, dripping, plastic-wrapped chickens into his bedroom, and I could hear the opening and closing of a fridge door. He had closed off all the rooms except the kitchen and the adjoining room which appeared to be his bedroom. He came back into the kitchen wiping his hands on his pants.

"What's the matter with them?" I asked. He shrugged.

"Always selling," he said vaguely. "You want to buy my house?" My heart gave a leap against my ribs and sweat broke out on the back of my neck. I took a drink to cover my nervousness.

"I'd like to talk to you about it," I said, setting down my glass.

"Have more," he roared, and filled my glass again. His mood changed abruptly and he sighed heavily, the lines around his mouth turning down. "I want to die in Old Country," he said. "Have brothers, sisters there. I go home." He looked sadly at the wall behind me where a small window between the cupboards gave a cramped view of the hills on the western edge of town. "I die with my people."

I doubted his honesty, he doubted mine, but we managed to strike a deal in a fairly short time. I knew I was being reckless, but I didn't care. I was desperate to have the house, to live in it, as if some hidden part of myself that my conscious self didn't have access to, had taken over my will.

I declined his offer to stay the night with him, I had no idea where he thought I might sleep, and went to the hotel. The next day I drove him to the neighbouring large town where there was a lawyer, we drew up the papers, I wrote a cheque, and the house was mine.

Nick asked for a month to sell his furniture, which I had said I didn't want, and to make his arrangements. I hoped privately that a month would be enough time. I didn't like his size with its hint of brutality, his abrupt swings of mood, and his way of narrowing his little eyes at me as if assessing the depth of my depravity.

There was running water in the house, but no bathroom. Nick had used an outhouse during the summer and a chamber pot in winter, so before I left the town that day, I made arrangements with a carpenter recommended to me by the café-owner, in whose café I had eaten my meals, to begin converting an upstairs bedroom into a bathroom. As I drove back to the city I was filled with an elation that I hadn't felt since I'd received the phone call about the prize, a deep satisfaction that things were going as they should, that puzzled me and disturbed me a little, at the same time as I enjoyed it.

"Don't bother to visit," I warned all my acquaintances. "It's too far away, and anyway, I'm going there to write. *I vant to be alone.*"

"No danger," Will, my closest and oldest friend said. "You'll be back by fall, if you last that long. Anyway, Cheryl and I will be in the East till late June or July." His manner was joking, but I detected an undertone that bordered on cheerful contempt. I didn't reply, a little surprised, faintly hurt.

I went back to packing my books and clothes and dishes, to sending out change of address notices, arranging to have my few pieces of furniture moved, and to paying a few farewell visits. I debated, then decided not to call my ex-fiancé, Louise. My frequent, prolonged absences during the past year, and what I swore to her was only her overactive imagination had broken our relationship. Anyway, I knew she was involved with a recently-divorced English professor. No doubt she'd hear about my move through the grapevine, the same way I'd heard about her new relationship.

At the end of the month I drove through a greening countryside back to the village, climbing slowly over many miles to that high plateau, and at last descending into the deep valley with the town spread out below me where my house waited for me. It was a soft spring twilight as I descended that long hill, the few lights in the town winking orange, and I had the sensation of sinking into some warm, dusky dreamworld. At the bottom of the hill passing the newly sprouting hayfields on the outskirts, I was seized by a wave of loneliness, so powerful that for a minute I thought I would have to pull over. I slowed, and as the outlines of the first houses grew sharper under the streetlights, the sensation diminished, grew less keen, till only a faint memory of it lingered.

Nick was gone, leaving me, for some unaccountable reason, with the beautiful old chair I had sat on during my first visit, a few other broken remnants of furniture, and a twenty-year accumulation of dirt. I hoped that the other old man, the writer, was still present somewhere in those dusty vacant rooms with their fading, stained wallpaper and their worn, linoleum-covered floors. Although what I meant when I thought that, I didn't try to articulate.

While I scrubbed the floors and carted out and burned old rags and ancient, mouldy Eaton's catalogues I found lying in the back of closets and in the crumbling cellar, I thought of the writer, that serious, bookridden child, a misfit in a community of work-obsessed, silent people. I found myself looking for his ghost in the bedrooms with their slanted ceilings, and in the decaying front porch where he had sat with his mother on summer evenings, and listening in the night for a hint of his child's voice echoing through the long years.

I began to convert the other back room opposite the kitchen into my study. I set my desk squarely in front of the big, old-fashioned window where I could lift my head and see the hills across the little river and the opening into the more distant coulee where I would one day find the relics of a dinosaur. I took paint remover and scrubbed away the white paint that marred the Golden Oak chair Nick had left me. Perhaps it had been there since the house had belonged to the writer's family.

I had been warned about small towns: how they were hotbeds of gossip, innuendo and outright lies, of deep-seated prejudices and antiquated attitudes, also, of the most disgusting hidden vices. But some had told me of their warmth, and of the concern of villagers for each other's welfare, of their appreciation of the past. What the people of the village thought of me didn't matter to me; I didn't expect to fit in, nor want to; I hoped only to find solitude and anonymity, to be better able to hold at bay all the temptations that accompanied fame, for I was sure they would ruin me as an artist.

I want to be a writer. I murmured the incantation to myself over and over again. I want to be a good writer. And silently, so silently that I never formed the words even in my own head, something in me murmured steadily, like the sound of the wind in the trees that lined the streets: I want to be a great writer.

The woman from the neat new bungalow next door came to visit. I was at my typewriter when I heard the front door close and a woman's voice calling, "Yoo hoo," down the hall. Startled, wondering if somebody had arrived without warning from the city, I hurried out to see who was there.

A short, middle-aged woman in a print housedress, the kind my mother wore when I was a child, was advancing down the hall, peering to the left and right, holding a cake still in its pan in front of her.

"Oh, there you are!" she said when she saw me. "I'll just put this in the kitchen" and disappeared into it. I followed. "Have you made a difference in here! That old Nick was so dirty! And when I tried to clean up for him, he got downright grabby, if you get my drift, so I had to leave him to stew in his own juice, if you know what I mean." She set the cake on the counter, turned, and seeing me standing in the doorway, she said, "I'm Palma McCallum, I live next door. I thought it was high time I came over and introduced myself."

"George . . ." I began.

"Barrett, I know," she said. "You wrote that book. I read it," she added, and went no further. She began to peel plastic wrap from the cake pan. "I didn't mind it," she said. "Heaven knows, there's lots worse than that."

"Would you like some coffee?" I asked, deciding to ignore her remarks about my book.

"Just the thing," she said. "We'll have some of my cake."

Palma had a husband, but I rarely saw him. He was always out at the farm seeding or summer fallowing or spraying or hauling wheat. I soon realized that she would be in my house everyday washing my dishes or dusting, if I didn't make it clear to her that I wanted few interruptions. I was a bachelor, after all, and she assumed that I was like all the others in the district, a man whose socks always needed mending, whose buttons were perpetually popping off and needed sewing on and who would starve if it weren't for the occasional casserole or pie fresh from her oven.

"That rug needs vacuuming," she'd say. "I'll just run over it . . ." but I would quickly intervene, "Now Palma, I'm not helpless. I can vacuum my own rug. Come and have a cup of coffee with me. I was just going to take a break." She would meekly follow me into the kitchen, checking behind me for dust on the windowsills, then sit while I made the coffee, chattering about her husband and her relatives and our other neighbours. Her sharp eyes took in everything, and I knew what she saw in the morning was all over town by afternoon. She kept bustling in without knocking until I took to turning the key in the door so that when she decided to drop in, she had to knock.

I had quickly recovered the régime I had maintained before my first novel was released: up at six, write till ten, then out for a long walk across the river, over the prairie and up into the hills behind my house, then back to my desk. The pile of pages by my typewriter grew thicker with each day that passed. It seemed to me, though, that my original idea was changing slightly, and I wasn't sure whether to wrench the novel back to that, or to follow this subtle new tone to wherever it might lead. I decided finally to let the writing go to where it seemed to want to.

When my writing had temporarily stalled and I had tired of scraping off old wallpaper or mending wiring or painting, and I found my thirst for human company too strong to resist, I strolled down to the café for a cup of coffee and a hamburger.

"Evenin', how's the carpenter?" Harry, the owner, always asked as I sat down. Then he'd pour me a cup of coffee without asking if I wanted one.

I soon began to see that the café was the centre of social life for a certain strata of local society: the retarded people who lived in the old peoples' lodge on the riverbank, the men who had never married, Hutterite men in town on business, strangers passing through, outsiders like myself — in short, everyone who was left after all the circles of friends and relatives had been cast. I found too, that because the town was located in the heart of what had once been dinosaur country, any scruffy-looking stranger might turn out to be a distinguished paleontologist from a distant university.

Occasionally, when I tired of my own company, and the café held no appeal, I went to the bar, which was in the old hotel, where, even if there were only a few oldtimers nursing their warm draft beer or a familiar face or two from the café, there was at least loud rock music playing and a pretty barmaid to look at. Later, I knew, the place would fill up with a stray oil crew or two and young farmers and ranchhands and their girlfriends, and the bar would grow raucous with a palpable current of violence that often erupted into fights.

One night I was surprised to find three middle-aged Hutterite men sitting quietly together, each with a glass of beer in front of him. I wondered if this was allowed, or if they were breaking rules. After I had been there for a while a pair of young Hutterite girls came in the outer door and put their heads around the corner of the entryway. They looked to be about sixteen or seventeen and they were grinning broadly and giggling so loudly that everybody, a dozen or so people, turned to see what was going on. Everybody except the Hutterite men who seemed to know without looking, who it was making the noise.

"What's that all about?" I asked Denise, the barmaid, who had come to ask me if I wanted another drink. She was only a few years older than the girls giggling in the doorway.

Denise laughed, turning her head toward them. She had a wry, flippant way about her that wasn't pleasant, but that intrigued me because it contrasted so sharply with her perfect pink complexion and her face with its small nose and sensual mouth and large blue eyes, all framed by her long, pale-blonde hair. She had a way of standing holding her tray that emphasized her full young breasts in the tight shirt she always wore. I had wondered if it was meant especially for me, but I had soon seen that she stood like that in front of all the men, as if she believed that a casual parading of her charms was part of her job description. Once or twice I'd thought of taking her home with me, I thought she could have been persuaded, but something held me back. The welcoming calm of my house, the sense of a presence that was always there, so that I never felt alone — I felt she would disrupt all that, that she might dispel it, and I wouldn't risk its loss.

"I guess they want to go home," she said. "Everything in town but the bar is closed." One of the old men who were waiting at the door each morning for the bar to open, and who sat in his usual place near the door, lifted his unsteady head, his greasy cap stuck on sideways, patted the seat beside him, and called to the girls, "Why doan youse come and sit with me?" The girls dodged back around the corner and their giggles reached such a pitch of hysteria that I thought surely the men would have to get up and tell them to be quiet or shoo them back to the van I had seen parked down the street.

When they didn't move, I said to Denise, "It doesn't seem to be bothering them much," nodding my head in the direction of the three Hutterites who were talking quietly together. She made a sour face and shrugged one shoulder so hard her breast bounced.

"I bet they'll catch hell on the way home. The men aren't supposed to be in here, so the girls know they can get away with it." She took my empty glass away without looking at it, her eyes meeting mine in a too-frank gaze that she practiced on most of her customers. "Hutterite women don't have much to say about anything."

I looked back to the two apple-cheeked girls in the doorway — I had never before seen anyone that description fitted — and studied their costume, the black and white polka-dotted scarves they wore over their hair, their ankle-length bright plaid dresses with the long aprons over them, and I saw that their faces shone with a childish innocence, unabashed as they were by the attention they were provoking from the audience that, except for Denise, was entirely male. I hadn't known there were still teenagers in Canada like that. I wondered if I could find a place for them in my novel and then dismissed the idea as silly.

Ten more minutes passed, the girls didn't tire of their game, and the three Hutterite men, one of them very drunk, slowly stood up. As soon as they began to rise, the girls let out a couple of delighted shrieks, pulled open the outside door and pushed each other out into the street. When I went out a half hour later, the van was gone.

Other than Palma only canvassers for the Heart or Cancer or Lung associations knocked on my door. And, of course, the Hutterites, who came selling freshly killed ducks and geese, frozen chickens, and fresh vegetables from their gardens which must have been vast. It was always the old man with the thin grizzled beard, Benjamin, who came, too old to work on the colony anymore, I guessed, and a young man who drove the van, carried the heavy sacks of potatoes or carrots and any large orders of birds.

I never bought much, but I always bought something. I even placed an order for some pairs of hand-knitted wool socks, in my case, good for nothing but wearing inside my winter boots since they were so thick and bulky. But I had first seen Benjamin when the house was still Nick's and I felt leery about disturbing a tradition.

One day they arrived at noon as I was taking a small roast out of the oven. It was too much for me, I had cooked it in order not to have to cook for a few days, and on impulse, I asked him and his driver to have lunch with me. Although he barely knew me, Benjamin accepted without a trace of hesitancy or surprise. I realized that such an invitation was in keeping with the communal tradition he lived by, and I knew too, that if I arrived at the colony at mealtime, it would be taken for granted that I would eat there.

Benjamin said grace before I had even thought of it, and then dug in with a good appetite.

"You should come visit us at colony," he said. "Our women cook you good meal."

"I'll have to do that," I said, although I had no intention of ever doing any such thing. I hadn't even any sure idea, beyond the direction, where the colony was.

"What you do for living?" he asked.

"I'm a writer," I said. "I'm working on a book." He put his fork down and looked hard at me, his dark eyes sharp.

"About this town?" he asked. I had to laugh.

"Heavens no," I said.

"Why not?" he asked, returning to his meal. "Lots here to write."

"I'm sure there is," I said, "but . . ." and couldn't think how to finish my sentence. "I'm finishing something I started before I came here."

The young man with him, William, hardly spoke at all, but he ate with ferocity, not lifting his eyes from his plate. Despite Benjamin's frail old age, it was plain he was the boss.

"Is William your son?" I asked.

"No," Benjamin said, "grandson. My boys men now, have sons of own."

"They live on the colony, too?"

"Two in Manitoba," he said, then gave me that sharp-eyed glance again. "Sure on colony. All on colonies. How else to live?" He gave a little laugh, more to himself, and I glanced at William, wondering why he never spoke. Benjamin must have seen me looking at William, because he said, apropos of nothing that I could tell, "It's hard to keep young ones on colony. They want to go. Some of them. Gets harder all the time."

"Oh?" I said.

"They want to see world," he said. "Television, cars, women." I kept silent. "They want to see world," he repeated, giving his old head a shake and reaching with his knife for the butter. "I tell them, the world!" He flapped his free hand as if to make the world vanish. "On colony we keep out bad things."

William kept chewing, his eyes on his plate, but red was creeping up his neck to disappear under his short, white-blonde hair. "We get him wife," the old man said, winking at me. "He settle down then." William swallowed hard, but still refused to look at us.

"You married?" Benjamin asked me.

"No," I said.

"Man needs woman," he pointed out.

"Oh, I suppose I'll get married one of these days."

"Have little ones," he suggested. "Not good for man to live alone."

When the two of them had gone, I thought about what Benjamin had said about me living alone. I realized then that although I had been living alone for a couple of months, I didn't have that empty, alienated feeling that being alone had always raised in me in the past. I felt as though someone was with me. It was peculiar, and I found myself wandering through my house thinking about it. It had to be the house, there was something about it, it exuded a warmth, I actually felt it welcomed me, it wanted me in it. But that's silly, I told myself. It's only your imagination. But there it was. Perhaps, I thought, it's the writer glad to have a kindred soul living here.

Still, I reminded myself, if it really were the dead writer, surely my work would be going better. My first novel had poured out of me, but this one seemed to be going in fits and starts. Often a couple of days would pass without my writing a line, and yet I couldn't quite put my finger on what the trouble was. I knew my characters; I knew where I wanted my characters to go; the setting was familiar to me as the city I had grown up in. Oh well, I thought, you hit a bad spell every once in a while. You can't expect it to be always easy and smooth.

Palma dropped in unexpectedly about five o'clock one afternoon when I was lazing around with a new novel an acquaintance had just had published. It wasn't very good, I didn't think, and I was wondering what I would say in my letter to her.

"Let's have a glass of wine," I suggested to Palma, glad to put down the book.

"Heaven's no! I don't drink," she said.

"Come on," I teased her. "One little glass won't set you on the road to ruin." She looked as if she was about to give me a lecture, then relented.

"Oh, all right," she said, "but you have to promise me, I mean *promise* that you won't tell anybody." The village was full of female teetotalers, all innocent and pious women who must have felt that not allowing a drop of liquor to pass their lips would somehow redress the cosmic balance for the kids who drank too much beer and rolled their trucks, the old reprobates nothing would ever change, and those ranchers and farmers who drank whisky to soothe their aches and to forget their bankers breathing down their necks.

"I see those Hutterites coming to you door all the time," she scolded. "Can you afford to buy so much? Don't be afraid to tell them to buzz off if you don't want to buy."

"Are you suggesting they aren't honest?" I asked. She hesitated, then nodded sagely.

"The young ones steal." When I looked surprised, she hurried on. "Nothing big or expensive, just little things, fasteners for their hair, cheap costume jewellery, things like that."

"I wonder why that is," I said.

"Well, then, it's what they believe," she said, pursing her lips smugly.

"What they believe?" I prompted. Behind her in the back yard the

June sun was shining warmly on the one tall cottonwood that was left — the others had had to be cut down, sawed into manageable pieces and hauled away before the dead branches could blow down on the house. I wondered if the dead writer's parents had planted them. His mother, I thought.

"That you can't own anything," she said, surprised at my ignorance. "They can't have rings or earrings or necklaces, they think that's sinful, and since they can't have money, they steal. You can't keep a young girl away from pretty things, you know. It isn't natural. Betty in the Co-Op has to keep a weather eye on them whenever they come into the store."

I was trying to decide whether this was true, or merely local prejudice. "Do you know they don't want their kids educated? They've got their own school on the colony, but if they get educated, the first thing they do is leave, and the elders can't have that. So they make it hard for the teacher. They're forever taking their kids out of school to help kill geese or babysit during harvest or whatever, anything to keep them out of school. And they all stop going as soon as they're old enough."

"Do . . ." I began.

"And they won't allow television or music except religious singing or even pictures on the walls. Now I ask you, how can you teach school without even pictures on the walls? Or tape recorders or radios?" She would have gone on and on, I saw no hope of stopping her if I had wanted to, but the phone rang and I went to my study to answer it. When I came back, she was rinsing our wineglasses in the sink.

"I can't think why I stayed so long," she said over the noise of the running water. "It was that darn wine. I never should have taken any. Now remember, you promised."

"A little wine won't hurt you," I said. "But I promise." She seemed to think I might put up a notice on the bulletin board in the café.

She set the glasses on the drainboard and wiped her hands vigorously on a paper towel. "I don't understand it at all," she said. "The men drive tractors and big, expensive combines, but the teacher can't even have a record player." She looked up at me, frowning, her lips pursed, as if I might be able to explain it.

"I don't understand it either," I said, finally. She went out into the hall and stood by the door. I followed her. "My sister taught on one of the colonies for a couple of years. That's how I know." She went out without saying good-bye, shutting the door clumsily so that it banged, leaving me standing in the hall watching her figure, muted and wavering through the frosted oval glass of the door, disappear down the sidewalk.

I had lived in the town about three months. I should have been finished the first draft of my novel, but there it sat, a thick enough pile of pages, but no longer the novel I had planned and begun in the city. I wasn't wholly lost, but neither was I able to find the tone I wanted and to hold it steady. Instead, it fluctuated from the driving, energy-filled narrative of the first novel with its wry, angry tone that the critics had loved, all the way to the other extreme — a calm, almost meditative voice that I didn't recognize and that was becoming harder and harder to break free of.

I picked up the stack of pages sitting beside my typewriter. They weighed satisfyingly heavy in my hands. I sat down on the old oak chair and flipped through them. There it was, that quiet, removed voice that made me think of the small river that flowed past my house — at night, when the moon was shining on it. Mixed in with passages of prose that might have come straight from my first novel.

I lifted my eyes from the pile of paper and stared out the window at the hills that were deepening into blues as night drew down over the countryside. I could see now that while in my first book I had dealt with every conceivable problem of urban life — the constant hurry, the obsession with matters of style and taste, the driving passion to get ahead, the unspoken urge to transcend it all — what I had not dealt with was the possibility of any other way of life. It was as if I had been so involved myself in that life that I couldn't even imagine any other way of living.

The more I wrote, the more it seemed to me that I was actually losing interest in that rich, perpetually exciting world. It had lost its urgency, had begun to seem dreamlike. I was having more and more trouble conjuring its colour, its sensuality, its speed. I even had moments when I felt I simply couldn't be bothered.

I sat for a long time looking out the window behind my desk at the moon-washed hills and the high, winding coulee eroded back into them, a deep shadow now, and I saw two deer moving haltingly down the slope, going to water at the river. Abruptly I pulled down the blind, blocking out the scented countryside, pulling the small room back into itself. I sat a while longer, then I went upstairs to bed.

It was after that I found the dinosaur bone. I felt I had been spending too much time in the café in the evenings and I vowed that when the urge to go for a mindless chat with Harry and a cup of his foul-tasting coffee came upon me, I would, instead, cross over the small footbridge at the end of the street and go for a walk across the prairie and up into the hills. I knew that once I was well away from the town the glimpses of deer or rabbits, hawks or even the occasional eagle, and the calm and beauty of the landscape would work its spell on me and I would forget how much I had wanted company. On one of these walks I went further than usual into the coulee, and spotting a white rock at the base of a steep clay cliff, I went closer to it to see it. I could tell at once that it was bone and of an animal so large there was nothing on the prairie to rival it for size. A femur, perhaps. The piece newly exposed was not big enough to identify definitely, but I knew if I chose to dig I would find more, much more. I stayed out till dark that night and when I returned across the little footbridge, the coyotes were yapping and howling in the hills as if to mourn what I had uncovered.

Summer came, and I had begun a second draft. I went occasionally to the café again, where absolutely nothing seemed to have changed in my absence. One night when I was there Benjamin and a young companion were just finishing supper in a booth near the back, across from another booth where four farmers were lingering over cups of coffee. Otherwise, the café was empty.

"Did you hear about what happened in Black River?" Harry asked me, leaning close over the counter and lowering his voice. I said I hadn't. "The council tried to stop the Hutterites from getting any bigger or starting another colony in their municipality. They passed some bylaws that would keep them from building on any new quarters of land they bought, so nobody could live on that land. Stopped 'em cold. But the Hutterites went to court and the news just came out today.

They beat 'em. Unconstitutional, the court said." He sighed. "To tell the truth, they don't bother me none."

"Funny they wouldn't want them around," I said. "I heard they're good neighbours, that they'll go help anybody who is in trouble."

"Oh, yeah," Harry said, still keeping his voice down. Benjamin and his companion came and paid their bill and left. Harry came back from the till and leaned on the counter beside me again. "They roll onto the place with their big equipment and all that help and they have that whole damn place seeded or combined by noon. It's really something to see." There was a roar of laughter from the booth where the farmers were sitting. One of them, still laughing, stood up, a toothpick in his mouth and his bill rolled in one big brown hand. He came up to the cash register.

"What's the joke, Dave?" Harry asked as he accepted the man's quarters.

"I was telling 'em about old Ben. He came up to me on the street in Mallard the other day. He was all upset. Saw a sign that said there was strippers dancing in the bar there." He had to stop talking for a minute because he had begun to laugh again. He shifted his toothpick. "So I said, 'What? Naked women dancing? It can't be true!' I get a kick out of teasing them Hutterites," he explained. "Especially old Ben, he's so serious. So Ben said, 'It's true, you see?' He was shaking his head he was so shocked. 'It's crazy,' he said. So I said, 'Ah, I don't believe it.' And I took his arm, pretended I was going to get him to come with me to see. I said, 'It can't be! Come on, let's go see!'" He had to stop again to get control of his laughter. "But old Ben, he took me serious. 'No No!' he says, and he pulls his arm away. 'I ain't going over there! It's crazy!' Christ," the farmer said, "I couldn't stop laughing." He went out of the cafe shaking his head and chuckling.

I paid for my coffee and walked slowly home through the soft summer twilight. There was nobody on the street or in the yards, everyone had gone indoors, and lights splashed out across the sidewalk now and then from rooms where families sat talking or watching T.V. I thought of the life I had left behind, and I was overcome by a longing for my old apartment in the city, for my friends and our familiar haunts, for the busy, full life we led, for the laughter we shared, and the talk, and the love.

When I got home instead of going straight to bed, I went into my study. I turned on the desk lamp and sat down, not really intending to work, but not yet ready to go to bed either. There was a passage, though, that I hadn't been able to turn to my satisfaction, that was what had driven me out to the café, and I picked up that page again and looked at it. I began to cross out phrases and re-write them in the space above the line of type. Slowly the futility of what I was doing swept over me and I tore up the page and threw it down.

It was no good. For months now I'd been wrestling with this book, fighting to keep it true to the concept I'd developed in the city. I'd twisted passages and ideas, I'd compromised, I'd left in that I couldn't bring myself to leave out even though I knew it didn't quite belong. And now I knew it was no good, it didn't work; in my desperation to match my first success I'd been kidding myself.

Would I ever again write anything that was worth reading? Was what I had accomplished so far worth what everyone said? At this moment of true insight it seemed of little consequence. I saw spread out before me all the world of art, of great achievements and there was a transparent wall between me and it and I knew I had not even breached it yet. Perhaps I never would. If I had been chosen, as I had believed, it was not in the simple-minded way I had thought, and the prize I had won meant nothing.

I moved to my armchair and fell into it. My eyes lit on the stained patch on the wall, high up, that spilled over onto the ceiling. I had tried everything to remove it, but it had resisted every effort, and now it was coming through the water-based paint I had applied over it.

I remembered then how the writer whose home this had once been, had written in an autobiographical essay about that very stain, how it had come to be there as a result of a chemistry experiment he had tried as a boy, that had exploded. And I knew then that my vision, or my revelation, or whatever I might choose to call it, had come from that dead writer. And I felt, with certainty that settled in my bones, that this was why I had come here. And I was filled with dread, and an overwhelming sense of the implacability of my fate.

I sat in the armchair in the shadowed corner of the room and sweat broke out on my forehead and ran down my backbone. To stay here for the rest of my life, to struggle day after day alone, with nothing but the hills and the wind for company. I can't do it, I said, over and over again. I can't do it. I won't, I won't do it. There has to be an easier way. And then, I can leave if I want to. I can leave.

When I had calmed myself I went upstairs to my bed and escaped into sleep.

In the morning I woke late to the ringing of the phone. I stumbled downstairs to answer it and stood in a patch of sunlight spilling in from the hall that faced the east while I talked. It was Will, phoning from the city to say that he and Cheryl had gotten up this morning and decided, without any warning, that today was the day they would drive down to see me.

"Fine," I said, heavily. And then, with a little surge of pleasure, "Fine," for I had remembered what had happened the night before and I felt wholly lost, as if the floor could no longer be trusted to hold me, or the entire house might float away, like a hot air balloon that had lost its anchor.

Later in the day I was vacuuming when I felt somebody was in the room with me. Turning, I saw Palma McCallum standing in the doorway. I hadn't bothered to turn the key in the lock.

"Hi," she said, and then, a little timidly, "Are you working?"

"Just housework," I said. "Want some coffee?"

"I'll just put the kettle on for tea," she said, and disappeared toward the kitchen. I pushed the vacuum cleaner out of the way and followed her. "Thurman and I are going to visit his sister in the city," she said, over her shoulder, as she ran water into the kettle. "I had a few minutes while he's out checking things at the farm. I thought I'd drop over and see if we can pick anything up for you."

"No," I said, "I don't need anything, but it was nice of you to ask."

"What's a neighbour for," she said, taking my teapot out of the cupboard and setting it on the counter. "You got any cream?"

"Cream!" I said, "Where would I get good farm cream?"

"Darn! I got some from the Hutterites that'll just go bad when I'm away. I was going to bring it over."

"I'm having some friends come from the city later today," I said. "They'll be staying a couple of days."

"And I'm going to miss them!' she wailed. For one awful moment I thought she might try to persuade Thurman to postpone their trip.

"You wouldn't like them," I said. "They're trendy city folk."

"I might like them a lot," she replied indignantly, so that I had to laugh.

Cheryl and Will arrived about five o'clock. I was watering the front lawn when they drove up in their big, old seventy Ford. I hurried to turn the hose off while Will got slowly out of the driver's seat, untangling his long legs, and stretched luxuriously. Cheryl jumped out, and before I could say hello, called, "Wow! This must be the ends of the earth! We've been driving for hours!"

She hugged me, brushing my cheek with her lips, my nose in her hair, and I smelled that good, womanly smell, perfume or whatever, that I hadn't smelled for what suddenly seemed an eternity. Will came around the car and we slapped each other on the shoulders and shook hands.

Later, when I served the whipped cream on the Saskatoon pie that Palma had claimed was only going to waste in her freezer, they were ecstatic. "I've never seen anything like it," he said. "It's like mayonnaise."

"Why can't we get cream like this in the city?" Cheryl asked. "Where does it all go?"

"I guess this's one advantage to living in the country," I said.

After dinner we went for a long walk through the town, up one street and down another, while people in their yards stared at us or said hello.

"Can we walk out there?" Cheryl asked, pointing across the river to the hills. So I took them across the footbridge and out onto the prairie, and eventually, up into the coulee where not long before I had found the partially uncovered skeleton of a dinosaur.

"How did you find it?" Cheryl asked, kneeling and gently brushing away the earth from around it. I remembered that she knew a little about archaeology. I wondered if that included old bones, or was it just cities?

"Pure luck," I said. "I was out walking and I just happened to spot what I thought was an unusual colour of rock. It must have just been eroded out because it was still white and chalky to touch."

"That's absolutely incredible," she said. "All the people who must come out here and you're the one to find it. I can hardly believe it."

"How long ago was that?" Will asked. He was kneeling too, bending to study the piece of exposed bone. "Aren't you going to do anything about it? I mean, phone the Museum of Natural History or the University?" I shrugged, then knelt too, a little embarrassed.

"Oh, yeah, eventually," I said.

"Why don't you take these little pieces home?" Cheryl asked. She held something in her palm and blew gently on it. "I think this is a tooth, or a part of one."

"Maybe I will," I said vaguely, but I didn't touch the piece she held. She set it down again and brushed a little dirt over it.

It was growing dark, but there was a gold half-moon riding the hills to the south. Cheryl gave me a puzzled look, then stood up, brushing her hands off on her jeans.

We sat in my living room drinking scotch. After a while Cheryl stood up and said, "All this good country air is making me sleepy. I think I'll go to bed." She yawned and stretched, unconscious of how desirable she looked with her round breasts pushed against the light cloth of her shirt. I had to drop my eyes before Will noticed me looking at her.

When she had gone, Will said, "So, this is where the great old man lived." Will taught English lit at the university, specializing in modern American. Come to think of it, I was surprised he hadn't come before. "It's not much, is it," he said, "to have produced a genius."

"They were poor people," I said. "But I think the house must have been comfortable enough, especially when it was new."

"Have you had any visitations?" Will asked, grinning.

"Not exactly," I said. "I mean, there haven't been any manifestations or any weird noises in the night, if that's what you mean." He raised his eyebrows questioningly and waited for me to continue, but I felt I didn't want to talk about it, at least, not yet.

We talked about people we knew in the city, about what was going on in the publishing world, about Will and Cheryl's plans to spend Will's sabbatical travelling in Europe.

"Louise had a one woman show at the campus gallery," he

remarked, not looking at me.

"Oh?" I said. "Has she made any progress from that series of dancers or whatever it was she was doing?"

"I didn't think so," he said. "The show was a disappointment, I think that was the general opinion."

"I'm sorry to hear that," I said. Her long back turned to me in the dim light of the bedroom, her dark hair falling over her shoulders.

"How's your writing going?" Will asked softly, and I could hear in his voice how long he had been waiting to ask me that.

"It isn't going very well," I said. It had cost me something to say that, but Will was, after all, my oldest friend, the one who had encouraged me most in my desire to write, who had stood by when nobody would publish me, and who hadn't deserted me when I went off the rails after the prize. "It keeps changing on me," I said.

Will set his drink down and leaned back, staring up at the ceiling.

"How?" he asked.

"I set out to do one thing and it slipped away from me. It turned into something else." I wasn't sure anymore that this was the problem, but I didn't know what else to say. "It . . . I've . . . lost my way, at least, I've lost the old way, and I'm not sure what the new way is, or if there's a new way." There was a long silence while both of us thought about this. "I mean, I think I'm maybe just at the beginning of something new . . . but it's not what I was doing before."

"Maybe what you're doing now is better," Will said slowly.

"Better?" I thought about this. "Are you trying to tell me you didn't like my first novel?" He glanced at me, then quickly looked away, and I realized that he hadn't.

"No," he said carefully, "that's not necessarily what I meant. But you must have known you couldn't keep doing that forever." He paused, then added, "I know there's a tremendous amount of pressure on a writer, once he's had a success, to duplicate it."

"I wasn't planning to keep doing that," I said, stung. But of course I was. I thought of how sweat actually broke out on the back of my neck and how my stomach tightened whenever I thought of how the critics who had so praised my first book would meet my second. I shuddered. A coyote far out in the hills behind the house had begun to yip, and a wind had risen. We could hear it blowing softly around the eaves and through the open windows of the house. I began to tell him how my life was, in this house, and what had happened to me in my study the night before.

"No wonder your work is changing," he said. "But what do you think it means?"

"It means that . . . I wasn't a writer before," I said. "I think, it means I had to undergo some kind of . . . profound change . . . before I could go on." I shook my head, then fell silent. I could hear the papers in my study scattering across the floor as the wind grew stronger. Let them blow, I thought.

"You'll be coming back to the city then?" Will asked.

The next day we went for a longer walk in the hills, this time carrying with us a few sandwiches and a bottle of wine that Cheryl and Will had brought. When we were far from the town, or any signs of civilization, we sat down on a grassy hillside and enjoyed the sun and the breeze and the scent of sage that was on the air all around us. Watching Cheryl lying on her back in the grass, one arm thrown across her eyes to shield them from the sun and her hair spread out around her head, I thought again of Louise, and regret swept through me.

"By the way," Cheryl said, taking her arm down, "that thing Louise had going with Bob Stewart is over."

"They were always fighting," Will said. "It was downright funny." Cheryl rolled over onto her stomach and grew silent, looking up at me where I sat above her on the hillside.

"Are you happy here?"

"I'm not unhappy," I said.

"Isn't it awfully lonely?" she asked.

"I only started to get lonely lately," I told her. "I swear I wasn't before."

"Nobody's even seen you for four or five months."

"I've been to the city a few times," I admitted. "But I didn't go to Saskatoon. And I had to fly to Toronto for a few days last month. I haven't been here the whole time."

"Just avoiding your friends, eh," Cheryl said, laughing.

"No," I said. "I was avoiding something else."

"The scene of the crime," Will said.

We decided to have supper in the café, which, for a change, was more than half-full when we arrived. We found an empty booth next to the row of stools at the counter and Harry came over to say hello, then left us to go back to 'chewing the fat', as he put it, with a couple of farmers in a back booth. Benjamin, the old Hutterite, was there, too, with a different companion, this one a tall, skinny twenty-year old in a black suit that was too short in the sleeves. They were eating supper in their usual booth near the back.

"This food isn't bad," Cheryl said, as we began to eat.

"Do you eat here often?" Will asked.

"No," I said, "hardly ever, but I come down occasionally for a cup of coffee in the evening." The waitress came back and refilled our cups. The café had begun to empty and it was growing dark outside. Cheryl and Will were planning to leave in the morning.

Will suddenly glanced up and I realized someone was standing beside me, leaning against the low partition that separated our booth from the aisle and the row of stools on the other side. It was Benjamin.

"Hello, George," he said. "You got visitors."

"Yes," I said, and introduced Cheryl and Will to him. His companion passed him, paid the bill, and went outside.

"You're in town late," I said.

"We . . ." he began, and was cut off abruptly, pushing almost over the partition into our booth. His hat fell off and tumbled up against Will's coffee cup. Somebody passing by had bumped into him so hard that he had been knocked almost off his feet. I could see by his expression and the way he was holding his upper arm that the collision had hurt him. We all realized at the same time that it had been deliberate. In the confusion, heads turning, voices raised, I looked from Benjamin to the young farmer who was walking fast toward the door. I saw him look back over his shoulder at Ben; I saw he was grinning, and there was a light shining in his pale eyes that was ugly to see.

"He did that on purpose!" Cheryl said, and then to Benjamin, "Are you hurt?"

"No, no," Benjamin said, reaching out to take his hat back from Will. He looked toward the door, but the farmer was gone. Suddenly Harry was there.

"He's drunk again," he said to us. He turned to Benjamin. "You know what Ernie's like when he's drinking. Don't pay any attention to him." Benjamin shakily set his hat back on his head, but didn't answer Harry.

"To do that to an old man!" Will said, his voice filled with disgust, and there were murmurs from people sitting near us.

"That Ernie, he goes too far," Harry said. "He'll wind up in jail yet." The shocked voices around the café were dying down now as people turned backed to their meals.

"I . . . I go find Joseph," Benjamin mumbled, ignoring our questions, and walked away, a slow, shuffling walk, not at all the way he usually moved.

"Somebody should call the police!" Cheryl said in a loud, indignant voice.

"Shsh," Will hushed her.

"Do you think there's anything we should do?" I asked Harry. The way Benjamin had walked away, the look on his face, as though he was lost or in shock. But I thought, probably Benjamin and Joseph are in the van by now, pulling out of town, on their way back to the colony. Harry shrugged and turned to watch the closed door as if it might have the answer written on it.

"Do you know that Ernie?" Will asked me.

"He's in here a lot or in the bar," I said. "I don't know him."

"Let's go," Cheryl said, in a low, choked voice, pushing her half-full cup away. Her cheeks were flushed and she wasn't looking at Will or me. We rose hastily, following her, paid the bill, and went outside into the summer night.

Benjamin was standing alone in the middle of the sidewalk, peering down the street, first one way and then the other. A couple of men in the shadows along the wall of the café.

"Are you okay, Benjamin?" I asked.

"I don't know where van is," he said, in a frightened voice. Will was the first to take in the situation.

"I'll run and get my car," he offered in a firm voice. "It won't take me five minutes, and if we can't find your friend, I'll drive you home." He started to sprint away in the direction of my house. I turned to the men standing by the wall.

"Do you know why Joseph left without Ben?" I asked. "Did he say anything?"

One of the men came forward into the light thrown through the door of the café and I saw that it was Martin Gutwin, a family man, not often in the café.

"He got in the van and drove away," Martin said. His lined, suntanned face was concerned, and he thrust his hands into the pockets of his pants. "It was the damndest thing! Ernie came barrelling out of the café and Joe was standing right there on the sidewalk by the van, waiting for Ben, I guess, and Ernie shoved him up against the van and swung on him."

Cheryl gasped, and Benjamin took a step toward Martin as if to ask more.

"Then, before we could do anything, Ernie jumped in his truck and peeled rubber outta here. We helped Joe up," he nodded toward the other man still standing back in the shadows, "and Joe got in the van and pulled out. I thought he was going after Ernie, but . . ."

"No, no, he never do that," Ben interrupted, shaking his head.

"He went that way," Martin said, pointing down the street. He laughed, turning to Benjamin, a strained sound. "Went off and left you, eh?"

"What's the matter with him, anyway?" Cheryl asked. "Doesn't he understand that these men are pacifists? That they won't defend themselves?"

"I guess he understands that pretty well," Martin said.

"This is incomprehensible!" Cheryl said. "This is terrible." At that moment Will arrived in their old Ford, the brakes squealing. Cheryl got in beside him and Benjamin beside her. I sat in the back, behind Benjamin.

"Are you sure you're not hurt?" Will asked him.

Will began driving up and down the few streets, all of us peering out the open windows.

"There!" Cheryl cried. The van was parked by the sidewalk in front of the Mountie's office. Will parked behind it under the old cottonwoods, their branches trailing over the car. The light from the streetlight was muted and erratic as it shone through the limbs of the big trees. We saw Joseph coming down the steps from the office where he had been pounding on the locked door. The old man was out of the car almost before we came to a full stop, surprising us with his agility, which had returned when he saw the van.

"They aren't here after five o'clock," I said to Cheryl and Will.

Joseph was striding down the walk with short, jerky steps and as Benjamin reached him, the top of his head coming just up to Joseph's shoulder, he touched Joseph's arm, but Joseph pulled angrily away from him. We couldn't make out Benjamin's words, but he seemed to be pleading with Joseph. The van's motor was still running and Joseph went to it, his long legs scissoring in an awkward, staccato way that expressed his agitation.

He began suddenly to shout at Benjamin. The old man followed him, pulling at Joseph's too-short jacket.

Suddenly Joseph turned hard and began to stride down the sidewalk toward us where we sat in the car, Benjamin still hurrying beside him, his head raised to look up at Joseph, still pulling at the boy's sleeve. As they came closer we could hear Joseph cursing. He paced wildly, up and down, cursing at the farmer who had assaulted him, raging, using language that must have horrified old Benjamin.

"Joseph, Joseph, nein, nein, remember . . ." and Joseph would jerk away, pace in the other direction, still cursing. His voice disturbed the calm of the peaceful little street. The old man began to cry.

He let go of Joseph's sleeve and came to us, standing on the sidewalk close to the open doors of the car.

"I don't know," he said, spreading out his hands helplessly. "I can't . . . He is . . ." We could see his tears glistening on his beard.

"I'm sorry this happened," I said. "I'm so sorry."

Joseph had stopped cursing and was standing half-way between the truck and our car in a patch of shadow. We could see his chest and hands, but not his face. He said something in German to Benjamin that sounded harsh and angry, a command. Benjamin went to him at once, remonstrating softly with him in German. Joseph turned away again, went back to the van and climbed in, slamming the door. Benjamin stood watching him for a minute, then came back to us.

"But . . . what happened?" she asked. "Why did Ernie do that?"

"He was just drunk," Will said to her.

Benjamin wiped his face with his sleeve, then touched his beard with fingers that still trembled.

"He's neighbour to us," he said. "We help him with his cattle, we help him cut hay . . ."

"Well, you certainly shouldn't help him anymore," Cheryl said, angry again. Ben ignored the interruption.

"At Christmas," Benjamin went on, "we sell him pair of socks. He said they don't match. We tell him, bring them back, we give another pair, but he . . . " Ben shrugged. "He still mad."

Will sucked in his breath. Cheryl and I were silent.

"We go to colony," Benjamin said, his voice soft, and he made a gesture toward us with his hands as if to hush us. "Many thanks." He started back to the van, hurrying now, as Joseph roared the motor. We watched him struggle up into it and shut the door. It squealed away from the curb and roared down the silent street. We watched until its tail-lights disappeared around the curve that would take it out of town and up into the hills where the colony was.

In the morning Cheryl and Will were up early, packed, and ready to leave for Saskatoon. We were subdued, as though what had happened the night before had affected us out of all proportion to its importance.

"It's a lousy day," I said. A cold wind was blowing and the sky was heavy with deep rainclouds that I knew from experience would hang there all day and yet not shed a drop. Such a hard, dry country, I thought.

"More coffee?" Cheryl asked. Will and I shook our heads, no. "I suppose we should get moving," she said. Will stared moodily out the small kitchen window.

"But the writer wrote about how beautiful it is here in the winter — the hills shining with snow, the sky above them a clear, endless blue . . ." I could hardly speak, such a heaviness had descended on my spirit. I half-wished Palma would burst in with her cheerful scolding. Cheryl had begun to gather the breakfast plates. Now she set them down and spoke directly to me, her blue eyes meeting mine.

"Come with us," she said. "Come with us now. You can come back for your furniture later." We stared at each other. Behind us Will moved.

"No," he said softly.

"Why not?" Cheryl asked him, surprised. But still he didn't speak, gathering his thoughts, or waiting for us to understand something he had already seen.

"You know why," he said to me at last. There was an intensity in his eyes I hadn't seen in years. "He'll stay here," he said to Cheryl.

For no reason that I could name, I had the impression that there was someone else in the room with us. The sensation was so strong that I couldn't stop myself from looking nervously around. Cheryl, seeing this, did too, then looked at me in a puzzled, questioning way.

"What is it?" she asked.

"Someone just walked on my grave," I said. We stood in the kitchen, the three of us, the normally bright room gloomy. "I'm afraid," I said.

"And so you should be," Will said, after a minute, but he was smiling.

I rode with them to the service station a block away and waited while they gassed up.

"I hate to see you go," I said, when the tank was full and Will had paid.

Cheryl put both her arms around me and hugged me hard, pulling me tight against her.

"You come and see us whenever you can," she said. When she stepped back to get in the car there were tears in her eyes. Will and I hugged, then stood back.

"Write to me more often," he said, putting one arm around my shoulders.

"Come more often," I said.

Cheryl called through the open window.

"Next time we'll bring Louise with us. You can show her that dinosaur bone." Will went around the car and got in the driver's seat. "I mean it," Cheryl said.

I watched them drive away as we had watched the Hutterite's van disappear the night before. Then I walked slowly back to the house where my manuscript waited on the table beneath the window that had the view of the hills and the mouth of the coulee where the dinosaurs had walked.

CHETAN RAJANI was born in Uganda and now lives in Ottawa. His stories have been featured in *Best Canadian Stories* and *The Literary Half-Yearly*. This story first appeared in CFM No. 66-67 in 1989, a special issue on Ontario writers.

The Letter Writer

CHETAN RAJANI

IT WAS EVENING and Manu-bhai the letter-writer was coming to the end of another day, under the Banyan tree in the centre of town. It was the quiet hour now, between the rush and bustle of the day-time crowd and the appearance of the first of the promenaders. Most of the stores along the east side of the square had closed for the day, their brightly coloured doors and shutters adding to the quiet scene a garishness not visible before. The last of these merchants were hurrying home, some on bicycles, some on foot. Soon many of them would return with their families, looking fresh and rested after a wash and tea, dressed in their casual clothes, to walk the river bank beyond the *maidan* before supper.

The emptying of the square was a signal for the middle-aged letter-writer in the undulating light and shadows of the tree to begin his own closing ritual of bringing his 'Office' in order. The ink wells of the small, folding, school-type desk that Lai Singh the *mistri* had designed and made specially for him were running dry and Manu-bhai busied himself with the task of filling them. His stock of bottles stood on the low cement *parri* that encircled the tree, and which served as his chair during the day and on which some of the promenaders sat at night to chat — his customers usually stood before him. The red bottle always came first and now he reached for it.

There hadn't been any wedding invitations to write today and the well with the red ink needed only a few drops to replenish the loss due to evaporation. He recapped the bottle after wiping its narrow mouth with the stained rag he used for just this purpose. Then he wrapped a corner of the cloth around his right third finger and, with a motion as deft as that of a young girl applying kohl to an eyelid, wiped the black rim of the plastic well before plugging it with a cork to protect it from the dust stirred up by passing carts, bicycles, and the occasional car. Then followed the well with the business black, reduced now to nib-scratching level due to the heavy, end-of-month rush. Then came the blue of the personal correspondence well which was half empty.

Reach, recap, fill, wipe-wipe, plug and put away. He did this methodically and with the economy and fluidity of motion that came from fifteen years of daily practice. Now the bottles could be put away into the black leather bag which also sat on the *parri* and which contained the implements and supplies of his trade as well as a few personal items stowed into a designated corner — he would not be needing any more ink for the evening as the returning day-labourers and promenaders brought only a little business. Clean the six holder pens, remove the nibs and clean them with a scrap of blotting paper . . . wipe the desk top . . . a fresh supply of paper from the ream in the drawer . . . there, all done now, except for the sorting of the day's letters which he always did after going to the water tap.

His next evening-ritual was the more personal one of what he liked to think of as 'bringing himself into order.' He walked to the municipal tap across the square with a towel, a bar of soap and his water tumbler. The tap was a meeting place for the town women during the day but was deserted now, and even the marks of their visits, their mingled footprints in the dirt around the cement stand and the gutter had dried into crusty molds which now crumbled under his buffalo-hide sandals. He turned the flaking, rust-blistered tap and briskly washed his face and hands. He wetted his hair, finger combed it, and then filled his tumbler with water for a long drink to slake the hot afternoon's thirst. The first gulp of metallic tasting water he always used for gargling and rinsing his parched mouth. He did this now with quick puffing and sucking motions of his cheeks, and then streamed the residue with his usual, unerring accuracy, with a loud *pwrrth*, into the gutter. He drank slowly, then went back to the tree, singing. The singing, too, was a part of the daily ritual. Today he sang, in a low airy voice which sometimes caught in his chest, the words to an old Hindi film song: *Awarah hoon, Aware hoon.* 'A vagabond am I . . .'

At the tree, he sat on the *parri* and began to sort the day's letters for the morning post-office run: a pile for the local, and one for the overseas — or 'foreign' as the townspeople so quaintly put it. Around him he could hear the evening chatter of the birds by the river and the music from the sweet shop across the street. From the direction of the town's houses he could hear the rattle of the two snack-vendors' carts approaching the square through a cobbled alley: the *chai-walla* and the *pakora walla.* He could smell them already, above the rich smell of rotting, fallen figs that surrounded the tree. Soon he would be able to have his evening snack of tea and a *samosa* and smoke one of the three daily *birris* he allowed himself to buy from the tea-vendor's wagon. He had almost finished his sorting when he happened to look up and noticed the young man standing across the street near Mithoobhai's Mithai Mart, watching him.

The young man was dressed in an outfit similar to the letter-writer's: a long white *kurta*-shirt and white draw-string pajama pants. He stood stiffly, half in the shadow of the roof overhang, his arms crossed at his chest. He looked familiar, and the letter-writer who knew all the people in the area — at least by face — tried to place him. The young man's nervousness, which was quite apparent to Manu-bhai was even more familiar and he instantly recognized its source. The letter-writer's lean face broke into a smile.

This one wants me to compose him a love letter — how long will it take him to muster up the courage to come and ask?

Manu-bhai was sure he was right. Over the years, be felt he had finely honed a certain ability to read people, an ability he was so proud of that he seldom considered himself wrong.

The letter-writer crossed his own arms at his chest in imitation of the young man and stared back at him. The young man turned and fled, disappeared behind the sweet shop.

The letter-writer laughed.

That night after the last of the stragglers had left, Manu-bhai walked home with his bag of supplies under one arm and the folded desk stung over his right shoulder by means of a strap. He found himself smiling again. And he began to sing: '*Tooh merah dulʻah, mai terrih dulahan* . . . you are my bridegroom and I your bride.' He chuckled. The prospect of another long-distance-love-affair customer after such a long time promised relief from the boredom of the daily routine and this lifted his spirits considerably. This would be something new, something different from the drudgery of the daily lies and numbers of business letters and the petty victories and scandals and flattery of personal letters. Just the thought of it filled him with a thrill, that secret voyeur's thrill that accompanies the event of being privy to something not one's own. It put a spring in his step, set his arms to swinging, and made the fingers of his free left hand trill in the air before him, as if on an invisible accordion, the bridge to the song's chorus.

He stopped suddenly and looked back. Sometimes these desperate types followed him home in order to make their fumbling-mumbling request in the privacy of an alleyway. They would come running up behind him like some street *goonda* and scare the breath out of him. Then, quite unlike a thug, they would stand beside him, shuffling their feet and meekly, imploringly, touch his arm. They would hum and clear their throats, glance this way and that — anywhere but into his face. 'A small matter,' they would begin, 'a personal matter, Letter-*sabib*.'

Nothing. The alley was empty except for a multi-coloured dog a few yards away, nosing at someone's back steps. The dog's tail stiffened and then wagged hesitantly. It stopped sniffing the garbage and sidled over to the letter-writer, as if dragging an invisible leash. Manu-bhai continued on his walk down the long alley toward the road home. The dog, sensing the letter-writer's essentially benign nature — or at least his indifference — followed at a distance, occasionally pausing to make forays into interesting smelling corners. Over his shoulders the letter-writer heard its paws padding on the packed-in dirt floor of the alley and mapped from the sound the mutt's course behind him.

On both sides of the alley there were houses, the windows of which threw onto the opposite floors and walls parallelograms of barred light, creating a topless tunnel of random geometric forms through which the shadows of the dog and man led each other, switching places in the areas of darkness. The letter-writer observed with a touch of amusement the phenomenon of their lurking shadows mingling and kaleidoscoping in the alley. Through the windows he glimpsed the activities of the inhabitants: a crew-cut head studiously bent over a book; a bespectacled nose sniffing the daily paper; the straining, pigtailed, *saried* back of a woman leaning over a stove. An invisible girl's sudden laughter resounded off the walls. Somewhere a baby was crying and there came a woman's soothing response. Snatches of music, emitted from transistors in these houses, followed him and faded briefly, only to be resumed louder at the next house where the same song was playing. Another house, another radio, the same song, approaching and fading.

And cooking smells assailed him, maddeningly aromatic cooking smells from which he catalogued the supper menu of each residence. The letter-writer who had eaten only a *samosa* with his tea that evening found himself salivating and thinking about the time when his wife was alive and always had a hot supper ready for him. He used to go home early in those days, closing up shop along with the rest of the merchants in the square and often walking with and chatting to whoever happened to be going in his direction. His wife, too, always put the radio on after she finished cooking, and listened to it while she waited for him.

When he reached the lane that led to his one-room brick house just off the main road, the letter-writer found himself hurrying up the garden path, the overgrown grass and weeds on either side brushing against his pant legs, leaving burrs attached to the cotton. And he realized that he had been expecting, somehow, miraculously, the door to be open and the lights to be on and the music to be coming through the screen door. But the house was silent and only its corrugated iron roof which reflected the moonlight displayed any signs of life: the movement of shadows of the Tamarind tree at the front corner of the house. The letter-writer stopped at the front steps, slightly embarrassed at having fallen into the same old trap of expecting miracles. The dog came up around him and sniffed the steps. The letter-writer ignored it. The dog snorted and yawned and then trotted away, its nails scratching and clacking on the flagstones of the path.

Inside, he turned on the lights, lighted the *Primus* stove and put on some water for tea. He walked all around the room, as he waited for the water to come to a boil. On the dresser sat a hand mirror and a shell comb. On the wall was a painting of the goddess Laxmi and above the door-way hung a torohana of mango leaves, dried and crumbled after so many years. A fine layer of dust covered everything. Now, in the harsh light of the single shadeless lamp on the ceiling, the letter-writer found the room unbearable — how he hated coming home to a house that smelt only of dust and kerosene fumes. He looked at an object and she was holding it. He looked at a spot and she was standing there. He dared not look at the bed.

After he had prepared his tea Manu-bhai went outside to sit on the steps. He took a sip of his tea and grimaced: he had never mastered the correct proportions of tea leaves, milk and *chai-masala* needed to make a truly great cup of tea. As he put the cup on the step beside him, he noticed that there was a full moon that night, and that the air was cool and redolent with the smell of eucalyptus from the trees that lined the road beyond the tangled garden. The sky was clear and stars boldly studded its inky blue expanse. From all around there came the *kurkeek-kurkeek* of cicadas.

He sat there for a long time, staring into the darkness, his tea untouched after the first sip and growing cold. A mosquito bite finally brought him around. He thought then of the young man who had fled and how his face had reappeared later in the evening, pale and ghostly in the square's only street light, timidly inching closer into the group of promenaders by the Banyan tree. The letter-writer smiled wanly, and scratched the side of his chin, feeling the black and grey stubble there. And he realized that he had forgotten to shave today. Again.

He will come to me yet with his request for a love letter. His shyness will fall under its own unbearable weight — like an overripe fig from a Banyan. Such is love's gravity.

It took the young man three days to work up the courage. He came early one morning when the letter-writer was still in the process of setting up his desk, and stood mutely before him.

The last time such a love-stricken youth had stood before him, shifting from one foot to another like a child before an angry parent, the letter-writer had taken great pleasure in making the boy go through the uncomfortable ritual of stating, very specifically, the nature of his request. When that young man had shyly intimated the personal nature of the epistle, the letter-writer had only pressed him further, querying in a rather loud voice for the *exact* nature of the 'personal letter' he had wanted written. The young man had cringed and, it seemed to the delighted letter-writer, visibly shrunk when a passerby looked toward them.

'Oh, a love letter it is you want me to write for you! Why didn't you say so in the first place?'

A man walking by had snickered, overhearing the words. The boy's dark face had turned to a shade of purple and Manu-bhai had finally stopped, realizing that to take the play much further would altogether endanger the transaction, for the boy's entire body seemed poised for flight, and for a moment, it seemed to the letter-writer, he would disappear in a puff of smoke by the sheer intensity of his embarrassment. He had not wanted to lose the young man completely for, whatever else, these types could be relied upon to provide steady, not to mention more interesting, business. And further, they were willing to pay more than the going rate per line, often three times as much.

Afterwards, recalling the incident, the letter-writer had been surprised, even shocked at how easily, how rapidly the good business sense he had cultivated and prided himself on had departed in the face of an opportunity to have a bit of fun. Fortunately, it had all turned out well and ended in marriage. The letter-writer did not want to lose this young man who was, if it were possible, even shyer than the last one.

'You want this letter written to whom?'

'A girl — a lady in . . .' the boy said, naming a small nearby town. He looked quite relieved.

The letter-writer smiled benignly. 'A love letter,' he said, casually.

'Yes, something like that.'

'You want me to write it or take dictation?'

'I will dictate.'

The letter-writer looked up from his ink wells, surprised. 'Name?' he asked sardonically.

'Mine or hers?'

'Hers, of course — her name, the recipient's name always comes first.'

'Yes, of course. Kusum is her name, Sahib.'

The letter-writer pulled out a sheet of paper and placed it with a flourish on his desk.

'Ink?'

'Yes, ink.'

'I meant what colour?'

'Colour?'

'Yes, what colour of ink would you like me to use?'

The young man's shoulders stiffened at the decision. His arms came up, scooping air, hands almost joined in the manner of prayer.

'In cases like this special ink is not inappropriate,' the letter-writer said quickly.

'Special ink?'

'Yes, may I suggest Peacock Blue — I have a small stock of it in my bag. Special stock it is — the best — but it costs a *pai* per line extra, you understand.'

'Yes, of course; whatever you suggest, whatever you think best — I leave it entirely in your hands.'

'Good,' said the letter-writer. He retrieved the small bottle of ink from his bag, uncapped it, and set it on the desk. He dipped his rarely used peacock pen into the ink and sat with the pen poised over the whiteness of the paper, watching the shadow it created on the shifting collage of light and shade from the light filtering through the leaves of the Banyan tree, a shadow oddly resembling the hood and fangs of a cobra poised to attack.

'Paper?' he said, lifting a corner of the sheet, about to go on and offer a choice of colours and scents which, in truth, he did not possess.

'White is fine.'

'As you wish. Please begin.'

'Dear Kusum, I am sorry for not having written to you as soon as I arrived home but . . .' the young man blurted out and then paused, as if surprised at the fact that he was finally saying those words.

'Go on.'

'I am thinking.'

'Well, I will start while you think.'

My dearest, sweetest Kusum, wrote the letter-writer, and waited. Then: *I have not written to you as promptly as I promised but* . . . and there he stopped.

Finally the young man said, '. . . but I ran out of paper and the cow was sick so I could not leave the house for three days and father would not give me money for the paper.'

I came home to find my mother in ill health, and had to spend three days attending to her.

'I am fine, how are you?'

And I have spent every single moment of those three days thinking of you. And every night, I have not been able to sleep for thoughts of you. When I look out the window of my room and see the moon's radiant face, I am reminded of yours. And when I hear a nightingale I hear your voice. As I sense the smell of jasmine lingering near our house, I feel a terrible longing for you. I fear I may become sick if I do not see you soon . . . wrote the letter-writer.

The boy dictated in long rambling pauses interspersed with moments where an occasional word emerged, or a whole series of them actually assembled themselves into a sentence. The letter-writer, who for the most part ignored him, wrote furiously, desperately fighting to ward off his own brand of speechlessness. When he had finished he realized that the young man had stopped dictating for some time now, and was staring at him. Manu-bhai felt exhausted. He finished by asking the young man his name.

'Vijay,' said the young man.

. . . *Forever yours, with love, Vijay-kumar,* wrote the letter-writer.

They both waited for the last of the ink to dry and then Manu-bhai read the letter aloud. When he had finished he realized that he had deviated considerably from the young man's dictation, but somehow the substance of the letter was essentially that of the young lover's.

'Good. It is a good letter, you got it down exactly as I said it.' After Vijay left, Manu-bhal put the coins the young man had given him for postage and writing fee into his tin cigarette case, and smoked a *birri* three hours before his schedule permitted it — while he re-read the letter. And as he read he remembered a time many years ago in the city where he had gone to college.

He had considered himself quite the poet in those days, and used to frequent a café near the university favoured by aspiring writers and artists. He had taken up smoking and though only a farmer's son, assumed the European style of clothing, jargon, and mannerisms favoured by the dilettantes of the day. The drinking of large quantities of coffee, and later, in his second year, wine, and talking about Life and Art had become an integral aspect of the new lifestyle that eschewed studies and praised decadence and curfew-breaking. The life in his parents' village, his childhood with his sisters, had receded further into his memory then, but not far enough, for it seemed to him that those memories owned the interminable, odious quality of an especially bad and sentimental Hindi film one had seen, and which plagued one's mind despite its obvious lack of merit. And he had fallen in love.

She was a student at a nearby girl's college; intelligent, beautiful, from a wealthy family, and completely ignorant of his existence. And he had been completely, fatalistically enamored with all those things about her, except the last which caused him no end of pain. Of course, he felt he had a good chance of winning her if only he could somehow draw her attention. Each night he sat at his desk in the hostel where he lived, drinking smuggled-in wine while he attempted to compose a love letter to her.

He had never written the letter, and a few months later, after an evening when he had heard her reading her poems at a mixed gathering in the Student Union Hall, and realized that she was already a better poet than he would ever become, after a night of anguish and self-recriminations, he had finally admitted to himself that be did not possess the courage to approach her. So full of self-loathing he had been, that the next day he had cut classes and very systematically got drunk; blind staggering drunk on cheap wine by four in the afternoon. He had been taken back to the hostel by some concerned friends to sleep it off, which he had done and then still hungover, had gone out again, this time in the company of the most decadent of his café acquaintances. He had gone, goaded by despair and emboldened by more wine, to *that* part of the city where he had vented his passions on, and found a modicum, if not of solace, then at least of a kind of warmth in the arms of a whore who did not in the least resemble she who had been responsible for it all.

Manu-bhal the letter-writer realized that he had now in his hands that letter he bad attempted to write then, some twenty years too late.

Each day after that, Vijay the lover came to the letter-writer's office in the cool, undulating shadows of the Banyan tree to see if a response had arrived for him. He would sit on the *parri* next to the older man and share a few moments of silence with him. It was pleasant under the tree, with the rich smell of rotting, fallen figs; a good view of the square's activities; under the tree, the branches of which sent down shoots which became roots, and roots that broke the surface at the base, oddly resembling intertwined human limbs. The letter-writer did not mind these visits and, indeed, came to enjoy and even look forward to them. The boy's mute, stolid personality seemed somehow well placed under the tree and was not at all intrusive. Having no real friends to speak of, Manu-bhai was always a little sad when the young man finally stood up and mumbled something about it being late, of the long walk home, and waiting parents, for it meant he would be alone again. Once when the boy had not appeared at his usual time, the letter-writer found himself unable to relax until the next day when he showed up, almost apologetic, mumbling something about visitors.

There came a response some two weeks after the letter was sent. The letter-writer picked it up at the post-office on his morning run. He could barely contain his excitement, and found himself impatient for the day to end and the young man's arrival so that he could open the letter. With a professional and practised eye, he examined the letter several times, and concluded from the script and type of envelope that it was also written by a letter-writer. He recognized the professional *letter-walla* imprint — besides, the girl, like the boy, was probably illiterate. This in itself was not unusual at all for he had dealt with other letter-writers before, quite common in the country in fact. No, what was unusual was the fact that the letter had been penned by a female hand — obviously and undoubtedly a female hand. True there was that woman in the south country, and also the one in the northeast, who were in the business, but he had heard from them only once each in his fifteen years in the trade. And he *knew* the letter-writer in that town, an old man who, from what he had heard, had been in the business practically since the turn of the century. The letter-writer's professional curiosity was soon aroused and then the impulse to open the letter without the young man being there came to him.

Although it seemed quite permissible to open the letter, professionally speaking — he was, after all going to read it anyway — the letter-writer hesitated before the decision. He could not bring himself to do now what he had never before done in his career. He put it away in his desk drawer where, between customers, he could reach in and touch it; run his finger along the flap seal, along the perforations of the stamp. He knew as he debated the issue, that even if he were to open it without the boy being there, it would do him no good. It was as if he, by a curious sort of reversal, had become the young man, the true recipient of the letter, and the young man the letter-writer, now somehow, strangely, empowered to decipher the contents.

The event of the letter so disrupted the beginning of Manu-bhai's day that his routine of setting up the desk was not even completed when the first customer came to him; from then on things got worse. The letter-writer was a man who depended on habit to see him safely to the end of the day, and now that he had veered so far off his course he found it difficult to do anything with his usual, easy manner. Everything he experienced had the opposite of its usual effect: the sight of the women going to the tap and the sound of their voices did not give him the same sense of comfort and company as before; and the activity in the square brought not a diversion but an irritating distraction. The day, it seemed to him, would never end, but end it did and dusk found the young man walking toward the letter-writer, and the older man waving the letter to him. Their dark, almost black forms played out a pantomime against the crimson-blue sunset beyond the *maidan*, and from across the street Mithoobhal the *mithaiwalla* watched the entire performance.

The young man seeing the letter in Manu-bhai's hand began to run. The letter-writer began to jump up and down on his *parri* seat, waving the dark rectangle even more excitedly. Passersby stopped to watch the spectacle. The older man handed the younger one the letter. The young man looked at it very carefully, and then gave it back to the letter-writer, who swiftly applied his letter opener — a miniature cutlass — to it, and unfolded the letter.

As was his custom the letter-writer first read the letter to himself in order to become familiar with the contents before reading it aloud to the young man. It seemed fine to read it now that the boy was here. The letter was the usual love letter, not as impassioned and poetic as the one he remembered writing, but a good one just the same. In fact it was a near duplication of his own, except for the stilted language, and the post-script. The letter-writer read the letter to the young man, who listened solemnly. When he had finished, the young man requested another reading, and Manu-bhai complied. Then Vijay asked to see the letter, and the letter-writer, not without a twinge of reluctance, acquiesced — it was, after all the young man's letter.

'Will you keep this safe-safe for me? I can't take it home — my mother may find it,' the young man said after carefully examining the letter — delicately holding it between trembling hands and peering judiciously at it.

'Of course,' said the letter-writer, 'most pleased to.'

'I will come back tomorrow to write another one,' said the young man, and turned to leave.

Then he turned around, as if he had suddenly remembered something. 'What were those lines at the bottom about —the ones after the space?' Manu-bhai did not respond immediately, but waited. The young man also waited. The letter-writer's lips set grimly at the thought of the postscript. He hoped that the young man would not persist. The young man would not budge. Finally the letter-writer spoke: 'Just more of the same same stuff — you know?. . . Look, I am an older and more modest man, and it is not becoming that I read aloud the impassioned words of a young woman — it was nice-nice, you understand? No? Yes, you are man, you understand.'

Post-script:
This girl is a snivelling, ugly, tongue-waggling shrew. Were it not for the fact that I am new in the business, I would not deal with her at all (and I may not do it again, anyway). What about him, is he the Dev Anand you and her make him out to be, or some puerile, lumbering, farm lummox?

Post-script:
Dear Letter-walli, it is very unprofessional to make such statements about one's clients, and, further, a habit to eschew if one is serious about making this one's business. To answer your question, he is neither lummox, nor film star, but a simple farm boy with a good heart. Please refrain from making personal comments in future letters.

Post-script:

Dear Letter-walla, I have to apologize for my indiscretions of the previous letter from this party. You are absolutely right, it is unprofessional and even unethical, not to mention cruel. I do not know what came over me. It was just that she was excited and giggly, that it was difficult to get even a straight word out of her. Also, business is slow, and what little there is of it, is boring. Besides, you are such a poetic, artistic writer that I was sure that you would not have minded this bit of fun. Forgive me for being so presumptuous.

Post-script:

Apology accepted, we will speak no more of it. I must admit to many similar urges, especially when I was younger and more impetuous, and did not understand the seriousness of the service we provide. I now have a bit of professional pride that keeps me from indulging in the occasional impulses that arise these days when business becomes too boring and monotonous to bear. But when one works for a living one must learn to put up with such things — it is not such a bad profession, you must agree.

Also, admit I must, to having written much poetry in my youth. A compliment from a colleague means a great deal. I thank you, but must say that you may have overestimated my talents (as this letter will surely prove!); frankly, I fear I had 'written over my head,' and am not likely to repeat such a performance — I do not know what came over me. Thank you just the same.

Post-script:

You are much too modest. Why, your last letter far surpasses the previous one. It is more powerful and sure of itself. Why did you ever stop writing poetry? Also, you are right, ours is a very serious business, and not without its rewards. Why, only yesterday, I got a few more clients and they were all so nice. It seems that the old man who did this job before is fast going blind and senile; all of his customers are now coming to me now and complaining of illegible prose, crankiness and so on. Sad for him but good for me. You see, I need the money. I have a son to support.

Dear Letter-walli,

Thank you again for your compliments. You may be right, the muse seems to be favouring me again. Why, only yesterday, at a free moment during the day, I found coming to me the opening lines to a story that I have long intended to write about our town painter, which I wrote down immediately.

In answer to your question: I stopped writing poetry because after my college days I believed myself to be a novelist, another Dickens or Tolstoy, or Turgenev. You see, life which had until then seemed so easy, showed me its other side. I fell in love and wound up with a broken heart. And my parents, who I had neglected in my college days, both passed away one within a few months of the other. Everything I felt then seemed too strong, too big to be encompassed within the form of a mere poem; an epic novel, I felt, was boiling within me.

Post-script:
Your heart was broken, and you had seen the death of those you loved, and then?

Post-script:
And then? And then I left the city and with the little money that came from my father's will, I set up house in this little town, a place I had chosen randomly, with my eyes closed, from a map at the bus station. For a year, I sat in my little rented room and wrote about all the people I saw from my window. I imagined their lives, and so began the great novel of peasant life. But it died, too, every word of it, on paper. I started to panic. Then I started to go outside every day, to write sketches, descriptions, anything to keep writing, to keep my hand in; but it was no use. There was something wrong, something missing, something I did not know that kept me from continuing. One day, a man who had seen me writing under the Banyan tree came up to me and asked me to write for him, a letter to his lawyer for some business or other in the city. Ad that is how, by accident and default, unwittingly and reluctantly, I came to my profession.

Dear Letter-walla,
Tell your young man something nice, and also, that the young lady has finally decided that she is going to broach the subject with her parents, and urges him to do the same with his. So, that is it for your life? You must be young, or else you have not told me everything. Surely you did not give up completely after that difficult time, surely you are working on your epic. They say it took Tripath twenty-five years to write Sarasvati Chandra. My late husband told me that. He is the one who taught me to read and write; a college fellow be was, just like you,

except he was a lawyer. I remember how difficult it was to read and write, but I persevered. Surely you too persevered?

P.S. What is your name 'letter-walla sahib' (it seems silly that we have written for so long and still do not know each other's names — mine is 'Kanchan')? Also, how is the story about the painter going?

Dear Kanchan-behn,

You are right, that is not all there was to my life. I worked at the profession, but without heart; it was just a means of making money, a way of using my small gift with words until I could start writing again. Around my twenty-fifth year, a distant cousin of my father's sent word that I should get married, that there was a girl from a nice family . . . By that time, once again, as in my college days, life had shown me its other side, shown me that everything I thought I knew was wrong; and it is difficult being a man alone in this world. So I said yes, and prepared myself for a life of marital drudgery. So disillusioned was I with life at that time, that I believed it was pointless to have any hopes of having the life I had always dreamed of, so I decided to accept whatever fate itself decided to give me.

Ah life! The vagaries of fate — of how the wheel turns in such unexpected ways. There I was, resigned to the idea of drudgery, there came what fate had in store for me: bliss. What can one say about bliss? Those were the happiest years of my life, unmarred except for the lack of a child; and how hard we tried.

Post-script:
So you are married.

Dear Kanchan-behn,

So I was married. She finally conceived but died in childbirth. I was heartbroken, again (I suppose I still am). Some say that I should remarry, that there is still time, still hope. But I do not know any more — no one can replace her.

P.S. Everything is going to work out. You see, his parents know the girl's family, have known them for years. It was only the young fool that did not know this; seems that he met her at a wedding in your town quite recently. Well there is going to be another wedding in your town soon. He is so happy now, he even talks. Having no one in the family to do this, he insists on my being the best man.

Dear Letter-walla,

You have still to tell me your name. How is the story going — that you did not tell me either? How will I recognize you at the wedding, what do you look like?

P.S. and, please drop the formalities, all this Kanchan-behn business. 'Kanchan' will do just fine. She is deliriously happy also.

Dear Kanchan (as you wish),

The day is drawing near, and I have not seen him for a few days. I do not miss him much, though I had enjoyed his company while it lasted. Life goes on. The story is just pouring out of my hand, and already I have discovered many more characters. There is a whole life-time of stories to tell, and the muse is with me, as she has never been before; all the metal of my youth is in the work, but tempered oh so finely tempered! And I have you to thank. Yes, you, for without all this writing about the past, all this thinking and mucking about in the mind, the story would not have happened.

Thank you.

I have decided not to attend the wedding as it would mean breaking my rule of 'professional non-involvement'; also, there is much writing to be done. I thank you once again for your company; it was pleasant while it lasted.

I will remain faithfully yours,
The Letter-Writer.

T.J. RIGELHOF was born in Regina, Saskatchewan and now lives in Westmount, Quebec. His publications include *The Education of J.J. Pass*, *Je T'Aime Cowboy and Other Stories*, and *Boy in the Blue Dress*, which was nominated for the Governor General's Award for Non-Fiction in 1997. This story first appeared in CFM No. 70 in 1990.

A Hole With A Head In It

T.F. RIGELHOF

> *I'm not running away from trouble, I'm walking away from an accident involving a personality double and a hole with a head in it.*

BUTCH HEARS THESE WORDS and repeats them to himself and the tape keeps rolling and one song unfolds and another passes by scarcely heard and then T Bone Burnett's advice to a faithless friend to

> *keep on shaking until you shake yourself loose*

gets inside his head and he stops merely listening and starts living the lyrics and remembering things he would rather forget:

> *I don't know what hold this rounder downtown has on you
> But keep on shaking baby till you shake yourself loose* . . .

And he shakes his head. It is a voluntary movement. He tells himself he is some kind of an idiot. And the shaking moves involuntarily from his head through his neck and down his spine as a shiver spreading through his ribcage and hitting his heart like a hammer blow and his arms tremble and his knees go weak. And Butch tells himself it is only tiredness, not illness. He is not sick. He is not going to get sick. He is not going to catch pneumonia. Or anything else. The only illness he suffers from is a kind of sickness of the head: he is a dunderhead, a fool, an idiot. He tells himself that he is some kind of an idiot. He tells himself that he is some kind of idiot to have come back to Montreal simply because Florio is sick and said he needed him. He tells himself that he is a fool for love. He tells himself that he is a fool for loving Florio the way he does. He tells himself things he has told himself a hundred thousand times since he arrived in Montreal at Florio's loft on The Main. A million times. A million million times since he has known Florio. But they do no good, no good at all:

I don't know what hold this rounder downtown has on you
But keep on shaking baby . . .

But his curses and imprecations against Florio's hold on him are as useless as the prayers he used to say over and over again when he was a good little Roman Catholic boarding school boy trying to shake himself free from the filthy, sinful habits his flesh was so prone to indulge under the covers late at night in the dormitory. Prayers. Hymns. He had hated praying. It had never done him any good. He had enjoyed masturbating far too much! But he had liked the hymns, he had liked singing. He had used the liturgical music to shut out the sense of sinfulness in his flesh. He wished he could use this music to shut out the words Florio inspires inside his head but the sentiments are too close to the bone. He needs music that he has heard a thousand times or more. He needs sentimental lyrics that will hug his skin like shrink wrap around a record album. He needs the kind of songs he sings and plays when he gigs at piano bars for lovers who need consoling. He needs the kind of music he was making for suburbanites in Kingston when he heard of Florio's illness and came running up to Montreal leaving broken hearts and a broken contract behind him. But Florio doesn't have any Tin Pan Alley songs around the flat anymore. All his old albums, all the music Butch once shared with him is gone now, and in its place are stacks of cassettes filled with the songs of singers he does not know. Like this one by T Bone Burnett.

T Bone Burnett, a self-titled tape, drew him to it first by the shadowy John Lennon face on the cover and then by Tom Waits "Time" on the second side. Butch has been teaching himself Tom Waits tunes and routines to lift his act a little from the doldrums to which it has descended in recent years, years that have found him more often gigging the piano bars of towns like Kingston and Cornwall and Peterborough, than playing Toronto and Montreal where he began when his talent was fresher and his looks were better.

T Bone Burnett. There is a hush to this tape that feels like being alone in a church, in a school chapel, in childhood. But oh, the words, the words are caustic with truths that keen in his head like banshees, witches, mothers. Mothers. Mummies. Butch tries hard not to think of his mother and what his mother will say when she hears that Butch has been in Montreal with Florio again. After all this time! "After all these years," he can hear Mummy begin, "you're still an idiot, Butch, when it comes to that man." And what will he say in reply? He can say that yes, he is an idiot. But he cannot say this to his mother. He can say this only to himself. And to Florio. And only to Florio when Florio cannot hear him. He hopes that Florio can hear the music playing on the stereo. Butch wants him to hear T Bone Burnett sing:

you say you love me but I get no love at all. . . .

Butch wants Florio to wake up and tell him that this time everything is different, this time he can have all the love that he has it in himself to give, that this time it is love forever and ever, amen. But this is a futile wish, a wish as futile as a child's prayer. Florio cannot answer any prayers. He is too sick, too drugged with prescribed antibiotics and painkillers, too pneumoniac. Butch is alone and cold and shaking. Shaken. Pneumonia is so often so much more than pneumonia these days for men who love men in their ways. He should get up and turn up the heat against the damp chill of early winter but all he can do is sit and rock in his chair and listen to this unsentimental, caustic music of love gone wrong, and try not to think too much of his mother's reactions. And try to think of Florio as he was in better days: Florio. Flow rio. The river that was and is Florio began forty years ago in southwestern Saskatchewan as Floyd Keller Junior, in a small hospital in a small town, on a clay white river in Cypress Hills country, within sight of an oil derrick his father had rigged. It was a dry well but a sticky, wet, messy premature son that Mr. Keller brought into the world. Later, Keller Senior would have good luck with oil and bad luck with his son, but at birth Floyd Junior was the fulfillment of a dream that went deeper into a father's heart than black gold. Butch knows this to be true. He has heard this story from Florio's father and he has believed it and has had his belief confirmed by photographs of the father with his infant son. It is one of the very few stories he has heard that he has ever believed about Florio's childhood. Still, he knows in general terms what that childhood must have been like. It cannot be that dissimilar from his own. He and Florio have long been two of a kind, sensitive prairie boys of artistic temperament, crybabies, sickly sorts. Butch grew up hating his weakness and despising his cowardice and trying to pretend that neither existed. But they existed, how they existed! In the womanish world that he had inhabited, the pretense had worked tolerably well. In Florio's more mannish world, a sorry history of self-contempt cut deeper, and consequently was denied more forcibly. The crude folk culture of oil towns and cattle lands had made Florio mouthy, a tall tale teller, a congenital and self-convenient liar, a truly maddening man.

 Rocking back and forth, Butch tries to keep time with the easy light swing of T Bone Burnett's country tunes played on traditional acoustic instruments. But it doesn't quite work because the music has subtleties that get lost in Butch's anger and resentments against Florio, against himself. Losing patience with himself and with the cowboy musician, he turns his chair a quarter turn so that he can see the face of Florio's longcase clock and rock to the easier rhythms of its pendulum. It is a pretty clock with an easy beat and it holds good memories for Butch. It was the first really fine present he'd bought for Florio when they first lived together. The clock had been broken but was still valuable and he had fixed it and made it as priceless as their love and friendship had been in those far-off days. Later, when things had soured a little, he had been glad to leave it behind — a parting gift. Butch watches time pass over the ornate face of the antique clock. He watches its golden sun set and its silver moon rise mechanically, and he looks out the window and sees that yes, it is evening now and he thinks that yes, it is evening in more senses than one. Everything in the world he has known and loved best is aging, shrivelling, dying stupidly, idiotically. Again and again, rocking back and forth, back and forth, Butch tells himself that he must get out of the chair, must do something. What? Do what? He could tidy the studio. He could set Florio's encrusted brushes to soak in tins of fresh solvent. He could turn some of Florio's more recent paintings, the ones that most disturb him, the ones that are too terribly chic, the ones that the Yuppie dealers fight to hang, the ones that are quite dead, to the wall. To do this would be to subtract something from Florio and to add something to himself, to assert that he has preserved standards that Florio has glibly tossed aside. But Butch doesn't have the energy to make such a statement. He has hardly enough energy to make a cup of tea but he is dreadfully thirsty so he does get out of his chair and says, "Yes, I must make some tea. I'm not coming down with anything. I just need to warm up a little."

Butch makes tea the way his mother taught him to make tea years and years ago, lifetimes ago. He now makes tea the way that tea was always made for the ladies who came to play Bridge and talk across the card tables in the front parlour of the big brick house on The Crescents in Regina, Saskatchewan, that was his family's home. It is the way that Butch has always made tea for his lovers. It is made by warming a silver teapot upside down over the jet of steam rising from a kettle of fresh water that has just begun to boil. It is made by spreading loose English Breakfast tea leaves across the bottom of the pot before adding boiling water. It is made by gently steeping the tea leaves for precisely six minutes — six minutes measured off by the grains of sand in an egg timer, twice upended. It is made by pouring the tea through a stainless steel strainer into milk that has already been poured into the bottom of a bone china cup. Florio's teapot needs polishing, the grains of sand are sticky in the timer, the strainer has stains, none of the cups any longer has a matching saucer. Butch closes his eyes to these details. He stands at a sinkful of dirty dishes and drinks his tea quickly. He wants instant energy. He wants to do something. He knows he ought to do some housework. He pours himself a second cup of tea. He leans against the counter. He closes his eyes. The taste of the tea takes him back to childhood and his mother's house and a manless world of women visitors and card tables and small sandwiches and dressing-up. Butch remembers his own very plain face and handsome hair that was blonde and curly. And long as a girl's. Butch remembers his Granny drying his hair in a big pink towel and brushing it until it shone like spun gold. Spun gold! — that is what his Granny called it as she dried it and brushed it back from his forehead and pulled the sides down over his ears.

Butch drains his cup and remembers how his mother would always come and inspect Granny's handiwork. He remembers how his mother would tease his hair to make it curlier and curlier until he looked like a small albino version of a Zulu warrior. He remembers how his mother would always ask her lady friends if he wasn't just the prettiest boy they had ever seen. And he remembers how those ladies always agreed that he certainly was pretty even if they did not prize prettiness in a small boy to the degree that his mother and grandmother did. And he hears his mother interpolating with an odd mixture of pride and regret that sometimes she has to literally drive him out of the house to play since he'd rather stay inside even on sunny days and read The Encyclopedia Britannica. And Butch sees himself bristling at those words. But bristling came later, much later, when he had actually started to read his way through the Encyclopedia from beginning to end. In the days of the afternoon teas, in the days before be had been thrust out of the brick house on The Crescents into the larger world of school, he had loved being petted and admired by his mother and her friends.

Butch opens his eyes and looks at the bottom of his empty teacup and stares at the pattern of leaves and remembers that once he could and did read the future from tea leaves; in Granny's house no two cups are the same. Each cup is handpainted with different kinds of English garden flowers and every cup and saucer is shaped differently from its neighbour on the walnut tea wagon. But they are all rimmed with gold and Butch drinks his tea from a cup decorated with pansies. The rim is chipped. Butch drinks his tea at the kitchen table with Granny and as soon as they are done, they go back to the sitting-room and a place is cleared for them on the small settee, and his mother's lady friends bring them their empty cups and Granny reads their fortunes in the tea leaves. Granny is clairvoyant and teaches Butch the secrets of her art: keep the handle to the left and use it as the starting point. Lines and symbols to the right side of the handle mean what the fates hold in store. Lines and symbols to the left are the things that come about through personal initiative. Acorns bring good luck. Anchors mean love. Angels are good news. Boots mean travel. Baskets are storks bringing babies. Brooms indicate changes. Clean sweeps. Bulls are dangers. Florio is a Taurus but this comes later in the tea leaves, in life. Castles are legacies. Cats are ill-omened loves. Coffins indicate death. Circles are money. Under D, there are devils and there are eggs under E and F has fountains and Granny takes him in his pre-school days through her alphabet of signs until Butch has mastered her diviner's dictionary. And he saw anchors and angels and acorns in all their lives. Now he sees coffins, coffins, coffins everywhere.

Tonight in Montreal at Florio's, among the coffins, he sees in his cup an anchor, a love. He thinks suddenly not so much of new-found love as of an old seashore and sees boats riding in a harbour at high tide. They bobble and the bubble of memory bursts and he sighs and thinks back to other boats bobbling elsewhere. Butch is a lover of the sea and always takes a winter holiday to the sand and sun and anchors of the West Indies. St. Vincent. In the summers, he goes to San Francisco or to the Aegean. He has watched many boats bob at their anchors at high tide. Butch closes his eyes and recaptures the bubble of memory he most wants and sees inside it the Tancook Island ferry. It is a vivid memory of Nova Scotia five years ago. It's a holiday. He was looking for Florio. In a way, he wishes that he hadn't found him. In a way he wishes that Florio was a past that he could revisit only in memory — dulled, distant memory. He straightens Florio's bedclothes and kisses Florio's stubbly cheek, then stretches and presses his nose against the grimed glass of the studio window and studies the passing lights of the cars on The Main:

"I suppose that your father could have your bed and you could take mine and I could sleep on the couch. How does that sound to you, Florio?"

"Don't fuss, Butch. Just leave things the way that they are. He won't stay overnight. Trust me."

"But what if he wants to stay, Florio? It's no good you telling me to just leave things as they are because things aren't always the way you want them to be, are they? We don't know his plans, do we? He hasn't said, has he? If he comes here expecting a bed for the night, we'll have to put him somewheres, won't we? And I don't want him in my bedroom and I'm not going to have you sleeping with me while he's here in the house, and I just can't stand to see what it does to the couch or to you or to the front room when you spend the night in here. So we'll put him in your bed if he stays and you'll have mine and I'll sleep in here, right?"

"If that's the way you want it, that's the way we'll do it, Butch, if he stays the night."

"So now you think that he may stay the night, do you!"

"No, I don't think that he's really going to want to spend the night under my roof. Stop fussing."

"But what if your father does want to stay? We can't just turn him away from the door. It isn't done, Florio, and you know it isn't."

"All the more reason to do it, isn't it? He expects me to be unconventional, Butch."

"It isn't a matter of unconventionality. It's hospitality. When parents come to visit, you give them a bed. That's the done thing."

"Well, we're not going to do it. I really don't give a damn if its the done thing or not, do you understand? Just leave everything as it is. You don't have to give up your bed. I don't have to give up my bed. Nobody has to sleep on the couch. If he stays too late tonight to drive back to Halifax, he can stay at The Windjammer."

"At this time of the season? For God's sake, talk sense, Florio! I'm going to change the sheets on both beds just in case he does stay. I'm not going to have your father sleep in your dirt. You can be very annoying, you know."

"And you know how to make more of a fuss than the guy who is waiting for Godot, you know. You really can forget about my father. I made a reservation at The Windjammer just in case he needs a place. He wouldn't stay with us for love or money, Butchie Godot."

"Jesus, why didn't you say so in the first place! You can be a real pain in the ass, Florio."

"Don't you just wish, Butchie, don't you just wish."

Butch was furious but Florio wasn't prepared to take any notice of him. Florio just burrowed deeper into the previous Sunday's *New York Times* and Butch took his fury back upstairs to the room that faced that part of the Atlantic Ocean that is Mahone Bay. From the window he looked down on the yachts that filled its basin. Nearer, almost at his feet, he watched sturdy, squat, straight residents of Chester, Nova Scotia buy fresh fish on the docks and taller, leaner, less upright tourists study the menus posted outside genteel restaurants that had established themselves as Florio's nearest and least dear neighbours. Watching the tourists approach and the locals retreat, Butch felt sad enough to cry for the seedy part of town that was being reborn. Butch didn't want Chester to be a chic summer place. He looked out across the bay. The passenger ferry was starting out on its hourly voyage to Tancook Island. Butch felt so suddenly sad that he sat down at the piano that was in the room and began to play.

Grieg. Butch no longer played Grieg as well as he once played him. Grieg required a certain softness and suppleness in the fingers that he'd lost. It wasn't the onset of middle age. It wasn't his anger against himself for his stupid quarrel with Florio. Butch's mother, like many other older people, managed to play Grieg well right into the arms of enraged senility. It wasn't getting older that had done it to him. It wasn't just plain tiredness.

No matter how tired, how frustrated his mother had been at the end of a long day of teaching the rudiments of piano to small children with largemouthed mothers, she had been able to make Grieg sing. She could still make Grieg sing. Butch cocked an ear to the piano and suspended his own playing and heard the way Mummy had taught him to play the piece. Lowering his fingers to the keyboard and playing, it sounded other than it should have sounded in the room and in his head. He punished his faulty fingers with great booming chords of his own invention. He hoped that he'd disturb Florio. He hoped that he'd force Florio to abandon his newspaper. He hoped that Florio would come upstairs and be kind to him, ravish him with kisses.

Grieg. It was this music played on an old upright Steinway with a cracked soundboard and chipped yellow keys that first drew Florio to Butch in the school in which they were held captive. It pulled Florio away from his Scott's stamp catalogue and down the long dusty corridor from the junior recreation room and into the doorway of the more private room where Butch practised, where Butch was supposed to practise church music. But Butch made his own music. Outside chapel services, there was little music to be heard in the priest-run boarding school to which Butch had been confined after his Granny's death and his mother's move to her sister's house in Peterborough, Ontario.

Grieg. Butch's Grieg. It was this music that brought Florio to him. It wasn't love. It wasn't friendship. Those came later. In the beginning, it was the boredom of Sunday afternoon broken by small melodious sounds that hinted of something larger.

Tires crunched against the gravel below the window. Butch's fingers collapsed to silence as he listened for the sound of the car turning into the drive and stopping. Hearing it, he raced downstairs. Florio was unmoved and brooding within a messy nest of newspaper surmounted by a half empty whisky decanter. There was solid hammering on the front door. "I'll get the door, Florio. You see to the newspapers. Please."

"Don't fuss so, Butch. My father isn't worth it. Me neither."

"Do shut up please and just pick up the damned funny papers."

"What funny papers? This is *The Times.*"

They'd only met once before. Years and years ago. But Floyd Keller Senior flashed a tight smile of recognition, pumped Butch's hand. "They still call you Butch, do they?"

"That's right, Mr. Keller. Do come in."

"I never forget a face. Hardly ever a name. Yours is George, isn't it?"

"I'm Butch to everybody since my Granny died," Butch said icily as he stared into Mr. Keller's face. He couldn't see anything of Florio's devastating handsomeness in it. Nor was there anything of the man he remembered meeting the one time that Mr. Keller had come to visit Florio at boarding school. That man had seemed tall, ramrod straight, tough, leathery. An oil rigger. This man was just crumpled, paunchy, bald, florid in an expensive way. An oilman. An Alberta oilman. Crude. Alberta Crude. Butch felt Florio's hand on his shoulder, registered the flash of homophobic rage in Mr. Keller's eyes. Butch stepped aside quickly, played the role of peacemaker and host as effortlessly as he could in the circumstances. He got Mr. Keller a large glass of Coke over ice and poured himself a Perrier while Florio lowered the amber level of Scotch in the decanter by another inch.

Seated in the armchair, glass in hand, Mr. Keller talked to them as a man who wore a dark blue ultra-suede jacket with a lighter blue shirt and a tri-toned blue striped tie with grey ripcord trousers and tooled cowboy boots was inclined to talk, Butch supposed. Mr. Keller had an immense amount of small talk and he addressed it to a point on the wall behind his son's ears. He gave the spot on the wall an inning-by-inning account of a baseball game he had seen in Montreal the previous evening. He told it about the cabbie who had taken him out to Olympic Stadium and the cabbie who brought him back to the Sheraton Centre. He told it of his dissatisfactions with Montreal's black taxi drivers. He told it of his great satisfaction with the Sheraton Centre. He told it of his distaste for parts of Montreal: St. Catherine Street was a drug and sex war zone. The Pope, he thought, was definitely somehow to blame for the blatant sexuality of the place. Perhaps the wall yawned but suddenly Mr. Keller was on to ice hockey. The wall must have been smiling encouragement. There was a torrent of tale-telling about the Edmonton Oilers. Inside stuff. The Oilers were his hometown team. They were winners. They were almost American. This led him to talk of the West Edmonton Mall, the largest dang shopping centre on the face of the earth. Florio yawned openly. Mr. Keller didn't seem to notice. He had the full and undivided attention of the friendly wall behind his son's head and began to lecture it on the virtues of the Free Market System, Supply Side Economics, Monetarism, Reaganism. Everything was Capitalized. Everything was Capital. Not quite. Butch stared at the wall and felt blistered for its sake as Mr. Keller declaimed against creeping socialism, PetroCan, the Canadian dollar, Israel. But the wall had strengths Butch lacked and remained impassive. Despite his ingrained good manners, Butch began to slump in his chair and stare at his own fingers and think about how little music was left in them. He looked up and smiled and tried to focus on Mr. Keller's antizionism but he'd missed a transition. The children of Moses had given way to the sons and daughters of Jesus and the wall had ceased being the preferred audience. Mr. Keller was speaking directly to them. And it wasn't just Jerry Falwell and The Moral Majority and maybe Jim-Keegstra-has-a-point-you-know. It was stranger and stronger than that: Mr. Keller had been re-baptized in the Blood of the Lamb. The Holy Spirit had newly descended upon him. He had been buried in the black waters and he had been reborn in the clear waters of The Resurrection. He had been born again. He was witnessing to Christ right there in the front room of the house in Chester by the waters of Mahone Bay. Butch was wide-awake in his worst nightmare — Florio's father was in their midst as an Avenging Angel. Butch felt hot and clammy, wet with fear.

With a pocket-sized New Testament open in his hand, Mr. Keller was saying,"Listen boys, this is not my word. This is not the word of any man. This is God's own word. And it says, 'the wages of sin are death.' Right here, it says that, just that 'the wages of sin are death' but no man has to die. All men are born to everlasting life. It says so, right here. And all you have to do to have eternal life is simply to accept the Lord Jesus Christ into your life. And if you want to accept Lord Jesus Christ into your life, all you have to do is to kneel right down beside me and say, 'Lord Jesus, come into my heart' and when He hears your prayer, He'll enter right into you and make you well. I've seen Him do it. I've seen Him enter men and women and drive the uncleanness right out of them. I've seen the downcast uplifted and the bent straightened."

Mr. Keller paused, looked deeply into his New Testament and sifted its words for words that would not fall on stoney ground. "I tell you that I've see men as queer as any you have ever met accept Christ into their hearts. Those men are married now and are the fathers of fine children. Junior, will you kneel down beside me now, son, and pray with me? And you too, George?"

Junior. George. The old names, the names of Christening rang out like bullets in Butch's brain. Floyd Joseph Paul Keller. George Anthony Benet. But they weren't bullets, there was no sense of violence in Mr. Keller, just the pathetic hopefulness of the true believer. The nightmare had come to very little. Still, Florio rose from the sofa like a great breaker from the sea and swept across the room to Mr. Keller and clenched him by the shoulders and spat in his face. Full in his face. Then the wave that was Florio retreated as suddenly as it had swept forward and it broke out the door and ran out to the wharf.

Face to the window, red with embarrassment, Butch followed

Florio's passage and watched him jump aboard the Tancook Island ferry. At his back, Butch heard Mr. Keller say, "I only want to help him. I only wish him the happiness of his own children. If he had daughters of his own, his mother would live again in them and he'd be free of her ghost. He needs a wife and daughters. He doesn't really need you, George. Let him go, please."

Butch looked at Florio's father. Mr. Keller's face was white and crest- fallen with a purple-red tracery of broken veins in his cheeks. He wasn't made of granite. He was traventine — soft and porous. Butch opened the window. He hoped fresh sea air would turn Mr. Keller to dust. It didn't. When he turned around and faced the room, Mr. Keller was sobbing into a large white handkerchief. Butch wasn't altogether certain what he could or should say. Florio's gesture had been so crude and melodramatic as to hint of something more deeply felt than the mere words that had been spoken. Not knowing quite what to say, Butch said the things he'd been taught by his Granny to say in awkward circumstances of any sort. It did the trick. Florio's father waxed nostalgic, showed him photographs of Junior as an infant, told him stories of infancy when Junior was so small and frail he, heh-heh, had to be basted with olive oil and kept in a roasting pan in the warming oven to keep him warm enough to live through his first prairie winter.

After Mr. Keller had left, Butch returned to the upper room and piano but he did not play. He gripped his knees with his hands and stared at the hard black and white keys. Ebony and ivory. "Ebony and Ivory." Paul McCartney. Stevie Wonder. The harmony of perfect opposites. Florio's music, not his. Florio's blindness, not his own, gripped him until Florio had returned a little repentant and much too late.

The Main is quieter now. Butch turns away from the window. Wrapped in bedclothes damped with sweat, Florio sleeps fitfully. He mumbles, he jerks, he calls out a name — Evelyn. He repeats it at intervals in moans and cries and whispers. It is the name of a dead woman who Butch never knew. He cannot summon memories of her to his friend's bedside. Not in the flesh. Butch has never met her as she existed outside Florio's imagination. He knows her only as Florio has painted her in the Neo-Expressionist paintings that now litter his studio. In them, Evelyn exists as a fierce shadow that has blacked out Florio's customary painterly concerns. In them, she exists as a blood red muse that has exploded Florio's painterly reputation for lightness and clarity of expression. She is the face of death that Yuppie gallery owners outbid one another to see grace their large white walls. Evelyn is the woman that Mr. Keller's prayers seemed to will upon Florio. Butch straightens the bedclothes and wipes the sweat from Florio's face. He would like him to wake but he doesn't.

While Florio sleeps, Butch seeks out Evelyn in the canvas images, but he cannot find the once living being behind the paint. He would like to see at least one true-to-life photograph of her. He tells himself that if he could see her, he could better help Florio cope with the memory of her. He suspects that some concrete sign of the nebulous figure in the paintings is to be found in the locked box that Florio has brought back from the house on Mahone Bay. Not finding images and souvenirs of Evelyn elsewhere in his trips around the studio, Butch has convinced himself that they are to be found in the locked box half-hidden under Florio's bed. It is a large box and very heavy and Butch has to get down on his hands and knees and has to exert considerable force to slide it out from under the bed and into the middle of the room He has done this several times in the last few days but each time he has done so, he has returned the box unopened to its storage space.

The box is made of wood and is roughly carpentered, and a protruding nailhead keeps digging into the floorboards and scrapes long ragged scars that Butch repeatedly scuffs out with a paint-soaked rag from a bucket beside the smallest of Florio's easels. It has been the automatic reaction of a person who has been doing things that they would be ashamed to be caught doing. But really, there is no one to catch him at it, is there? Florio will probably not wake till morning now, right? Butch inspects the box once more. It is a fairly ordinary wooden box of the kind that his generation of university students used to pack and ship books from home to school and back again. It is constructed out of a single sheet of ½ inch plywood, a length of 1x1 pine, two hinges, a clasp, a handful of screws and two short lengths of rope for handles. It will never be an object of beauty but it has been made interesting by the shipping labels it has accumulated as Florio has trundled it from one art college to another, from one studio to the next, from life with one lover to life with another. Beneath the labels, there is a worn coating of black paint.

Florio is open if not entirely truthful about almost everything in his life and always has been with Butch. But he has not been open about this box and the things it contains. In all the years Butch has known Florio to have owned the box, it has never once been opened in his presence and it has always been kept locked with stout padlocks. Butch now has the key in his hand. All he needs to do is to insert the key and turn it and remove padlock from clasp and lift the lid and all of Florio's secrets will be his for the taking. Butch wishes that it wasn't this easy. He wishes that the box was covered with dustballs. He imagines sweeping the lid with the back of his hand and watching the grey turn black and spiderwebby. He thinks of himself rummaging for a clean rag and wiping both the back of his hand and then the exposed surfaces of the box. But all he has to do is to insert the key and turn it. He inserts the key, he turns it, the padlock falls open. He removes it from the latch. He lays it aside. He lifts the lid and a welter of notebooks and large brown envelopes and loose photographs come to light. Layered like the remains of an ancient empire, it is the most recent that lies closest to hand. Butch turns layer upon layer upside down on the floor beside the box until nothing stands between himself and the time he went in search of Florio and found him living in the house on Mahone Bay and Mr. Keller came to visit.

The first photograph is of Florio on the Tancook Island ferry, his back to the mainland. He is smiling with a familiar lust. The object of his lust is obviously the person holding the camera and that person is obviously Evelyn for it is she who is the subject of the thick layer of photographs accompanying it. In some, she is dressed; in others, she is semi-dressed; in the rest, she is undressed.

Naked, Evelyn is a narrow young woman, elongated in head and body. Her neck is thin, blunt, chiselled into high squared shoulders that frame the flat planes of her chest. Her breasts are small knobs that tilt upward no matter which way the rest of her leans. Two-thirds of the knobs are dark nipple. Like a boy, Evelyn is straight to the hips and flares out angularly. Her pelvic bones rise against her flesh like ploughshares. Are they the swords that pierced Florio's heart? Is there ever any understanding of heterosexuality? It is only in her lower groin and her legs that Evelyn becomes curvaceous. Her legs are long and beautiful. Looking at them, admiring them, Butch thinks of the women who model stockings for Hanes. Butch thinks also of his mother. Mummy's legs are still very fine. He does not have his mother's legs but he does have his mother's perfectly formed feet. Butch smiles broadly as he notices that Evelyn's beautiful legs terminate in ruined, large, unshapely feet. He cannot imagine Florio kissing those arches, sucking those toes like Florio has kissed his arches and sucked his toes. Florio is capable of many things but sexually, he is always aesthetic. If her feet are not an attraction, what in her is? Butch is drawn to the clump of black hair at her groin and the lighter clumps of hair in her armpits and the great shaggy mop of bleached hair that envelopes her head. Hair has always been the thing that has been most seductive. He thinks of Florio's rich mat of chest hair. He thinks of ways in which it can be twisted around his finger. He goes back to thinking of Evelyn. It is her hair that would attract him if he was attracted to her. But he is not attracted to her in her nakedness.

Semi-naked, Evelyn is curvaceous calves sloping into curving thighs creasing lace and satin lingerie into narrow tight folds. This is somewhat more attractive but what is a body without a face? Nothing! Faces are everything to him, more than hair. It is faces that he loves and it is only in the pictures of Evelyn fully dressed that Butch sees her face. To him, a human face is as full of signs and portents of fate and destiny as the bottom of a teacup. But Evelyn's face is an empty cup against which he recoils. How, he wonders, could Florio have loved such a face? Perhaps it was personality, perhaps it was the things she had to say, could say, did say that drew Florio to her. Florio can always be drawn sexually with words, with music. Perhaps she sang? Butch digs deeper, shifts from pictures to poems carefully printed in an unfamiliar hand in a lined schoolbook: there is one title standing for all — *Astral Liars*.

> *cross my eyes: I find the point of power.*
> *In it, I place myself. Feet first. Then head.*
> *Head. Arms. Legs. Straight. Straight,*
> *symmetrical, all crossings undone. Eyes closed,*
> *I begin to see doubt take its leave of my senses;*
> *I count the breaths of its passages:*

one, two, ... ten. Then,

*I turn to the beach with feet plowing furrows
in the young dunes: their hollows like mine
break the wind-bitten slopes into sudden terraces
that will last long enough for dune grass to SEED
a patch of vegetable memory. just that, only*

*that [.....] a fact
that [.....] stills
the error
in my way.*

*A sand mite
bites the heel
that feeds
it, i
hurry over the rise and fall
before the bed
of heaven,
it's sheets
still troubled
from a storm
rising
the night
fishermen
are moored
in morning
lanterns snuffed
tridents sheathed
the fish
mock them
the lover
worships
in me
the love left
so easily.*

*The altar of the beach has no candles, no books, no incense
just a priesthood of fine young men tumbling in front
a candy-striped tabernacle. Rosy. Crossed, they bruise
their thighs, toss balls high in the air.*

*This is it:
always IT
in games of tag
the losers
HAVE THE GREATER FUN
running the DUMB SHOW
fast or slow
striking the angles
commanding the waves
Picasso was not Charlemagne
nor are you but a picture
cure a toothache
my jaw throbs
where you entered me I
watch balls sail
above the coven
to greater communion
with a dog
wetted liver
brown and fiercely proud
of the bleached head
I
worry
in the sands
my jaw throbs
where you entered
me
a picture in the sand
like this —*

and then a single scrawled line of ink outlining an animal form that might be a dog with a crown on its head and a belly full of puppies or perhaps a goat half-liquid with milk. Butch does not know, cannot say because the line drawing such as it is, in his estimation, is pretty piss poor. And the poem or poems? Are the words meant to be all parts of one poem or many? Butch goes back and reads them again and tries to see a meaning beyond that which seems to him obvious: after a night of lovemaking in which oral sex has played a prominent part, Evelyn rests her sore jaws by watching young men play volleyball on the beach and she adopts their dog for company and it all puts her in mind of something she has seen somewhere by Picasso. Or is the artistic reference something just dropped in to make it more appealing to Florio? Who knows? Who cares? What is there really to care about in any contemporary poetry, Butch asks himself? The real poets nowadays are the songwriters. Has any living poet written a line as good as Tom Waits's

And the shroud tailor measures you for a deep-six holiday . . .

Thinking about it, Butch starts running the lyrics of "The One That Got Away" through his memory and wishes that he could so simply say of Evelyn

The corpse is froze, the case is closed

but he can't and so he returns to her poetry, sifts the pages of the notebook some more, encounters this

SIGNED,
thus —
This is my mark
remember me
like a dinosaur
I dally
I. Dali.
Isadore, Isabel
a joke old as dinosaurs
or me or goats

like you asking me
as king
daddy
dada
Amin
Amen
All men
Idi [.....]
Like birds of a feather
whores always flock together
Life is in the liver
Hell has as many seasons as heaven
Sing a song of puppy love, the dog has left its manger
If you sing along with me, I won't feel any stranger

Butch reads no further. He has read enough, he thinks, to get a handle on the kind of poet and person she is, was, for Florio. She was a whore, Florio! She was a whore with a heart as twisted by psychological complexities as any woman, as all women her age are, Florio! Butch dismisses her and wishes that the night was over and Florio was awake and feeling better, getting better, recovering and this detritus of another life could be forgotten, hidden away, rammed and jammed back in its box, consigned to a rubbish tip, incinerated, destroyed, whatever. But that cannot be and so Butch plunges deeper into the box, uncovers layers of life long before Evelyn entered the picture. He digs deep, deep down in the box, turns up a picture of Rue Ontario:

RUE ONTARIO. It could have been the title of a manifesto if the English artists and musicians of the French Quarter had been given to making public pronouncements, but it was only the name of a nondescript street transecting the district. There were jazz clubs in sub-basements and working class diners and hole-in-the-wall needletrade workshops and big sprawling capacious coldwater flats over top of automobile parts suppliers that smelled of rubber and grease. Butch had his own flat on Rue Ontario and gave parties that were open to whoever found their way to his door. He gave many parties, was spendthrift with the money Granny had given him so that he could study music at

McGill and qualify as a music teacher in case his performance skills were not up to the standard that his mother had willed into him. And it was there, in the middle of a party, that Florio walked back into his life after four years of heart-breaking absence and abstinence. Florio had been studying in Italy with sculptors of oldfashioned outlook and temper and training. With them, he had studied anatomy — practical and theoretical. With them, he had mastered the science of calibrating the body top to toe. With them, he had learned to celebrate the male body, front and back. He had learned the effects of aging and dissolution on flesh and muscle. He had broken his right arm in four places when his Vespa was run into the face of a cliff by a drunken industrialist in a Mercedes. An industrialist, who Florio later claimed, had taken him to a villa high in the hills while he recuperated. This industrialist, he alleged, had catered to his every whim, in and out of bed. He gained many things from this experience but he did not regain his full strength in his right hand. He had given up all thought of sculpture; he had turned to painting. He had returned to Canada. He had returned to his first and greatest love.

Back from Italy, in Butch's world of Rue Ontario, Florio stood out. While the other artists grew their hair shoulder-length and stopped shaving, Florio went to a Sicilian barber every week and had his hair cut close against the scalp with a straight razor and the ends singed with flaming sulphurous matchsticks. On his upper lip, the barber crafted a perfect rectangle of clipped whiskers. While others wore sandals and jeans and workshirts and oversized sweaters and carried knapsacks, Florio wore grey suits and black shirts and bright ties and European loafers and carried an ancient leather briefcase. While others talked about Chicago blues bands, Florio combed second-hand record stores for jazz albums featuring the jazz pianist Bill Evans. While other painters on Rue Ontario slavishly imitated the most abstract of their teachers' expressions without altogether forsaking the impression of the old guard, Florio quarreled with everyone at Art School. He was thought a philistine because he admitted to watching more than just hockey games on television. But he could not be ignored; he had an immense talent for realism, he had a wonderful capacity for self-promotion, he had a scathing tongue and articulate principles and he was the first in that set to openly flaunt his homosexuality. He knew exactly who he was and what he was capable of doing. Butch admired him immensely. Butch was unable to articulate much of anything about himself or his music and he could not say anything of the love that consumed him and the appetites that ruined him for women. He responded the best way he knew how: he became a Bill Evans imitator.

Butch sighs at the memory of it, at the memory of a time in Montreal when nobody could make a living playing jazz. It is into those days and those appetites that he most wants to retreat in his thoughts as he drifts into sleep slumping over Florio's box. Drifting sleepwards, Butch is grasped and held under the control of a foreign power. Evelyn's power? A pair of eyes float eerily over the sheaves of photographs and leaves of paper. The eyes are depressingly blank, drugged. Butch tries to find lips, ears, nose, nostrils, cheeks, chin to attach to the eyes but there is only a jaw, an uncompromising jut of jaw. A voice tells him that Evelyn's cheeks are the cutting edges of a determined mind, that her nose is a wedge that sunders all opposition, that her nostrils are a sea of nervous energy, that her ears are tight coils of stubbornness. A voice tells him that Evelyn is his opposite. Butch does not believe this voice. Florio's emotional range is narrow, he tells himself, and Florio has loved them both. But then he is crying and his tears nudge him back into consciousness and the words from a song on the T Bone Burnett album that has been repeatedly replaying itself in the background comes clearly into his mind and shakes him awake

>*Oh your poison love has stained the lifeblood in my heart and soul dear*
>*And I know my life will never be the same*
>*For my pleadings have all been in vain for you and you alone dear*
>*And you know you are guilty of the shame . . .*

Butch returns to the teapot and pours himself another cup and thinks about clearing up the mess he has made of Florio's things, and about putting himself properly to bed for the night. The longcase clock has struck one. He returns to the box by the bedside and carefully begins to replace all that it contains. In his haste to do so, Butch plunges his right hand deep down and through a miscalculation of distance to the floor, jams his fingers and a searing pain takes his breath away:

It is Sunday afternoon in the late fifties and the boys at the boarding school have been given a free afternoon and everyone wants to head downtown and see a movie, but some people don't want other people to tag along with them, and Florio gets dumped upside down into a garbage can full of cold baked beans and potato parings behind the Refectory. And Butch comes to his aid immediately and tries to dislodge him but Florio thinks that it is one of his attackers returning and flails and kicks and topples the can with a horrendous crash and clatter and a stream of profanity. Father Prefect overhears and comes quickly out from the priest's parlour but does not comprehend the situation and frog-marches both boys to his office and lectures them on the need in boys their age for good physical exercise that toughens the body and fortifies the soul. They are deprived of their liberty and exiled to the baseball diamond where Father Prefect, garbed in a white T-shirt and black trousers and white tennis shoes, waits with a baseball bat and more boys. It is not their first experience of this kind of detention. Butch is outfitted with shinguards and a catcher's mitt and a facemask and a chest protector. The other boys are given outfielders' gloves. Florio is handed the ball. Father Prefect takes the one and only bat in hand and swaggers up to the plate. The boys arrange themselves around the diamond. They will stay there until they make three outs against Father Prefect's batting. They will stay there all afternoon. Father Prefect once had a try-out with the Brooklyn Dodgers as a left-handed first basemen and played a couple seasons of double A. Father Prefect makes them run three laps around the outfield after each of the outs. Butch plays catcher because there is almost nothing for him to do behind the plate. Father Prefect swings at everything that isn't beyond the reach of the catcher. Florio pitches. Father Prefect hits and hits and hits and then there is a liner that screams through the infield knocking Florio from the mound before being snagged in the webbing of the shortstop's glove. An out. "Three laps around the outfield boys. No walking. No talking." They huff and they puff and drag themselves into home plate and then drag themselves back into position and someone else pitches and Butch has nothing to catch as Father hits and hits and hits as he finds his groove and stays within it. And then, the unexpected: a foul tipped to the catcher's glove is caught and held despite the flame of pain that brings tears to Butch's eyes. He hurls the mitt and ball into the dust and plunges his fingers inside his mouth. "Put that mitt back on, fellow, and get back into position. You could have had an easy out. Remember, a man who can play with a little pain is always a winner in life. Play ball." And the pitcher pitches before the batter and Butch are ready and it comes straight into the catcher's mitt and snaps Butch's wrist backwards. The world goes black and a jagged white line divides it down the middle.

Florio visits Butch in the infirmary and gives him a teddy bear as a present. Butch has three broken bones in his left hand. He can still feed himself but Florio wants to do something to make him feel better so Butch lets Florio spoon food into his mouth like a mother does for her child. But Florio cries and Butch strokes his arm and then the food is put aside and they are holding one another tight and kissing like children do as they crush the teddy bear between them. A shadow falls over them and Father Prefect stands between them and the light and snarls, "That's not the way for men to behave, lads. We'll have none of that, we'll have none of that ever again. You'll both be men before I'm done with you." And the teddy bear is confined to a cupboard inside Father Prefect's office until Graduation Day.

All of this returns in an instant and with it the full force of the hatred that Butch feels against so many elements of the past he shares with Florio. Had it not been for that school, they would never have met in the ordinary course of things. That is the only good that Butch has ever been able to attribute to their high schooling. The priests were reputed to be civilized men and they undoubtedly knew many fine things from the foreign worlds in which they had travelled. But those travels and studies had also diminished the practical sense within them. When it came to handling boys, when it came to fulfilling their holy function to act *in loco parentis*, the priests became cruder than the crudest of parents. It has taken years and years for Butch to begin to make even a little sense of what that school did to him and to Florio and to untold other sensitive boys of artistic temperament. The priests gave everybody a new name for a start and the nicknames they bestowed were an expression of the crudest and vilest values of the folk cultures from which their alleged civilization was supposed to purge a man. The nicknames were seldom honorific, frequently satirical and always descriptive in a sneering sort of way — even the brightest "Brains" among them was levelled by his moniker. And along with the names went attitudes that were as rough as any found on the prairies when it was still frontier: the priests, despite their education, sponsored cruel practical jokes, allowed crude and ugly prejudices, systematically persecuted individualism in any form and bullied all sensitivities. Why? Why was it that they had been great levellers rather than uplifters of the human spirit? It was not enough simply to say that religion had taught them that young boys were allies of the devil. There was more to it than that. There was something far more primitive in their responses to the boys, something that had to do with a real contempt for all living things, something that allowed them to eat great semi-raw hunks of beefsteak at every opportunity, something that allowed them to feed the boys in their charge any vile thing that was not actively poisonous. Butch reins in his thoughts and runs cold water over his fingers to take away the sting of past and present misadventures. The priests were as cruel and as crude as cowboys, and far less romantic.

Cowboyism. It is this as much as anything that makes Butch loathe the effect Evelyn has had on Florio. She has done to him what the priests had never been able to do to him: she has not only split him away from Butch's friendship and love, she has returned Florio to much-too-much of the world that they had bravely withstood in the priests and fellow students. Under Evelyn's influence, Florio has exchanged suits and ties for denims and cowboy boots. Butch can see the boots — six pairs of them — neatly aligned alongside Florio's full length mirror. Under her influence, Florio has exchanged all the music that Butch had given him for Ricky Scaggs and Randy Travis, K.T. Oslin and K.D. Lang, Nanci Griffiths, The Sweethearts Of The Rodeo, Dwight Yoakum and David Lynne Jones, Ian Tyson, Ricky Van Shelton, The O'Kanes, Steve Earle and dozens more. Under her influence, Florio has grown nostalgic and paternalistic and paternal and sentimental about dogs and children. Under her influence, for all Butch knows, Florio might even have gone horseback riding. And it is this recognition that be does not know enough about her yet that sends Butch back to the box and the layers of Florio's life that can be seen and studied:

Early in January, 1984, Florio started a half-year sabbatical from his college teaching job in Montreal by moving out to Nova Scotia and renting a house in Chester. The house was the property of an art historian from Boston and contained everything Florio hoped such a house would contain: there was wine in the cellar, Danish cutlery and earthen tableware in the kitchen, garden produce and wild berries in a freezer on the enclosed back porch, cupboards stocked with home preserves, well-worn furniture covered with bright throws and cushions from New Mexico, an out-of-tune Steinway in an upstairs room filled with sheet music and an almost antique but still faithful stereo together with a huge collection of Deutsche Grammaphon Archiv recordings plus the best of the British Invasion — Beatles, Stones, The Who. There was also a fully equipped artist's studio in a third floor attic naturally lit by oversize skylights. The only thing wrong with the house was that the heating system was inadequate everywhere except in the attics. So Florio pulled an old couch into the studio and toppled a sleeping bag on top of it and forgot about the rest of the house except the kitchen. He was happy to be on his own. He made itemized lists of things he wanted to accomplish. He made drawings for the paintings he intended to paint. He discovered a plethora of photographic equipment and a bathroom that did double duty as a darkroom.

February was a time of severe winter storms and Florio was unused to Maritime winter. The storms terrified him. He cowered inside the house and hoped against hope that the power wouldn't fail but it did. Repeatedly. At the end of February with the coming of the worst of the storms and the longest blackout, he gave up and jammed a few things into a rucksack and drove to Halifax airport in an old truck that came with the house. But just before his flight to Montreal was called, it was cancelled. Another storm was sweeping into the region. Florio was despondent. Lacking the will to do anything else, he sat down in the lounge. The place was jammed with Newfoundlanders, stranded but carefree. The authorities were urging everyone to take a bus back to town and wait out the storm at a Halifax hotel. Florio returned to his truck and found a young woman sitting inside. She told him that she hated crowds as if this explained everything. If he was going back to

Halifax, she told him, he could give her a lift. He gave her a lift all the way to Chester and his house, and she entered his life as they shook the wet and tiredness from themselves, opened a jug of the art historian's best homemade wine, heaped a whole lot of bedding on a big double bed and crawled inside and got gloriously drunk.

The woman told Florio that her name was Early Spring. This was a joke. Her name was Evelyn Airleigh Sprung. This was not a joke: she had a Vermont Driver's Licence to prove she was who she said she was, although she also had a fistful of credit cards in other names. As a joke of his own, Florio called her Cinnamon because she sprinkled that spice on everything she ate — including his private parts.

Evelyn Airleigh Sprung travelled light. She brought with her the clothes that she wore, a carryall, a handbag. When she first undressed and shivered her way into Florio's bed, she was wearing a pair of lime green lowcut Sporto Portage Pacs. Portage Pacs are reputed to keep feet warm and dry because they have uppers of oil-treated chrome-tanned leather that is supposed to defy mud, rain and snow. These uppers are triple-stitched to bottoms of vulcanized gum rubber with crepe rubber soles for traction. It is the vulcanized gum rubber that has been dyed the same shade of green that the Soviet automaker Lada uses on some of their exports to Canada. It was these shoes that interested Florio the most in all her possessions. They were the only thing practical about her. Her socks were out at heel, her dress was summer weight cotton, her home-knit woollen sweater of many stripes and more dropped stitches was threadbare, her coat was a mothnibbled fur jacket with a rip under the right armhole and missing buttons.

She had no scarf nor hat nor gloves. But in her carry-all, she carried a black silk dance dress that was slit high on the thigh, black lace underwear, a pair of thong sandals with high high heels, an Oriental shawl, squares of Chinese silk, costume jewellery, belts, an ebony cigarette holder, a copy of Rimbaud's *Une Saison En Enfer:*

> *J'ai de mes ancatres gaulois l'oeil bleu blanc, la*
> *cervelle étroite, et la maladresse dans la lutte.*
> *je trouve mon habillement aussi barbare que le leur.*
> *Mais je ne beurre pas mas chevule . . .*

which she had translated in the margin

White-blue-eyed I of my Gallic
past narrow-skulled clumsiness
my clothes are as barbaric
but I don't butter my hair ...

Later, she gave him poetry of her own but then, just then, she produced a brass pipe and hashish and a drug-induced end to February: Evelyn Airleigh Sprung's handbag contained uppers, downers, LSD, Angel Dust, Demerol, cocaine. There were also edible lotions and perfumes. She slept with a switchblade knife under her pillow alongside her packet of contraceptive pills.

March. Evelyn sat and knitted for hours on end. Then she unravelled all that she had knitted. When she did this, she insisted that Florio call her Penelope Homebody. He thought that this was very funny. Sometimes she pored over technical photography books all through the night and then confessed she had never owned a camera. Sometimes she pretended not to eat anything for whole days on end even though Florio found the empty preserve jars exactly where she had half-hidden them. Florio was infatuated by her freakiness, her bullying sexuality and her drugs. He loved her indifference to time and space, her photogenic postures in bed, her games with his mind.

Butch sits at Florio's bedside and reads all this in a diary that Florio has kept of those days and nights of a Nova Scotia winter. As he reads, Butch keeps filleting photos of Evelyn from the pile he discarded earlier. He continues to discard the ones of her in states of undress. He is interested in her face, in her eyes. But Evelyn's eyes are depressingly blank, drugged. He looks to her lips, ears, nose, nostrils, cheeks, chin. And again and again he notices that her jaw is an uncompromising jut, her cheeks are cutting edges of a determined mind, her nose is a wedge that sunders all opposition, her nostrils are full of nervous energy. Her ears are tight coils of stubbornness. Butch knows that he will never understand her and he marvels that Florio can seemingly love her. He says he loves her, over and over. They talk of getting a dog. They talk of having a child. To comfort himself, Butch mashes bananas in a bowl and makes a stack of peanut butter and banana sandwiches and eats them while he reads more of Evelyn's poetry:

The house within the house
is rich with the silks and velvets
of the rising sun
lace curtains and patchwork
a negress sleeps on a four poster bed
a poet fluffs her pillow
all rhymes turn reasonable
in violent light
stroke me to sleep
I am washed with snow
I am burned with moonshine
what kind of deal will you give the dealer?

I am a loaf of bread
I am salt in the water
You take me shopping
and all we find is an iron-buckled seachest
big enough to drown ourselves.

Vermont is green, I am ripe.

April. May. Both months are missing. June. In June, Butch came to Nova Scotia in search of Florio. For several weeks, Florio had answered no letters. There was no telephone, no point of contact. Butch had grown worried and as soon as one gig ended and before another started, he was on a flight to Halifax and in a Tilden rental car to Chester. He had found Florio in the house overlooking Mahone Bay living on his own and making a mess of it. The house was squalid. It hadn't been cleaned in weeks. He came to Florio's rescue without quite knowing what was what. Florio was in a very odd mood. He seemed glad to have Butch cook and clean. He even seemed glad of Butch's company in bed, and at the breakfast table, but that was all. Florio was lifeless, stale, enervated. He could not even paint. He seemed haunted by a ghost that he would not name. And then, out of the blue Mr.

Keller sent a telegram from Montreal that he was arriving the next day. And he came. And Florio spat in his face and fled the house and jumped aboard the Tancook Island Ferry. And Butch consoled Mr. Keller as best he could, and Mr. Keller went away and Florio returned from Tancook Island, a little repentant and very late and they had a row. What a row! Butch had told Florio that there was no excuse, none on the face of the earth for what he had done to his father. And Florio had said there was and had told him this:

Florio's father was a geologist employed by the Standard Oil Company. Mr. Keller directed an exploration rig in Alberta, far north of the Drumheller fields. It was very isolated — there were no towns, no schools, no other children but Florio — Floydie as he was then — was happy. Floydie watched the riggers drill test holes in sweat-stained undershirts and filthy chinos and heavy steel-toed boots. They were muscular sunburnt men who teased him mercilessly and yet did anything and everything he asked them to do for he was the only child in their lives at that moment. They had children of their own, most of them, but those children were far away in Montana and Ohio and Texas. Floydie was their mascot. They dragged him along with them when they played ball against the crews on neighbouring rigs. But this was not often. Mostly they kept him awake at nights as they sat by their campfires and swapped tales about booze-ups and wide-legged wild women daft as geese. Floydie's mother hated him listening to such things from such low company. She wanted him to sit quietly beside her and fall asleep early in the evening listening to the things she had to tell him about a very different kind of people — her kind of people — the ladies and the gentlemen of England's Home Counties. She told him that an English gentleman — and he was one! — never lied and never bragged and never ever discussed women in a low way and always played cricket with a real bat not the sort of club these boorish men used for their rounders. She would not call it baseball.

 Mrs. Keller filled Floydie overfull with stories of England and English public schools and she taught him mathematics, history, Latin, geography and literature. Literature was her greatest love and ally. And sketching. She taught him to sketch the wilderness in a pretty way. Twice she took Floydie back to England with her and stayed with her father. His grandfather Kendall rode to hounds, glorious in a red coat and high black boots. Floydie was proud that his mother was a real lady. Even the riggers said she was a lady! Even in England and in its bone-chilling dampness, Floydie remembered the stinking hot sunshine of Alberta and heard the voices of the riggers who were not gentlemen but were he-men, real men.

It was August and it was afternoon and it was hot and filthy and stinking at the well-head. Oil had been found. Maybe. There was sour gas. For certain. Floydie ran to the cool shade and artificial air of the trailer — his mother insisted upon calling it a caravan — that housed them. His mother gave him a tall glass of lemonade with a cube of ice and mixed herself the same but added lots and lots of gin. He sat down beside her and let her hand ruffle his long blonde hair and pet him. He was the immediate centre of her interest. It was almost always so. Sometimes, he had to share her with a book whenever a new packet of romantic novels had just arrived from Mills & Boon courtesy of her father. But that day, she was bookless. Floydie did not want to see her so. She was unhappy when she was bookless. So he asked her to read some Dickens to him. She had been reading to him from *Bleak House*. He loved that particular story. He knew that his own inheritance from his grandfather was quite safe and would not undo him. He did not, however, know then what inflation would do to it and that the interest on principal from which it was intended he would live like a gentleman through all the days of his life was inadequate even in the days of his art studies in Italy. He listened quietly, his eyes closed. Mrs. Keller's voice was trained for such reading and it was almost like music and then there was a crash and Mr. Keller burst through the door. His father startled them because he was filthy with grime and roaring with excitement. It was an uncommon sight. Mr. Keller was in the habit of washing up outside at the stream with his men and changed both his clothes and manners before solemnly entering the trailer. Caravan. The riggers liked to joke about this outside his father's hearing. Now, Mr. Keller stood there, stiff and angular, in clothes that stank of oil. Crude. Face-smudged, he had something to say but couldn't say it. He was too happy. "We've hit it. We've hit it. We've hit it," he repeated. When he could speak, he said, "Honey, I've already been on the field phone. They want to see us in Texas. Then you and me are going to have us some kind of a holiday, Peg."

His mother's flesh went as cold as the ice in their lemonades. Floydie wanted to jump up and dance around the room with his father but his mother's arms gripped him like thin steel cables. She said, "But what about the boy? Have you thought about Floydie in all this?"

"Of course, I have, Peg! What kind of man do you think I am! I've arranged everything. Floydie will be going away to boarding school. We've put it off long enough. I've talked to the priests. He's half a year underage but they'll take him as a favour to me."

"You've arranged it, have you? Without asking? You want to take everything from me. You mean to send him away to the priests. You want to kill the child in him. You want to crush me. I might as well kill myself as have you do it. I tell you, you shan't do it, I won't have it, I'll kill myself first." Her mouth frothed with anger. The foam turned hard on her lips. As hard as her words. Floydie could not listen to her but he could not break free of her grip. He looked at her lips and thought of her spittle as meringue: he thought of the egg whites rising up the sides of her mixing bowl and turning over and over as she whipped them with a fork.

"If the strike is as big as I think it is, we'll be able to send him to England to study with the Greyfriars in a year or two but the money isn't there right now, Peg, as you bloody well know. Besides, we need some time together right now, you and me, girl. And he needs friends his own age. Other boys. You can see that, can't you? You can see that he needs happy parents and a happy life, can't you? Won't you please try to see that I've got all our best interests at heart?"

As he attempted to reason with his wife, Mr. Keller's flat Canadian twang grew tender. Floydie could hear the tenderness. He thought about the pet rabbit his father had given him. The company truck had run over a wild rabbit and his father had lifted a bit of living fur free from the entrails and brought it home to the caravan wrapped in his shirt. Floydie had nursed the newborn rabbit with an eyedropper. It had lived a few days and then died of fright and loneliness. His father had told him that this was proof of how much a boy needed friends. His mother had whispered in his bedtime ear that the dead rabbit was proof of how much a child needed its mother. Suddenly aware of his son, Keller caught hold of Floydie's arm and wrestled him free of Mrs. Kelter's grasp. "Go play outside!" he shouted.

As he walked away from the caravan, Floydie heard his mother's complaints rise on the air like the shrieks of crows. Floydie hurried off to the bushes by the stream that was his special hiding place. He stayed hidden for a long time.

"Floydie, son, your mother — women — are the devil." His father sweating, red-faced, out of breath found him. "I love your mother, Floydie, you do know that, don't you? But it can stare her right in the face and she can't see it, can she son? What is to become of you if you spend all your life listening to her books and her complaints? This isn't England. You're almost a teenager — you do need to be with boys your own age. What is the sense in talking about England right now? I simply can't afford it and I won't have her father educating my son to be a smarmy Englishman. I simply won't have it! And do you think she'd stay here with me where she belongs beside her husband if you were in England? A wife is supposed to stand beside her husband. When we married, she swore before God that we would raise you as a Roman Catholic and a Roman Catholic like me you are going to be. The priests will see to that. I know that she calls herself an English Catholic but that isn't the same thing at all. You need priests to explain the whys and wherefores of that sort of thing to you. Your mother means well. Tomorrow, we'll drive into town. The three of us. The priests gave me a list of things you'll need to have at school. We'll buy them and pack them in that old steamer trunk and send them off. It's a good school. It's my own old school. Buck up, Floydie. Go show your mother just how happy you are. And son, I know that you don't want to leave us. But no one ever wants to leave home that first time. Your mother will come around. She's in a funk now but we've seen her in a funk before, haven't we? Go and cheer her up son!"

Floydie walked slowly back home to the caravan. He thought of his mother who could be as cold and white and as easily crushed as one of her meringues. He thought about running away from home and taking her with him. He thought about going home to England with her. He thought about being a gentleman to her lady. He knew about chivalry. He thought about being her knight in shining armour.

There was screaming coming from the caravan. Floydie ran and stumbled forward and crashed to his knees at the threshold and fell inside. From the floor, Floydie could see straight through another open door into the bathroom. He saw his mother. She, too, was on the floor. Her mouth was open and screaming. At the sight of him, she put her hands to her face. They dripped blood. A broken glass lay beside her. One of the riggers pushed him aside roughly. Another rigger, more gently, lifted him up and carried him outside. As they passed his father, Floydie spat in his face.

That was the end of his childhood.

That was the seminal experience in his life, so he said.

After this, the only hand he ever allowed to ruffle his hair was Butch's. After this, no one was ever allowed to read aloud to him at bedtime. After this, when he was very unhappy, he called out to Butch and Butch came running and made music to sweeten his life. His mother meant to save him. She botched it. She really botched it. She didn't even kill herself. She simply went mad. She locked herself within a prison of her own making. From inside the walls of one private hospital and then another, she laid waste her family's fortune except for the legacy that was supposed to see him right for the rest of his life but hadn't.

Butch had not believed the story. It was too artful in the telling. Florio was always artful when he lied. Meringue. Rabbits. Spittle. Blood. Suicide. Madness. Butch did not know quite what to believe any longer about the events that had brought Florio to the boarding school and into his life. Year by year, the story had changed, shifted its focus. There were always oil wells in the background but sometimes it was a gusher, other times a dry well that had precipitated a crisis between his parents. Sometimes the quarrel had ended with his mother attacking his father with a carving knife, and other times, the knife was in his father's hands. This time it was broken glass and a suicide attempt. What had been the real story? In an attempt to drive a wedge between boys whose friendship was too particular, Father Prefect had once called Butch into the office and had told him that Florio was a Juvenile Delinquent who had been sent to the college to be reformed. Butch had been unbelieving. Very confidentially, very privately, Father Prefect had whispered into his ear while fondling Butch's knee that Floyd

Keller Junior had attacked both his parents with a hunting knife after they had brought him back from Edmonton where he had run off with one of the oil riggers. There had been too much artfulness in that story as well: Juvenile Delinquent! Runaway! A hint of Homosexuality!

But he told Florio that Father Prefect's story was more believable than the story of the meringues and the rabbit and the broken glass and they had quarreled. How they had quarreled! And always as ever the fighting between them had turned away from the immediate circumstances and they had thrashed one another with recriminations for past offences. They had fought dirty, as dirty as they had ever fought and it had ended things between them once more. Florio had announced grandly that he was no longer covering the waterfront exclusively but had been swinging both ways for some time and had now discovered that some women meant a great deal more to him than most men. He announced that he was well on his way to becoming a father. He announced that he was thinking very seriously about getting married. And Butch had packed his bags and had walked out of Florio's life forever and ever amen.

Hah! What a joke that was. The two of them might separate again and again but they could never divorce. Too much held them together, had always held them together, would hold them together until death. Butch had flounced out of the house at Mahone Bay and gone off to France with the first hard, rugged body he met at the next piano bar he worked, as he had flounced out and off too many times before. But this time bad been different. Florio had never before spoken so openly of bisexual instincts, had never before spoken so emotionally of fatherhood and family life. Butch had attributed all of that to whatever it was that bad gone on between Florio and his father. And it had seemed a reasonable assumption at the time. He had not known Evelyn beyond the mere fact that there was a woman somewhere bearing Florio's offspring within her. It had not moved him very much to know of this, had not moved him in the way he should have been moved. He had felt betrayed. He had felt jealous. He had felt enraged. He had not felt sympathetic. He had not felt compassionate. He had not felt joy that Florio was bringing something new and vital into the world, someone who would outlive them and keep their memories alive in ways that music and paintings never could. He had felt abandoned and left alone. And he had left Florio alone except for one or two parting shots hurled across the Atlantic. He was more ashamed of this than of any of the other failures to love in his crowded life.

And so it had been from mutual friends and not from Florio himself that he had heard of the deaths of the woman and her child. The baby was stillborn. Evelyn had died a week afterwards of complications. And love had failed once more and he had not come running back to Nova Scotia. Those deaths had not healed the breach between them. They had broadened it. Away from the friendly and familiar influence Butch had always brought to bear on him, Florio went strange, very strange, turned his art into a shrine to the memory of Evelyn, turned the shrine into a money-grubbing business and turned his life as an artist into a career as empty and as junky as the Yuppie culture that now controlled The Main. And in all these turnings, Florio had kept his back to Butch, never once called out for help and consolation.

The function of the artist is to disturb. . . .

Butch is disturbed by the way his mind is running. Butch is disturbed by the fact that he cannot keep his thoughts straighter, more focused. He knows that he now has to come to better terms with Evelyn and her dead daughter. He knows that he cannot delay this any longer. He knows that he must work his way free of the woman of the poems, of the notebooks, of the photographs, of the paintings, as once he had to work himself free of the woman on the floor dripping blood from her wrists. That was frightening but no more frightening than this. Evelyn seems a madwoman to him. What were her poems but hysteria? What were her sexual proclivities except obsessions? But none of this really matters. What really matters is to be as dispassionate about her as possible. Without this, how can he be any help to Florio? Butch needs a refuge from his feelings about her. Buddhists, Florio once taught him, have three refuges. Buddhists take refuge in the Buddha, in the company of monks and in the Four Noble Truths: life is suffering; suffering has a cause; the cause of suffering is desire; desire can be overcome by following The Eightfold Path. One must seek right action and right speech and right understanding will follow and flow into right alertness, right . . . There are steps to the path that he cannot now remember but Butch does remember that life according to the Buddha is a river never returning. A river flows. Florio. Florio is his refuge, his monastery, his law of life. This has always been the case, this will always be the case until death parts them finally and irrevocably:

> *The function of the artist is to disturb. His duty is to arouse the sleepers, to shake the complacent pillars of the world. He reminds the world of its dark ancestry, shows the world its present, and points the way to a new birth. He is at once the product and the preceptor of his time. After his passage we are troubled and made unsure of the too easily accepted realities. He makes uneasy the static, the set and the still. In a world terrified of change, be preaches revolution — the principle of life. He is an agitator, a disturber of the peace — quick, impatient, positive, restless and disquieting. He is the creative spirit working in the soul of man.*

Butch has not thought of these words of Dr. Norman Bethune in some time. He thinks of them now only because they too are in Florio's box. They are there in Butch's own handwriting on the pale blue paper of an aerogram — a five-year-old aerogram postmarked from the villa in the south of France where he fled with his hard rugged pick-up love after the debacle in Nova Scotia. There are pin holes in the top and bottom of the aerogram. Did Florio read it to Evelyn? Is it something he pinned to the wall of his studio at Mahone Bay? Is it something in which he found consolation after her death and the death of his daughter? Butch tries to keep his thoughts from wandering off in these directions. The thing to do, he tells himself, is to focus on Bethune's words not Florio's reaction to them. Bethune's words once meant something very important to him; why else had he so scrupulously copied them out by hand on an aerogram and posted them to Florio so soon after their quarrel? He could not remember the reasons why he had done so. But they had meant something to Florio as well. Why else had he saved them and pinned them to the wall.

*The function of the artist is to disturb. His
duty is to arouse the sleepers . . .*

The function of the nurse is to quiet the disturbed. Is every nurse an enemy to every artist? Is this why Florio has called him to his bedside? Does Florio really imagine him to be the enemy of his art?

Butch realizes that he is losing his focus again. He knows that he should get up and do something useful. He knows that he should put himself to bed. But first he must do something about the box and its contents. He begins to put all of Florio's hidden life back into the box that holds secrets. He puts them back as carefully as a spy. He has been a spy. He locks the box and pushes it back under the bed under the dead to this world weight of Florio. As he pushes, he keeps one eye on Florio's sleeping face. He does not want him to wake. He can't afford to let Florio find him snooping into the hidden life.

In his own bed on the camp cot he has erected near enough to Florio to be able to hear every cry he might make in the night, Butch asks himself what would have happened if Florio had awakened while the box was out and open? He does not know the answer. He does not know what rages or insights or forgivenesses Florio can manage in his illness. Should he attempt to find out? Should he open the box again in the morning, drag it into the middle of the room, scatter photographs and diaries and poems very which way and rub Florio's eyes awake to it?

Florio should be made to look at the things that he has done to Evelyn and to Butch and to his other lovers and to himself in the pursuit of his art, shouldn't he? But even as Butch imagines doing this, he fluffs his thin pillow and slumps back into the thin mattress and wills himself to fall asleep as he hugs his teddy bear. But his will doesn't triumph. Something niggles him. He knows that there is something that he has quite forgotten to do. What? He rises from the cot and views the room by the light of the small lamp that is forever lit to hold back the total darkness that has always terrified him. His eyes spy the old aerogram lying forgotten on the bedside table. Butch recovers it swiftly and squashes it into a tight ball and looks around for a place to throw it. And then he thinks again about this thing he has done and he rolls the ball of thin blue paper back and forth in the palm of his left hand with his thumb. What is he to do with Dr. Bethune's words, his message to Florio from a state of mind he cannot fully recapture?

> *The function of the artist is to disturb. His*
> *duty is to arouse the sleeper, to shake the complacent pillars . . .*

Bethune's words re-emerge line by carefully printed line as the paper is unwadded and pressed flat against the surface of the table and smoothed out by Butch's fingers. Unwrinkled, the words are no longer quite so clearcut as they were only moments ago. They no longer look nor read like the small incisions of a very sharp scalpel. In those early years in Montreal, Florio had used art like a sword. For the Florio of those days the only art that had mattered was the art that fought against British and American imperialism, the art that conserved realism and celebrated social solidarity. Florio had made his mark among the free egalitarian fraternity of Rue Ontario by denouncing American art in all its guises, while promoting Canadian social realism in every guise he could unearth, including the naive and primitive painters who lodged otherwise unappreciated in the boardinghouses of that quarter. And Florio had resisted the prevailing lies: popular culture was not going to save anybody from anything; new technologies were not going to make anything better for anybody:

Nobody in power offered Florio permanent teaching positions anywhere when his studies were over and gallery owners were dismissive of his work. He struggled and Butch supported them by playing ragtime piano and boogie-woogie in a cocktail lounge, and it was a life of sorts. Florio took occasional lovers who drove trucks or worked with welding torches or plied the Seaway in iron and coke boats. Butch played jazz wherever and whenever he could and picked up hard rugged bodies of his own in bars. Florio sketched people on Rue St-Denis and then he painted what he'd sketched in the privacy of his studio. When he began, the people he painted were simple *habitues* of the street, students, hangers-on, revolutionaries. But a decade came and went and the revolutionaries grew older and became Pequistes and powerful, and Florio's portraits of their younger selves made it seem to them that Frederick Taylor while still alive and retired in Mexico had been reborn among them, and the workers Taylor had painted in the Angus shops of the thirties had given birth to the sons and daughters of the Paul Sauve Arena of the mid-seventies.

Butch stares at Dr. Bethune's crumpled and straightened old words

> *The function of the artist is to disturb. His duty is to arouse the sleepers, to shake the complacent pillars of the world. He reminds the world of its dark ancestry, shows the world its present, and points the way to its new birth. . . .*

but his thoughts have moved along to the words of another doctor, Florio's physician. Florio had not seen a doctor on his own initiative. When Butch first arrived in the studio on The Main he had found Florio almost too weak to be moved from his bed. It was a scary shuffle to get him out of bed and down his stairs and into a taxi and up to the Royal Victoria's Emergency. Luck had been with them that night. Butch sat for three hours in a small, stuffy, overheated green room with no distraction other than a television set suspended overhead at a wrong angle to the chair upon which he sat clutching his overcoat and Florio's leather jacket against the company of other people as frightened as himself. He sat among the walking wounded of a premature Montreal winter and watched doctors and nurses who looked scarcely half his age come and go through a door that the public could not use. And he worried lest none of them would have the patience and tact to get to the bottom of Florio's illness.

He needn't have worried quite so much: the doctor who claimed Florio's dossier was their age, a man of experience, cultured enough to recognize Florio's paint-daubed clothing as an artist's working clothes, patient enough to probe Florio's psychological defence mechanisms and find an opening through which he could get the information he needed to diagnose something beyond common garden variety influenza. There was influenza, but there was also malnutrition and stress and a kidney inflammation and insulin deficiency and more than adequate grounds for more testing than would be done in the normal course of events. As if to undercut the threat of this, to provide at least temporary reassurance, the doctor said, "Mr. Keller needs at least a couple of weeks in bed. He's worn out from too much work and not enough good food. He has viral and bacterial infections. I can prescribe something for them. He can't be admitted in his present condition unless there is no one to care for him at home. He has to be kept warm and quiet and well-fed to prevent pneumonia from developing."

Butch had done his best. Even so, fever had developed and then pneumonia and the doctor, bless him, had made a house call and taken further blood samples. Tomorrow, maybe, they'll hear from the doctor who will have heard from the lab. In the meantime, Florio sleeps.

Butch knows that Evelyn is at the heart of Florio's darkness. He knows that Evelyn has split Florio from his work. Evelyn has robbed Florio of his painterly gifts and left counterfeit coin behind. Butch knows that Florio cannot live without painting. Butch knows that Florio cannot really recover so long as his studio is home to all the Neo-Expressionist canvasses he has done of Evelyn. They exhaust him. They threaten to destroy him. Its isn't just that they explode his reputation for lightness and clarity of composition. It isn't just that they deflect attention from the great strengths and true values in his more customary painterly concerns. It isn't just that they are an anomaly that defeats Butch every time he tries to compose his thoughts about them. It is all this and more, much more. Evelyn is dead, dead, dead. Butch feels her deathly presence in every nook and cranny in the studio as if the twenty paintings stacked against the walls with Evelyn inside each and every one of them were a sort of nuclear furnace melting down Florio's life.

They leave him cold. Butch feels cold, ice cold. He rises from the camp cot and goes over to the paintings and turns them outwards towards him and lines them up along the wall. They are large canvasses and there is room for viewing only a few at a time. The first three that he looks at, the last ones in the series in order of composition, remind Butch more than a little of the sort of thing Claude Breeze did in the sixties: *Lovers In A Landscape*. A man and a woman are flayed monsters of sexuality. The woman has been gored by a bull of a man. She is a matador dying but there is no bullring and no afternoon Spanish sunlight. The landscape is nowhere and nothing but sensuous abstraction. It is as near to Abstract Expressionism as Florio has ever gone. It is a great betrayal of the things that made his art honest and personal and sincerely felt. Butch hates it and the ones to either side of it and all the others in the series enough to want to pick up the sharpest knife he can find and cut the canvasses to shreds. He wants to reduce them all to a heap of narrow ragged strips of canvas clotted with paint. He wants to kick apart the heavy wooden stretchers that hold the images taut against his consciousness. He wants to fall into a trance of vandalism and destroy Evelyn utterly in all the forms that Florio has given her. He wants to disinter all that remains of her inside Florio's box of souvenirs and make a fire of her. He wants to fall into a frenzy of violence against her until his arm grows so tired that he is merely hacking at her rather than slicing through her. He wants to burn her at the stake and reduce her to ashes after first drowning the life out of her like a common medieval witch. But he does nothing. There isn't a knife honed sharp enough to defeat her. There isn't a fire hot enough to destroy her. She is a poison against which there is no antidote. Butch knows that he can do nothing, nothing at all, against the death she brings.

Butch returns to his bed and tries to calm himself with thoughts of his mother. In his thoughts, she is always Mummy, although Mummy does have a name. Mummy's name is Estelle Mary Grant Benet. Benet was her erstwhile husband, Butch's father, but he is long forgotten and his name remains only because Mummy has never surrendered anything she has been given. Butch does not know much about him, only the little that Mummy has told him and this is truly very little. Mummy has always told him a great many too many things about altogether too many people in whom Butch has not had the slightest interest. His mother has spoken of his father rarely and always in this dismissive way: "I could never trust your father for a moment in the company of other women. He was a womanizer of the worst sort." She has never told him what a better sort of womanizer might be like.

Butch finds it easy to think about Mummy. Mummy is inescapable. She is always there, just at the edge of mental consciousness, right at the centre of emotional response. If Florio was to wake up, he thinks, and smile and say, "Butch, a penny for your thoughts," he would say, "You're a spendthrift, Florio, I wasn't thinking about anything at all." He would say this because he doesn't like talking to Florio about Mummy. It's too disloyal. He cannot quite say why. But it doesn't matter. Not here. Not now. Florio isn't awake and he never smiles in his sleep and he'd never say anything so conventional as "A penny for your thoughts." So Butch is left to talk to the teddy bear that he has brought with him to Montreal. Butch likes to talk to Teddy about his mother as if he was talking to a stranger on a train or to a sleeping lover whose name he can't quite remember. It is only to perfect strangers and to sleeping lovers and to Teddy that he can say, "I think most mothers resent their sons at least some of the time and I guess that there are some mothers who resent their sons most of the time but honestly, I sometimes think that Mummy resents me all of the time. You know I try not to take this personally anymore, not at least, too personally. Mummy has been badly used by men. Mummy has been abused by recent history but women like her have taught people like me where to take a stand with the men in our lives. We owe them something for their pains."

In bed, into his old and nearly threadbare teddy, he whispers, "I've read Marx too. I'm not a dumb fucking machine. I looked at Mummy's life and I learned how to use the dialectic of history to my own advantage. Mummy is nearly seventy but she stopped counting years and years ago. She is just fifty-ish. Even so she expects me to remember her birthday. Always. Every August 22nd, Mummy expects me to bring her flowers and a bottle of good champagne, some scent or something in silk from Holt's and a chocolate cake that I've baked myself. She doesn't expect a card and she doesn't want me to wish her a Happy Birthday but she does want her chocolate cake and I have to have baked it myself or there's a flood. She expects all this even though she knows that her birthday is on the same date as Florio's. The last time she went into a flood was last Christmas, you remember, Teddy. I forgot to order her a poinsettia. I had to run out and pick one up at a florist's just before closing time. It was a wretched thing. Mummy went on and on about it and I got angry and pitched it right into the garbage. She didn't mind that very much. But then I went and called her Mother instead of Mummy and she flooded again and stopped speaking to me until

January 6th. The Epiphany is a major feast in her books. She forgives everyone everything on the day that the Three Wise Men brought gold, frankincense and myrrh to the stable in Bethlehem. It's an old custom left over from her childhood. I don't understand it although it was supposed to be a part of my childhood too."

"I have grown up but Mummy has only ever grown old. Have you noticed how Roman Catholics never think that they are the least bit superstitious? They'll tell you that there is nothing in the least bit irrational in their religion. So they're suckers for astrology. Mummy regards herself as a gifted astrologer. She casts her own horoscopes. She is a Sun in Leo on the cusp of Virgo with her moon in Libra with Cancer rising. This, she says, means that she is frank, open-hearted, generous and has a marked dramatic flair. These signs, she says, make her a sincere and affectionate lover who is highly appreciative of affection freely returned. The planets that rule her, she says, attract her most and make her most attractive to refined and harmonious people who join her in easy alliances. These same planets, she says, have given her a hatred of small details and a preference for doing things in a big way. These planets, she says, make her quick to anger but just as quick to forgive. These planets, she says, have given her strong interests in food and hygiene, a liking for very good clothes and a dependence upon the accomplishments of her child. I know these things by rote. These are the things that Mummy has been telling her friends year after year after year. Some of her friends have come to believe her. Some of her friends think that she is a gifted psychic. I keep trying to tell her that everything she says of herself must also apply to Florio. They have more than the same birthdays, they do have all the same signs. But she just ignores what I say about him, I mean about the things I say in his favour. I myself am a Sun in Scorpio with Moon in Virgo on the cusp of Sagittarius with Capricorn rising. This makes me suspicious, sceptical, critical, reserved and calculating. I'm forceful, blunt and sarcastic, courageous, bold, daring. There is a love of the elemental in me and a fascination with the sea, Teddy, isn't there?"

Butch looks at Florio asleep and promises the teddy bear that he has carried everywhere with him since boarding school days that if it is truly time for Florio to die, that if the disease within him is AIDS, his ashes will be dropped in the sea on the shore of Mahone Bay where the ashes of

Evelyn and the stillborn child now rest. Until then, he will put them both to sleep by singing the Tom Waits song "Time" that T Bone Burnett still sings in the part of his brain that never forgets a song

And they all pretend they're orphans
And their memories are like a train
You can see it getting smaller as it pulls away
And the things you can't remember
Tell the things you can't forget
That history puts a safe in every dream

And she said she'd stick around until the bandages came off
But these momma's boys just don't know when to quit
And Matilda asks the sailors, 'Are those dreams or are those prayers?'
So close your eyes son and this won't hurt a bit
And its time, time, time
And its time, time, time
And its time, time, time that you love
And its time, time, time . . .

BARBARA GOWDY was born in Windsor, Ontario in 1950 and now lives in Toronto. Her publications include *Falling Angels,* and *We So Seldom Look on Love.* This story first appeared in CFM No. 74/75 in 1991, the 20th anniversary issue.

Ninety-Three-Million Miles Away

BARBARA GOWDY

AT LEAST PART OF THE REASON why Ali married Claude, a cosmetic surgeon with a growing practice, was so that she could quit her boring government job. Claude was all for it. "You only have one life to live," he said. "You only have one kick at the can." He gave her a generous allowance and told her to do what she wanted.

She wasn't sure what that was, aside from trying on clothes in expensive stores. Claude suggested something musical — she loved music — so she took dance classes and piano lessons and discovered that she had a tin ear and no sense of rhythm. She fell into a mild depression during which she peevishly questioned Claude about the ethics of cosmetic surgery.

"It all depends on what light you're looking at it in," Claude said. He was not easily riled. What Ali needed to do, he said, was take the wider view.

She agreed. She decided to devote to herself to learning, and she began a regime of reading and studying, five days a week, five to six hours a day. She read novels, plays, biographies, essays, magazine articles, almanacs, the New Testament, *The Concise Oxford Dictionary, The Harper Anthology of Poetry.*

But after a year of this, although she became known as the person at dinner parties who could supply the name or date that somebody was snapping around for, she wasn't particularly happy, and she didn't even feel smart. Far from it, she felt stupid, a machine, an idiot savant whose one talent was memorization. If she had any *creative* talent, which was the only kind she really admired, she wasn't going to find it by armouring herself with facts. She grew slightly paranoid that Claude wanted her to settle down and have a baby.

A few days before their second wedding anniversary she and Claude bought a condominium apartment with floor-to-ceiling windows, and Ali decided to abandon her regime and to take up painting. Since she didn't know the first thing about painting or even drawing, she studied pictures from art books. She did know what her first subject was going to be — herself in the nude. Several months earlier she'd had a dream about her signature in the corner of a painting, and realizing from the conversation of the men who were admiring it (and blocking her view) that it was an extraordinary rendition of her naked self. She took the dream to be a sign. For several weeks she studied the proportions, skin tones and muscle definitions of the nudes in her books, then she went out and bought art supplies and a self-standing, full-length mirror.

Halfway down the living room she set up her work area. Here she had light without being directly in front of the window. When she was all ready to begin, she stood before the mirror and slipped off her white, terrycloth housecoat and her pink flannelette pyjamas, letting them fall to the floor. It aroused her a little to witness her careless shedding of clothes. She tried a pose: hands folded and resting loosely under her stomach, feet buried in the drift of her housecoat.

For some reason, however, she couldn't get a fix on what she looked like. Her face and body seemed indistinct, secretive in a way, as if they were actually well-defined, but not today, or not from where she was looking.

She decided that she should simply start, and see what happened. She did a pencil drawing of herself sitting in a chair and stretching. It struck her as being very good, not that she could really judge, but the out-of-kilter proportions seemed slyly deliberate, and there was a pleasing simplicity to the reaching arms and the elongated curve of the neck. Because flattery hadn't been her intention, Ali felt that at last she may have wrenched a vision out of her soul.

By now it was close to supper time, Claude would be home soon, so she stopped work for the day. The next morning she got out of bed unusually early, not long after Claude had left the apartment, and discovered sunlight streaming obliquely into the living room through a gap between their building and the apartment house next door. As far as she knew, and in spite of the plate-glass windows, this was the only direct light they got. Deciding to make use of it while it lasted, she moved her easel, chair and mirror closer to the window. Then she took off her housecoat and pyjamas.

For a few moments she stood there looking at herself, wondering what it was that had inspired the sketch. Today she was disposed to seeing herself as not bad, overall. As far as certain specifics went though, as to whether her breasts were small, for instance, or her eyes close together, she remained in the dark.

Did other people find her looks ambiguous? Claude was always calling her beautiful, except that the way he put it — "You're beautiful to me," or "I think you're beautiful" — made it sound as if she should understand that his taste in women was unconventional. Her only boyfriend before Claude, a guy called Roger, told her she was great but never said how exactly. When they had sex, Roger liked to hold the base of his penis and watch it going in and out of her. Once, he said that there were days he got so horny at the office, his pencil turned him on. She thought it should have been his pencil sharpener.

It was hot, standing in the direct sun. Between her breasts a drop of sweat slid haltingly, a sensation like the tip of a tongue. Watching herself in the mirror she covered her breasts with her spread fingers and imagined a man's hands . . . not Claude's — a man's hands not attached to any particular man. She looked out the window.

In the apartment directly across from her she saw a man.

She leapt to one side, behind the drapes. Her heart pounded violently, but only for a moment, as if something had thundered by, dangerously close. She wiped her wet forehead on the drapes, then, without looking at the window, walked back to her easel, picked up her palette and brush and began to mix paint. She gave herself a glance in the mirror, but she had no intention of trying to duplicate her own skin tone. She wanted something purer. White with just a hint of rose, like the glance of colour in a soap bubble.

Her strokes were short and light to control dripping. She liked the effect, however . . . how it made the woman appear as if she were covered in feathers. Paint splashed on her own skin, but she resisted putting her smock on. The room seemed preternaturally white and airy; the windows beyond the mirror gleamed. Being so close to the windows gave her the tranced sensation of standing at the edge of a cliff.

A few minutes before she lost the direct sun, she finished the woman's skin. She set down the palette and put her brush in turpentine, then wet a rag in the turpentine and wiped paint off her hands and where it had dripped on her thighs and feet. She thought about the sun. She thought that it is ninety-three million miles away and that its fuel supply will last another five billion years. Instead of thinking about the man who was watching her, she tried to recall a solar chart she had memorized a couple of years ago.

The surface temperature is six thousand degrees Fahrenheit, she told herself. Double that number and you have how many times bigger the surface of the sun is compared to the surface of the earth. Except that because the sun is a ball of hot gas, it actually has no surface.

When she had rubbed the paint off herself, she went into the kitchen to wash away the turpentine with soap and water. The man's eyes tracked her. She didn't have to glance at the window for confirmation. She switched on the light above the sink, soaped the dishcloth and began to wipe her skin. There was no reason to clean her arms, but she lifted each one and wiped the cloth over it. She wiped her breasts. She seemed to share in his scrutiny, as if she were looking at herself through his eyes. What she saw was a serene woman, probably a recent immigrant, a woman apparently unaccustomed to closing the curtains and to going to the bathroom to wash herself. From his perspective she was able to see her physical self very clearly — her shiny, red-highlighted hair, her small waist and heartshaped bottom, the dreamy tilt to her head.

She began to shiver. She wrung out the cloth and folded it over the faucet, then patted herself dry with a dish towel. Then, pretending to be examining her fingernails, she turned and walked over to the window. She looked up.

There he was, in the window straight across but one floor higher.

Her glance of a quarter of an hour ago had registered dark hair and a white shirt. Now she saw a long, older face . . . a man in his fifties maybe. A green tie. She had seen him before this morning — quick, disinterested (or so she had thought) sightings of a man in his kitchen, watching television, going from room to room. A bachelor living next door. She pressed the palms of her hands on the window, and he stepped back into shadow.

The pane clouded from her breath. She leaned her body into it, flattening her breasts against the cool glass. Right at the window she was visible to his apartment and the one below, which had closed vertical blinds. "Each window like a pill'ry appears," she thought. Vaguely appropriate lines from the poems she had read last year were always occurring to her. She felt that he was still watching, but she yearned for proof.

When it became evident that he wasn't going to show himself, she went into the bedroom. The bedroom windows didn't face the apartment house, but she closed them anyway, then got into bed under the covers. Between her legs there was such a tender throbbing that she had to push a pillow into her crotch. Sex addicts must feel like this, she thought. Rapists, child molesters.

She said to herself, "You are a certifiable exhibitionist." She let out an amazed, almost exultant laugh, but instantly fell into a darker amazement as it dawned on her that she really was . . . she really *was* an exhibitionist. And what's more, she had been one for years, or at least she had been working up to being one for years.

Why, for instance, did she and Claude live here, in this vulgar low-rise. Wasn't it because of the floor-to-ceiling windows that faced the windows of the house next door?

And what about when she was twelve and became so obsessed with the idea of urinating on people's lawns that one night she crept out of the house after everyone was asleep and did it, peed on the lawn of the townhouse next door . . . right under a streetlight, in fact.

What about two years ago, when she didn't wear underpants the entire summer? She'd had a minor yeast infection and had read that it was a good idea not to wear underpants at home, if you could help it, but she had stopped wearing them in public as well, beneath skirts and dresses, at parties, on buses, and she must have known that this was taking it a bit far, because she had kept it from Claude.

"Oh, my God," she said wretchedly.

She went still, alerted by how theatrical that sounded. Her heart was beating in her throat. She touched a finger to it. So fragile, a throat. She imagined the man being excited by her hands on her throat.

What was going on? What was the matter with her? Maybe she was too aroused to be shocked at herself. She moved her hips, rubbing her crotch against the pillow. No, she didn't want to masturbate. That would ruin it.

Ruin what?

She closed her eyes, and the man appeared to her. She experienced a rush of wild longing. It was as if, all her life, she had been waiting for a long-faced, middle-aged man in a white shirt and green tie. He was probably still standing in his living room, watching her window.

She sat up, threw off the covers.

Dropped back down on the bed.

This was crazy. This really was crazy. What if he was a rapist? What if, right this minute, he was downstairs, finding out her name from the mailbox? Or what if he was just some lonely, normal man who took her display as an invitation to phone her up and ask her for a date? It's not as if she wanted to go out with him. She wasn't looking for an affair.

For an hour or so she fretted, and then she drifted off to sleep. When she woke up, shortly after noon, she was quite calm. The state she had worked herself into earlier struck her as overwrought. So, she gave some guy a thrill, so what? She was a bit of an exhibitionist . . . most women were, she bet. It was instinctive, a side effect of being the receptor in the sex act.

She decided to have lunch and go for a walk. While she was making herself a sandwich she avoided glancing at the window, but as soon as she sat at the table, she couldn't resist looking over.

He wasn't there, and yet she felt that he was watching her, standing out of the light. She ran a hand through her hair. "For Christ's sake," she reproached herself, but she was already with him. Again it was as if her eyes were in his head, although not replacing his eyes. She knew that he wanted her to slip her hand down her sweat pants. She did this. Watching his window, she removed her hand and licked her wet fingers. At that instant she would have paid money for some sign that he was watching.

After a few minutes she began to chew on her fingernails. She was suddenly depressed. She reached over and pulled the curtain across the window and ate her sandwich. Her mouth, biting into the bread, trembled like an old lady's. "Trembled like a guilty thing surprised," she quoted to herself. It wasn't guilt, though, it wasn't frustration, either, not sexual frustration. She was acquainted with this bleached sadness — it came upon her at the height of sensation . . . after orgasms, after a day of trying on clothes in stores.

She finished her sandwich and went for a long walk in her new toreador pants and her tight, black, turtleneck sweater. By the time she returned, Claude was home. He asked her if she had worked in the nude again.

"Of course," she said absently. "I have to." She was looking past him at the man's closed drapes. "Claude," she said suddenly, "am I beautiful? I mean not just to you. Am I empirically beautiful?"

Claude looked surprised. "Well, yeah," he said. "Sure you are. Hell, I married you, didn't I? Hey!" He stepped back. "Whoa?"

She was removing her clothes. When she was naked, she said, "Don't think of me as your wife, just as a woman. One of your patients. Am I beautiful or not?"

He made a show of eyeing her up and down. "Not bad," he said. "Of course, it depends what you mean by beautiful." He laughed. "What's going on?"

"I'm serious. You don't think I'm kind of . . . normal? You know, plain?"

"Of course not," he said lovingly. He reached for her and drew her into his arms. "You want hard evidence?" he said.

They went into the bedroom. It was dark because the curtains were still drawn. She switched on the bedside lamp, but once he was undressed, he switched it off again.

"No," she said from the bed, "leave it on."

"What? You want it on?"

"For a change."

The next morning she got up before he did. She had hardly slept. During breakfast she kept looking over at the apartment house, but there was no sign of the man. Which didn't necessarily mean that he wasn't there. She couldn't wait for Claude to leave so that she could stop pretending she wasn't keyed-up. It was gnawing at her that she had overestimated or somehow misread the man's interest. How did she know? He might be gay. He might be so devoted to a certain woman that all other women repelled him. He might be puritanical . . . a priest, a born-again Christian. He might be out of his mind.

The minute Claude was out the door, she undressed and began working on the painting. She stood in the sunlight mixing colours, then sat on the chair in her stretching pose, looking at herself in the mirror, then stood up and — without paying much attention, glancing every few seconds at his window — painted ribs and uplifted breasts.

An hour went by before she thought, He's not going to show up. She dropped into the chair, weak with disappointment, even though she knew that, very likely, he has simply been obliged to go to work, that his being home yesterday was a fluke. Forlornly she gazed at her painting. To her surprise she had accomplished something rather interesting: breasts like Picasso eyes. It is possible, she thought dully, that I am a natural talent.

She put her brush in the turpentine, and her face in her hands. She felt the sun on her hair. In a few minutes the sun would disappear behind his house, and after that, if she wanted him to get a good look at her, she would have to stand right at the window. She envisioned herself stationed there all day. You are ridiculous, she told herself. You are unhinged.

She glanced up at the window again.

He was there.

She sat up straight. Slowly she came to her feet. Stay, she prayed. He did. She walked over to the window, her fingertips brushing her thighs. She held her breath. When she was at the window, she stood perfectly still. He had on a white shirt again, but no tie. He was close enough that she could make out the darkness around his eyes, although she couldn't tell exactly where he was looking. But his eyes seemed to enter her head like a drug, and she felt herself aligned with his perspective. She saw herself — surprisingly slender, composed but apprehensive — through the glass and against the backdrop of the room's white walls.

After a minute or two she walked over to the chair, picked it up and carried it to the window. She sat facing him, her knees apart. He was as still as a picture. So was she, because she had suddenly remembered that he might be gay, or crazy. She tried to give him a hard look. She observed his age and his sad, respectable appearance . . . and the fact that he remained at the window, revealing his interest.

No, he was the man she had imagined. I am a gift to him, she thought, opening her legs wider. I am his dream come true. She began to rotate her hips. With the fingers of both hands she spread her labia.

One small part of her mind, clinging to the person she had been until yesterday morning, tried to pull her back. She felt it as a presence behind the chair, a tableau of sensational, irrelevant warnings that she was obviously not about to turn around for. She kept her eyes on the man. Moving her left hand up to her breasts, she began to rub and squeeze and to circle her fingers on the nipples. The middle finger of her right hand slipped into her vagina, as the palm massaged her clitoris.

He was motionless.

You are kissing me, she thought. She seemed to feel his lips, cool, soft, sliding and sucking down her stomach. You are kissing me. She imagined his hands under her, lifting her like a bowl to his lips.

She was coming.

Her body jolted. Her legs shook. She had never experienced anything like it. Seeing what he saw, she witnessed an act of shocking vulnerability. It went on and on. She saw the charity of her display, her lavish recklessness and submission. It inspired her to the tenderest self love. The man did not move, not until she had finally stopped moving, and then he reached up one hand — to signal, she thought, but it was to close the drapes.

She stayed sprawled in the chair. She was astonished. She couldn't believe herself. She couldn't believe him. How did he know to stay so still, to simply watch her? She avoided the thought that right at this moment he was probably masturbating. She absorbed herself only with what she had seen, which was a dead-still man whose eyes she had sensed roving over her body the way that eyes in certain portraits seem to follow you around the room.

The next three mornings everything was the same. He had on his white shirt, she masturbated in the chair, he watched without moving, she came spectacularly, he closed the drapes.

Afterwards she went out clothes shopping or visiting people. Everyone told her how great she looked. At night she was passionate in bed, prompting Claude to ask several times, "What the hell's come over you?" but he asked it happily, he didn't look a gift horse in the mouth. She felt very loving toward Claude, not out of guilt but out of high spirits. She knew better than to confess, of course, and yet she didn't believe that she was betraying him with the man next door. A man who hadn't touched her or spoken to her, who, as far as she was concerned, only existed from the waist up and who never moved except to pull his drapes, how could that man be counted as a lover?

The fourth day, Friday, the man didn't appear. For two hours she waited in the chair. Finally she moved to the couch and watched television, keeping one eye on the window. She told herself that he must have had an urgent appointment, or that he had to go to work early. She was worried, though. At some point, late in the afternoon when she wasn't looking, he closed the drapes.

Saturday and Sunday he didn't seem to be home — the drapes were drawn and the lights off . . . not that she could have done anything anyway, not with Claude there. On Monday morning she was in her chair, naked, as soon as Claude left the house. She waited until ten-thirty, then put on her toreador pants and a white, push-up halter top and went for a walk. A consoling line from *Romeo and Juliet* played in her head: "He that is stricken blind cannot forget the precious treasure of his eyesight lost." She was angry with the man for not being as keen as she was. If he was at his window tomorrow, she vowed she would shut her drapes on him.

But how would she replace him, what would she do? Become a table dancer? She had to laugh. Aside from the fact that she was a respectably married woman and could not dance to save her life and was probably ten years too old, the last thing she wanted was a bunch of slack-jawed, flat-eyed drunks grabbing at her breasts. She wanted one man, and she wanted him to have a sad, intelligent demeanour and the control to watch her without moving a muscle. She wanted him to wear a white shirt.

On the way home, passing his place, she stopped. The building was a mansion turned into luxury apartments. He must have money, she realized . . . an obvious conclusion, but until now she'd had no interest whatsoever in who he was.

She climbed the stairs and tried the door. Found it open. Walked in.

The mailboxes were numbered one to four. His would be four. She read the name in the little window: "Dr. Andrew Halsey."

Back at her apartment she looked him up under "Physicians" in the phone book and found that, like Claude, he was a surgeon. A general surgeon, though, a remover of tumours and diseased organs. Presumably on call. Presumably dedicated, as a general surgeon would be.

She guessed she would forgive his absences.

The next morning and the next, Andrew (as she now thought of him) was at the window. Thursday he wasn't. She tried not to be disappointed. She imagined him saving peoples' lives, drawing his scalpel along skin in beautifully precise cuts. For something to do she worked on her painting. She painted fish-like eyes, a hooked nose, a mouth full of teeth. She worked fast.

Andrew was there Friday morning. When Ali saw him she rose to her feet and pressed her body against the window, as she had done the first morning. Then she walked to the chair, turned it around and leaned over it, her back to him. She masturbated stroking herself from behind.

That afternoon she bought him a pair of binoculars, an expensive, powerful pair, which she wrapped in brown paper, addressed and left on the floor in front of his mailbox. All weekend she was preoccupied with wondering whether he would understand that she had given them to him and whether he would use them. She had considered including a message: "For our mornings" or something like that, but such direct communication seemed like a violation of a pact between them. The binoculars alone were a risk.

Monday, before she even had her housecoat off, he walked from the rear of the room to the window, the binoculars at his eyes. Because most of his face was covered by the binoculars and his hands, she had the impression that he was masked. Her legs shook. When she opened her legs and spread her labia, his eyes crawled up her. She masturbated but didn't come and didn't try to, although she put on a show of coming. She was so devoted to his appreciation that her pleasure seemed like a siphoning of his, an early, childish indulgence that she would never return to.

It was later, with Claude, that she came. After supper she pulled him onto the bed. She pretended that he was Andrew, or rather she imagined a dark, long-faced, silent man who made love with his eyes open but who smelled and felt like Claude and whom she loved and trusted as she did Claude. With this hybrid partner she was able to relax enough to encourage the kind of kissing and movement she needed but had never had the confidence to insist upon. The next morning, masturbating for Andrew, she reached the height of ecstasy, as if her orgasms with him had been the fantasy, and her pretenses of orgasms were the real thing. Not coming released her completely into his dream of her. The whole show for him: cunt, ass, mouth, throat offered to his magnified vision.

For several weeks Andrew turned up regularly, five mornings a week, and she lived in a state of elation. In the afternoons she worked on her painting, without much concentration though, since finishing it didn't seem to matter anymore in spite of how well it was turning out. Claude insisted that it was still very much a self-portrait, a statement Ali was insulted by, given the woman's obvious primitiveness and her flat, distant eyes.

There was no reason for her to continue working in the nude, but she did, out of habit and comfort, and on the outside chance that Andrew might be peeking through his drapes. While she painted she wondered about her exhibitionism, what it was about her that craved to have a strange man look at her. Of course, everyone and everything liked to be looked at to a certain degree, she thought. Flowers, cats, anything that preened or shone, children crying, "Look at me!" Some mornings her episodes with Andrew seemed to have nothing at all to do with lust; they were completely display, wholehearted surrender to what felt like the most inaugural and genuine of all desires, which was not sex but which happened to be expressed through a sexual act.

One night she dreamed that Andrew was operating on her. Above the surgical mask his eyes were expressionless. He had very long arms. She was also able to see, as if through his eyes, the vertical incision that went from between her breasts to her navel, and the skin on either side of the incision folded back like a scroll. Her heart was brilliant red and perfectly heartshaped. All of her other organs were glistening yellows and oranges. Somebody should take a picture of this, she thought. Andrew's gloved hands barely appeared to move as they wielded long, silver instruments. There was no blood on his hands. Very carefully, so that she hardly felt it, he prodded her organs and plucked at her veins and tendons, occasionally drawing a tendon out and dropping it into a petri dish. It was as if he were weeding a garden. Her heart throbbed. A tendon encircled her heart, and when he pulled on it she could feel that its other end encircled her vagina, and the uncoiling there was the most exquisite sensation she had ever experienced. She worried that she would come and that her trembling and spasms would cause him to accidentally stab her. She woke up coming.

All day the dream obsessed her. It *could* happen, she reasoned. She could have a gall bladder or an appendicitis attack and be rushed to the hospital and, just as she was going under, see that the surgeon was Andrew. It could happen.

When she woke up the next morning, the dream was her first thought. She looked down at the gentle swell of her stomach and felt sentimental and excited. She found it impossible to shake the dream, even while she was masturbating for Andrew, so that instead of entering *his* dream of her, instead of seeing a naked woman sitting in a pool of morning sun, she saw the sliced-open chest in the shaft of his surgeon's light. Her heart was what she focused on, its fragile pulsing, but she also saw the slower rise and fall of her lungs, and the quivering of her other organs. Between her organs were tantalizing crevices entwined swirls of blue and red — her veins and arteries. Her tendons were seashell pink, threaded tight as guitar strings.

Of course she realized that she had the physiology all wrong and that in a real operation there would be blood and pain and she would be anaesthetized. It was an impossible, mad fantasy; she didn't expect it to last. But every day it became more enticing as she authenticated it with hard data, such as the name of the hospital he operated out of (she called his number in the phone book and asked his nurse) and the name of his surgical instruments he would use (she consulted one of Claude's medical texts) and as she smoothed out the rough edges by imagining, for instance, minuscule suction tubes planted here and there in the incision to remove every last drop of blood.

In the mornings, during her real encounters with Andrew, she became increasingly frustrated until it was all she could do not to quit in the middle, close the drapes or walk out of the room. And yet if he failed to show up she was desperate. She started to drink gin and tonics before lunch and to sunbathe at the edge of the driveway between her building and his, knowing he wasn't home from ten o'clock on, but laying there for hours, just in case.

One afternoon, lighthearted from gin and sun, restless with worry because he hadn't turned up the last three mornings, she changed out of her bikini and into a strapless, cotton dress and went for a walk. She walked past the park she had been heading for, past the stores she thought she might browse in. The sun bore down. Strutting by men who eyed her bare shoulders, she felt voluptuous, sweetly rounded. But at the pit of her stomach was a filament of anxiety, evidence that despite telling herself otherwise, she knew where she was going.

She entered the hospital by the Emergency doors and wandered the corridors for what seemed like half an hour before discovering Andrew's office. By this time she was holding her stomach and half believing that the feeling of anxiety might actually be a symptom of something very serious.

"Dr. Halsey isn't seeing patients," his nurse said. She slit open a manila envelope with a lion's head letter opener. "They'll take care of you at Emergency."

"I must see Dr. Halsey," Ali said, her voice cracking. "I am a friend." The nurse sighed. "Just a minute." She stood and went down a hall, opening a door at the end after a quick knock.

Ali pressed her fists into her stomach. For some reason she no longer felt a thing. She pressed harder. What a miracle if she burst her appendix! She should stab herself with the letter opener. She should at least break her fingers, slam them in a drawer like a draft dodger.

"Would you like to come in?" a high, nasal voice said. Ali spun around. It was Andrew, standing at the door.

"The doctor will see you," the nurse said impatiently, sitting back behind her desk.

Ali's heart began to pound. She felt as if a pair of hands were cupping and uncupping her ears. His shirt was blue. She went down the hall, squeezing past him without looking up, and sat in the green plastic chair beside his desk. He shut the door and walked over to the window. It was a big room; there was a long expanse of old green and yellow floor tiles between them. Leaning his hip against a filing cabinet, he just stood there, hands in his trouser pockets, regarding her with such a polite, impersonal expression that she asked him if he recognized her.

"Of course I do," he said quietly.

"Well —" Suddenly she was mortified. She felt like a woman about to sob that she couldn't afford the abortion. She touched her fingers to her hot face.

"I don't know your name," he said.

"Oh. Ali. Ali Perrin."

Her eyes fluttered down to his shoes — black, shabby loafers. She hated his adenoidal voice. What did she want? What she wanted was to bolt from the room like the mad woman she suspected she was. She glanced up at him again. Because he was standing with his back to the window, he was outlined in light. It made him seem unreal, like a film image superimposed against a screen. She tried to look away, but his eyes held her. Out in the waiting room the telephone was ringing. What do you want, she thought, capitulating to the pull of her perspective over to his, seeing now, from across the room, a charming woman with tanned, bare shoulders and blushing cheeks.

The light blinked on his phone. Both of them quickly glanced over at it, but he stayed standing where he was. After a moment she murmured, "I have no idea what I'm doing here."

He was silent. She kept her eyes on the phone, waiting for him to speak.

When he didn't, she said, "I had a dream . . ." She let out a disbelieving laugh. "God." She shook her head.

"You are very lovely," he said in a speculative tone. She glanced up at him, and he turned away. Pressing his hands together, he took a few steps along the window. "I have very much enjoyed our . . . our encounters," he said.

"Oh, don't worry," she said. "I'm not here to —"

"However," he cut in, "I should tell you that I am moving into another building."

She looked straight at him.

"This weekend, as a matter of fact." He frowned at his wall of framed diplomas.

"This weekend?" she said.

"Yes."

"So," she murmured. "It's over then."

"Regrettably."

She stared at his profile. In profile he was a stranger — beak-nosed, round-shouldered. She hated his shoes, his floor, his formal way of speaking, his voice, his profile, and yet her eyes filled and she longed for him to look at her again.

Abruptly he turned his back to her and said that his apartment was in the east end near the beach. He gestured out the window. Did she know where the yacht club was?

"No," she whispered.

"Not that I am a member," he said with a mild laugh.

"Listen," she said, wiping her eyes. "I'm sorry." She came to her feet. "I guess I just wanted to see you."

He strode like an obliging host over to the door.

"Well, goodbye," she said, looking up into his face.

He had garlic breath and five o'clock shadow. His eyes grazed hers. "I wouldn't feel too badly about anything," he said affably.

When she got back, the first thing she did was take her clothes off and go over to the full-length mirror, which was still standing next to the easel. Her eyes filled again because without Andrew's appreciation or the hope of it (and despite how repellent she had found him) what she saw was a pathetic little woman with pasty skin and short legs.

She looked at the painting. If *that* was her, as Claude claimed, then she also had flat eyes and crude, wild proportions.

What on earth did Claude see in her?

What had Andrew seen? "You are very lovely," Andrew had said, but maybe he'd been reminding himself. Maybe he'd meant "lovely when I'm in the next building."

After supper that evening she asked Claude to lie with her on the couch, and the two of them watched TV. She held his hand against her breast. "Let this be enough," she prayed.

But she didn't believe it ever would be. The world was too full of surprises, it frightened her. As Claude was always saying, things looked different from different angles, and in different lights. What this meant to her was that everything hinged on where you happened to be standing at a given moment, or even on who you imagined you were. It meant that in certain lights, desire sprang out of nowhere.

Greg Stephenson lives in Toronto. This story first appeared in CFM No. 81 in 1993.

Periodic Table of Escape Velocities

GREG STEPHENSON

AT FIRST THE NURSE couldn't find any record of my sister. Finally she confirmed that a Sampson had been admitted, but couldn't find the doctor. I sat in the waiting room and listened to the nurses discuss the patients according to their condition, not their name. Was my sister the cardiac arrest, the gunshot wound, the drug overdose? Eventually a doctor appeared and motioned for me to follow him.

"You're Sam's brother?" he asked. Judging from his tone, either he didn't believe we were related or else he suspected I was somehow responsible.

"Her name's Charlotte," I answered. "Our last name's Sampson, which must be where the 'Sam' comes from."

The doctor impatiently scratched out her name on the chart and asked me to spell Charlotte. I wondered what was so important about a name. Maybe I'm used to Charlotte's preoccupation with her name, though "Sam" was new to me. Up until a few months ago, when I'd last seen her, she was calling herself Charley.

I must have been about six, and Charlotte four, when she first talked about changing her name. My name's Lyle, but it took Charlotte a while to master the first i, so it came out "isle." In response, I shortened her name to the last syllable: "ought." I tried to explain to her that was as much as we could do to shorten or modify our names. Unlike a Jonathan or a Christine, which offer lots of abbreviations, my sister and I were stuck. We could give ourselves new names, call each other whatever we liked, but underneath it all, she would still be Charlotte, and me, Lyle. There was nothing to do but accept it, I told Charlotte, and concentrate on what we could change. Mom said the names were our father's choice — her turn was supposed to have come with the next child, but our father was dead before that could happen.

The doctor wasn't listening to me, and called my sister Cheryl. He managed to get my name right, but he only had to look at *Lyle* sewn onto the chest pocket of my coveralls. I hadn't had a chance to change, but had come straight to the hospital.

"We don't know why," the doctor said, "but it's some type of coma. She's stable, but responds only to pain."

Before I could stop him, the doctor leaned over and ground his knuckles on Charlotte's breastbone, calling out her name as if she was at the other end of the hall, not two feet away. She grimaced slightly, but I barely noticed. I didn't have time to think *this is a hospital and he's a doctor* before I had him up against the wall with my arm against his throat, telling him if he ever did that to her again I'd break all his ribs.

Charlotte looked as if she'd abandoned her body, cast it aside like a set of clothes. I held her hand, which was cool and unresponsive. For a moment I felt reassured, as if we were kids again, when holding hands would have been enough. "It's Lyle," I said, and squeezed her hand gently. I wanted to ask her why she was there, and assure her everything would be all right. But the phrases sounded hollow and pointless even inside my head, and if they didn't comfort me, wheat use was there in voicing them? Charlotte, when she was conscious, had managed always to ignore my words of caution, as if she were tuned to a different frequency whenever I spoke. Nothing I could say would be of any use now, regardless of whether she was capable of hearing me. I looked at her, so uncharacteristically still and serene on the gurney, and I wondered which of us was more helpless.

A security guard appeared soon after and escorted me out. All I could think of as I crossed the parking lot was that nothing ever changed, but just got more complicated. Charlotte had been responding to pain all her life, but this time it was inside, private, beyond anything I could do or any questions I could ask.

The basic principle by which a household cooling system operates is pretty easy to grasp. There's an enclosed space to be cooled, a heat exchanging mechanism that turns the warm air into cold, and a thermostat that governs the system. The technical details can be enormously complex, but usually breakdowns are simple — a blown fuse or a perished gasket. Sometimes it's plain exhaustion. I'm confident I can isolate and correct the problem. It's up to the customer to deal with the warranty.

    I repair fridges and air-conditioners for a living — officially I'm a climate-control technician. Some would say I'm underemployed, but I'm not ambitious. The one drawback about the job is the people. Invariably they resent me, if only because I'm a sudden reminder of their own helplessness. Plus, by the time they admit there's a problem, the milk is off, the beer is warm, or the house is as hot as a furnace room. Ultimately the customer is irrelevant, just a device to let me in and then sign the cheque when I'm done. Aside from that, it's me versus the appliance. As Charlotte used to say — not meaning it as a compliment — I have a mechanical mind. A process of elimination, maybe a few inspired guesses, and a pool of water on the floor and the spoiled food in the garbage are the only evidence that I was even around.

    I started working part-time for a company that leased appliances, the first job I got when I came to Toronto to attend university. Evenings and weekends I hauled three-hundred-pound appliances up narrow stairs only to find the door jamb had to be ripped out to get the thing inside. And the boss never wasted two reliable workers by pairing them up. I was always supervising guys just out of detox or off a Greyhound, who had a hard enough time concentrating on the cash at the end of the day. It was supposed to be a promotion when I was put in charge of repossessing on lapsed payments, but I'm not really a people person, at least not when it comes to snatching televisions when the kids are watching cartoons or pulling frozen pizzas out of the fridge so I could cart it off. I realized I was more comfortable with machinery than people, and transferred to a refrigeration course at technical college.

I didn't know it at the time, but I was training for a recession-proof job. One of the components of most fridges and air conditioners is eating away the ozone, and as the ozone disappears, it gets warmer down here. All of which means more demand for air conditioners. I don't take credit for seeing the connection between vanishing ozone, global warming, and refrigeration, but it's not entirely accidental that I've ended up with guaranteed job security. As I tried to tell Charlotte, it's the result of planning, initiative, carving a niche overlooked or undervalued by others. Sometimes the world cooperates, as in my case, but even if it conspires against you, no one can take away your goals or your initiative. Momentum and inertia — they obey the same laws.

Charlotte refused to see my point, and twisted the argument every time I pointed to my success as an illustration. Air-conditioners, for Charlotte, rated slightly below chain saws on the enemies-of-the environment scale. It wasn't that I was just part of the problem by not being part of the solution. I *was* the problem, since my livelihood depended on the continuing depletion of the ozone layer. My paycheck translated into skin cancer, drought, and melting polar ice caps, according to Charlotte. I couldn't see any difference between my situation and that of a welfare worker — we're both in the business of alleviating suffering, and if the planet were a more hospitable place, we'd both be out of a job. Charlotte claimed the only connection between poverty and the ozone layer was the fact that she was poor and unemployed because her life revolved around a principled rejection of ecological destruction. At least my convictions were consistent; Charlotte drank as much cool beer as I did, and slept undisturbed through humid summer nights thanks to central air.

Charlotte, when she followed me to Toronto, signed up for art school. I've got nothing against artists, but sooner or later they have to eat and sleep somewhere other than at their brother's. Whenever I brought this up, Charlotte talked blithely about the fortune to be made in graphic arts or set design. Material possessions, she implied, were an indication of some deeper moral weakness, and besides, credit cards were the best bet, given the certainty of imminent economic and environmental collapse. She waited on tables while she went to school, moved into some warehouse with a bunch of her friends, and ended up selling her handmade earrings on the street.

I suppose there'll always be a market for earrings, just like people always need fridges, and I'm an asshole for saying *I told you so*. But who's strapped to the hospital bed while the world hurtles toward Armageddon, and where are all those artist friends whose company she preferred to mine? The thing is, she ignored my advice when we were younger, and how do you teach someone to pay attention when they never learned to listen?

The doctor, after reviewing the results of blood tests and a brain scan, told me that everything was normal. He seemed puzzled that she didn't just sit up and stroll out the door. I'm no doctor, but I wanted to tell him that there's an instinct for survival, and it functions kind of like a heat-exchanging mechanism. When it breaks down, whatever's on the inside won't last until the expiry date. People aren't like appliances — I know that. But I also know Charlotte, and suddenly I feel like I'm six years old again, when I thought she was just a slow learner, unable to distinguish between what's outside and what's inside and the importance of keeping them separate.

Charlotte's roommates had fled. Some woman who lived on the top floor of Charlotte's building showed me how to get in through the fire escape. The place was empty inside, painted entirely in black. Even the cat was black — Charlotte's cat, the lady told me. Everything else had either disappeared with the roommates, or the landlord was holding it hostage for back rent.

I didn't want the cat, but the lady claimed it was my sister's. Charlotte would never have left her cat, the lady said, which is the only reason she knew that Charlotte was still in there. When the cat wouldn't shut up, she broke in, then called the ambulance. So I have a cat, as well as a few shirts and a boom box with a Patsy Cline tape that apparently was in the apartment when they took Charlotte away. That's the extent of my sister's possessions, aside from a few paintings she left at my place — untitled and incomprehensible. I don't know the name of the cat, which is thin and sullen, and still hisses when I offer my hand.

As soon as I got home, the cat headed for the bedroom and cowered under the dresser, then started howling. I turned on the Patsy Cline tape and dropped my sister's shirts on the floor, thinking that maybe familiar sounds and smells would help. The cat didn't shut up till I left the apartment to get a beer and hopefully a bit of privacy, which is normally what I enjoy at home.

Why a cat? No job, no roommates, a future increasingly remote from the present, yet had a cat. I suppose the presence of a cat left some room for hope. After all, they have to be fed, looked after. But it could have been inherited from one of the roommates, or just a stray, attached to Charlotte only through coincidence. And who saved whom?

The last time Charlotte had expressed interest in pets was when we couldn't have any — our mother's allergies. I found Charlotte in the neighbor's garage with a tabby one day, snipping its whiskers with scissors. She didn't think it cruel, or even bother to ask whether whiskers would grow back. All she wanted to know was what whiskers were for, whether for balance or to test the width of holes a cat could squeeze through. Once released, the terrified cat managed to squeeze under the garage door, which was only a few inches off the concrete, and we never saw it again. Charlotte looked for it for weeks, chasing every tabby she saw, examining roadside carcasses, poking around inside drainage pipes narrow enough to trap a cat. We never did locate the cat, and the function of whiskers remained a mystery to Charlotte.

I'm not suggesting Charlotte got a cat to revive an abortive childhood experiment. But there is a pattern — even chaos generates its patterns — and you have to start somewhere. The dewhiskered cat is just an example. All through high school, for instance, Charlotte selected courses I'd already taken, substituting art for shop. She knew I'd organized and saved all my notes and assignments, and she copied them all. None of the teachers caught on, partly because she was so careless that she never distinguished herself the way I did. Except in art, and that was her doing.

Clothes around the house and toys in the yard, toast crumbs in the butter and library books left on the bus — for as long as I can remember, I was picking up after Charlotte. She went through childhood and then school, scattering bits of herself everywhere. And me, I followed her around, tidying up, making excuses and trying to teach her at least to close the door if your room is a mess, make sure no one is looking when you stuff your pockets with things you don't plan on paying for.

Charlotte had a different doctor, in a separate section of the hospital. The psych ward. I had to talk to the doctor before I was allowed to see her. He kept me waiting an hour.

"She's conscious now, but still in restraints," he began. "There's some evidence of self-mutilation."

"She's an artist," I explained, thinking he was talking about all her earrings and nose ring, or maybe her tattoo. But then he calmly traced his finger back and forth across his arm, then across his chest.

"She was trying to commit suicide?" I asked.

He shook his head. "That's different. Besides, there are scars. But recent."

He waited for my answer. I didn't know what to say. Charlotte used to be fascinated with blood, not connecting it to injury. Scrapes and bruises didn't count, only sharp cuts where you had to pinch the wound to force just a narrow bead of crimson. It was the healing process that fascinated me — two days, and all evidence had disappeared, without even the reminder of a scar. But as far as I knew, we had behaved as normal children do, our curiosity innocent.

"How would you describe your upbringing?" the doctor asked, obviously thinking I was already on his side.

"Ask Charlotte. She's the one in hospital."

"Why don't you ask her," he said mildly, "then come and tell me what she says?"

I didn't move, knowing that there's no such thing as simple offers or innocent curiosity in psych wards. Again the doctor didn't say anything for a moment, leaving me more than enough time to take him up on his offer but not so much that I could get up and walk the other way, out of the hospital.

"Your sister won't answer questions," he continued, his tone different now, confident that I had already agreed to something. "She's conscious, but refuses to respond at all. You'll have to speak for her, get us started."

I shook my head as I stood, reminding myself about the security guard. "Not unless she wants me to," I answered. "It's her that's your patient, not me."

The doctor stared at me, but this time he looked away first. He wrote something on the clipboard, then made a big deal of looking at his watch and putting his pen in his pocket.

"As you wish," he said as he stood. "You can see her for five minutes."

She had a room to herself, painted a soothing pink, not the normal industrial green. Sunlight streamed through the window, though the latticework shadow of the iron grate fastened to the outside of the window fell like a net across the bed. I stayed for two hours, waiting for someone to kick me out. But the only person who came in the room was a nurse, who checked the iv and the restraints, all without looking at me even once. Charlotte was so quiet and still, she looked like an angel, all in white except for her black hair against the pillow and her arms and legs tied as if they were afraid she was going to rise up and disappear through the ceiling. I didn't say a word, but just sat by the bed, thinking *It's only a phase, a pause for the ice to melt. Like swallowing an ice cube, you can feel it, dead inside, a lump in your stomach. We just have to wait for it to thaw, that's all.*

When I left, I leaned over to kiss Charlotte on the cheek. She didn't so much as blink, not even a flicker of her eyelashes as I brushed my lips on her cool, smooth cheek.

Patsy Cline sings about falling to pieces, endless tales of heartbreak, abandonment or just drifting apart. As far as I can tell, she describes Charlotte's condition as accurately as any of the high-tech hospital equipment managed to do — what is the more faithful reconstruction of Charlotte's collapse, Patsy Cline songs or a brain scan? Astrophysicists tell us the universe expands in spite of the gravitational pull stars exercise on one another. Gravity, wherever its center, is not enough — a truth Patsy Cline took as axiomatic.

To cats, the laws of science and the mysteries of human behavior present no enigmas. Either the food dish is full or empty, the litter box clean or filthy, and the person who fills the dish and empties the box is either present or absent. Charlotte's cat I have named Shadow, because she disappears the moment I turn on a light and she's so black I can't see her in the dark. But even if I can't see her, I know she's there. Dependent on me, Shadow nevertheless recognizes no debt, and prowls the perimeter of the apartment or sits at the window as if an escape will magically appear. I tell her there's nowhere to go, it's a hostile world on the other side of the door, but she either ignores me or treats me like a predator whenever I'm home. When I'm gone, she knocks things over — plants, mugs left on the counter, anything under ten pounds and more than a foot off the floor. The lady below me has already complained to the super, who didn't believe that it was only a cat making all the racket.

"You'll have to spade your cat unless she shuts up," he warned me. At first I thought he wanted me to kill it with a shovel and bury it in the flower bed. But the next time I saw him, he gave me the name of a vet and said something had to be done, and I should get her declawed at the same time. Otherwise she'd ruin the parquet floors.

Shadow and I have one thing in common — aside from Charlotte, that is. My Coldspot fridge, which is at least as old as Patsy Cline tunes. Solid as a bank safe, it sports rounded corners, a gentle dome-like curve on top, and a handle that you pull like a slot machine. I can hear the fridge kick in from the other side of the apartment, feel like an approaching train the throbbing through the bottom of my feet on the kitchen floor — it purrs like Shadow never will, which I suppose is why the cat is as fond of the fridge as I am. Old Coldspots look and sound sturdy, and can be renewed indefinitely with spare parts and a few simple tools.

Without warning, my father died suddenly of a massive heart attack, or so I'm told. One theory about hearts is that they're like wind-up watches. They have a certain number of beats, and that's it. Transplants are one option, much like a watch-spring can be replaced. What I wonder, as I keep Charlotte company, is whether she's exhausted something equivalent to a watch-spring. She used to be wound-up and now she's wound down. I tell myself we are more than the sum of our organs, and heartbreak is not a medical term. Her heart ticks away like an idling engine, her pupils contract and dilate, but she sees nothing, feels nothing. I think of my trusty Coldspot, squat, inanimate, and reliable — cold comfort.

At the hospital, they pay more attention to the plants I've put on the windowsill than to Charlotte. She's no longer in restraints, and will walk around, though only if someone leads her. Otherwise she just sits in bed, listless and inert. The real doctors don't even look in anymore, but send their clerks, who get no further than vague diagnoses about dysfunctional childhoods and profound withdrawal. One of the nurses goes out of her way to be friendly to me, though she talks as if I'm the only one in the room.

"Just give her time," the nurse said, as though we only have to wait for Charlotte to come out of hibernation. But the only time that's important is what's already passed. If only I could give that to Charlotte, roll it up tidily like a soft round ball of wool and hand it to her and say *here, try again.* We can break the sound barrier, but nothing exceeds the speed of light — the cosmic blueprint makes no provision for second chances in this universe.

The nurse assured me that Charlotte's not on any drugs, and I asked in a roundabout way whether they would need my approval to kick-start her with electroshock.

"It's you that should worry about getting electrocuted, staying here most of the night, then going off to work all day."

I shrugged, as if I had nothing better to do with my time, but the nurse laid her hand on my shoulder and looked at me with a concerned expression.

"You're wearing yourself out, Lyle," she said. "Isn't there someone else who can visit while you take a break?"

I said. "There's no one else."

"Then take some time off. Really, Charlotte won't miss you."

I stared at the nurse's hand until she took it off my shoulder, then I snapped, "It's you she wouldn't miss."

The nurse put her hand back on my shoulder, as though I was just having a temper tantrum and she knew me better than I did. "There's nothing I can do to help her," she explained, "and not much you can either, especially if you don't look after yourself."

I didn't want to admit it, but the nurse was right. I couldn't concentrate, and once had to go all the way back across the city to check on something that still wasn't working after I'd left — I'd forgotten to plug it in. But I can't stop visiting Charlotte, and it's not as if the nurse couldn't just put her hand on Charlotte's shoulder instead of mine, touch her for some reason other than to check for injuries or search for hidden silverware.

In high school Charlotte skipped all her physics classes except the optics section, and those she attended only because she got to experiment with prisms and study the symmetry of crystals. She missed the demonstrations of centrifugal and centripetal forces. Charlotte is governed by centrifugal force, I'm more of a centripetal person. The nurse wouldn't understand this, and the doctors don't care, but this is the reason I can't abandon Charlotte. It's not just that we're family — and the only family either of us has got — but we balance each other. I'm sure there are reasons for our defects, but they don't interest me — the damage can't be undone. What's important is that I have adjusted to my imbalance, but Charlotte can't. Like laundry on the spin cycle, she's a prisoner of centrifugal force, limp and helpless and all wrung out.

I distract myself and take comfort in the good news about black holes, invisible regions with intense gravitational fields that swallow even light. Black holes could be like cosmic toilets — a new theory claims that they are in fact tunnels to other universes. Time goes backwards in these tunnels, which ultimately end in white holes, the origin of a new universe. Verification of this theory presents a problem, since these tunnels offer only one-way travel. Still, there is an ultimate elsewhere, even if we can't see it.

"Our mother, Charlotte, you remember as vague and shapeless, prowling the darkened house in her dressing gown all day, complaining of noise, smells and dust. She was constantly retreating into the next room, and even though she rarely left the house, she had an attitude of elsewhere. You reacted by saying I'm *here*, and I said *Pretend I'm not.*"

Charlotte didn't appear to be listening, but she hadn't seemed to tire of my voice, either. As if her problems were simple amnesia, I filled the room with stories from our childhood, recalling in detail things I never knew I'd remembered. I thought at first that maybe I'd trigger something in Charlotte — when you erase a file on a computer disk, it doesn't just disappear, but is rearranged so it's unrecognizable. I thought maybe the same thing had happened to Charlotte, and she might recognize herself in my anecdotes. But nothing generated a response, so I closed my eyes and talked till I was hoarse. When I left, I shut the door tight, as if to keep the words floating in the room for Charlotte to absorb on her own. As I crossed the parking lot on my way out at night I always paused to examine her room from the outside. The window, subdivided by the grid of the bars, looked like leaded glass from a distance. It was too much to expect her silhouette in the window — all I wanted was a flickering shadow, some indication the room was occupied. I had to settle for the fact that she never turned the light off, at least not until I was out of the parking lot.

I sensed progress, though it couldn't be measured. When I examined Charlotte's eyes, I saw more than just my own reflection — there was inner life, however remote. Charlotte might look and behave the same when the nurse intruded, yet I was convinced that she was listening when we were alone. I cautiously embellished the past, rearranged the chronology and even added incidents. She looked confused when I introduced a husband, who subsequently left her for Patsy Cline. The words flowed out of me as if I were as helpless as a musical instrument, and our inverted past took on a life of its own, surviving collisions both with itself and with our real past. I was impressed with the resilience of my imagination, which nightly was exhausted but somehow renewed itself during the day.

The authorities, however, saw no change in Charlotte's condition.

I was in no position to argue — they would undoubtedly have found bedspace for me if I revealed my belief in Charlotte's preference for a fabricated, alternative life.

"We've decided she needs stimulation," a doctor said, ambushing me on my way in one night. Just behind him was a young woman in street clothes. She bobbed her head eagerly in agreement, but her smile faltered when I refused her hand.

"Stimulation?" I asked. "Like maybe I take her on the subway at rush hour, or to a wrestling match?"

The doctor glanced at the woman, then turned back to me. "Wendy is a social worker, and we've agreed that she can do more for your sister than the hospital can provide."

"It's a structured environment," Wendy said reassuringly, looking earnest now.

"So's this," I said. "You want to dump her — in some rooming house where stimulation means watching TV all day and squashing roaches at night."

The doctor left at that point, and it was up to Wendy to try to convince me Charlotte was better off out of the hospital. "The doctor says there's been no improvement so far, so an extra month won't make any difference."

"That prick hasn't even looked at my sister for three weeks. I know she's improved. She can come live with me —"

Wendy shook her head and cut me off. "She needs supervision."

"But she can't even protect herself."

"I promise I'll get her the best available space. That's all I can do."

"No," I shouted, "what you can do is —" I caught myself when Wendy stepped back and looked around nervously, as if she was ready to summon help. I quickly mumbled an apology and escaped before help could arrive.

We were given a week while Wendy looked for a placement. I pretended to be cooperative, and told the nurse that I would escort Charlotte to the lounge and maybe off the ward, just to get her used to other people. The first time, they sent an orderly along with us, but they were too short-staffed to watch us all the time. Charlotte looked at me expectantly, puzzled by my silence. I didn't even attempt to explain to her why she was out of her room, surrounded by strangers who carried on animated conversations with themselves or just stared off into space.

"Listen, Charlotte," I said abruptly, taking her hand and looking around for anyone in a white lab coat. "If you don't want to come with me, just say no."

Charlotte didn't take her eyes off the man who was trying to wash his hands in his water glass, but when I stood and moved toward the door with my lunchbox, Charlotte rose and followed. We were alone in the elevator, and it only took me a minute to take the extra pair of coveralls out of my lunchbox and pull them on over Charlotte's robe. I'd already covered the name tag with some white adhesive tape, and I put the lunch box in Charlotte's hand.

"You're my apprentice," I said as the elevator doors opened on the ground floor, and I kept up a steady stream of conversation as we approached the exit. "The best therapy is to keep busy, focus your mind on details. We'll be partners, a team."

Maybe it was just being outside in the dark, but Charlotte suddenly seemed small and vulnerable, a target for any passing menace. She looked lost inside my coveralls. Only the pale skin of her face and hands, and the white adhesive tape on her chest were visible in the dark.

"Or you can just sit in the van if you like," I said hastily, silently urging her to stop looking back over her shoulder. "Listen to music, wait for me to finish my jobs."

A couple of people stared at us as they walked by, and I grabbed Charlotte's arm. "This is it," I said. "It's too late to go back."

An orderly I recognized from the ward had just come out the door, obviously looking for someone. I tried to shield Charlotte from his sight, but he saw both of us and called to the security guard inside. Charlotte wouldn't run, so I threw the lunchbox aside and took her in my arms. She weighed so little that she wasn't even awkward cradled in my arms, and it was then that I realized how little was left of her. One wrong step, and I'd snap her brittle bones as I fell. I stopped and let them catch up with us. I stood in what I considered a posture of surrender, but even so, the orderly tackled me, then grabbed me by the throat and squeezed my windpipe like a tube of toothpaste. Black spots danced before my eyes, and his voice faded until all I could hear was the roar of blood in my ears.

He sat on my back until the police came and put me in the backseat, shutting the doors so I couldn't get out, couldn't hear a thing anyone said. My vision was still blurred, but I could see Charlotte near the entrance to the hospital. She was facing me, an orderly clinging to each of her arms. I couldn't make out the expression on her face, though her arm was raised as if in a farewell gesture. Then I saw it was only one of the orderlies, holding her by the wrist as he struggled to remove the coveralls.

"We could arrest you for attempted kidnapping," the policeman began after everyone else had disappeared.

"She's my sister," I said dully, and looked at the pool cast by a streetlight on the grass where the orderly had tackled me. I could see the indentation where he'd pressed my head into the grass, and the hollows at the end of the ruts left by my sliding knees. The adjacent grass, where Charlotte had stood watching while they held me down, was undisturbed. It was as if she hadn't even been there.

    I tried to put myself in Charlotte's shoes, where effect is detached from cause and consequences inhabit different dimensions than actions. All I could feel was an emptiness, not a void, but an emptiness waiting to be filled. I didn't listen to the rest of what the policeman said, didn't attempt any further explanation. I climbed wordlessly from the car when he opened the door, and then stood, looking at the window of my sister's room. Someone had turned off the light, though all the other rooms on the floor were lighted. It looked as though there was a gap in the wall, and I tried to convince myself it wasn't just a darkened window, but a tunnel.

THOMAS WHARTON lives in Peace River, Alberta, and has published the novel *Icefields*. This story first appeared in CFM No. 87 in 1994.

Dream Novels

THOMAS WHARTON

Dream Novel

WHEN THE LIBRARY of Alexandria was burned, this book alone survived the flames: a novel devoid of any vestige of figurative language. No metaphors or memorable images disturb the orderly progression of the staid sentences, no rhetorical devices make a plea for the reader's emotional involvement. Only those aspects of human existence which are empirically verifiable are recorded. A character may glance in passing at a rain puddle in the street, the surface ruffled by the wind, but from this stimuli will come no bittersweet recollection of a long ago lakeshore where the last embraces of a dying love were shared. The words enter your reading mind not like caravans or a shower of coins, but only as words: direct, denotative, utilitarian markings on a page.

You shake the novel, bang it against the arm of your chair, convinced it must be damaged in some way. You read doggedly on, but the work is so completely literal, so much like a textbook written in rational, cold-light-of-day prose, that it repels you, freezes your willingness to enter its dry, schematic world. Much to your dismay, this novel that is not a novel loses you along the way somewhere, and you feel no need to flip back and find out what may have been missed. Such perfect, clinical sentences, specimens of a rigorous grammatical functionalism, eventually fade into a sort of background noise, like a hum of electronic machinery down a distant corridor. Your thoughts drift elsewhere, meandering after your own desires and memories, while your eyes continue to move mechanically along the lines of text and down the page.

Inevitably, as this afternoon set aside for reading settles into evening, the thick, heavy book drops from your fingers over the side of the deck chair, and you close your eyes, submerging without resistance into the nebulous landscapes of dream. And it is then, to your delight, that a wondrous transformation takes place. The novel comes to you at last as it should be, its coldly logical structure broken into tremulous fragments, distortions of perspective and sensation, the monotonous chronicle of mundane events it presented in daylight now heaved and buckled like an earthquake zone, emitting bright flashes of beauty, magic, and myth. At last, in darkness and dream, through the dry veins of this desiccated novel, a blood called story flows.

You wake with a start, to find yourself shivering in the cool night air. Stumbling indoors to make a cup of tea, you hope to scribble down at least some impressions of that mysterious, terrifying novel read by your dreaming mind. Only then do you discover with regret that the dream novel has vanished, shredding away out of the reach of memory in the kitchen's cold fluorescent light. You step back outside to pick the book up off the deck, and flip through it sadly, finding only what was there before you fell asleep: the original mass of lifeless words, a two-dimensional plane, flat and unresponsive to your hungry gaze.

Only in dreams can you hope to rediscover its magical avatar.

Novella

With a subtle promise of sensual delight, and an unrepentant romanticism, the novel draws you in, charms you, seduces you away from any other books you may be reading at the time. This is unexpected, of course, because you only picked the novel up in the airport bookshop as something that might lessen the tedium of a long transatlantic flight. In fact, you wanted only that, a diversion, a distraction: something undemanding to keep mind and body at a distance from one another during a period of cramped, enforced inactivity. Nothing that might tax your intellect, or stir up emotions that would be useless and inconvenient in the metal shell of an airplane at forty thousand feet. The fact is, you didn't even care if, by the end of the flight, you hadn't finished the novel. You read a few pages after takeoff, sighed, stuffed the book in your travel bag, and settled back to watch the in-flight movie.

Back at home, after unpacking and a shower, you lie on the bed and glance up at the bookshelf, crowded with all the other novels you've been meaning to read when you get some time to yourself. And now you have that time, those who might bother you aren't yet aware of your return. But you can think only of the novel you started to read on the flight. Retrieving it from the travel bag, skimming again through its first few pages, you find that an image takes shape, a face, and a body, forming from the personality of its prose. Not the image of the author, of course, someone you've never heard of before, but the face and form of the novel itself. You see it as a pale, passionate young woman, perhaps somewhat like Mary Shelley at the age she wrote Frankenstein. And when that happens, when the book has a face, a character, a shape that makes it distinct from any other novel that claims your attention, something strange happens. You find it amusing to imagine falling in love with this fiction, formed of the novel as it unfolds. There is, you are certain, no cause for concern. This is not the kind of novel you habitually desire, the kind you prowl through used bookshops on dull, rainy evenings in the hope of encountering. Not only that, but you have often noticed that you yourself have no gender when you read, and for some reason you imagine that this phenomenon will help keep you from losing your perspective. There is no danger of your being truly swept up in this game, is there?

Yet your growing relationship with the novel proves to be a tempestuous one. This slight, transparent work of fiction proves to be jealous of all other novels, especially the three glossy paperbacks you left on your nightstand with the intent of finishing them when you returned from your trip overseas. These have to be hidden in a drawer if there is going to be any peace between you and the novel that now claims all of your affection. Novella, as you call her (although you are not absolutely certain the novel is completely feminine), manipulates and evades your responses, your advances, with such infuriatingly childish and worn-out histrionics, that you can't understand why you continue to put up with it. After all, aren't you an old hand at this game, haven't you calmly resisted the allurements of far more desirable fictions in the past? No, you are confident that you remain in control of the situation. In fact, though you dare not admit it to Novella, you secretly get the most exquisite pleasure out of pretending that she is really a lost book you read once, years before, in adolescence, and have always yearned for.

But soon you are forced to admit that this playful liaison has become a true passion. You find yourself wondering who else is reading Novella, and what revelations are being awarded to that other reader, who may be more diligent and tirelessly faithful than you. It tortures you think that the novel may only reveal the true depth and beauty of its passionate, tormented soul to someone other than yourself.

Now is the time to prove to yourself that you can still turn away, close the book, part with it amiably, in friendship, without bitterness, regret, or an ugly scene. And yet you keep reading, even if it means your utter ruin.

Deserted Novel

This novel is not, as you had anticipated from the bas-relief depiction of a shipwreck on the cover, a novel about a castaway on a desert island. The novel is the island, and in reading it you become its solitary castaway. You begin by salvaging whatever you can from offshore, swimming naked during the first few pages to that sinking wreck of your expectations, broken there on the rocks off the margin and soon to be washed away by the pounding waves of words. Huddling with the book at night, alone, you console yourself with the knowledge that you chose to read it, you chose to be here, just as Robinson Crusoe's historical original was left on a desert shore at his own request.

You bring what you can to your crude shelter within the novel, trying to make for yourself a habitable space in the midst of this fearful desolation. Everything you build now is temporary, makeshift, constructed for survival and prone to collapse when the elements grow fierce. But this now is your space: you can start anew here, discover an entire new world and be recreated by it.

And yes, you've been waiting for that archetypal moment to occur:

you're not a naive reader, you know that one day you will find a footprint, a definite trace, the evidence that someone else is here with you, the presence of another mind, another text, someone else reading. You long to find this other reader, this other text, to have it teach you its lexicon, its way of living within, and outside of, the novel.

Then it hits you, a crazy and frightening surmise: every single word is a footprint, one of the traces for which you've been searching. Against the white page they suddenly appear for what they are: the words of another language, the language of this foreign space that is the novel, not at all deserted but quite the opposite, one upon which you have blindly established all your old preconceptions and imperialistic ways of reading.

Anti-Novel

Not merely a dense work of prose but one that has collapsed in on itself, no longer a novel but an abyss, into which you pour your patience, your powers of concentration, your time, and your willingness to be carried away by a great story well told. The novel swallows all that down without thanks and demands more. You grow exhausted as you continue, there is no lessening of the novel's inescapable attraction, its ability to absorb all your formidable reading energies. Your eyes become dry and sore, the muscles in your back scream for relief, your whole body slumps and sags forward, threatening to topple right over into the pages of the book itself.

Then the novel's gravitational power extends to the physical objects that surround you as you continue, irresistibly, to read. Was it your imagination, or did the ashtray slide an inch or two closer to the edge of the lamp table beside your easy chair? No, it was not a trick played by your fatigue, for the cigarette in the ashtray has burned to ashes, and even the steaming coffee in your cup has been sucked down to cold dregs.

The pull of the novel increases, accelerates. Other books fly off the shelf on the other side of the room and disappear into the novel's deepening gulf. Your room begins to collapse inward in a spiral around you like an Escher drawing, until you are no longer sure where the world ends and the book begins, or whether book and world have changed places. You realize you are in the grip of a true anti-novel, one that condenses infinite space rather than creating it. And even as the light in the lamp bleeds away and spirals down into the inky blackness, you find yourself unable to hang on. You feel that it is unjust in the extreme, that you are a diligent reader, you are always careful to give a novel as much of your heart and mind as you possibly can, which is often difficult in an age that does not leave a person much time for reading, but, after all, don't novels deserve such effort and consideration for all the pleasure and enlightenment they've given you over the years? But now this, surely this is going too far, you protest ineffectually to yourself, to the universe which, of *course,* is now inside the novel with you and is incapable of providing any objective evidence that things once were otherwise.

Ghost Story

It jumps and thumps on your bedside table after you've turned out the light and settled your head into the well-fluffed up pillow, forcing you to get up and read a few more pages in an effort to placate the disturbed ghosts that haunt its pages. And it seems that the novel rearranges sentences and paragraphs while you are not reading, adds or removes words in order to get your attention in the most absurd and upsetting ways. It rubs out stately, graceful turns of phrase and puts shocking scatological terminology in their places. You begin to wonder whether you are actually reading a novel or whether the physical book itself is perhaps an illusion, an apparition, composed of bits and pieces of one of the many, too hastily consumed works of fiction that you've read in the past and that have sunk unnoticed to the bottom of your psyche, rising up at odd moments in this spectral form, especially when you are tired, overworked, scraped raw by the frustrations of daily life. You briefly consider calling a psychologist, or perhaps an exorcist, but you abhor the inevitable professional condescension of those who would scoff at the idea that fiction could be haunted, more than you fear its troublesome but not really malevolent antics.

You know that unquiet texts usually have some forgotten secret they are compelled to reveal, a tale they want uncovered and told, or some skeleton to be dug up from the cellar and exposed in the living world, the world in which they insist they still have a place, a voice, a body of text. But after all, they're dead, they're finished, and that's that. Why persist as disembodied wraiths, cluttering up perfectly quiet, respectable, ordinary novels, when there are new stories to be told, and nothing good will come of disinterring what has been buried by time?

It's no use. The hauntings do not cease merely because logic and decency would have it so. You are forced to consider what these textual ghosts might want from you, what story it is that they wish to have told. In the end, you are reading only these ghostly disruptions, having abandoned the novel you thought you were trying to finish and put aside for another. The ghosts of this haunted novel are triumphant, they will have their proper resting place, in your imagination.

Insta-Novel

For those readers with no time for relaxed, contemplative involvement in fiction, this novel offers a delightful alternative. The substance of its original nine-hundred page bulk has been judiciously plucked, abridged, pulverized, filtered, dried, and reconstituted; then this concentrated version is repackaged in a contemporary and easily accessible form.

And yet, despite what you initially fear, this is still the finest quality literature, straightforwardly thematic, engaging, innovative, devoid of the extravagances of authorial self-indulgence, and savoring of a keen insight into the human condition. Poignant, riveting, and unobtrusive enough that it can be enjoyed while watching television, working at the computer, talking on the cell-phone in rush-hour traffic.

And perhaps best of all, no unpleasant after-images or ethical dilemmas linger past the reading to trouble the rest of your day.

This is, in short, the latest innovation in the technology of effort-lessness: a novel that allows you to not read.

Novel: A Schematic

Reading aloud, and hearing the echo of your voice ringing along vast, metallic spaces, you understand that almost nothing remains of this once lively and daring work of fiction. Where are the characters you had read about so often in summaries and literary companions, the fiery clashes of personality, the human truths wrung from doubt and anguish? All that remains is the barest of scene setting, and an absolute minimum of narrative, consisting only of a coldly functional pattern of plot lines, angular traceries dispassionately connecting incident to incident. The novel seems to be little more than a schematic diagram, waiting for some heroically tenacious reader to supply the electric current of imagination through the system, to leap across those silent, empty, synaptic chasms disclosing barren landscapes of geometry and silence.

It may be that the author planned the novel with the help of some computer program incapable of the kind of mistakes that have been called portals of discovery, but then abandoned the method as too rigid and lifeless. Or, what you are reading may not be the novel itself, but rather a flow chart left by an earlier reader, attempting to keep track of the vertiginous complexities of a wonderfully rich and digressive fictional tapestry, one that has sadly been lost, and of which you never retrieve more than is disclosed in the interstices of this paper-thin skeleton.

There is one other possibility. Sadly, it may be that everything but these sinuous, functional plot lines has disintegrated under the swift corrosives of deconstructive criticism. The structural arrangement of underlying vectors and forces has been revealed, but in the process the flesh and blood has burned away.

Reading Novels

There is no way around it: one cannot begin this novel until it has been decided just how it is to be read. A certain methodology, an approach, must be arrived at in advance, and adhered to, if you hope to turn this unashamedly intimidating assemblage of words into a novel.

The book rests there, on the other side of the room from you, on a well-lit table, looking harmless enough. But you dare not go any nearer just yet. There are so many questions to be answered.

Will your reading be informal? dutiful? spasmodically somnolent? intrusive? deferent to public opinion? forensic? psittacic? influential?

Will it be traditional? irreverent? over? under? through? light? heavy? the new? the first? the last?

Would it be best to read anxiously? symbolically? coldly? blindly? geographically? piously? aloud?

Will you read by the light of a lamp? divine grace? a campfire? welding torches? tracer bullets? the Tao Te Ching? the moon?

Will you grip the book in suspense? in incredulity? in a paroxysm of rage? in extremis? in bed?

Don't make the mistake of opening the book until you know. And don't expect the novel to make this decision. It's having enough trouble of its own deciding how to read you.

The Novel in Its Lair

It would be foolhardy to meet this novel face to face, to read it without some kind of highly polished surface, a mediating presence to deflect its terrifying power to turn you to stone. If you can find a way to read the novel's reflection, and finish it off at one sitting, you can wear the book around your neck as a token of your bravery, if such was your intent. But if you would rather linger with the novel, in spite of its terrifying powers, you'll find a surprisingly beautiful story that, while it may be made up of little more than ingratiating and rather pitiful scraps offered like the sad and useless junk advertised in the back pages of glossy magazines, might cause wings to sprout from your shoulder blades, or allow you to feel, pulsing within your light-filled body, the weightless and fiery heart of an angel.

Perverse Novel

It is difficult to read. The pages only open at that particular moment in the day, one you can never predict, in which you have no desire for words, but instead wish to be out of the house, into the spring air, strolling briskly along the street, meeting friends, or wading the grassy fields, simply watching clouds drift. At such a moment, while buttoning up your coat and putting on your overshoes, you turn and see the book lying open (you're certain you closed it after the last reading) on the sill of the window where you left it. You turn back, sit down against the wall, and read, wearily, against your will, grudging each moment that keeps you away from the real world outside, but unable to overcome the lethargy that this novel instills in your limbs. If only you could open the book when you wished to, the rest of the day would run smoothly and efficiently. But the novel will allow no such order in your life.

Delphic Novel

The reader who climbs these heights, trembling with fear and hope, is puzzled and discouraged to learn that the promise of symmetry, verbal nakedness, clarity is not kept. In ancient Greece the oracle spoke through a hole in the rock, from which nothing other than the flat and cryptic verses might emerge to guide the supplicant in the interpretation of the riddle. And so it is with this novel.

The questions asked of the delphic novel are always asked at the last possible moment, or too late, to ward off the fate that brings one here to read in the first place. The reader seeks continuance, a story going smoothly along the same groove in which it started out. No crisis or dramatic upheaval, unless of course it turns out to be an upheaval that brings the characters back full circle to the stable state in which they began, and in which one learned to love them. But the oracle speaks of change, and worse, of a changing world that perhaps will not include the reader in its transformations.

Body of the Novel

The thin dry epidermis sloughs off rather easily as the first pages are turned: a light, superficial, one might almost say dead layer of interest is exposed here, penetrating no dark sub-regions of emotion or insight, opaque, giving some slight indication of the deeper matter but remaining essentially a thin carapace to protect the inner bulk from the depredations of predatory, scavenging readers.

But there is a faint glow upon these introductory surfaces, a pale radiance, rising outward from its own intense living core, as if the deeper tissues of the novel has nourished and rendered these outer foliations.

Probing further, reading more carefully, reveals tiny, circumstantial threads of trickling text leading to larger veins of weighty matter, vigorous action proceeding from stimuli, characters responding to subtle and often mysterious dictates and impulses. Slowly the contours of a system of connection and significance are perceived, lying deep within, cushioned from a superficial examination by layers of seemingly gratuitous, but stabilizing and insulating verbiage.

But a reader cannot expect to plumb without risk to the ultimate core of the novel, for eventually a page thick with vivid words will give way to a dense, unyielding, bone-white ground, the skeletal framework upon which much of the novel's sanguine vitality depends, but which, when laid bare, reveals that the fleshiest of novels is only a facade upon the wordless anatomy of death.

Marginal Novel

I unearthed it in a used bookstore, a gorgeously bound book, a true find, tucked away amid outdated travel guides and moldering paperbacks with garish photographic covers. A book from a former age, its smooth, only slightly yellowed pages like sepia-tint photographs of slow, dreamy mornings, mornings devoted to enchanted, irresponsible reading.

But once at home, I wondered why I hadn't noticed this irritating preponderance of marginal notes made by an earlier reader. There were few at the beginning of the book, but, flipping through, I discovered to my annoyance that the jottings proliferated, cluttering up the clean white space on either side of the stately print, like refuse collecting along the curb of a wide, bustling thoroughfare.

These graffiti, most of them obviously written with a cheap pen that blobbed ink, distracted me from the grace and symmetry of the printed word, driving me to maledictions and the grinding of teeth. Try as I might to stay with the story, there was no avoiding this other, earlier reader's comments and queries. There was no way I could simply pretend they were not there: when I turned a page and found another of these cramped, handwritten blotches, I was compelled by simple human curiosity to glance at it. I had to know if that earlier, perhaps long dead, reader stumbled upon something that I missed, if he or she had an insight that I was too impatient, or unintuitive, or mentally slothful to have. Or, conversely, I would have been overjoyed to find proof that this other reader was far behind me in the perception of subtle qualities, that his or her notes were clumsy, groping queries about literary matters so elementary that I could safely relax and enjoy my own, obviously vastly superior reading of the novel.

But what I unfailingly noticed was that the reader had underlined the most seemingly inconsequential passages, lending them a kind of numinous aura of importance, and then scrawled notes about these passages that employed indecipherable abbreviations and a private lexicon of crypticisms. In each instance I was left completely in doubt as to whether this other reader was possessed of a great, piercing intellect, a genius for uncovering the truly wondrous gold that lies hidden to most readers, or whether here were nothing more than the intellectual droppings of an irritating poseur, one who obviously believed that merely filling the margins of a book meant one had thoroughly studied and absorbed its subtleties, its deep and rewarding meanings. I eventually swayed toward the latter view, if only because the very fact of handwritten scribbles in such a fine book was testimony enough to the character of their author.

But it wasn't long before I caught myself turning the pages of the novel only for the sake of the marginalia. In themselves they begin to tell a more involving story than the one contained within those white borders now desecrated. I was now reading a detective novel of my own making, trying to piece together the life and character of the person who had made those maddening notations, those clues to identity. Was it someone I knew, another obsessive reader in this prosaic provincial capital, or someone unknown, a passing stranger from another city, another counter who dropped this volume off at that used bookshop solely for the wicked satisfaction of imagining some other reader ensnared in its marginal labyrinth.

On the penultimate page of the novel, to my horror, was revealed the most heinous sin: a grocery list scrawled along the top and down the side of the page, the unkempt letters clinging like bats to the cornices of the text, and punctuated at bottom with a bloated phone number inscribed in mulberry crayon. A somewhat familiar phone number, upon reflection.

A sudden shock of deja vu overcame me at that moment. I felt convinced that I had read this novel, years before, in another place, another time. And there could then be no doubt whose life was scribbled on the edges of these pages for the world to read. Could it be possible I had forgotten this novel, that I had been the kind of reader who could forget it, even after laboriously filling it with the detritus of my dull, groping sensibilities?

Had I swept so much of my own past into the margins?

Renewable Novel

The garden is the ideal spot to sit back and read this novel, morning the ideal time to begin. On the soft, pliant green paper, dew has collected overnight. And yet each page, as it draws towards its last few words, slowly turns yellow, sere and faded. As the finished pages accumulate, they fall softly from the book to the soil of the garden, across which the shadows of the trees moved in their daily progression. When the cool breezes of evening stir these fallen pages, it seems best to leave them where they lie. Soon the first snows of winter cover them.

In the spring, the pages of the novel are the first signs of green to emerge, their unfolding corners poking up out of the melting patches of snow. Gathering and binding them reveals the same wonderful novel, concerning the tumultuous lives of the same characters, and yet everything about them and the world they inhabit has been completely transformed, as if seen now through the eyes of a morbid, housebound narrator suddenly recalled to life.

Two Novels

The first one to be read is a huge novel-cycle, seventeen lengthy volumes in all, that deals only with a few pivotal moments in the life of its young protagonist: a young girl who has a seemingly trivial but in fact life-altering epiphany one spring day while stepping off the bus on a downtown corner. This leviathan of a novel enters at infinite length into her growing self-awareness, her character, both past and yet to be, seen in the sensual, aesthetic, metaphysical, and radiant light of these few moments on a slushy street, the girl on her way to a piano lesson, amid the smells of exhaust and spring runoff, the sounds of the bus door closing and the brakes hissing, the sight, far above the cold office towers, of the wintry pall of cloud shredding away to reveal a warm, aegean heaven.

And yet this vast, proliferating mass of words can only be described as a page turner, breathtaking and suspenseful. Amazingly, it seems to take a very short time to read. Perhaps this is because a novel of such immense size contains long passages that one can skim over, like a pelican above the surface of a lake, without quite realizing it, yet without ever losing sight of that barely submerged gleam, which is both a form in motion and the movement that it defines.

This colossal novel comes with a companion volume, a brief coda that summarizes the rest of the character's life, and the life history of her city, after the moment described in the forty-seven parts of the first. The second novel is only fifty-nine pages in length, printed in a large, grade one primer typeface with generous margins.

Because it is so brief, and within its few pages so much is concentrated, each word in this companion volume seems a dense lump of ore which must be carefully analyzed, weighed, examined from all angles, before one can confidently proceed to the next. The second novel is almost unbearably aware of its own importance, like a gourmet dinner that consists of a few slices of food on a vast white plate, morsels requiring exquisite concentration to spear with the dainty fork, break apart with the tongue and the teeth, and reverently swallow.

In consequence this novel built of sparrow's bones, compact and delicate, seems to take years to read. One must take days off before continuing, to savor to the full that which has just been digested, whether it be several pages or only one or two words, or to recover from the burdensome significance of its scrupulous prose.

Art of the Novel

As the shrink wrap is stripped from the book, a novel is revealed that has been turned inside out. In the store, you were intrigued by its plain, rough jacket. No giant black typeface, no blurbs or other hype, just the title and the author's name. Its very unavailableness was inviting and you bought it, sealed up as it was in transparent plastic like a head of lettuce with its unsightly brown spots hidden from finicky shoppers. If one wants this head of lettuce, the chance will have to be taken. You're a daring reader, you decided to judge this book by its cover. And when you finally got it unwrapped, the words on the inside leapt out, fantastical, flamboyant, burning across slick, glossy pages like festive rockets. The content of the novel, it seemed, was the hype: the effort to tantalize with a catchy precis of the story, a hint of the grand and furious adventure it might take you on, but never really would as there was nothing more to be read than this dazzling promise.

And since this is an inside out novel, with the dull but essential content on the outside, and the roaring and the tumult within, the effect upon you is also the opposite of what an ordinary novel would produce: you flip through the pages with a breathless superficiality, convinced in advance that this is a great work and you are among the discerning few who have discovered it.

Typeface, layout, cover art, texture of the paper, even the length and width of the pages: these delight you and keep the pages turning. What was once the intangible, ineffable grace abounding to the most demanding of readers has become simply a tactile pleasure. Holding the cool leather binding in your hands, stroking with your fingertips the smooth creamy paper, you believe you are absorbed in the finest prose you have ever read. If there is any fiction going on here, it is the fiction that the reception and appreciation of a novel's qualities are independent of its presentation on the physical page.

Ephemeral Novel

Lightness: a powdery dust of character, a plot like a puff of smoke in a breeze, details that seem to float, suspended, like distant ice-capped mountains. The more you read, the heavier and more solid you feel yourself to be. No other novel, however weighty or intimidating, could raise such an absolute barrier to your entry. Its very fragility has rendered it invulnerable.

Conquest of the Novel

One that has become unreadably littered and crowded because nothing is ever lost: each character, each brief incident or circumstantial detail refuses to remain in its place and be absorbed, subsumed into the growing structure of the novel; once read, phrase and image pack up their belongings and set up camp at the outskirts of the next scene, crowding in upon the chapters and incidents that are to follow.

The confusion, you imagine, is somewhat like that of the teeming, cosmopolitan mass of people that gathered in the wake of Alexander's army as he thundered across Asia, decimating armies and subduing kingdoms, refusing to halt and let the dust settle even for a moment on his expanding empire. A tent city rapidly filling with refugees whose towns were sacked, homes burned by the conquerors, delegations from besieged fortresses who vainly petition for an audience with Alexander, supplicants for clemency, research grants, and royal favor, worshippers of the divine king himself, war correspondents, the merely curious and the opportunistic, bewildered multitudes of the suddenly unemployed, escaped slaves, acrobats, magicians and fakirs, shoe menders, merchants, prostitutes, real estate speculators, military observers, thieves, cutthroats, lawyers.

And like Alexander, you, the conquering reader, ignore this tent Babel simply because it is behind you, it is of no consequence in the grand scheme. That is, until the day your generals fearfully inform you that entire companies of your soldiers, once happy to drill, march, and face vastly superior forces, now spend their time exploring the myriad delights of Tent City, playing bloodless games of chance, listening to storytellers and musicians, dallying with young men and women taken as war booty, anything rather than press forward any further into unknown lands, where the likelihood of a spear through the intestines or an axe cleaving worn armor draws ever nearer for those who have survived thus far with a whole skin.

The utter and complete assimilation of the novel is threatened by this swelling city of detritus. You cannot allow the past to bog down the swift approach of the future, the end. This excess baggage of multiplying meanings and ramifications must be jettisoned. But what can you do? If, as Alexander considered doing, you wheeled your remaining troops about to face the threat dogging your heels, another city would surely spring up behind you, the city of what might have been.

Ironically, the very swiftness and success of your reading has led to this unforeseeable dilemma.

Remember that there came a night that Alexander slipped out, cloaked and unobserved, into the streets of the tent city, and as he crept past booths and tents, and lingered by pavilions filled with the voices and music and perfumes of all the nations and peoples and songs he had conquered, he understood that here was his real empire. Many of the people he met and talked with had never heard of a king named Alexander and scoffed at the possibility that their city had only come into existence because of him. Wisely, Alexander considered the many cities he had founded in his own name across Asia, and acknowledged to himself that this haphazard patchwork of babbling tongues was in fact the true Alexandria. And perhaps, when at last he came to the end of the earth and could march no further, he could come to dwell here, in Alexandria the Unconquerable, and spend the rest of his days listening to the storytellers weave tales of all the wonders that are not seen in the noise and dust of conquest.

Poignant Riveting

What can one say about this breathtaking, timeless work that would give even a hint of the pleasures awaiting the reader?

Strangely formless and yet somehow blending into an organic entity, it is more than a novel, and at the same time cannot be anything but a novel. A plurality of worlds take shape and substance in the reader's mind, interpenetrate and fade on the ever-changing canvas, a ceaselessly rewritten tableaux. And each character, each event, each discrete and isolated unit of novelistic substance, is complete in itself, a world unto itself, not merely a part contributing to a whole. A fantastic vision of reality, and yet nothing more than that reality.

The writing is often so perfectly transparent, so clear and unobtrusive, that it becomes ambiguous merely because, as a transparent focusing medium, it allows vision beyond ordinary human sight.

The novel is divided into twenty-six sections, which connect in convoluted but precise ways with each other like the sides of a giant, complex, and transparent polyhedron. And when each section is read through, every poignant and compelling rivet of detail in place, each strand and filament aligned, imagery and metaphor enter into a new relation and take on unforeseen significance, until at last, by the end of the novel, a radiant unity, a new Jerusalem, is revealed, the grail at the end of literature.

It Will Live in Your Imagination

That's what the blurb on the back cover said this novel would do. So you bought it, started reading, fully aware that the promises on the covers of books are either wildly exaggerated, or, at the very least, ridiculously inaccurate for the sake of popular appeal.

And now you find yourself damning the reviewer who enticed you into this novel by telling you the novel would get inside your head and take up residence there, for much to your shock and annoyance, it has. The blurb was neither hype nor misrepresentation, but awful truth.

You cannot simply toss the book away and forget about it. You were too polite, too accommodating, and that opportunity has passed you by. Having made itself at home, the novels bumps around inside your head at all hours of the day and night, hangs its wet, abundant undergarments across your tidy plans and dreams, pollutes every corridor and room with mysterious, alien odors, refuses to share in the daily chores, invites unwanted, noisy guests unacquainted with the notion that a welcome has an expiry date, leaves the kitchen a mess and the bathroom a horror.

Now it has come down to a painful decision: one of you is going to have to find new accommodations. You stand there in the hallway, steeling yourself for this unavoidable and unpleasant confrontation, while the novel lies sprawled on the sofa, staring vacantly at the television, its bare feet propped on the snack-cluttered coffee table, its thick, dull fingers prodding the remote control.

Novel in Analysis

The number of possible readers, authors, and narrators have been multiplied to infinity: implied, apparent, ideal, insidious, reliable, unreliable, and serendipitously-appearing just-in-time, binary, tertiary; narrators within narrators within narrators, controlling, absolute, omniscient, omnipotent, omnivorous, omnibus-driving. The real reader, if he really exists, and his equally doubtful counterparts, real narrator and real author, are swallowed up in the squabbling crowd.

This is ridiculous, and you won't stand for it another second. You want your old, comfortable way of reading back. Or do you? Just who is it that is making this plea, anyhow? How dare you insist on your own rights and wishes in the midst of this multitude?

Unread Novel

The book sits on the shelf. Although it is one of the great treasures of your personal library, you've never felt the need to take it down and actually read it. You have been told or have read about its content, its political orientation, its philosophical underpinning, and that has been all you needed to know. You are convinced it is the novel you have been waiting for, the one to justify your existence, its title on your lips without hesitation whenever you're asked to name a favorite book.

From time to time you take the handsome leatherbound volume down from its place of honor on the shelf, run your fingers up and down the ridges on the spine, riffle the pages and let the book fall open where it will. Words and phrases catch your eye fleetingly and you come away with a faint and suggestive intimation of a story, a world. It is enough.

Perhaps, you muse, the truth is that you are really afraid to read the novel in its entirety: you would rather not have your illusions of perfection destroyed. Perhaps those few tantalizing and wonderful fragments are, by incredible coincidence, the only ones worth reading, and if read in context, embedded in the cold pudding that makes up the rest of the novel, they would lose their force and distinctiveness, and you would sink with them, the stale, flat taste of binding glue on your tongue.

A Novel Is a River

A faint haze of smoke hangs about the first pages of the novel, smoke from the smoldering fires along the edges of the stubble fields up above the valley, smoke that has drifted down and mingled with the evening mist rising from the wide flat river, its whorls and currents melting and shimmering like liquid metal, rippling as it passes under the piers of the bridge, as if there is only a thin veneer of water over a flat expanse of mud the color of milky tea, the bridge where older couples taking their evening walk pause to look down at the river's curving sweep, watching kids on bicycles plunge up and down the undulations of the grassy bank, or perhaps two or three sullen teenagers wandering along the gray sand flats below, picking up and discarding scraps of driftwood, slapping offhandedly at the clouds of mosquitoes spawned by the recent rains and now frantic as the evening air cools, birds sweeping low along the shore darting after insects, and a magpie, a flash of white and black in the gloom that seems to descend in funereal stages, you look down at the face of the water and vaguely imagine how it might feel to climb over the railing and plunge into that murky current, the water no doubt colder than it looks, and this reminds you of the swimming pool, yesterday, where, in the vaulted, echoing space, with its humid reek of chlorine, amid the high, shrill voices of splashing children, you stood, reader, on the wet sloppy edge of the pool in your sandals, the cool gusts of air off the water tickling the hairs on your bare and embarrassingly thin legs, talking to the woman treading water in the pool, a woman you know well, but who, in the water, was transformed, distracted and removed by the element she was immersed in, sweeping her arms, pedaling with her foreshortened legs, aloof to your dry, superior stance, not looking at you, blinking water out of her eyes, with a new and attractive seriousness lent her by her efforts to keep afloat, a distant, watery grace, but no, you decide, the river would not be a pleasant place to swim, because it is slipping away, flowing away out of your life here in this town, on this bridge where you linger, uncertain what to do with your evening, the wind picking up a chill now, time to turn up your collar and head home, the river will be left to its ceaseless, unmatched passage through the long night.

Novel and Reader

How many times have you read it? There is no telling. The first encounter was in childhood, that much is certain, and the novel became the absolute central core of your being, around which all else in your life rotated, at greater or lesser distance.

And each time you turned to it in the following years, you found the novel's radiance shrinking to a smaller and smaller point of distant light, until at last it was lost in a firmament of other books, hidden by all the whirling debris of impulse and responsibility.

The question is, of course, whether you remained at the center of your existence, while the novel receded, or rather it was the novel that held to its place, powerless to keep you from drifting away in the infinite remoteness of a fathomless universe.

Novels You Desire But Will Never Read

A wordless novel. A novel that can only be read in the dark. A novel of maps. A filthy scatological novel that reveals how everything that lives is holy. The Prospect: a lost novel by Kafka. An edible novel. A novel about light. A novel that can't help dreaming of all the novels it might have been. A novel of passion that immolates itself and then rises from the ashes. A novel written from within the consciousness of the world soul.

A novel that is "a sphere and yet is as many thousand spheres, solid as crystal yet all through its mass flow, as through empty space, music and light: ten thousand orbs, involving and involved, and every space between peopled with unimaginable shapes...."

A novel of infinite Dickensian plot-strands that are never brought together at the end but go on and on forever. A novel that changes depending upon where it is read. A novel whose story you can switch, when you get bored, like television. A novel written by a paranoid bureaucracy, to be read only by the same. A novel that removes your memories and gives you its own. The novel that you know will be the last one you read in this life.

Geoff Hancock has devoted his life to fostering and promoting the art of short fiction. This tribute was compiled without his knowledge in recognition of his remarkable achievement as an editor and unsurpassed contribution to Canadian fiction. — *Bob Hilderley, Publisher*

Tribute to Geoff Hancock

ANN COPELAND (aka Anne Bernard)

"In a strange way, this 25th anniversary publication represents a coming full circle for me. In 1973, two years after arriving in Canada, I set myself the task of learning how to write short fiction. When I finished "Siblings," I sent it off to CFM. I had written it under the name Anne Bernard. When nothing happened, and months grew long with effort to write other stories, I decided that maybe changing my pseudonym would bring more luck. So I became Ann Copeland. Then . . . one day, a letter addressed to "Anne Bernard" arrived. It was from the new editor of CFM, Geoff Hancock, who had found my story in a slush pile as he cleaned up his inherited office. I still have this typed acceptance letter somewhere. In his excitement over the story, he said, as he hurried to get to the typewriter, he tripped over the cat! I always considered that whole episode a kind of good luck omen for my writing more fiction. When "Siblings" won the CFM Contributor's Prize later that year, I was thrilled.

Over the years I have found Geoff (whom I have never met) to be an editor with a keen sense of what makes a fiction work and also a reader with a generously open mind toward experiment in words. That he has sustained editorship of CFM this long — through various setbacks and frustrations — is a real tribute to his belief in the importance of fiction-writing. We need more such editors!

DOUGLAS GLOVER

Geoff Hancock is one of those rare creatures in the realm of Canadian letters — a tub-thumper, a promoter, an unabashed enthusiast, an editor with a mission, and a man who has always put writing ahead of personal gain. Over the past 25 years he has discovered and published some of the best writers this country has produced, and I won't say what it's gotten him, though he hasn't gotten much, except the affection and gratitude of an awful lot of writers. If there had been a half-dozen Geoff Hancocks instead of just one, Canada's literary landscape might have been a lot less sub-Arctic than it is today ... I wonder who will take his place.

THOMAS WHARTON

Geoff Hancock's CFM prefaces have been a inspiring reminder to brush the cobwebs off the smithy of my soul, and work at the craft of writing with total engagement.

ROHINTON MISTRY

As he has done for so many, Geoff Hancock provided me with encouragement at a very crucial stage — at the start of my career. For this, a heartfelt thank you.

BARBARA GOWDY

Geoff Hancock is a great editor and is widely recognized as such, but what might not be as well known is that he is a kind man, aware, as only another writer can be, of what it takes to make fiction. Early in my career, when few editors could be bothered to even send me a rejection letter, Geoff published a story of mine in Canadian Fiction and he was solicitous and enthusiastic to a degree far beyond what I thought a writer of my unrenown deserved. Since then I've been a devotee of his magazine and especially his highly original prefatory musings, and I have come to believe that his obstinate devotion to Canadian letters and Canadian fiction writers is one of the marvels of literature in this country.

T. F. RIGELHOF

I thank Geoff for realizing early on that whatever I was doing, I was worth publishing because I wasn't jiving. I honour him because he has brought a singular force, emphasis, excitement, ballsiness, voice to Canadian Fiction Magazine.

MATT COHEN

Only a crank with the persistence, drive and infinitely eclectic taste of Geoff Hancock could have foreseen the explosive development of the Canadian short story and made CFM into its most effective showcase as well as the magazine where the best new story writers are usually to be found.

FRANCES ITANI

Congratulations on the launching of the 25th anniversary issue. You have supported the creation of this exquisite and exacting literary genre, the short story, for a very long time. My best wishes for the next phase of your life and activities. I hope it will bring you many personal rewards.

SHARON BUTALA

I've always thought that CFM was, if not the best, one of the very best literary magazines in Canada, and it was Geoff Hancock who made it so. All we fiction writers are thus indebted to him for creating such a venue, and maintaining its high standards for 25 years.

GUY VANDERHAEGHE

Geoff Hancock and his editorship of Canadian Fiction Magazine has contributed much to the flowering of the Canadian short story in the past 25 years. Not only has he published established writers, but more importantly his keen and discerning eye has recognized the talent of new ones. All writers of fiction ought to be grateful to him.